Dear Readers,

This book is part of a new edition for the whole series of stories about the Gibson Family. It has brand new covers and I hope you like them as much as I do.

I'm writing letters to readers for each book, sharing some of what was going on behind the scenes when I wrote the stories. Talk about a trip down memory lane!

When I wrote *Ridge Hill*, I thought it would be the final one in the series. I knew from my own reading that in longer books you needed more than just one pair of central characters, so in *Ridge Hill* I also focused on Annie's brother Tom and her son William. And of course, Annie couldn't be allowed to marry Frederick Hallam and have no problems from then onwards or there would be no story to tell. So I made his grown-up daughter very hostile to her father's second marriage.

This is a basic fact of writing: there have to be problems for the characters to overcome or there isn't a story worth telling.

In my personal life, I had been on extended sick leave with chronic fatigue syndrome, but as I recovered, I decided to take early retirement and concentrate on my writing. My day job didn't fill me with the utter joy that writing did – and still does!

My publisher and I were really happy with the positive response to this series, and I was eager to go on with the stories about Annie Gibson. But in one sense I was being thrown into the deep end! A five-part series as my first one ever. It's a long time to keep readers interested.

But I knew I hadn't finished Annie's story, so I settled into conjuring up ideas for two more books. And as always, the ideas came to me when I was lying in bed, just waking up and very relaxed. And the rest, as they say, is history. The publisher liked the ideas. I wrote more stories about the characters I loved, and the books have continued to be read and reprinted.

I hope you enjoy this third book in the Gibson Family series.

Anna

Anna Jacobs

ANNA JACOBS

Ridge Hill

The Gibson Family Saga:
Book Three

HODDER

First published in Great Britain in paperback in 1996
by Hodder & Stoughton
An Hachette UK company

This paperback edition published in 2015
by Hodder & Stoughton

3

A CIP catalogue record for this title is available from the British Library

Paperback ISBN 978 1 147 361709 4
eBook ISBN 978 1 444 71442 5

Typeset in Plantin Light by Palimpsest Book Production Limited,
Falkirk, Stirlingshire

Printed and bound by Clays Ltd, St Ives plc

Hodder & Stoughton policy is to use papers that are natural, renewable
and recyclable products and made from wood grown in sustainable
forests. The logging and manufacturing processes are expected to
conform to the environmental regulations of the country of origin.

Hodder & Stoughton Ltd
Carmelite House
50 Victoria Embankment
London EC4Y 0DZ

www.hodder.co.uk

With love to my aunt and uncle
Connie and Jim Heyworth

I

Bilsden: December 1848

A man tramping across the moors paused to wipe the rain from his forehead and stare down at the smoky valley in the distance. He spat and stood for a moment, scowling at the town in which he had grown up and cursing under his breath. He had never intended to return to bloody Bilsden. Never! But now – well, where else should he go to die but the place he'd been born? That seemed right, somehow. Though he wasn't going to die for a while yet. Years, probably.

'Is that it, Dad?' The boy beside him was thin, though tall for his eight years. He stood shivering in the bitter wind that promised more rain before long. Both he and the man were soaked to the skin, in spite of the sacks tied around their shoulders to keep off the worst of the weather.

'Aye. That's Bilsden, son.' The man squinted down at the huge square bulk of Hallam's, the largest mill in town, and the rows of mean terraced dwellings huddled around it. The only greenery was in the streets near the park. And even that had been given to the town in memory of Thomas Hallam. 'Bloody Hallams!' he said automatically. If they hadn't sacked him, he wouldn't have had to leave.

'It's not as big as Bolton, is it, Dad?'

'It's big enough to hide us, Jim, and that's all that matters.' For as usual, the man had left a trail of debts and resentment behind him. Head on one side, he calculated how long it would take to get into town and sighed. He was bone tired now and it had been a while since either of them had eaten. Nor had they found anyone to give them a lift across the tops, as they'd hoped.

The last carrier who'd passed them had flourished his whip at them when asked for a ride. The man on foot had cursed the driver, who had turned round to yell, 'Go an' earn your bread like the rest of us do, you thieving rascals. Then you can afford to pay for your rides. My loads have to earn their way!'

The boy waited, but the man still did not move. 'Ain't we goin' to move on?'

Spitting another gob of phlegm into the vegetation at the side of the road, his father nodded and picked up his bundle. Once he would have made nothing of a walk like this, but recently his great strength had faded and he had started to cough blood. He knew what that meant. No need to pay a sodding doctor to tell him. But he'd cheat death for a while yet, just as he'd cheated those who sought him. He snorted with bitter amusement. The very illness that threatened his life had also saved it, for he was a gaunt figure nowadays and his once luxuriant hair had fallen out, leaving only a dirty grey fringe around his bald pate. Even his own mother wouldn't recognise him.

'We'll change our names here, lad,' he said as they tramped along.

'What to this time, Dad?'

The man narrowed his eyes and considered. For a moment inspiration eluded him, then he noticed the smears of black smoke rising from the tall chimneys below them. 'Black,' he decided with a grin. 'We'll call ourselves Black. Frank, I'll be, an' you can be Jemmy.'

The lad nodded, accepting this as he accepted everything else his father did. The only thing in life that really frightened him was the thought of being put into the workhouse. But his dad had saved him from that, turning up when his mother died and taking his only legitimate son away with him. The boy who would call himself Jemmy from now on shouldered his bundle and started walking doggedly on, pausing when his father stopped to cough, moving when his father moved on again.

The going grew easier as they began to move down the slopes into Bilsden and they both speeded up. The wind did not keen around them as shrilly here and there was the promise of food and warmth ahead. The man was not without money for all his protestations of poverty. He just hated to spend it on anything but himself and his booze, the last pleasure left to him, or so he told the boy every night as he headed for the nearest public house.

If Annie Ashworth had known that this man was back in town she would not have slept at night, however soft her bed. The sight of him would have brought back memories of a night of horror it had taken her years to forget. If Annie's brother Tom had seen the man, he would have beaten him senseless, as he had longed to do years ago. But Annie didn't know. And although Tom saw the man several times, he didn't recognise him.

The newly-named Frank Black blended easily into the life of Claters End and it was to be quite a while before either Annie or Tom found out that he was back.

In the Bilsden Ladies' Salon, in the very best part of High Street, Annie Ashworth, born Annie Gibson, was standing staring out of the window at the people passing by. For once, the salon was empty. Most of the ladies who patronised it had already ordered their new gowns for the Christmas festivities and her workpeople upstairs were busier than they had ever been. A thriving business, her salon. But she would be leaving it soon, leaving it to marry Frederick.

At this moment he would be telling his daughter. Her

own family already knew and accepted the fact that she would be marrying him. So why did she feel uneasy? Why could she not settle to anything today?

She stood there for a while longer, then shook her head and turned round. Enough of this. The decision had been made. For the second time in her twenty-eight years she was in love and longing to be married. Only this time nothing was going to go wrong. So she had better start designing her wedding gown and trousseau. She did not want to let Frederick down in any way. A smile softened her face as she thought of him, then she picked up a pencil and began sketching.

In a fine house near the top of Ridge Hill, Annie Ashworth was the subject of a bitter confrontation. Beatrice Hallam stared at her father in horror. 'You can't mean that! Oh, no, I don't believe it!'

'Why not?' Frederick managed to keep his expression calm, but he could feel the anger rising. His youngest child had always been difficult. Today it was particularly hard not to give her the good shaking she deserved. He had known that she would not be pleased about Annie, but he had not expected quite that depth of revulsion in her voice when he told her the news.

'Father, you can't possibly *marry* a woman like that!' Beatrice moved towards him, her hand outstretched, then, when she saw him step backwards, she let the hand drop, buried her face in her handkerchief and began sobbing loudly.

He growled in his throat as he looked at her. She was more like a spoiled child than a young woman of twenty-one, as this theatrical performance proved. Christine's fault, that. His late wife had always been overindulgent with Beatrice. They had been more like sisters than a mother and daughter. And he had to take some of the blame for the way

Beatrice had turned out, because he had cared so little about the pair of them that he had not intervened.

In the three years since his wife's death, he had found a female relative to keep his daughter company. Jane Ramsby, a distant cousin of his wife's, had been living in genteel poverty since her father's death and was grateful to be given such a comfortable home. She was willing to put up with Beatrice's moods and spitefulness as no one else would be.

'I mean exactly what I say, Beatrice. I'm going to marry Annie – and the sooner the better.'

Beatrice gasped. 'You mean – you mean you *have* to marry her? Oh, that's disgusting! And at your age, too. Could you not just buy her off, provide for the child? After all, women of her class are used to such arrangements.'

With an effort, he kept his voice steady. 'Let it be clearly understood, Beatrice, that my desire to marry Mrs Ashworth stems from my love for her, not from any sense of obligation.' He had not loved his first wife. Christine had been rich and well connected in the cotton towns around Bilsden, a good match for the ambitious son of a rising mill owner. But she had not stopped whining and cringing away from him from the very first marriage night to the hour she breathed her last.

As Frederick saw the disbelief in his daughter's eyes, he added sharply, 'If you need me to say it bluntly, then I will. Annie and I have not yet shared a bed. Annie is as respectable as you are, believe me, Beatrice.'

His voice softened as he said Annie's name and his daughter sucked in an angry breath as she heard it. 'Then make her your mistress!' she begged. 'Other cotton masters take mistresses. With your reputation, that would cause little comment in the town. Cotton men are not known for their fidelity.'

'The cotton industry which you so despise, miss, and the

men who work in it, are what have given you a dowry large enough to buy the sort of effete gentleman whom you apparently desire for a husband.'

'Reginald is *not* effete! He is most truly a gentleman. Why, his grandfather was an earl.'

'Barrence is a nothing sort of creature, fit only to spend the money others have earned for him!' Frederick had disliked Reginald Barrence on sight, and the feeling had clearly been mutual.

'Reginald is a poet. He cannot concern himself with such mundane considerations as money.'

Her father bit back the comment that Reginald's poetry was as lifeless as Reginald's thin body, wispy dust-coloured hair and bony white hands. And for one who had his mind on higher things, the man had concerned himself very actively with the question of Beatrice's dowry and the marriage settlements, proving to be a shrewd bargainer.

Frederick walked over to stare out of the window at what Beatrice referred to grandly as 'the lake', but which he called, more accurately he felt, 'the lily pond'. How that annoyed her! He smiled at the thought, but the smile faded quickly. He despised her pretensions and the way she was ashamed of the mill her grandfather had built. After the first heat of his anger had passed, he turned round again, 'The decision to marry Annie is mine and mine alone, Beatrice. I've already written to your brother and sister to inform them.'

'I'm sure they'll be as pleased about it as I am!'

There was nothing to be gained from arguing with her, so he added with the bluntness for which he had once been famous, but which had softened in the last few years, 'I think I also need to remind you, Beatrice, that if you want the rather generous dowry that I've promised your dear Reginald for taking you off my hands, then you had better keep a civil tongue in your head when you call upon Mrs Ashworth.'

'One does not call upon one's inferiors.'

Where did she get her silly pretensions? Annie was worth ten of her. 'We'll be calling on her tomorrow.'

Her eyes met his, she opened her mouth then closed it again.

'I insist, Beatrice.'

She gave an angry sob. 'A woman from the Rows! Why, her father was one of your own mill hands!'

'And a good one, too. It's men like John Gibson who make the money you spend so carelessly.' A genuine smile lit Frederick's face for a moment as he thought of Annie's family. Tom, her brother, was as tenacious and hardworking as she was, running the family junk yard, expanding his provision supply business and dipping his fingers into half a dozen other small schemes. Give Tom Gibson time and he would likely make a fortune.

Like brother, like sister. Annie was a sound business-woman, shrewd and intelligent. It was one of the things he loved most about her, that eager questing brain of hers, though most of the men he knew would be amazed at that. Other men wanted a wife as housekeeper and mother to their children. Well, he'd had one of those and it had not suited him at all. Christine had bored him within a week, and he had come to despise her within a month.

The Gibsons were very different to his own family, full of warmth and vitality. John Gibson's second brood of children were shaping well, too, now that their fool of a mother was dead, for Annie had taken them and her father in hand, moving them out of the Rows to live with her. Though she had failed in one thing. A grin lifted the corners of Frederick's mouth briefly. Recently John Gibson had married for a third time, and married hurriedly, because he had fathered yet another child, his fourth living son. Well, Frederick hoped that he, too, would follow John's example and father more children, one or two, anyway. He realised that Beatrice had spoken and dragged his attention back to her. 'Sorry. My thoughts wandered for a moment.'

Her pale skin flushed to an unlovely shade of pink. 'They always do when you're talking to me, Father. I said that if Mrs Ashworth is not compromised, surely there is no need for you to marry her in such haste? People are bound to talk about that.'

'I don't give a damn what people say. And why should we wait? I'm not getting any younger.'

She made a scornful noise in her throat. 'No, you're not. That woman must be thirty years younger than you!'

'Nonsense! Twenty-two years younger, actually.' He spoke wearily, wanting only to end the interview and the melodrama upon which Beatrice seemed to thrive. 'I shall marry Mrs Ashworth as soon as it can be arranged, immediately after Christmas, if possible. And that is my final word.'

Beatrice burst into genuine tears. When her father's expression merely shifted from irritation to boredom, she stumbled from the room, sobbing hysterically, pushing past her companion, Jane, on the stairs and locking herself in her bedroom. There she poured out her troubles to Mabel, her new lady's maid, who truly understood how her mistress felt about this coming marriage. Indeed, the maid's indignation nearly equalled that of her mistress. For Mabel had known Annie Gibson years ago when they were both maid-servants in Dr Lewis's house and it galled her to see how well Annie was doing for herself.

In the drawing room, Frederick was pacing to and fro, seething with anger. The family portrait on the wall caught his eye and he stopped in front of it. The painter had been skilled enough to catch the essence of them all. Christine's vapidity, his own cynicism – yes, he admitted that now. Mildred, his elder daughter, looked amiable enough, though her foolishness showed in her expression. She was off his hands now, thank goodness, living in London with a small son of her own and two stepdaughters.

The portrait had been Christine's pride and joy, but he would have it moved before Annie came to live here. He was sick of looking at the damned thing. His younger son's arrogance showed clearly on his face, even at the age of twenty. Like Beatrice, James was ashamed of the mill which had made the family fortune, but give him his due, he was making his own way in the world, doing quite well for himself as a lawyer in Leeds, especially since he had married the only daughter of his senior partner.

And Oliver, Frederick's elder son. He sighed. The charm showed clearly, magically caught in a few smears of coloured oil. Oh, yes, that fatal charm that had greased Oliver's path through life and made his mother and sisters adore him. Well, Oliver had made an utter mess of his life, marrying Adelaide, an extravagant woman with no fortune, and then getting himself killed in a riding accident before he could even father a child.

Frederick reached up to unhook the picture and dumped it on the floor. He had no doubt that James and Judith would make some pretence of welcoming Annie into the family, in public at least, as would Mildred and her husband. And Adelaide would do as she was told, for fear of losing her allowance. It was his younger daughter who was going to give them trouble.

Well, he would just have to protect Annie from Beatrice's spitefulness as best he could. 'Ah, Annie, love,' he muttered as he turned to leave the room. 'I don't want to wait, not a single day.'

The next morning, Beatrice, her eyes still puffy from weeping, accompanied her father to make a formal call upon

Mrs Ashworth. As Mabel had said, 'Best get it over with, miss, for your father's not a man to be denied.'

Annie, forewarned by a note from Frederick, stayed home from the salon and sat waiting for her visitors in the parlour of Netherleigh Cottage. She could not sit still, but moved over to stare at her reflection in the mirror, twirling one auburn curl absently round her finger. Yes, this dress really suited her, showing off her slender waist and neat curves. Its full skirt fell elegantly down over six frilled and starched petticoats, the weight of which was dragging at her five-feet-two-inch frame. She sometimes wondered how wide and heavy skirts would get.

Fiddling with ornaments that needed no straightening, she moved aimlessly round the room. She was not used to sitting idly with her hands unoccupied, but she had no doubt that Beatrice was making this visit under sufferance and she did not intend to be caught with a piece of common mending in her hands. She gazed out of the window for the umpteenth time. 'Ah! At last!'

As the carriage drew up in front of the house, Lally, the new maid of all work, pattered along the hallway, standing ready to open the door the minute the knocker sounded.

Annie smiled. Lally, aged thirteen and scrawny as an underfed fowl, was rapidly learning the ways of the gentry and was clearly determined to make a success of her new position. Already her accent was changing, becoming more genteel, and her face was filling out with Kathy's good food.

'Mr Hallam and Miss Beatrice Hallam to see you, ma'am,' Lally announced at the parlour door, then hurried back to the kitchen to confide in Kathy, 'Miss Hallam looks as sour as a lemon and she's got that many spots on her face, you'd never believe she's a lady. *And* she's been crying. Her eyes are all puffy. Mr Hallam smiled at me as nice as you please, though. It fair does your heart good to see how he looks at Mrs Ashworth, doesn't it?'

'Yes, well, you just stay here and make sure everything's ready, in case Annie wants to serve them tea. I've got the tray ready.' Kathy fussed around the kitchen, preparing the day's meals. She felt guilty that she was hiding away here like this, but she had begged Annie not to make her join them in the parlour.

She went across to peer fondly into the cradle in the corner, where her first-born, Master Samuel John Gibson, was sleeping soundly, then she went to give the stew a stir. She was no fine lady and never would be, she thought, glancing at her reddened hands. The prospect of entertaining someone like Miss Beatrice Hallam made her shudder. Mr Hallam was not nearly as terrifying as Kathy had expected, but she could never see herself calling him Frederick, as he had said she must. Just let him make their Annie happy, Kathy prayed every night. Their Annie had had enough trouble in her life. She deserved to be happy now.

In the parlour, Annie greeted Beatrice with composure, her heart warmed by the loving glance Frederick exchanged with her from behind his daughter's rigid back. 'How kind of you to come and visit me, Miss Hallam.'

'Oh, do call her Beatrice,' murmured Frederick. 'After all, you're going to be her stepmother soon, aren't you?'

'Beatrice,' repeated Annie.

The girl said nothing, just inclined her head, but the gesture of greeting was contradicted by the angry glance she threw at her father.

'Won't you sit down?' Annie asked. 'The sofa by the fire is very comfortable.'

Beatrice went to sit on the edge of the nearest armchair.

Frederick came forward to clasp Annie's hand in his and draw her close enough to kiss each cheek in turn. 'You grow lovelier by the day, my dear.' He did not attempt to lower his voice.

Beatrice stared across into the flames of the blazing fire. Tears welled into her eyes at the thought of this woman taking her dear mother's place. She blinked several times in an attempt to clear them.

Annie had not missed the tears and she stifled a sigh as she sat down. Frederick had probably had to coerce the girl into making this duty visit. Thank goodness Beatrice was getting married herself in the spring! 'And have you made all your preparations for Christmas, Beatrice? There's so much to do at this time of year, is there not?'

With her father's eyes upon her, Beatrice had to force out a response. 'I daresay Jane will attend to that sort of thing for us. She usually does. I had expected to spend Christmas with my sister, Mildred. In London, you know. The people in London are *so* much more cultured than those in Bilsden.'

'Instead of which, Mildred and her family have agreed to come and spend Christmas with us here in the wilds of Bilsden,' Frederick bared his teeth at Beatrice in a smile like that of a tiger waiting to pounce the minute his prey moved. 'My son James and his wife Judith will be joining us as well, so I'm hoping to persuade you to marry me early in the New Year, Annie, my dear, while we have all my family gathered together.'

Beatrice's lips curled. Persuade her, indeed. As if a woman like that would need persuading to marry her father. But to her astonishment she heard Annie demur.

'Don't you think we should wait a little, Frederick?'

'No. I don't.'

The look he gave his intended could only have been described as 'hungry'. Beatrice flushed scarlet. It was shocking to see a man as old as her father looking at a woman like that.

Frederick's attention was all on Annie. 'There's no reason whatsoever for us to wait, love. Can't I persuade you to marry me next month?'

Annie's breath caught in her throat as she looked at him. She had still not grown used to the warmth that welled up in her whenever she saw him. Or to the way he made her feel when he kissed her. How could she have thought for so long that what lay between them was merely friendship? Or that she could marry Daniel Connor just because he had been courting her for years and she had grown used to him? For a moment, she forgot Beatrice, forgot everything, as she said, 'I suppose there's no real reason why we shouldn't.'

His face lit up. He had an almost uncontrollable urge to swing Annie into his arms and dance round the parlour, but with Beatrice sitting there like a sour-faced spinster aunt, he confined himself to catching hold of Annie's hands, raising them to his lips, one after the other, and kissing them lingeringly. 'My dear, I know it's a trite thing to say, but that really will make me the happiest man on earth.'

There was silence for a moment, then Annie moved away from him and sat down.

'We must invite Annie over to Ridge House, must we not, Beatrice?' Frederick prompted, going over to stand by the fire. 'Show her her new home, let her choose a sitting room for herself.'

'Yes.'

Frederick glared at his daughter.

Beatrice added in a toneless voice, 'I shall look forward to your coming to call upon me, Mrs Ashworth.'

'Tomorrow afternoon?' Frederick prompted.

Beatrice forced the words out. 'I hope that will be convenient, Mrs Ashworth?'

Annie nodded.

Frederick took over the conversation again. 'I'll send the carriage for you, Annie, love.'

'Thank you.' Annie would rather have walked up the hill to Ridge House, but she did not want to arrive at Frederick's house looking rosy and windswept.

'Good. And now we must settle on our Christmas festivities. Would you and your family come and dine, then spend the evening with us at Ridge House – shall we say the Saturday after Christmas?'

Annie hesitated. Her family would be awkward and uncomfortable in his grand house.

He could read her thoughts. 'We don't want people to say that I'm ashamed of your family, Annie, or that I shan't welcome them into my home after we're married. I'm sure Beatrice agrees with me about that, do you not, my dear?'

'Yes, Father.'

He sighed and moved away from the fire. 'We must go now, I'm afraid, Annie.' He allowed Beatrice to precede him out of the house, then pulled his intended back into the hallway for a moment and took her into his arms. 'The girl's as mumpish and spiteful as her mother. Don't let her upset you, my love.'

Annie raised one hand to caress his cheek. 'It's only to be expected that she would resent anyone who replaced her mother. Treat her gently, Frederick.'

'I'll do what's needed to protect *you*, my dear. You've no need to worry about Beatrice. She always manages to look after herself.'

Annie smiled up at him. 'I'm not exactly helpless, either. I've been fending for myself ever since I was twelve.'

But in spite of her brave words, her smile vanished the moment the carriage had pulled away, and when she went back into the house, it was not to go and tell Kathy how the visit had passed, it was to return to the parlour and sit staring thoughtfully into the fire.

In spite of her own reassurances to Frederick, Annie was not looking forward to the visit to Ridge House, or to living there with Frederick's daughter. Even one month of Beatrice would be too long. How they would go on together for three months, she did not like to think. Still, if that was the price she had to pay for marrying Frederick, then she would pay it gladly, for there was nothing she wanted more than to be his wife. Nothing. And what could Beatrice do to her, anyway, except make the atmosphere uncomfortable?

2

The Gibsons: December 1848

Annie's announcement that the whole family was invited to visit Frederick Hallam's home on the day after Christmas Day was followed by a stunned silence, then, 'Nay, you can't take folk such as us to eat our mutton in Ridge House!' her father protested.

'Oh, Annie, I couldn't do that, I just couldn't!' One of Kathy's hands crept up to clutch at her throat, a sure sign of deep anxiety with her.

'I really need you to come,' Annie insisted.

'Why should you need us to do that, love?' John looked at her in puzzlement.

'Because if you don't accept Frederick's invitation and come openly to Ridge House from the start, folk will say I'm ashamed of you and they'll think that Frederick won't have you in his house. And neither he nor I want that.'

'Well, I for one would love to come.' Tom's voice was bracing. 'It's a fine house and I mean to have one like it myself one day, so you lot'll just have to get used to visiting fancy places. And Frederick Hallam's all right when you get to know him, Dad, not at all like he used to be when he was our master at the mill.' He grinned across at his wife, Marianne, as he spoke and she smiled back. She understood how ambitious her Tom was.

Kathy nipped John's arm and looked at him pleadingly, hoping he would get them out of this. He shook his head. 'Nay, you don't need us up there on the Ridge, Annie, love.'

Marianne moved across to slip her hand through John's other arm. She was already a great favourite with her father-in-law. 'Annie's right, you know, Dad. It'd be better if you did go. And don't worry.' She gave him a cheeky smile and a wink. 'Just let any ogres try to eat you up while I'm there!'

John was weakening. 'I shouldn't know what to say to him – or to his family.'

'We'll be there, too, you know,' Tom said. 'You'll not be on your own.'

John looked at his wife. 'What do you think, Kathy, love?'

'Oh, Annie, surely it'll be enough for you to come down here to visit us once you're wed?'

Annie hardened her heart. 'No.' She went across to put her arm around her stepmother's thin shoulders. 'It would hurt me to live like that. Please don't ask me to, Kathy. I love you all and my marriage won't change that. I want my family to be able to visit me at Ridge House any time they please. Think how lonely William would be if Mark and Luke and Rebecca couldn't come up to see him? And what about little Samuel John? He's my half-brother. Is he never to come and see me, either?'

It was the thought of the children that did the trick. It would be wrong for them to suffer for her cowardice. Kathy gulped and said in a breathless frightened voice, 'Well, for the childer's sake. All right. But I don't know how we'll go on. Whatever shall we talk about to them grand folk?'

John nodded his agreement with that. 'I shan't dare open my mouth.'

Tom slapped his father on the shoulder. 'Just talk about the same things you talk about to folk that aren't grand, Dad. The weather. The children. When we're going to get that railway branch line through to Bilsden.'

The young folk made much less fuss about the coming visit. Ten-year-old William was looking forward to it, since he would be going to live in Ridge House when his mother married. He was quite sure that everyone he met wanted to be his friend and he would not have flinched even from visiting Queen Victoria and her family at Windsor Castle.

Twelve-year-old Rebecca, who was fascinated by the 'rich folk' she saw in the salon, was eager to see Frederick Hallam's house, which rumour said was an absolute palace. As usual, over the next few days, she rehearsed what she would say and how she would behave, and she nagged her brothers to practise with her.

Mark, too, was delighted at the prospect of going to Ridge House. Working at the junk yard and dealing with customers had given him a confidence in himself far beyond his years and he looked much older than fourteen going on fifteen.

But poor Luke, a year younger in age than his brother and many years younger in confidence, was as fearful as Kathy, and nothing would convince him that the visit would be anything but a horrendous ordeal. However, like Kathy, he would force himself to do it for Annie's sake. Their Annie had looked after them when Luke's mam died – he had never forgotten how she brought them all here to Netherleigh Cottage to live with her, nor had he forgotten the squalor they had left behind. So if Annie insisted on this visit, if she *needed* them to get used to visiting grand houses, then they owed it to her to do so. Whatever it cost them.

The following day Annie sat in Frederick's carriage and stared out of the window glumly at the rain as the horses clopped slowly up the steep part of the hill. She was dressed in one of her smart new gowns, dark green with tartan edging to the three layered flounces, and a floppy tartan bow at the high neckline. Over the tight bodice she wore a matching dark green jacket with a fur trim around the bottom edge. She was, as she had joked with Kathy, dressed to dazzle them all.

She hadn't admitted it to her family, but she was feeling nervous about her new life. Not about Frederick – she had no doubt that he loved her as much as she loved him – but about the things that went with Frederick. His family. His friends and colleagues. His big house full of servants. His way of living. And there was William, too. How would her son adjust to his new life? How would Frederick get on with him? Frederick had never bothered much with his own children from the sounds of it, so why should he spend time with hers?

She was lucky to have found a new seamstress for the salon, to cope with the extra work the wedding would entail, but she was designing and putting the finishing touches to her own trousseau herself, sewing until late at night, thanks to the clear light of the gasolier in her bedroom. Everyone had thought she was mad having gas lights put in upstairs as well as down, but she had insisted. And she had had them fixed in the salon's workroom, too. You needed good light for the fine sewing.

She sighed at the thought of her business. She loved designing clothes and would miss the bustle and companionship of the salon once she was married. She and Frederick had still not had time to talk about what would happen to it, but she did not need telling that it would look bad, indeed it would be unthinkable, for the wife of Bilsden's leading mill owner to continue working there. But she had no intention of selling the salon, or even letting go of it completely. It was her own creation and she loved it. There must be some way to compromise.

She nodded to Frederick's gatekeeper as the carriage turned into the drive and then stared at the house, seeing it with new eyes, now that she was going to live there. It was a large square construction, built of stone, with a grey slate roof and a portico which rose two storeys to shelter the entrance.

The front door was opened by Mrs Jarred as soon as Annie got out of the carriage. The housekeeper was to show Annie over the house after the formal call upon Beatrice. 'Welcome to Ridge House, Mrs Ashworth. If I may say so, all of us servants hope you'll be very happy here.'

'Why, thank you. And I hope that we shall all get on well together. I shall be relying on you most of all to show me how things are done.'

When Mrs Jarred opened the doors of the drawing room, it was to reveal eight ladies staring at the newcomer, most of them with hostile, assessing expressions on their faces. At the rear of the group, slightly separated from it, sat Beatrice's cousin Jane, looking apprehensive. She nodded her head once to Annie, then stared down at her tightly clasped hands, the very picture of the poor relative, sitting on the fringes of family life and afraid to draw attention to herself. It made Annie angry to see her. How could Beatrice treat a relative like that?

The following quarter of an hour would have been amusing if it had not been so uncomfortable. Then Mrs Dawton, who had been silent most of the time, stood up to go. She hesitated, then said in a flustered voice, 'It was nice to see you again, Mrs Ashworth. I do hope you and Mr Hallam will be happy. Such a surprise to everyone – but a pleasant surprise, of course.'

Beatrice glared across at her guest. Annie watched everything thoughtfully. Did the girl really expect the other Bilsden ladies to be as open with their resentment as she was? Their husbands would ensure they did not offend Frederick Hallam, if nothing else did, for he dominated the business life of the whole town.

As the group settled down again, Annie noticed the woman nearest to her looking unhappily from Beatrice to Annie, as if nerving herself up to speak. Mrs Bagley, newcomer to the ranks of mill-owning families. She had only had one dress made at the salon so far. A timid little woman, Annie had thought.

Eva Bagley had not forgotten her husband's injunction to 'make sure you butter the Ashworth woman up. No, I don't care what her background is, or how upset that silly young bitch is about the marriage. Without Hallam's goodwill, I'll be lost, and you make sure you remember that while you're up there on Ridge Hill.' Eva tried to do as Michael had instructed, but her voice wobbled as she said, 'My husband and I were – we were delighted to hear the news about you and Mr Hallam, Mrs Ashworth. We – we hope you'll both be very happy.' She realised that everyone else had fallen silent and she cast a scared look sideways at Beatrice who was not attempting to disguise her anger at this speech.

'Thank you.' Annie gently led Mrs Bagley on to talk about her children and her preparations for Christmas, feeling Beatrice's eyes on them the whole time.

For perhaps ten more minutes, the conversation faltered from one neutral subject to another. Annie's face began to feel as stiff as if the smile had been glued on.

Then two more ladies began to make their farewells, and as the others all followed suit, there was an air of relief about them.

Annie moved swiftly forward and linked her arm in Beatrice's, ignoring that young woman's gasp of outrage and keeping a tight hold of the arm that tried to jerk away from hers. She propelled Beatrice forward into the hallway and kept hold of her, chatting affably while the visitors' cloaks and mantles were brought and carriages called for those who possessed their own vehicles.

Mrs Bagley paused on the doorstep and risked another breathless remark to Annie. 'I do hope you'll come and call on me one day, Mrs Ashworth. I'm at home every second Thursday morning.'

There was a hiss of indrawn breath from Beatrice and her arm jerked again in Annie's.

Annie held it firmly. 'I'd love to call on you,' she said loudly. 'I'll bring Beatrice with me, too, if she's free. After all, I shall have to get used to my new duties as her stepmother, shan't I?'

Only when they'd gone did she allow Beatrice to tug her arm away and storm back into the house. Of Cousin Jane there was now no sign.

'How dare you maul me around like that?' Beatrice stood glaring at Annie. 'Who do you think you are, behaving like that in front of my friends?'

'I'm your stepmother-to-be, as well as a guest in your father's house.' When Beatrice would have moved towards the imposing flight of stairs that led up from the back of the hall, Annie strode forward and barred the way. 'Don't ever behave like that to me in public again, Beatrice.'

'I don't know what you mean.'

'Oh, I think you do.'

Annie turned her back on Beatrice and walked across the hallway to tug at the bell pull. 'Ah, Mrs Jarred. I'm ready to see round the house now, if that's convenient for you.' She ignored Beatrice, still standing scowling at her from the stairs.

Ridge House was huge. A dozen bedrooms upstairs, two recently installed bathrooms in the family's quarters, servants' rooms in the attics – without bathrooms or even fireplaces. That would have to change. Servants needed to keep clean, too. Downstairs a series of spacious rooms which included a library.

'The master usually sits here of an evening,' Mrs Jarred confided, looking round her at the book-lined room.

'What a lovely room! I hope he'll let me sit here with him.' And she hoped, too, that Beatrice would not join them.

The kitchen, servants' sitting room and the utility areas were at the back of the house. Across the yard from them was a stable complex almost as large as Annie's present home, with the gardener's and coachman's cottages across another paved yard behind that.

Saved by Mrs Jarred for last, on the ground floor at the side of the house was a gigantic room with a high ceiling. 'Mr Hallam built it when his children were nearly grown up,' Mrs Jarred said, pride ringing in her voice. 'It's only used for special occasions, of course. Not even Lord Darrington has a ballroom like this. Lovely, it looks, when all the chandeliers are lit, though they're a terror to get the wax off afterwards.' She turned to confide, 'The master's given orders for us to get it ready for a reception after your wedding.'

Annie nodded. Frederick had said nothing about his plans for their wedding as yet, but she might have guessed that he was going to thrust his marriage down the throats of Bilsden's elite.

As they moved around the house, Mrs Jarred took the opportunity to introduce Mrs Ashworth to all the staff they met, which naturally turned out to be all the indoor servants who were dying to see their new mistress – everyone except Beatrice's maid, that was, for she was attending her young mistress just then.

When the tour was over, Annie turned to the housekeeper. 'Is there somewhere we can speak privately?'

Mrs Jarred nodded, worry creasing her forehead. You never knew what was going to happen with a new mistress. 'If you'd like to come into my sitting room – I could offer you another cup of tea, perhaps?'

'No tea. Just a chat.' Annie waited until they were both sitting down. 'The servants' quarters seem to be somewhat in need of refurbishing.'

'Well, things are beginning to wear out,' Mrs Jarred admitted.

'More than wear out. They're a disgrace.'

Mrs Jarred nodded.

'I daresay it never occurred to Mr Hallam to look at them, but Beatrice ought to have done something about it all.'

Mrs Jarred struggled to find a tactful way to agree with this and failed.

Annie leaned forward. 'Let's be honest with one another, Mrs Jarred. We both know that I used to be a housemaid and then a lady's maid myself. I'm not ashamed of that. I was good at my job. And I think my background makes me understand a housekeeper's problems better than a lady born and bred might do. I hope we shall get on well here. It won't be my fault if we don't.'

Mrs Jarred nodded to herself in satisfaction as her mistress-to-be was driven away without seeing Miss Beatrice again. Mrs Ashworth might have been born in the Rows, but she looked and spoke as much the lady as anyone in the town. In fact, she looked a good deal more the lady than Miss Beatrice did, for Mrs Ashworth had clear pale skin and elegantly modelled features. Quite a beauty, in fact. No wonder the master was so taken with her.

When the carriage deposited Annie in front of the Bilsden Ladies' Salon, one of a row of tall terraced buildings in the best part of the town centre, she thanked the coachman for his services and ran lightly inside, relieved to have that ordeal over. Now to get some work done.

But there was a further ordeal facing her inside the salon. Rebecca, who had been keeping watch, tugged Annie into the small retiring room almost before she had come through the front door. 'Mrs O'Connor's waiting to see you, our Annie. Miss Benworth put her in the back fitting room an' I made her a cup of tea. She's cryin' – Mrs O'Connor is, I mean, not Miss Benworth.'

Annie's heart sank, but she didn't hesitate. Her old neighbour Bridie O'Connor had been like a second mother to her over the years and whatever her son Daniel's faults, Bridie was not to be blamed.

As Annie opened the door, Bridie rushed across the room. 'Annie, love. Oh, Annie!'

The two women embraced, then Annie persuaded Bridie to sit down again and rang for a fresh pot of tea.

Clutching Annie's hand, Bridie stared at her with red-rimmed tearful eyes. 'Oh, love, what went wrong between you and our Danny?'

'We agreed that we wouldn't suit.'

'There's more to it than that, I know there is. I said nothing good would come of him changing his name to Connor and acting the gentleman.'

Annie did not intend to reveal that when she had told him she could not marry him, Daniel had tried to blackmail her out of all she owned. That news would break Bridie's heart. 'Well, we did quarrel, as you might guess,' she said, carefully feeling her way.

'Folk quarrel all the time. They usually make up again afterwards. They don't go off an' marry other people. There's you engaged to Mr Hallam, an' our Danny's run off with Parson Kenderby's daughter. He didn't even come to see us, just left us a note. Tell me what happened, love. What went wrong? I shan't be easy till I know. Mick said I should leave well alone, but I can't sleep for worrying about our Danny an' what's to become of him now. He always was a headstrong lad, always.'

Rebecca came in just then with the tea tray. She cast one

swift assessing look at Bridie's tearful face, then took away the old tray without a word. Nobody's fool, Rebecca.

Annie poured a fresh cup for each of them while she worked out what to say. 'Danny was in financial trouble, Bridie. He was counting on my money to sort it all out. He'd arranged to sell the salon without even telling me. I didn't want that. I – I also found that I didn't want to marry him, for that and – well, I'd made a mistake about my own feelings. Danny grew very angry. We quarrelled bitterly, I'm afraid.' That was the best she could manage.

'But why are you going to marry Mr Hallam now?'

Annie looked her straight in the face. 'That's why I didn't want to marry Danny. I realised that it was Frederick I'd loved all along. I hadn't admitted it before – not even to myself. Frederick and I had become friends, but he knew I would never become his mistress. And – and I didn't think he would ask me to be his wife.' After a pause, she added, 'I love him very much, Bridie. I was just – fond of Danny.' Till I found out what he was doing, she added mentally. Now she hated him.

Bridie stared at her and sighed. 'Sure, I knew there was something else behind it all. But our Danny has the devil's own temper and I was afraid – but I see now that you couldn't marry him if you loved someone else.' She fiddled with her gloves. 'I knew he was pushing you into the marriage, love. I couldn't help noticing. I just thought you didn't want to lose your independence.'

'Mmm.'

But Bridie was tenacious when something concerned those she loved. 'What I don't understand is why *he* has gone off to marry the parson's daughter. I didn't even know he was acquainted with her. We don't go to St Marie's.' Bridie and all her family, except for Danny, were staunchly Catholic. She looked at Annie and added, 'Tell me about her, love. I need to know.'

'Danny had met Helen several times when he came to visit me. They – they got on quite well from the start.' Annie hoped Helen would forgive her for her next revelation. 'When Danny and I quarrelled, it was Helen who asked him to marry her. She has quite a bit of money, you see.'

Bridie stiffened. 'She asked him! The hussy!'

'I think she had grown – more than fond of him. And she's quite wealthy. She knew he was in financial trouble and she thought she could help.' You didn't tell someone like Bridie that a woman could lust after a man, as a man did for a woman, but Annie had come to the conclusion that that was how Helen felt about Danny.

'She's still a hussy.' Bridie stirred her tea so hard that it splashed over the edge of the cup, then asked, 'What's she like?'

'Very nice.' Before Annie's quarrel with Danny, Helen had been one of her best friends. 'I like her. And I'm sure you'll like her, too.'

'If I ever see her. The letter said they'd gone off travelling. Our Rory read it to us.'

'Yes. Helen loves travelling.'

'And Rory says the building business has closed down.'

'Yes. I'm afraid so.' But she had heard that Daniel Connor had paid all his debts before he left. Or rather, Helen had.

Bridie heaved a heavy sigh. 'I'll never see him again.'

'Of course you will!'

'No. No, I won't. He'll be ashamed of us. Me an' Mick aren't the sort of folks he'll want to introduce his grand new wife to. If you can call her a wife. Goodness knows where they'll be getting married.'

'In London, probably. Helen has an aunt there who is very fond of her. I should think they've gone to stay with her.' Annie managed, by talking cheerfully of her own visits to Helen's aunt in London, to calm Bridie down, then

Rebecca brought word that Mick was waiting outside with the cart to take his wife home.

Before she pulled herself up on to the cart, Bridie gave Annie a big hug and sniffed away another tear. 'I'd rather have had you for a daughter-in-law, love. I shall never feel comfy with this one.'

'You will. You'll like her once you get to know her.' Annie stood back to wave them goodbye. She could not, she found, hate Helen. Indeed, it was Helen's intervention which had stopped Danny trying to blackmail Annie, and for that she would always be grateful. Somehow, she could not have borne it if Frederick had had to pay off Danny to prevent him blackmailing her.

But grateful or not, Annie hoped that she would never see the pair of them again. She did not know whether she could even bear to nod to Daniel Connor in the street.

3

Christmas 1848

The pleasures of Christmas Day were threaded with sadness for Annie. It was the last time she would spend it with her own family, and these were her last few days of living at Netherleigh Cottage. How proud she had been of the house when she moved in over three years ago! And how small it had come to seem once it was filled with her family. She had been very happy there, though, happier than at any time since her mother died when she was ten. Goodness, what a long time ago that seemed now!

'A penny for them,' said Tom, flipping a coin up and down in front of her face.

'I was miles away, remembering our mam.' Annie patted the sofa beside her. 'Come and sit down with me for a minute, Tom Gibson, and tell me how you and Marianne are getting on. I've hardly seen you since your wedding.'

He grinned. 'We're getting on very well indeed, thank you.' His voice became a little hoarse with emotion as he added, 'Marianne is all I could ever want in a wife. I'm the luckiest chap on earth, I really am.'

'She looks very well. And the baby doesn't show yet.'

'That's a good thing, or the old biddies of Bilsden would have a feast of gossip on it.' He blew a kiss across the room to his wife who was chatting animatedly to his father, then he smiled to himself. 'And I think Dr Lewis has just about forgiven me now for getting his precious daughter in trouble.'

'These things happen.'

'Only if you let them. I shan't let anything else hurt my Marianne.'

Annie shivered. 'Don't say things like that. No one can prevent another person getting hurt. It's part of life.'

'I can and I will,' Tom said firmly. 'She's come down in the world by marrying me, but I'll make sure we rise again together. She'll want for nothing, my Marianne won't. I intend to make a fortune for her and keep her in the lap of luxury for the rest of her life.'

Annie looked across at Marianne who was cuddling little Samuel John on her knee and laughing down at him. 'I don't think she's interested in fortunes, Tom. I think she's more interested in having children and in you two making a happy family life together.'

'Well, I'll see she has that, too. Not too large a family, I hope, though I'd like a couple of sons and a daughter who looks just like Marianne.'

Annie looked sideways at him. 'You're changing. Did you know that? What's happened to the rough lad I grew up with, the one who didn't believe in marriage?'

'He's gone for good.' But the cheeky old grin peeped out again for a moment as Tom said that.

Annie smiled back. You would never describe her brother as good-looking, but happiness had brought a glow to his face that was very attractive. It was an undistinguished face, with crinkly brown hair and a nondescript nose, very like his father's. But Tom's eyes held you. They were so very shrewd and knowing, as if they knew all about things you wouldn't even dream of. John's eyes were soft and kindly. Her gaze went across the room to where her father was smiling at her.

'It's a good do we're having today, isn't it, lass?' he called. 'I'm that full I don't think I'll want to move an inch for the rest of the afternoon.' He turned back to Kathy. His third wife was a lovely woman, that she was, even if she was no beauty. She had the kindest nature of anyone he'd ever met, which was much more important than good looks.

Eh, but he was a lucky man. It frightened him sometimes to think of it. He'd escaped from the mill before it destroyed him, and he had interesting and well-paid work in his children's junk yard. There was good food on the table every day and fine warm clothing to wear, even to go to work in. And all of it was down to their Annie – and Tom, of course, but it was Annie who had set it all off by marrying Charlie and saving her pennies so carefully.

And now his eldest lass was to wed again, and wed into the gentry, what's more. That thought brought a shadow to his face. Would Annie really be happy with Mester Hallam? John worried about that. Hallam was used to ordering folk around. She wouldn't take much of that, his Annie wouldn't. And there was William, too. How would a noisy lad like that go on living in that big posh house? You couldn't help noticing that William was around.

A door banged in the kitchen and footsteps pounded towards the parlour. John grinned. Talk of the devil!

William burst into the parlour, followed by John's second brood, as he often thought of them, Mark, Luke, Rebecca and Joan.

'You said us children could have our presents after we'd sided the table and washed up!' Rebecca, as usual, spoke for the group.

Mark, who considered himself too grown-up to be classed as a child or to clamour for presents, went across to sit on the window seat. He was tall for his age, much taller than Annie now, with straight dark hair and brown eyes. He would be quite good-looking when he filled out, she thought, watching him, but he had a lad's extreme thinness still, with bony wrists protruding from his shirt cuffs. He had a good brain inside his head, though, Mark did, and was a real asset at the junk yard.

Luke went to hang over the back of his father's sofa, a quiet presence in any gathering. She nodded to him across the room and he responded with his usual gentle half-smile. He had his dad's crinkly brown hair and lack of height, and his face was unremarkable, but there was something very likable about Luke, now that he had regained the confidence that his mother had beaten out of him as a child. He would always be quiet, but he could speak out for himself nowadays if he had to. He had become a keen and skilful gardener since their move to Netherleigh Cottage. Sometimes, she thought that gardening was his real love in life, and he only worked at the yard because his family expected it.

Annie's gaze passed on to Joan, who, at eight, was starting to lose her baby fat and shoot up. She had a sharp-featured face, with her mother's mousy hair, and she was a solemn little thing, nearly as quiet as Luke. But her smile was a delight, for it lit up her whole face and quite transformed it, so that you'd swear then that she was a pretty child. She was staying close to Rebecca, as she always did, even in a family gathering.

William bounced across to flop down at his mother's feet and tug at her skirt when she didn't immediately pay attention to him. 'You said we could have our presents if we cleared up and washed the dishes. And we've done all that, Mother.'

Annie's hand rested on his head and she smiled down at him. It frightened her sometimes how much she loved this son of hers, for all that he'd been fathered upon her in a vicious rape. He was an attractive open-faced boy, and however many times she studied his face looking for resemblances to his real father, she had never caught any signs of brutality or slyness in it. Indeed, he was almost too open at times, blurting everything out as soon as it popped into his head. He would get hurt by life if he didn't harden himself. She ruffled his wavy dark red hair and chuckled as he said, 'Don't, Mother!' For some reason, he hated the way his hair curled and was always damping it down to try to make it lie flat.

She was glad he knew nothing of his real parentage. He was at the age to worry about such things. Charlie Ashworth had been a good father to him and since Charlie's death, William had transferred some of his allegiance to his grandfather, who was teaching all three lads to be a bit handy around the house. It always surprised Annie what quiet authority John could exercise, and without any apparent effort. When she and Tom were children, they had never dared disobey their father. Only with his wives was John weak, and that did not matter with a wife like Kathy.

She realised that everyone was looking at her and pulled her thoughts back into the present. 'Kathy, if you'd care to go and inspect your kitchen, we'll see whether these rascals deserve their presents.'

Just at that moment, there was a hammering on the door and a voice yelled, 'Mester Gibson! Mester Gibson!'

Tom was on his feet instantly and had opened the front door before his father even reached the door of the parlour.

A man almost fell through into the hallway, panting and flushed from running. Neil Binns, who collected junk for the yard and helped out as needed. 'Mester Gibson! Someone's broken into t'yard.'

A chorus of voices expressed shock and dismay.

'Quiet!' It was John. He moved forward to stand beside Tom. 'Come inside, Neil lad, an' tell us what's happened.'

'Me an' my family were walking back from church, an' as we passed the yard, I noticed t'gate were swinging loose.' Neil sucked in air. 'I knew you'd never have left it like that, so I went inside to see if everything were all right. Someone's broke into th'office. Made a right mess of it, they have. Papers everywhere. I've left my eldest lad there to keep an eye on things an' my missus has gone to fetch the constables. Eh, it's a bad do. And on Christmas Day, too.'

Within minutes the men of the family were striding down the hill into town. William, who had known his mother wouldn't want him to go, slipped out of the back door without asking her and joined Luke at the rear of the small procession.

'Was there any money there, Tom lad,' John panted, trying to keep up with his eldest son.

'I'm not stupid. I never leave owt valuable at the yard.'

The constables, who had been celebrating Christmas like the rest of the world, did not send anyone until half an hour after the Gibsons arrived. By that time, Tom had checked everything and found that nothing much was missing.

John came in again from the back with Mark. 'There's nothing been took as we can see. 'Eh,' he said, sadly, looking at the mess. 'Why do folk do such things? He'd no need to smash stuff up like that. That's just wicked spite, that is.'

When a constable at last turned up, he took down all the particulars and promised to make enquiries, but did not hold much hope of catching the culprit. 'Better get yourself a watchdog,' he said as he prepared to leave. 'A big fierce one.'

'I'll do better than that,' Tom said grimly. 'I'll pay someone to keep watch here at night from now on.' He felt a sense of outrage that anyone could dare break into *his* yard and mess with *his* things.

'Ah. Very wise. Well, there's nothing else we can do now.' The constable tipped his hat and walked away.

'I've got a good strong padlock up at home,' John said. 'One of the lads can fetch it an' we'll fix it on the gate before we leave. This lock's beyond repair.'

'I'll go back and get it!' William volunteered, jigging about in excitement.

Tom looked at him sternly. 'Does your mother know you're with us?'

William wriggled. 'She won't mind.'

'So you didn't ask her?'

William stared at the ground.

Tom snorted. He knew very well how overprotective Annie was with William sometimes. 'I think you boys had better all go back home now. Mark can fetch us that padlock. Me and Dad will have another check round here, then we'll fix things up before we leave.' What a rotten thing to happen on Christmas Day.

When the two men got back to Netherleigh Cottage, the Gibsons made a determined effort to enjoy the rest of the day. Kathy brought a big platter of home-made sticky toffee and raisins and nuts into the parlour.

'Oh, good! I'll hand those round, then, shall I?' William was up at once.

He was going through a growing phase, Annie thought, and you could never seem to satisfy his appetite lately. And a rebellious phase, too. He wanted to be with the men, not with her. He was going to be tall, and probably quite strongly built. Fred Coxton had been a huge man, she remembered suddenly, her lips twisting with disgust. She had been glad when Tom heard that Coxton was dead. 'Don't hand anything round till after the presents have been given out, William.' Annie spoke more sharply than she had intended and her son looked aggrieved.

'Nay, sit yoursen down, lad.' John pointed to the rug in front of the fire. 'You're as fratchy as a laying hen today.'

William heaved a sigh, but did as his grandfather ordered.

The Gibson family made a big ceremony of the Christmas present-giving nowadays, though all of them, even Joan, remembered the days when there had been no presents to give. For the past few weeks, the children had been labouring secretly to make gifts for each member of the family, and there had been much giggling in corners as pairs of them plotted together.

Suddenly the shadow on the day lifted and faces took on an expectant look again.

'Mark, you hand the presents out,' Annie commanded, 'and Rebecca, will you help him? And no one's to open anything till I say so.'

William pulled a face of disappointment, but soon forgot that as he surreptitiously felt the packages that were piling up in front of him. They were wrapped in odd scraps of paper to conceal the contents, but you couldn't disguise the shape of the things inside. When every present had been handed out, they went round the circle, with each person opening one present in turn. For over an hour, laughter and cries of delight filled the room, and if John paused to flick a tear from his eye at the sight of his family gathered around him like this, no one commented.

Even Tom's eyes looked overbright as the ceremony proceeded. They all knew this was the last time things would be done this way. By next Christmas, Tom and Marianne would have their own family, and it was even possible that Annie would, too. However close the Gibsons' family ties, things would never be quite the same again.

That night, in the Shepherd's Rest, the man known as Frank Black was in such a foul mood that his usually talkative son sat in silence next to him.

'Cunning bastards!' he grumbled into his beer. 'They must be making a mint o' money in that junk yard. But they've got it hid away somewhere.'

Jim just nodded. He knew better than to interrupt or comment when his father was in this mood.

'To think o' Tom Gibson doin' so well, when poor Billy Pardy's lying in a pauper's grave! Not right, it isn't. Not bloody right.'

'Did you know this Tom Gibson before, Dad?'

Frank gave a hoarse chuckle. 'I knew his sister better. In a manner of speaking.'

When he didn't elaborate, the boy sighed and kept quiet. His dad had been a bit touchy lately. And his cough was getting worse. That soaking on the way to Bilsden hadn't done it any good at all.

A little later, a woman got up to sing and everyone started cheering and clapping. She had a loud voice, but it was obvious that the crowd was not pleased with her efforts. Calls of 'Where's Rosie?' and hoots of disapproval filled the air. In the end, Seth Holden beckoned her off the stage and she returned to serving at the bar.

Frank went home quite early, for him, and he was not as drunk as usual. He continued to look very thoughtful for a day or two.

He was plotting something else, the boy reckoned. Even at Christmas his dad had gone out 'on business'. He hadn't taken his son with him, so the boy reckoned he'd been breaking in somewhere. He'd done it before. And he never took his son with him when he did that, for which the boy was thankful. He didn't want to risk getting sent to prison. He'd heard what it was like in those places. As bad as the workhouse, they said.

But his dad didn't seem to have got what he wanted. Well, he rarely did. Most of his schemes came to nothing. Folk weren't as stupid as his dad liked to believe.

Perhaps the joy of Christmas Day at Netherleigh Cottage made the visit to Ridge House the next day seem even more difficult. Annie and her family were dressed as smartly as anyone in town, and her father's new solid gold watch chain, a Christmas present from her and Tom that had rendered him momentarily speechless, was prominently displayed.

They all sat in the parlour waiting for Frederick's carriages to arrive. As if they needed carriages when they could just have walked up the hill! But Frederick had insisted on sending the carriages.

Rebecca was the one to voice their feelings, as usual. 'What if them lot look down on us, our Annie?' she asked.

'That's up to them,' Annie said firmly. 'We shall behave politely, whatever they say or do.' She looked at the young people, sitting around self-consciously in their best clothes. 'You won't forget that, will you?'

Four heads shook vigorously. The fifth head did not move.

'William?' Annie pressed.

Her son turned to her, lower lip jutting out stubbornly. 'I shall be as polite as I can – but not if they say anything bad about you, Mother. I won't put up with that.' He had already had to face a few snide comments in the town about his mother marrying Mr Hallam. All the children had. William had come home with a split lip one day, but he'd been grinning, and he'd told his grandfather that the other chap now knew better than to say anything about William's mother again.

Before Annie could say anything else, there was a clopping sound outside.

'The carriages are here!' shrieked William. He rushed out into the hallway to throw the front door open, yelling, 'Come on, everyone!'

As they got out of the carriages in front of Ridge House, Frederick came outside to greet them, ignoring the icy wind that stung faces and sucked the warmth out of even well-wrapped bodies. He kissed Annie's cheek and then offered his arm to Kathy. 'I'm so glad you were all able to come today. Let me escort you into the house quickly, Mrs Gibson. It's freezing cold today. I shouldn't be surprised if we don't have snow before tomorrow.'

Kathy looked round in panic for Annie, but Annie was taking her father's arm, so Kathy could not avoid taking Mr Hallam's arm.

In the big drawing room Frederick's family were gathered, four of the ladies ranged on two huge sofas with their full skirts spread out around them, and Jane, in her usual plain dark garb, sitting a little to one side on a hard-backed chair. The men were standing up. It was conspicuous that one side of the room had been left vacant for the visitors, as if the two groups were not intended to mingle.

Mildred poked Beatrice in the side, and Beatrice stood up and walked slowly across the room, for once not relishing her role as her father's hostess.

Annie went to meet her. 'I hope you had a good Christmas, Beatrice.'

'Delightful, thank you.' Beatrice stood there as stiffly as a wax doll. It was hard to feel superior to a woman who looked as elegant as Annie Ashworth did.

Frederick stepped into the awkward silence that followed. 'Let me introduce everyone.'

The need to keep up his wife's morale gave John the courage to face these posh folk on their own ground. He repeated each of their names as he was introduced, muttering the name again under his breath as he moved on, so that he would remember which person was which. He was gratified to see the pride in his future son-in-law's face as he introduced Annie to his grown children. No doubting the love there. No doubting it at all.

Adelaide took a deep breath and prepared to make

conversation. Her father-in-law had made it very plain that if she wanted her allowance to continue, she must do the pretty towards Mrs Ashworth and her family. 'Whatever Beatrice says, we'd better keep the evening going smoothly,' she had told Mildred before they came downstairs. 'You know how stubborn your father can be when he sets his mind on something.'

Mildred had sighed. 'Yes, he's not to be moved, so we must just make the best of a bad job and hope that this Annie woman won't be too bad. Beatrice is a fool for making such a fuss. She won't change his mind.'

Now, looking at Annie, Mildred's lips tightened. Trust Beatrice to exaggerate. Why, Mrs Ashworth was extremely ladylike and even her voice could not be faulted, for she spoke clear unaccented English, with only a faint northern accent. In fact, she spoke better English than Mildred's father, for Frederick Hallam never made any attempt to disguise his northern origins. She must have learned to talk properly as a maidservant. The good ones usually did. And Mrs Ashworth's dress was truly beautiful, a dark blue watered silk with touches of white lace at neck and wrists, against which Annie's hair shone in all its auburn glory. Mildred began to feel a little more hopeful. Perhaps the marriage would not be such a disaster after all.

When the adult visitors were seated, Frederick rang the bell. 'I daresay you children will be glad to escape up to the schoolroom, eh?'

'Yes, sir,' said William, adding wistfully, 'if that's where the children usually go.'

'My grandchildren are up there with their nurse and governess,' Frederick said. 'Some of them are about your age, so you'll be able to play together.'

William nodded in resignation. Who wanted to play with two strange girls? The only girls William had any time for were his young aunts, Rebecca and Joanie. Most other girls were stupid.

Frederick looked at Mark, who was nearly as tall as his host and who was wearing his first ever evening suit. 'You look as though you'd be more at home with the adults, young fellow.'

'Yes, sir, I think I would. Thank you.' Mark looked around. It didn't seem as if the evening was going to be much fun, but he intended to use it to learn all he could about the ways of the gentry. One day he intended to be rich himself, like their Annie and Tom. He had already decided that. And he wasn't going to spend his life working in a junk yard, either. There were better ways to earn a living than that, ones where you didn't get so dirty.

Marianne sat down and exchanged remarks with Mildred across the fire. Tom watched his wife for a moment with a proud smile on his face, then roused himself to talk about the new railway line to Mildred's husband. Jemmings seemed to have invested a lot of money in railways, mere branch lines, too. Tom wondered if that was wise. He would never put all his eggs in one basket himself.

The evening limped along. When a meal was served, Frederick led the way into the dining room with Kathy on his arm and seated her in the place of honour next to him.

Unaware of the honour in that, Kathy just felt relieved, because Frederick Hallam at least was not hostile. Beatrice filled her with terror.

Several pairs of eyes watched carefully and betrayed their relief as Annie's family showed that they knew how to handle their knives and forks.

Annie hid a smile. Did they really think we'd eat our peas with our knives? She turned to James Hallam and asked him about Leeds, allowing him to talk uninterruptedly about the city he had grown to love, so that afterwards he told his wife that the Ashworth woman wasn't nearly as bad as he had expected, thank goodness.

'Your father's not stupid enough to marry an ignorant trollop. I found Mrs Ashworth very pleasant myself. And her family are decent folk, at least.' Judith's tone was sharp. She had already had a surfeit of Beatrice's complaints and grumbles, and thought her father-in-law's cutting remarks to his daughter unworthy of a gentleman. She could not wait to get back to her own well-ordered home.

At one stage, John got up to open the door when the maid was carrying out a loaded tray, which made Beatrice raise her eyebrows at Adelaide and pull a scornful moue that made Kathy wince. Next time the maid was ready to remove the tray of dirty dishes, Frederick got up to open the door for her, giving his daughter a challenging smile as he did so.

A flustered maid rushed down to the kitchen to report all this.

'How are them Gibsons coping, then?' asked Cook, who was sitting with her feet up now that crisis time was past.

'They're a nice polite lot, her family are,' said Winnie, 'even if they do talk broad. Politer than his lot, that's for sure. An' they're enjoying their food, too.'

'What about their table manners?' demanded Mabel, who was sitting in a corner, watching and listening, but saying little.

'Their table manners are as good as anyone else's. It's *his* family as are picking at their food an' twitching around. An' that Mr Jemmings has spilt his wine again. He drinks too much, that one does.'

'Well, they're still from the Rows, those Gibsons are,' said Mabel, 'an' it's bound to show, if you ask me.'

The other servants did not ask her, but they didn't contradict her, either. No one liked Mabel, but she was as thick as thieves with the young mistress, so it didn't do to cross her. She had a way of getting her own back on you, Mabel Clegg did. They'd all suffered from her spite, though nobody had been able to prove anything.

Peggy, the chief chambermaid, clattered down from the schoolroom, accompanied by William, who had insisted on helping to carry down the trays of dirty dishes.

He stood in the kitchen doorway, looking round with an open friendly smile on his face. 'Hello. I'm William Ashworth. I shall be coming to live here in a week or two.' He went over to Cook and offered her his hand. 'Peggy says you cooked the meal, Mrs Lumbley, and it was jolly good. My grandma's a good cook, but she can't make desserts like those.' He licked his lips involuntarily at the memory.

Mrs Jarred came forward, holding out her hand before Mabel could say anything spiteful. 'I'm the housekeeper.'

He nodded and shook her hand. 'Mrs Jarred. My mother told me how you showed her round the house the other day. When I come to live here, will you show me round, too?'

'It'll be my pleasure, Master William.'

He grinned. His mother had said the servants might call him that. Luke and Mark had been teasing him about it ever since.

'Well, I suppose I'd better get back upstairs now. Those girls said I shouldn't be helping Peggy, but the trays are jolly heavy, and my grandfather says we should all help one another, so I didn't pay any attention to *them*.'

Upstairs, Rosemary Jemmings, the elder of Mildred's two stepchildren, looked up as he entered the nursery. 'You shouldn't have done that,' she declared yet again, scowling at William and poking her chin out as she spoke. His action angered her all the more because she and her sister Philippa were spending most of the visit shut up in the schoolroom with the maid who looked after their little half-brother, and

Miss Mimms, their governess, who was determined to keep them out of Mr Hallam's way. As if she and Philippa didn't know how to behave in company. 'No, you definitely shouldn't,' she added, when he didn't immediately rise to her taunt.

'Oh, shouldn't I?' William glared at the girl to whom he had taken an instant dislike, but snapped his mouth shut on a further riposte. He had promised his mother to behave himself. Rosemary Jemmings was only a girl, he told himself, and a silly one at that. Very silly. Not worth getting upset about. And look at the dress she was wearing, a dreadful fussy frilly thing. He didn't know why the dress was wrong, he just knew it, and his eyes lingered on Rebecca for a moment as if for confirmation of that. Her dress wasn't all frills waffling around her like that girl's. Rebecca's dress looked – it looked all right.

'Are those your dominoes, Rosemary?' Luke asked, ever the peacemaker. 'I like playing dominoes.'

She turned to look at him uncertainly. He was older than William, almost a man. 'All right. I'll give you a game.'

Rebecca pulled a face at William. 'Come on. We'll play cards.'

When the governess poked her head through the doorway again, the children had all settled down, and Joanie was solemnly dressing and undressing Philippa's doll. She was so shy and humble that Philippa, who was constantly bullied by her elder sister, was enjoying the feeling of superiority and was quite happy to play with Joanie. Miss Mimms sighed in relief and went back to chat to the nursery maid. The two women worked too closely together for the governess to stand on her dignity about the difference in their stations.

Downstairs in the kitchen no one was laughing at William. 'Well, he's a lively lad, that one is, Mrs Lumbley,' said Mrs Jarred.

Cook looked fondly after him. 'I do like a boy as enjoys his food,' she said. 'An' as polite as you please, too.'

'Amazing, isn't it?' Mabel asked, but did not explain her cryptic remark. She continued to feel furious every time she thought of Annie Gibson becoming mistress of all this, and ordering her, Mabel, around. Mabel always thought of *her* as Annie Gibson, because she knew what a sham Annie's marriage to the old loony Charlie Ashworth had been, even if no one else did. And she knew who had raped Annie, too. You could learn a lot when the bedroom walls were thin, and Annie had confided everything to her friend, Ellie Peters.

If Mabel could ever find any way to show Annie Gibson up for the cheap scheming upstart she was, then she would do so. It was a shame the way Miss Beatrice cried herself to sleep at nights, thinking of her father's coming marriage, a proper shame. Mr Hallam was treating the girl cruelly in Mabel's opinion.

Well, Mabel would not hesitate to use her knowledge about Annie Gibson and her son if the opportunity arose. 'It isn't *right*, a servant marrying a master,' she muttered, as she got undressed that night. 'It just isn't right.' Especially when that servant was Annie Gibson, whom Mabel had always hated.

4

January 1849

'Cheer up, love. This is a wedding we're getting ready for, not a funeral.'

Tom's teasing was completely lost on Annie. She was standing in the middle of the parlour, feeling stiff and ill at ease in her sumptuous ivory satin and lace gown, worn over a padded horsehair crinoline and several layers of lace-trimmed petticoats. She raised the hem to peer down at her varnished slippers, to make sure the satin rosettes were holding firm. Everything, every single detail, had to be perfect today.

She looked around and tears misted her eyes. She was leaving Netherleigh Cottage for good. She would miss this house, especially the parlour. They had all been so happy together here.

'Leave her be, Tom lad,' John Gibson said softly.

Marianne stepped forward and took her husband's arm. 'Come on, Tom. It's about time we got off to church. That carriage has been waiting outside the house for long enough.'

Tom nodded, but first he walked over to Annie and took hold of her arms, pulling her forward to plant an awkward kiss on each cheek. He and his sister had never been the sort to go in for kissing and hugging one another, but this was a special moment. 'I'll miss you, love,' he said, in a voice grown husky. 'Don't grow too grand for us.'

Annie kissed him in return, then pushed him away, trying,

but not quite managing to smile. 'I'm only going half a mile up the hill.'

'Yes, but it'll be like another world up on Ridge Hill, I reckon. So don't forget us lot down here, eh?'

Annie gave him a mock slap. 'It's not likely I'll grow too grand for my own family, is it? Besides, you live on Ridge Hill as well now.'

He chuckled. 'We're as near the bottom of the hill in Throstle Lane as this house is – among all the clerks an' shopkeepers. But me an' Marianne will be living near the top one day, though maybe not as high up as you. Why, only the Darringtons live higher up the Ridge than your Frederick does.'

'And as they never come to Bilsden any more, they don't count,' she responded. The Darringtons might have been lords of the manor in the old days, but they lived in London nowadays and folk said that the old house on the moors was falling to pieces.

John watched with a smile of quiet satisfaction on his face as his younger daughter Rebecca followed her elder brother out of the parlour to wait in the hallway and peer at herself in the mirror there. Rebecca was to be Annie's only bridesmaid in church, Joanie being too shy and Beatrice having declined that honour. Today, Rebecca was absolutely full of herself in her first satin gown. She'd been rehearsing for days how to walk down the aisle and how to behave at the reception afterwards.

He turned back to look at Annie. It seemed so long ago, the day she'd been born. He and his first wife had just moved into Salem Street and had been so proud of their brand new home at the better end of the Rows. His face softened unconsciously at the memory. 'You were the first babby to be born there,' he said aloud.

'What?'

'You were the first babby to be born in Salem Street,' John repeated.

Annie pulled a face. She always did nowadays at the thought of Salem Street.

'I can't believe you're twenty-eight an' about to wed the richest man in Bilsden,' he continued. 'Eh, it only seems a minute since you were a babby in your mother's arms.'

'I can't believe it's all happening, either,' she replied, her voice so quiet he had to strain to hear. She had felt unreal all morning.

John moved across the room and pulled her into his arms for a hug. 'You look a real beauty today, my lass,' he said softly.

She didn't pull away, but twisted her head to stare at herself in the mirror. The wide bell of her skirt swayed around her at the slightest movement, the lace frills fluttering with it and a froth of lace veiling the rich colour of her hair. Then she looked back at her father, linked her hand in the crook of his arm and kept it there, taking comfort from the solid warmth of him. 'Oh, Dad, I don't think I've ever felt so nervous in my whole life as I do today!'

'Me neither, lass. How I'm going to walk down the aisle of St Mark's in front of all them posh folk without tripping over me own feet, I don't know. But they'll all be admiring you, you're that bonny. I wish your mother could have seen you today. She'd have been proud as a peacock, she would that.' With one rough fingertip, he touched the silk flowers holding her veil on to the gleaming auburn curls, then he sniffed and moved away from Annie to shake out a big clean handkerchief and blow his nose vigorously. 'An' I'm supposed to be cheering you up, not makin' us both weepy. Our Kathy would give me what for, if she could see me now.'

'You look very smart, too, Dad.'

He nodded. 'We all do – thanks to you.' He patted his watch chain absent-mindedly. It was a great comfort, that chain was. Only a man of substance would own a real gold watch and chain. Eh, fancy Tom and Annie giving him a present like that!

'Well, that's one thing I should know about, isn't it, clothes?' Annie answered lightly. 'I'm Bilsden's leading modiste, after all.'

'You'll not be a working woman from now on,' he said, shocked. 'You'll be able to leave all that sort of thing to Mary Benworth an' look after your husband.'

It was no use arguing with him, so she didn't try. To John Gibson, wives lived for their husbands and families, and nothing would ever change his feelings about that. Kathy, once Annie's apprentice and then her housekeeper, was cast exactly in that mould, as were most of the women they knew, those who could afford to stay at home, anyway. Poor women had to go out and earn money as well as their husbands. This house was Kathy's little kingdom, and her husband and child were the most precious treasures in her life. But Annie doubted she could ever feel like that, ever subordinate her whole life to her husband. Even to Frederick. And Frederick seemed to understand that, thank goodness.

She let go of her father's arm, to pace restlessly round the room. Why did people have to make such a big fuss about getting married? 'That carriage is taking a long time.'

'Well, they won't start without us, love.' John sat down in a chair, patted his pocket as if about to pull out his pipe, recollected that he couldn't go to church smelling of tobacco and gave her a sheepish grin.

At that moment he looked very much like Tom, same stocky figure, same springy brown hair – though John's was greying now – and what Annie always thought of as cheeky eyes. Gibson eyes, her father called them.

Lally rushed into the room without knocking and announced in a voice breathless with excitement, 'It's here. The carriage is back!' She and Rebecca had been standing in the hall with the front door open, watching for it, in spite of the cold.

Rebecca was waiting by the front door, holding Annie's new fur-lined cloak, a present from Frederick. She draped it carefully around her half-sister's shoulders and stroked the fluffy fur that trimmed the neck. 'Isn't it lovely? I want one just like that when I'm grown up.'

As the carriage made its way down the hill to St Mark's, it passed groups of men gathered on street corners. Even in her present state of abstraction, Annie could not ignore the anger on their faces or the jeers that sometimes greeted the sight of the carriage. She was startled by that. Frederick Hallam did not usually arouse hatred in those who worked for him.

'What's the matter with them, Dad? Why are they shouting at us?'

'Dawton's is on short time again.'

'Dawton's is always on short time.'

'Aye, well, there's been some trouble there as well this time. Injuries, and a death. Dawton's isn't like Hallam's, love. They don't look after their workers. Folk don't like it when workers get themselves killed through an employer's meanness. It makes them hate all employers.'

She shivered. The hatred of those thin-faced men was almost tangible, and she could see the hunger in their eyes, too.

Outside the church, a group of idlers was standing staring at the nobs as they entered, but at least this lot did not look angry or call out. Among them was a gaunt man who was coughing so hard that Annie could hear him even before the carriage door was opened for her. He was a tall man and when he paused for a moment to gasp for breath, his eyes met hers over the heads of the other bystanders. There was such malevolence in his glance that she gasped. Who was he? He didn't look familiar. And yet – there was something about those eyes.

Then she forgot everything else as Rebecca helped her out and straightened her skirts.

'You look lovely, our Annie,' Rebecca whispered.

'So do you, love.' Annie smiled at her father and concentrated on the matter in hand. 'Come on, then. Let's get the fuss over with.'

And after that the day rushed past so fast that Annie didn't have another moment to think about what she was doing, or to brood about the huge changes that were taking place in her life.

It was nearly ten o'clock at night before the bridal couple escaped from their well-wishers and took refuge in the luxurious suite that the master of Ridge House had previously occupied alone.

When the door had closed behind them, Frederick came up behind Annie and put his arms around her. 'Welcome into my life, Mrs Hallam,' he murmured in her ear.

'I can't believe it.' She leaned against him with a tired sigh, trying not to show how tense she was now feeling.

But he could tell. Already he could read her moods better than anyone else, except perhaps Tom. 'You're nervous about tonight.' It was a statement of fact, not a question. 'We should have gone away, then we could have escaped from our damned well-wishers sooner.'

'I didn't want to start our life together in some strange hotel.' She looked over her shoulder and tried to smile up at him. 'And it was you who insisted on all the fuss, not me.'

'I wanted to celebrate marrying you, my love.' She moved away and he watched her fiddling with the new gold band on her left hand. She was avoiding his eyes and tension was radiating from her. 'You *are* nervous, aren't you, my darling?' he repeated gently.

She swallowed and the word came out as a whisper, a mere breath of air. 'Yes. I'm sorry.'

'I thought you would be.'

'Did you?' She should have realised that. He knew that the only time she had lain with a man was when Fred Coxton had raped her. She had told him a little about that, not wanting to start their life together on any false premises. And she'd been surprised to see tears in his eyes when she'd finished her tale. She squared her shoulders unconsciously now, as she always did when facing an ordeal. She was almost as ignorant about making love as any pampered virgin. She had tried hard not to let her fear of tonight show, but it had lain there all week inside her belly like a heavy stone. Would it hurt this time? Would she disappoint him?

Frederick stepped forward and turned her round to face him. As she raised one hand to caress his face, he pressed his lips against it. 'I think that tonight we should just sleep together.' A mocking smile twisted his mouth briefly. 'Like brother and sister. Till you get used to sharing my bed.'

But she shook her head. 'No. That would only – only postpone it.'

'You sound like someone facing torture.'

Deep red suffused her face. 'I feel stupid and ignorant, ashamed of my fears. But Frederick, I'm not going to let anything come between us. Not tonight, or any other night.' She did not allow the shiver to do more than start.

He stared down into her green eyes and placed two very gentle kisses one on either side of her beautiful soft mouth. 'Then let me undress you, my brave little love,' he murmured. 'Let me play lady's maid for you tonight, so that I can show you how wonderful our loving will be.' With slow tender fingers he began to unfasten her dress, then when she stood there, blushing and clad only in her chemise and one petticoat, he waved towards the dressing room. 'Go and finish getting ready. I'll be waiting for you when you return.'

And he was waiting, there in the darkness, with a single candle beside the bed to guide her across the unfamiliar room, into the unfamiliar embrace of a virile, attentive husband. And from there, they soared together towards the biggest surprise of all, the ecstasy that a man and woman can share if they truly love one another.

Afterwards, she nestled in his arms and let out a long sigh. 'I didn't know it could be like that.'

'It isn't always.'

Her voice was growing sleepy. 'I do love you, Frederick.'

'And I love you, Annie girl.'

'I'll try my hardest to make you a good wife.'

He chuckled in her ear. 'I'd rather you tried to be a loving wife, thank you very much. Good women can be very tedious. Look at my daughter-in-law, Judith.'

She gave him a mock slap. 'You know what I mean!'

He settled her into the crook of his arm. 'Don't try to be anything but yourself, darling girl. I married Annie, not a copy of Mildred and Judith.' Or Christine, he thought and scowled into the darkness.

'But—'

'And *never, ever* apologise for yourself or your background. That's what made you. Be proud of it. As proud as I am of you.'

It was a funny sort of conversation to start off a marriage, but Annie never forgot those words for as long as she lived. And as she sighed into sleep, she felt loved as she had never been loved before. Warm and safe in her husband's arms, she felt a whole woman at last. Nothing could hurt her now. Not as badly as it had in the past, anyway.

5

Tom and Marianne

Tom enjoyed Annie's wedding, especially the reception afterwards, when he could rub shoulders with Bilsden's richest citizens. Hallam's friends and family hadn't known how to take him, for he refused to be subservient or cowed with them. Why should he? He was as good as they were. Better by far than that pale droopy fellow Beatrice was engaged to, who had come up to Bilsden specially for the wedding. What a milksop Reginald Barrence was, Tom thought scornfully when he was introduced, with his lisping voice and his languid air! And what an ugly woman Beatrice Hallam was, with an ugliness that came from inside.

He looked at his own wife, radiant and happy. With Marianne beside him, golden hair gleaming and all the glory of her young womanhood radiating from her, Tom felt like a king. He moved around the huge room, hiding a smile as he listened to the mill owners discussing the Ten Hours Act and complaining about how it was affecting their operatives. Did they really think that workers with more free time would be a threat to freedom? And how stupid to predict calamity and ruin from all this, as a couple of employers were still doing, even six months after the application of the Act. Why, the Act had caused no trouble that Tom could see, and he moved around the town more than most folk did, so he should know.

He found himself growing particularly angry as he listened to Jonas Dawton, the only owner who had set up a relay system for his workers, staggering the women and children's hours to try to avoid disruption and lowering of the men's hours to match those of the women and children. Even that had not saved Dawton, though. The fellow was on the brink of ruin. Everyone knew that. And as far as Tom was concerned, Dawton was a villain as well as a fool and deserved all he got. Tom had heard tales about conditions in that mill of his, and why folk got injured more often there. No wonder Dawton was hated in the Rows. No wonder lately he had started going around with two stout guards riding on the back of his carriage. As if two guards would save him when a mob got really angry.

'One day,' Tom said thoughtfully to Marianne, as they were being driven home in his new brother-in-law's carriage, 'I'll be richer than most of that lot, maybe even as rich as Frederick Hallam. An' I won't do it by killing children, like that Jonas Dawton does.'

'We're rich now,' she replied, linking her arm in his and leaning her head against his shoulder.

He grinned in the darkness. 'Well, we're going to be even richer, then.'

He woke up later than usual the next morning and lay in his warm cocoon for a few moments, stretching luxuriously. By the dim light from the shaded lamp that Marianne always liked to leave burning in the upstairs hallway at night, he stared at his wife, then reached out to curl one lock of her soft blond hair around his fingertip. He raised it to his lips and kissed it. Each day that they'd lived together since their marriage, his love for her had grown stronger. Other women had never roused this tenderness in him, not even Rosie, whom he had known for years before he met Marianne.

Marianne sighed and turned over in the bed, the gentle swell of her stomach pressing against him and sending a surge of fierce pride through him. His child. What would it be, a son or a daughter? He wanted a son – what man didn't? – but a daughter like Marianne would be wonderful, too, a little girl with soft blond hair and her mother's big solemn blue-grey eyes.

Very carefully he eased himself from the bed, stilling for a moment when Marianne frowned and muttered something in her sleep. Then, as her breaths sighed back into regularity, he slipped out from under the covers and tiptoed across the room to push his feet into his new leather slippers, and creep down the stairs to the kitchen.

In spite of his warm dressing gown, he shivered. The house felt icy this morning. Perhaps they were due for some more snow. January was usually a hard month, with only the greyness and cold of February to look forward to. Pity the poor devils who could not afford the coal to keep themselves warm.

There was the sound of a key in the back door and he went through into the kitchen just as Megan, the daily maid, came in. 'Ooh, sir, you're up already, an' I haven't even got the fire burning properly.' She put down the loaf and rolls she'd picked up from the baker's as she passed through town and the smell of them made Tom's mouth water.

'Here, I'll do the fire. You get the breakfast ready.' Tom took pleasure in building up a good fire. He opened the damper of the big black-leaded stove and seized the poker to lift the ash-covered mass inside and let air into the glowing coals that had been left overnight. Embers winked at him as he set the poker down and waited for the flames to blaze up. The kettle was already warm and wouldn't take long to boil now, because it always sat waiting on the hob. He enjoyed the little household routines like this one, enjoyed very much being master of his own home.

By the time he went through into the tiny dining room,

Megan had got a fire lit in there. Within seconds, she had brought him a cup of tea. 'Breakfast won't be long now, Mr Gibson.' At the door she stopped and suddenly clapped her hand to her forehead. 'There, if I didn't nearly forget it!' She fumbled in her apron pocket and brought out a crumpled piece of paper. 'I was asked to give this to you. A little lad knocked on our door with it last night.' She set the paper down and bustled out again. She was a placid sort, not overly curious.

Tom picked up the piece of paper, which had his name printed on the front in uneven letters. It was folded up and fastened in several places with sealing wax. Not a business letter, surely, but who else would be writing to him or taking such trouble to keep the contents of the letter secret? He frowned as he broke the seals and unfolded the paper, then he drew in a shocked hiss of breath as he saw the name on it.

Dear Tom
    I need to see you urgent. Plese. I woodent ask only its that urgent.
    Rosie

He reread it, grunting in exasperation before screwing it up and poking it into the fire. He stood watching till the paper had all been consumed, then he took the poker to break up the blackened flakes of paper, so that no one would guess that he'd been burning anything.

'Damn!' he said aloud. 'Damn and blast!' What the hell was up with Rosie? He'd finished seeing her a while back, once he and Marianne had started to get serious about one another. He'd missed her at first. He'd known her for years. Well, a man had his needs and Rosie was a cosy armful, plump and pretty. He could never have married a woman like her, but she was a good sort and he wished her well.

He sighed as he tucked into the platter of ham and eggs that Megan set before him. If Rosie was in trouble, he'd better go round to see her later. He didn't like to think of her wanting for anything. He frowned. Seth had said a while back that she'd left the Shepherd's Rest, where she'd sung for the evening customers as well as serving at the bar for the past year or so. Tom had just assumed that she'd left to move on to better things, or else she'd found herself a new fellow. He'd been too engrossed in Marianne to find out exactly what Rosie was doing, but he knew that she could look after herself.

When he'd finished eating, he went to have a shave and wash-down in the scullery. No fancy modern bathrooms here like they had at Netherleigh Cottage. Marianne didn't seem to mind, but he minded for her. She deserved better.

He left Megan humming as she dusted the dining room. He took a cup of tea upstairs with him, in case he woke Marianne while he was dressing. She was already awake, so he brought the lamp in from the landing and turned it up full. She lay there, looking all flushed and drowsy. If it had been a Sunday and they'd been alone in the house, he'd have been tempted to climb back into bed with her. 'I'm turning into a real lazybones,' she said, yawning.

He pushed the cup closer and bent over to kiss her. 'It's the baby that's sapping your strength. You stay as lazy as you please, love. There's nothing to get up for, after all, and it's still freezing cold downstairs. Megan's seeing to everything.' He was dressing even as he spoke, working efficiently, with his mind already on what he would do that day.

'Shall you be coming home to lunch, Tom?'

'No, I'm afraid not. I've got to go and see someone.'

She pulled a face, but didn't protest or ask whom he had

to see. He saw so many people that she could never keep track of them. 'I might go round to visit Ellie, then. I promised to tell her about the wedding.'

He nodded and plopped a farewell kiss on her brow. 'Aye, she'd like that. Pity she and your father can't get wed yet, then she could have come to the wedding with him. It's daft, really. It's not as if he loved your mother. Why does he have to wait to marry again?'

'It's just the done thing. They don't want people to talk, or to say that they've been . . .'

As she hesitated, searching for words, he filled in for her with a grin, 'Anticipating marriage. Like we did.'

She smiled back. She had no regrets about the coming baby.

At noon Tom left the junk yard and walked briskly towards Claters End, passing the Shepherd's Rest, in which he had a half share, on the way. It was doing a thriving trade already, though it would get much busier in the evening. He must try to find another singer. Seth said the new girl they were trying out had a voice like a mill hooter. You could hear her clearly enough, but you didn't really want to.

The huddle of alleys and courts in Claters End looked more ramshackle every time he went there. 'They should pull this lot down,' he muttered to himself. 'It's a real eyesore. They've been talking about it for long enough.' Rich folk thought all the Rows were slums, but Salem Street was as different from Claters End as Ridge Hill was from Salem Street.

He wrinkled his nose at the stench of the drains as he turned into Bobbin Close. His feet automatically took him to Rosie's door. It seemed strange to knock and wait for someone to open it to him, when he'd once been as free to come and go here as if it were his own home.

'Come in!' yelled a voice.

He pushed open the door into the downstairs room, which was living room and kitchen combined. It was empty. 'Hello! Rosie, are you there?' Whatever she wanted, he intended to sort her problem out quickly and leave. He didn't want folk thinking he was visiting her again.

'I'm up here in the bedroom, Tom. Come on up.'

'Why can't you come down?'

'Because I'm in bed.'

'I'm not interested.'

Her voice grew shriller. 'I'm not well, you fool. Having a man in bed with me is the last thing I want at the moment. Especially you.'

He frowned and started to climb the narrow twisting stairs to the one room above. It was a luxury in Claters End to have two rooms to yourself. But he'd seen Rosie right when he stopped visiting her, and he'd agreed to pay the rent on this place for a year, until she sorted her future out. He'd owed her that, at least.

Rosie was lying in bed, staring across the room at him, and the contrast between her and Marianne made him scowl and wonder what he'd ever seen in her. Rosie looked much plumper than she had before and her face was pale, framed by dark curly hair that was lank and uncombed. That was unusual for her. One of the things he'd liked about Rosie had been her cleanliness and sweet-smelling softness.

'What's up, then?' he asked, even before he had finished climbing the stairs, which led right into the room, without banisters or guard rails to protect the tenants from falls. 'Have you been ill?'

'You might say that.' She lay staring at him for a moment longer, then held out her arms. 'Don't I get one kiss, at least? For old times' sake.'

'No, you bloody don't.' He remained where he was. 'I'm a married man now. I don't go round kissing other women.'

Besides, he had to think of Marianne. If Rosie was ill, he'd best keep his distance from her.

She gestured to a bundle beside her in the bed. 'Well, you'll have to come a bit closer if you want to see this.'

'Why should I want to see it? Look, I only came here because you said you needed help urgently. I'm a busy man. Just tell me what you need. I'm not in the mood to play guessing games, Rosie Liddelow.'

'Don't you want to see your son, then, Tom Gibson?'

'*What!*'

'You heard me! Come over here an' meet your son.'

'That baby's not mine!'

She tossed her head at him. 'Of course he's yours. Do you think I'd lie to you about something like this?'

'But we haven't—' He broke off. 'Oh, hell!'

'Yes. The day you were mad at your father for giving Kathy a baby. You came to see me to get away from your family. I must have been soft in the head to let you touch me.' She smiled. 'Funny really, isn't it? You did just the same thing you were mad at him for.' But Tom didn't smile and he looked angry at the news. She'd been hoping he'd show her a little affection today, for she was feeling down, but instead he was bristling with suspicion.

'Why the hell didn't you get rid of it?'

'Don't you think I tried? The little bugger wouldn't budge. I didn't mind taking a dose or two to shift it, but I wasn't havin' anyone poking around inside me with a bit of wire. My sister died of that sort of meddling. I decided that I'd rather have the bloody kid than take that sort of risk.'

Tom walked slowly forward to the bed and leaned over as she uncovered the baby's face. 'Oh, hell!' he said again. The baby looked just like his new half-brother Samuel John. No one could ever doubt that it was a Gibson.

'There hasn't been anyone else. It's definitely yours, Tom,' Rosie said again.

'Yes, I can see that.'

She looked puzzled to have made her point so easily.

'It's the spitting image of my dad's new baby,' he explained curtly. He turned away for a moment, feeling sick with disgust at himself. If Marianne ever found out that he'd fathered a child on another woman while he was courting her, she'd hate him, and he wouldn't blame her a bit. 'I don't want anyone to know it's mine,' he said abruptly, taking the two strides needed to cross to the small window and staring down into the filthy alley outside. The light was dim inside the bedroom, even in the middle of the day, because little sunlight got through to the crowded dwellings in Bobbin Close. When she spoke, Rosie's voice sounded uncertain, as if she were near to tears, but he hardened his heart.

'There's only one person as knows it's yours, Tom, but she'll hold her tongue.'

'Who the hell knows?' he demanded, swinging round. 'Why did you have to tell anyone at all?'

'I t-told Widow Clegg – in case I died having it, so that she could ask you to look after it.'

'Oh.'

There was silence for a minute, then she spoke again. 'You'd have done that, at least, wouldn't you, Tom? You wouldn't have let your own child go on the parish, surely?'

He nodded and growled out, 'Aye, I'd have done something. Of course I would.'

Rosie sniffed, picked up the baby and cuddled it to her. 'It was a hard birth, in case you're interested. Dr Spelling said he doubted I'd ever have another child.'

'Mmm.' What could you say to that? He wasn't interested, actually. He wouldn't care if he never saw Rosie again – as long as he knew she was all right, of course. And he most definitely didn't want this child. It was Marianne he cared about, and only Marianne. 'Why did you send for me now, Rosie?'

'You rotten bastard, Tom Gibson! You're not even interested in your own son, are you?'

She looked so wan and unhappy that he felt a bit ashamed of himself. His voice softened as he said, 'I'm sorry, love, but I've got a new life now. I left you well provided for. I thought we'd parted friends, but I never expected something like this to happen.'

'It took two of us to get him, you know.'

'Aye. I must have been a right bloody fool.'

Tears were rolling down her cheeks now, big fat tears. 'I cared for you, Tom, really cared. I never played you false, not once. An' I haven't been with a fellow since, neither.'

He opened his mouth to protest and she cut him off savagely. 'Oh, I knew you'd never marry me. You made that clear enough from the start. A wench as serves in a bar and sings to the customers for pennies wasn't good enough for *you*. You allus was determined to get on. I knew you'd wed someone more respectable than me, but I thought,' she gulped and fought for self-control, 'I thought we might've stayed friends, at least, an' – an' seen each other occasionally. Especially now.'

He opened his mouth to say something comforting, to tell her that he'd always be her friend, then he shut it and waited for a moment, watching the tears falling, feeling guilty as all hell. But he had to think of Marianne, he reminded himself again, Marianne and his unborn child. 'Well, we can't stay friends, an' that's that. Marianne's – she's not the sort of woman you play false. An' besides, I don't want anyone else now.'

'Well, you've *got* someone else now, Tom Gibson. You've got a son. I don't care if you never touch me or speak to me again, but I want my son – *your son, too!* – to have a better start in life than I did. I don't want him to have to beg for help like I'm having to – not ever. I'll make sure of that, at least.' She gave a hiccup of bitter laughter that sent more tears coursing down her cheeks.

Tom shuffled his feet and ran one hand through his hair. 'What a bloody mess!' The words were out before he realised it.

Rosie was sobbing unrestrainedly now, great gulping sobs that twisted his guts with pity. 'Oh, you needn't worry, Tom Gibson. I won't cause no trouble for your fancy wife, not as long as you help me with him.' She was still clutching the child to her.

He stayed away from the bed, though all his instincts were urging him to take her in his arms and wipe away the tears. 'All right, then. All right. You didn't think I'd let you want, did you? Or him.' He just couldn't say the words *my son*. 'I'll help you. Of course I will.' As she tried to wipe her face on a corner of the grimy sheet, he muttered something under his breath and stepped forward. 'Here, take my handkerchief an' stop that bawling. It won't do either of us any good. We have to think what to do next. Think what's best for everyone.'

The baby had woken up by now and started whimpering. Rosie stroked its cheek and lifted her eyes accusingly. 'You haven't even asked to hold him.'

'Nor I won't.' Tom thumped one fist into the other. 'I can't afford to get fond of him, can I? Can't afford to have him recognise me in the street when he grows older, either.'

When the child continued to howl, she flopped her breast out and shoved it into the open mouth. The wailing stopped instantly. Her face softened as she looked down at her baby. 'He's a greedy little devil, this one is, just like his dad. I've getten right fond of him already.'

'What've you called him, then?'

She shrugged. 'I dunno.' She was pulling herself together now, getting some of her old spirit back. 'How about Thomas, after his dad?'

'Don't be bloody stupid! Call him – call him Albert.'

'Why Albert?'

'After the Prince Consort.'

She sighed in exasperation. 'I know who the Prince Consort is. But why call the lad that?'

'Because I don't know anyone called Albert, nor do you. And lots of folk are calling their sons Albert nowadays. The name won't make anyone wonder who the father is.' He grinned briefly. 'Unless you've been having a fling with the Queen's husband as well?' The grin faded as she scowled up at him.

'Always the careful one, aren't you?' she sneered. 'All right, Albert it is. Though I'll call him Bert, I think. Albert's too much of a mouthful for me.'

'Right, then. I'll send you some money. Regular.'

'Thanks very much.'

'On condition you keep my name right out of this.'

She looked at him then, her lower lip wobbling. 'Oh, Tom, you'd no need to say that. Not to me.'

His voice was gruff and he avoided her eyes. 'No. No, of course not. I'm sorry I said that, Rosie, love.'

But in spite of his efforts to look away, their eyes met across the room and held for a moment. 'It was good between us, wasn't it?' she asked softly.

He nodded. It had been good. Fun. Then he realised he was weakening and pulled himself together. 'But it's over now, Rosie. Completely. It has to be.'

There was silence for a few moments, apart from the snuffling and gulping of the baby as it sucked down its mother's milk.

'Why don't you go back to work at the Shepherd's Rest?'

he asked abruptly. 'We haven't been able to find another singer like you.'

'I might as well. If you an' Seth'll have me.'

'You've got a job there for as long as you want,' he said rashly. 'I promise you that.'

'Do you?'

'Yes, damn you!'

She nodded. 'All right. I'll start next week.'

'Make sure you get someone reliable to look after Albert, though. And—' Tom paused, 'make sure he gets some proper schooling as he grows up, too.'

He was speaking as if he never intended to see her again, she thought bitterly. Her Tom.

'They're going to build a proper infants' school in the Rows soon,' he was saying, not noticing how she was looking at him. 'Frederick Hallam's always been in favour of education for his workers, an' he's pushing the Council to do it. Send him there. Just don't let on who the father is. But you'll probably be married to someone else by then.' Strange how the thought of that was not comforting.

She looked down at the baby. 'Poor fatherless little lamb.'

'I mean that, Rosie. I don't want Marianne finding out.'

'Aye. We have to protect your precious bloody wife. How are you going to stop the rain falling on her, though?'

He gave a snort of reluctant laughter. 'Don't be daft.' He hesitated again, then added, 'And I'll make sure he gets a good start for earning his living. Later.'

She leaned back against the pillow, weary now. 'All right, Tom. You can go away now. I've got what I wanted an' I know you're anxious to leave. Give me a bit of money before you go, though, love. I've run right out, not working and hiding here like I'd done something wrong. I haven't even been able to pay Widow Clegg for her help. Good job she trusts me.'

Somehow, when it came down to it, he was reluctant to leave her there, alone and unhappy. 'I'll send money, then. Regular. Don't waste it. You'll have to be a bit more sensible from now on. Think about him, as well as yourself.' He knew Rosie of old. Once she got a desire for something, she forgot all else until the craving was satisfied. A woman of sudden enthusiasms. A singing bird once. A little kitten another time. They'd both died. And then she'd wept over them.

But she hadn't had any sudden fancies where men were concerned. He'd known that she was in love with him, known it for years, but he'd said nothing. What was the point? He didn't feel the same way about her, and even if he had, he'd never have married a woman like her. He realised she was speaking again and blinked at her.

'I'll tell little Albert that. Your father didn't even want to touch you, son, I'll say, but he did send you money. Regular. And I didn't waste it.' She was getting angry again. 'Oh, go on. Give us the bloody money and get out, Tom Gibson! You make me sick.'

He pulled the loose change from his pocket and slammed it down on the rickety chest of drawers without even looking to see how much there was. 'There.' Then he turned and ran down the stairs, slamming the door of the house behind him. Once outside he slowed his steps to a fast walk as he stepped out of the narrow alley into the street. 'Damn,' he muttered again under his breath as he walked. 'Damn!'

Behind him, in the mean little room, Rosie put her head into her pillow to muffle her sobs.

When he got to the yard, Tom ignored the sandwiches that Megan had packed for him and threw himself into planning his latest venture. A cheap eating house near the Rows. Somewhere that folk could get a plate of hot food for twopence and a feast for fourpence. Somewhere they could get either a cup of tea or a drink of ale. There was a need for such facilities. Respectable places for working folk to go for a treat when they were flush with money. He'd seen how popular eating houses were in Manchester. It'd be easy to get the food. Half the farmers around dealt with him now and he was getting a name among the better class of folk for his cheeses, his fresh eggs and his pure creamy milk.

He tried to concentrate on his planning, to keep the memory of Rosie sobbing at bay. He rather thought his eating house would do well. Those who worked for Hallam's were on full time. It was only Dawton's that was struggling. So it was a question of finding some premises and a good manager, and then keeping an eye on things. Maybe there'd be a vacant warehouse or shop he could use. He grinned. He'd ask his almighty brother-in-law. Hallam owned half the bloody town, after all.

But every now and then as the day passed, Tom would stop his calculations and stare into space, remembering the bright blue unfocused eyes of his son, the son he could never acknowledge, and remembering, too, the pain in Rosie's dark eyes. He had hated to see that, but he did not dare give way to his fondness for her. He just did not dare. Rosie was his past, but Marianne was his future.

In the early afternoon Marianne knocked on the door of Park House, though it felt strange to do so at her old home. Ellie Peters answered it herself.

'Eh, love! What a treat to see you. I was hoping you'd come round this week.' She enfolded Marianne in a big hug and drew her into the house.

'Is Dad at home?'

'No, he got called out to one of the farms.'

'Well, I'll just have to make do with you, then, shan't I, Ellie?'

'Get on with you! Come and tell me every single thing you can remember about yesterday.'

Marianne described every detail of the wedding and the reception afterwards. 'Mr Hallam's family behaved politely, coolly but politely. I think they've accepted Annie now – all except his youngest. Oh, Ellie, it makes me shiver sometimes, the way Beatrice looks at Annie. Tom says I'm just being fanciful, but I think she'll try to do Annie a mischief, if she can. I really do.'

Ellie nodded. 'Everyone says how spiteful she is.' When she and Jeremy Lewis were married, then she would be able to visit Annie at Ridge House herself, but just now she felt it better that she stay in the background, which was why she had turned down Annie's invitation to the wedding. She was dreading the sensation it would cause in the town when Dr Lewis married his own housekeeper, not quite the sensation that Annie's marriage had caused, but bad enough. Sometimes Ellie had trouble believing the marriage would ever really happen, because she'd loved Jeremy for so long without hope.

Even her own father still hadn't got used to the idea of her marrying their mutual employer, though her mother had perked up when she heard about it. But Elizabeth Peters had only perked up for a while. Most of the time, her mother continued to need locking away and watching, or she would spend her days scrubbing the same patch of floor dozens of times. It upset Ellie to see her, but her father was always very patient and loving with his wife, trying his best to behave as if nothing were wrong. And Elizabeth Peters was quieter in his company, almost normal sometimes.

Marianne's voice brought Ellie out of her sad thoughts. 'Now, that's enough about Annie's wedding – when am I going to see my little sister?'

'We can go up now.'

Marianne stared down at little Catherine. She still found it strange to see how closely her half-sister resembled her. She wondered if her own child would look like this, and she wondered, as she always did, who Catherine's real father was. They would never know, but you couldn't help wondering about it. Catherine would grow up thinking that she and Marianne were full sisters and shared the same father. And Jeremy would be the child's father to all intents and purposes. He'd be a good father, too, even though Catherine was not his. He loved children.

Suddenly, fiercely, Marianne hoped that her father and Ellie would not wait too long to get married and that they would have a lot of children. He deserved some real happiness, after his years of chill misery with her mother. And he'd always wanted a large family. She would speak to him the very next time she saw him, and persuade him not to wait much longer. Convention would not be outraged, surely, if a man trying to bring up a baby on his own sought a second wife to be a mother to the child? Not if it were handled properly. Not if the new Mrs Hallam spoke up for her friend.

As Marianne stepped out of Park House, she heard a roar in the distance. The day was still, the air damp and sounds were carrying further than usual. 'What's that?' she asked Ellie.

'I don't know. Perhaps you'd better wait. It sounds like . . .' her voice trailed away.

'Sounds like what?' Marianne prompted.

'Sounds like an angry crowd.'

They both stared at each other in dismay.

'It couldn't be—' Marianne faltered. 'Not in Bilsden.' For there were occasional riots elsewhere. She read about them sometimes in the *Bilsden Gazette*. But people didn't riot in Bilsden. Thanks to Frederick Hallam's lead, most of the mill owners treated their operatives reasonably. She'd heard Frederick boast that a bit of common sense and care saved a lot of money, and a lot of trouble, too, in the long run.

But everyone in town knew that Jonas Dawton's workers were not happy. There'd been windows smashed at his mill only a couple of nights ago and slogans daubed on his walls. *BLOOD*, someone had scrawled. *CHILDREN'S BLOOD EVERYWHERE. YOURS WILL BE NEXT, JONAS DAWTON.* Megan had seen it herself when she was passing through town and had told Marianne. Tom had been angry about her telling Marianne, and then Marianne had grown angry with him.

'I don't want wrapping up in cotton wool!' she'd yelled at him.

'I'm only trying to protect you.'

'What from? Life? I've been helping my father in his free clinic for years. I'd be doing it still if it weren't for this.' She indicated her belly.

'You bloody wouldn't. I'm not having my wife—'

'Tom Gibson, you'd just better get one thing straight. I'm a woman, not a toy. And I'm a doctor's daughter. I won't be treated like a silly little fool who'll faint at the thought of trouble.'

They'd made it up, of course, vowed not to quarrel again. But she had meant what she said.

Now, somewhere in the distance a woman screamed and the crowd roared again, more loudly than before. Another scream followed, cut off quite suddenly. Then there was a shot and everything went quiet.

'You'd better come inside,' said Ellie. 'Wait till we're sure it's safe before you leave.'

Marianne nodded.

Sam Peters came back to Park House an hour later and told them about the near riot at Dawton's mill. 'A little lass was scalped today when her hair got caught in the machinery.

I were nearby and they called me in till they could get Dr Spelling. But there was nowt he could do for her. She died crying for her mammy.'

'We heard someone scream.'

'It was the mother. She went mad afterwards. We had to hold her down, or she'd have attacked Dawton herself. He was watching it all through that big window in his office. But he didn't come down to say he was sorry or offer to help with the funeral, even. Not that devil. Eh, that poor woman. She was still screaming as they took her and the child's body home.'

'I thought I heard a shot.'

'Aye. It was one of those bodyguard fellows. He pulled a pistol on the crowd. It stopped them breaking in to get at Dawton, but it made them angry, too. Good thing he only fired over their heads. If he'd injured anyone, they'd have had him, pistol or no pistol.'

Marianne felt sick and reached for Ellie's hand. 'How is the mother?'

'How do you think?' Sam asked bleakly.

'Is there anything we can do?'

'Send her the price of a proper funeral. Dawton's workers have been on short time for a while now. You know how folk like to give their dead a good send-off.'

Marianne fumbled in her purse. She knew Ellie's dad would have little saved, for he followed the Bible and gave all he could to the poor. 'Here. Can you give that to her?'

'Aye.'

But Marianne could not get the thought of how that mother would be feeling out of her mind, and when she spoke to Tom about it, asking if they couldn't do something more to help, the two of them had another quarrel.

'Sam shouldn't have told you about that!' he shouted furiously.

'Oh, yes, he should. I've told you before – I won't be overprotected.'

'I shall have something to say to him about it tomorrow.'

'If you do, you needn't come home to me, Tom Gibson. I'd be ashamed to turn aside from trouble—' She broke off, horrified at what she had just said. 'Oh, Tom! We're quarrelling again.' She held her arms out to him and they clung together.

But however tactfully he coaxed, she would not promise to stay away from trouble. 'I care about people,' she insisted. 'I can't just turn aside and pretend nothing's wrong.'

He could sense trouble brewing in the town. Dawton was causing it, and he didn't seem to care. But as Annie had said, you couldn't protect people from life, not even when you loved them. Things happened all the time, good and bad things, all around you. He didn't like feeling helpless, though. He didn't want anything upsetting his Marianne.

6

Ridge House: January 1849

During the few days following their wedding, Annie and Frederick stayed mainly in his suite of rooms or in the library, talking, playing silly card games that he taught her, drinking tea or champagne, making love, according to the time of day, and generally getting to know one another better. He teased her about this 'at home honeymoon', but he admitted that he was enjoying it as much as she was.

It was the longest time she had ever spent doing nothing, as she called it to herself, and while she was enjoying it for a while, she soon realised that it wouldn't do for her as a way of living.

The servants had been warned in advance by Frederick not to disturb the two newlyweds and to turn all callers away from the house. Beatrice had been sent, protesting, to spend a few days with James and Judith in Leeds; William had not yet moved up to Ridge House; and Jane Ramsby, although still in residence, had made such an art of not intruding upon the daily life of other members of the family that it had not even occurred to Frederick to give her any instructions to keep out of the way.

'Aren't you glad I didn't let you take me to London?' Annie asked lazily on the third day.

He grinned at her. 'Very glad.'

She was half-lying on the couch, nestled in his arms. 'Even in my wildest dreams, I didn't imagine it could be like this between two people.'

'It isn't usually so wonderful.' His tone was bleak, but he didn't go into details. His sense of what was proper did not permit him to discuss his frigid first wife with his warm and loving second wife. 'Now, what do you want to do with the rest of the day, Mrs Hallam?' He loved calling her that, loved the sense of secure possession it gave him, after nearly losing her to Daniel Connor's trickery.

'Well, we have a few things we need to talk about.'

He turned her to face him. 'Now why does that sound ominous? What, for instance?'

She kissed his cheek, then moved away before he could return the kiss. 'Perhaps because this first thing isn't an easy topic. But it has to be discussed.'

'Oh?'

She took a deep breath. 'My salon.'

'Ah, I wondered when you'd get round to that.'

'We should really have discussed it before, but you rushed me off my feet.' Her smile said she didn't mind that at all, then the smile faded. 'I – I don't want to sell the salon, Frederick. In fact,' the words came out in a rush, 'I want to stay involved. In a reduced way, of course.'

'And have people saying I can't support my own wife?' he teased.

'You know that isn't likely.'

He was frowning now. 'But people will talk if you go to work there every day – and besides, there's no need for you to work and I don't want you going out to the salon, serving a bunch of foolish women. I want you here with me.'

'But you'll be going to work at the mill, or going to the Exchange in Manchester, or whatever else you do with yourself, so I won't actually be with you most of the time.'

It was his turn to pull a face. 'Well, I want you where I can find you, if I decide to take some time off. That's a different matter.'

'Not to me. Anyway, I wasn't intending to go into the salon every day, and I certainly wasn't going to attend to customers any more.' She pulled a cheeky face at him. 'I know the wife of the great Frederick Hallam can't do that. But I could design clothes from here and pass the designs on to Mary. I know the women she'll be designing for and what suits them. And I shall still want to design my own clothes and have them made up at the salon. People won't be surprised at that, surely?'

He was doodling with one fingertip on her sleeve, tracing the lines of the green-and-white striped merino and silk that clung so tightly to her trim figure, then billowed out below the waist over a ridiculous number of petticoats. 'Have you never bought yourself clothes designed and made by someone else?'

'No. Why should I? It'd be a waste of money.'

'You can afford to waste money now.'

'Waste money!' Her voice was horrified, her whole body suddenly rigid against him. 'I shall never be able to waste money, Frederick Hallam, *never*. I've had to work too hard for it.'

'But this is my money. And I'd be more than happy to waste it on you.' But he knew her answer before she spoke, for he had already offered to buy her some jewels and been rewarded with an uninterested shrug.

She looked up at him, very serious. 'That doesn't matter. I shall never waste anyone's money if I can help it, whether it's yours or mine. It would seem wrong, immoral even. I've seen too many people going hungry in the Rows. I'd rather help them than waste my money – or yours.' As she nestled back into his arms, she added, 'So what are we going to do about the salon?'

It was, he realised suddenly, much harder to assert your authority over a wife who was also a friend, who looked at you with the confidence that you would understand her needs. The man who had never hesitated to tell Christine exactly what to do found himself asking Annie, 'What exactly do you want to do about the salon, my love?'

'I want to continue designing clothes from here, visit the salon once or twice a week maybe, just to talk to the staff and keep an eye on things – we could say that was to do with my own clothes – and, and I want to keep making money for myself.'

He sat up and swung her round so that she was sitting facing him. 'And if I say no?'

'I don't think you will.' Her eyes were on his, trusting, loving.

'I'd like to.' His voice had a throb of anger underneath its usual mellow tones. 'I don't want to share your attention with anyone or anything else.'

'That's not possible, Frederick, love, whether I retain an interest in the salon or not. After this honeymoon period, you'll be away for most of each day. What do you expect me to do with myself then? Sit and watch out of the window for you?' Her voice had taken on a sharper tone, and it also was beginning to carry an undertone of anger, just like his.

He looked at her, opened his mouth, shut it again, then smiled ruefully, knowing the answer even before he asked, 'Won't running this house take up your time? And paying calls upon other ladies?'

She gave an unladylike snort. 'I have Mrs Jarred and a whole pack of servants to look after the house, not to mention the outdoor servants working in the gardens and the stables. Paying calls won't take all day, Frederick Hallam, and you know it.' She sighed. 'In fact, I rather suspect that it's going to bore me to tears – though I do realise that it will be part of my duties as your wife, so I'm prepared to do it.'

He thought of how Christine had always complained that her days were taken up with domestic crises caused by the stupidity of servants, and of the hours she had spent primping in front of the mirror – in vain, for her face had never had any trace of beauty, nor had her clothes shown any elegance. He remembered, too, the fuss Christine had made each time she was pregnant. Five times he had gone through that, to get his four live children.

'Frederick?'

He didn't hear Annie. He was trying to face the fact that a woman who could create and run a successful business would take managing a house, even a large house like this one, in her stride. 'You know,' he said slowly, 'I have to confess that I hadn't even thought about how you would occupy yourself during the day, my love.' Though he'd dreamed of how they would spend their evenings and nights. And he'd looked forward to taking her into Manchester occasionally to the Gentlemen's Concerts, or to dine with acquaintances there – though that would be a lot easier once Bilsden had its own railway line.

'Well, think about it now, Frederick. I shall need something to occupy my mind. And – and besides, I shall need the money.'

That surprised him so much that he couldn't speak for a moment. 'Why on earth should you need the money? I have more than enough for us both.'

'I'll need the money for William, of course. He has no claim on you, Frederick, but I want him to have enough capital when he grows up to start his own business, or,' this was a recent, rather daring idea, 'go to university, or – or whatever else occurs to him.' If the new Owens College in Manchester became a proper university, as Frederick said it might, then this was distinctly possible.

He could not prevent himself from speaking stiffly. 'I'd

assumed that, as his stepfather, I'd be paying for his education and I'd fully expected to set him up in something later, too. I'll be quite happy to do that, you know. I like William.'

She laid her hand on his, sensing his hurt. 'I'm glad you like him, love, but I wouldn't be happy about you paying for his education. He's not your son, after all.'

'And what if we have children? Shall you still insist on running the salon, Annie?'

'I don't know. We'd have to see. I – I didn't have an easy time with William. I had to take to my bed and let Charlie and Tom look after me for the last week or two.' Truth to tell, having more children was something she'd avoided thinking about. She was, she thought guiltily, a very unnatural woman by other people's standards. 'We didn't talk about anything that we should have before we got married,' she added, with an involuntary sigh. They'd just rushed headlong into marriage like a pair of heedless youngsters. You'd think they'd have known better at their age. 'Do you want to have more children, Frederick?'

'Yes. Well, one or two. *Your* children.'

'You have three children already and your grandchildren.'

His grimace was eloquent. 'I hardly know my grandchildren. Mildred's son is too young and her stepchildren are always whisked away to the nursery when they come to visit me, and when they do appear, they seem frightened to open their mouths. And I see just as little of my son's children. Judith has her nursery at the far end of her house.' It had not occurred to him to make an attempt to get to know any of his grandchildren, either. Not until now. Not until he'd got to know the Gibsons and seen how they cared about one another.

'Well, I've no intention of banishing William up to the nursery when he comes to live here. I enjoy his company,' Annie smiled, 'and his enthusiasms. He'll be lonely at first, missing Mark and Luke. You won't mind if he dines with us when we don't have company, will you?'

The idea had not even occurred to him, but he didn't suppose it would matter. 'No, of course not. But I have to warn you that I think Beatrice will mind very much.'

'And how much attention must I pay to Beatrice's whims?' Annie was careful to keep her voice calm and expressionless. The two of them hadn't worked out how to deal with that problem, either. His answer made her relax visibly.

'Pay as much or as little attention as you please. You're the mistress here and as far as I'm concerned, you'll be in charge in every way. Luckily Beatrice will be leaving soon. Now, let's—'

Annie put one finger over his mouth, smiling as he kissed it, but still holding herself away from him. 'So I may retain my interest in the salon?'

He shrugged. 'You're a very tenacious woman. Very well, Annie.' But he didn't look happy about it. 'For the moment, you may retain your interest in the salon, but secretly, if you please.' He had no desire to be a laughing stock among the other masters in Bilsden. 'We'll set up a room here as a studio, and give it out that you're interested in art. Have you ever tried sketching and painting?'

'Good heavens, no! Unless you're really good, and a man, there's not much money to be made from it. Helen taught me that.' She broke off as he burst out laughing. 'What's so funny?'

'You are, my love. You and your obsession with money. I have more than enough money for the two of us, you know.' Only Jonas Pennybody, his lawyer, knew exactly how much.

'Well, I suppose I could pretend to be interested in sketching and painting. If I have to. If it would make you feel better.' As far as she was concerned, sketching was something to pass the time for idle ladies who would have been better doing something useful with their lives. Few people had Helen Kenderby's talent.

'Then give it a try. And it'll be useful if you have some sketches to show people. A few landscapes, perhaps?' He raised one eyebrow quizzically as he felt her body tense against him.

'I'll feel a proper fool if you show people what I've done.'

He chuckled. 'Not you, Annie mine. If you can't draw decent landscapes yourself, I've no doubt you'll find someone who can draw and paint, and use that person's work.'

Reluctantly she smiled back at him. 'Yes. I can always do that, I suppose.'

'And there's one more thing while we're having this discussion.'

'Yes?'

'You need a lady's maid.'

Her smile faded instantly. 'Do I have to? I'll feel a fool having someone else to help me dress and undress.'

'You definitely have to. Not only would it be thought very strange if you didn't, but I won't have you wasting your time on caring for your own clothes. Shall I ask Mrs Jarred to find someone?'

'I'll ask her myself, thank you, but,' her eyes were determined, 'I intend to have the final say. I won't have someone I don't like, just for the sake of it.'

'All right. And now,' he sat up and stretched, 'I suggest we take a stroll through the grounds. It's cold but fine, and even two love birds like ourselves can't spend all day sitting in front of the fire. There are plenty of dry paths, so you won't get your feet wet.'

She was up in an instant, pulling him with her. 'What a wonderful idea! Better still, let's go for a walk over the tops. And who cares if we get our feet wet?' She grinned at him. 'After all, we each have several pairs of boots, do we not?

And servants to clean them afterwards. And what's more, if it's really necessary, I'll allow you to buy me some more pairs.'

He chuckled.

Then another new experience began for him, that of having a wife to stride beside him, to relish the bracing air and exercise, to beam at him as they walked, a wife ready to talk of anything and everything that an intelligent mind could cover.

He was, he realised as he got ready for bed that night, quite besotted with Annie, and the difference in their ages, the difference that he had feared so much, seemed not to matter at all. Especially when he took her in his arms and felt as ready to make love as he had ever done in his youth.

Of course, the idyll could not continue. On the day Beatrice was due to return from Leeds, Frederick went off to the mill in response to an urgent note from Matt Peters, and Annie went to bring William back to his new home.

She lingered in the kitchen of Netherleigh Cottage, enjoying a cup of tea and a long chat with Kathy, hearing how well little Joanie was doing at the new school for girls that had just been opened by two spinster sisters from the south, teasing Lally, who had become more a member of the family than a maid of all work, and telling them more about life up at Ridge House. Already, her old home seemed very small to Annie. Already, there seemed to be a distance between herself and Kathy, the distance inevitable between people who no longer lived together.

Just as Annie was starting to feel sad about that, William clattered into the kitchen, flushed with excitement, words tumbling from his lips. 'I've brought the rest of my things down. Shall I load them into the carriage?'

'No. The coachman will see to that.'

'Well, I'll go and help him, then.'

'No.' She caught William's shoulder. 'Just show Robert where the things are. It's his job to load them and he might be offended if you tried to help. You have to learn some new ways now, William, gentry's ways.'

He shrugged and went off to do her bidding, but could be heard chatting brightly to Robert as the coachman loaded the carriage with the boy's bags and treasures.

Five minutes later William came pounding back inside to announce that everything was ready. 'Aren't you ready to leave yet, Mother? I'm dying to explore Ridge House. I still can't believe I'm going to live there.' He went across to hug Kathy. 'I'll be back to visit as often as I can, *Grandma*!' He still thought it a great joke that Kathy had married his grandfather, and that he had an uncle who was still a baby.

'Go and fetch your dog, then.' Annie pulled a face at Kathy. 'I don't know how the staff up there will take to an indoors dog, and I'm sure that Beatrice will hate it, but you know how fond William is of Brutus.'

'Aye. You can't keep the pair of them apart. We'll have to get oursen another dog now, I reckon,' Kathy said. 'The other childer will miss Brutus, an' I will, too. Remember old Sammy an' how he loved it living here?'

Annie nodded. Sammy had seemed like the last link with her first husband, Charlie. The old dog had taken on a new lease of life for a few months after the move from Salem Street, then had faded rapidly, dying peacefully in his sleep, to William's great grief. 'I must go now, Kathy. Remember, I'm sending the carriage down for you on Wednesday and you're coming up to have lunch with me. Wear your grey merino.'

'Eh, Annie, love, I'm still not sure—'

'I thought we'd sorted all that out?' She turned to the

little maid. 'I'm relying on you, Lally, to see that she comes. And to look after Samuel John while she's away, too.'

Lally nodded, her wiry frame radiating self-confidence and determination.

Kathy sighed and shook her head at Annie. 'Well, if you insist, then, love. But I'll never feel comfortable in that grand place of yours. Never.'

'You will, once you get used to it – and the children will, too.'

'Aye. Mayhap.' But Kathy didn't sound convinced.

Outside, William was waiting with his dog on a brand new leather leash, chatting away to the coachman as if he were an old friend. Annie kissed Kathy goodbye and turned to smile apologetically at Robert. 'I do hope William hasn't been talking your ear off and that Brutus won't make too much mess in the carriage.'

'No, ma'am.' Robert's eyes were twinkling. It'd be great to have a lad around the house again. William was a taking young fellow, with his mother's direct gaze and frank speech. All the staff were pleased so far with Mrs Hallam, who was a most considerate mistress, not like Miss Beatrice, though they were predicting storms when Miss Beatrice returned from Leeds and saw the changes that had been made. Even the outside staff had found Mrs Hallam very approachable and interested in their doings, and Nat Jervis had said she was a real lady, wherever she had been born, a rare compliment from that dour man.

At Ridge House, Annie found another carriage standing outside the front door, with the undercoachman and a gardener unloading luggage from it, luggage that she recognised as belonging to her stepdaughter. The process was being supervised by a stocky figure in black who could only be Beatrice's maid, the one indoor servant Annie had not met yet.

'Beatrice must be back,' Annie said. 'Please, William, remember what I told you and don't let her make you angry. She's only here for another few weeks, then we'll have the place to ourselves.'

'But you don't like her, do you?'

'Between you, me and Brutus, no, I don't like her at all. But I won't give her the satisfaction of showing it.'

'Then I won't, either. Mark says it'll reflect on you if I don't behave well.' Mark had given William a talking to about how to behave in his new house, and so had Tom. William was getting a bit fed up with people telling him what to do, as if he was a stupid young child who didn't know anything. At ten, 'nearly eleven', as he always told people, though his birthday was not until September, he was just starting to shoot up and to feel the first approaches of manhood. He was jealous of Mark, who was now having to shave every day or two, and whose voice had deepened perceptibly.

The maid's back had been turned, but as she swung round to see who had arrived, Annie gasped aloud. 'It's Mabel Clegg! What on earth is she doing here?'

'Who's Mabel Clegg, Mother?'

'She used to work at Dr Lewis's with me.' Annie snapped her mouth shut. No use rehashing old feuds.

For a moment, resentment burned in Mabel's eyes, then, as Annie moved towards her, she lowered her lashes and bobbed a maid's curtsy.

One hand on William's shoulder, Annie paused. 'Good morning, Mabel. Are you Beatrice's maid now?'

'Yes, ma'am.'

'So you got your wish, then.'

'Yes, ma'am.'

The anger lurking in Mabel's eyes did not surprise Annie. Mabel Clegg had always been one to hold a grudge. In fact, it was Mabel who had told Annabelle Lewis when Annie became pregnant. If anyone here should be holding a grudge, it was Annie herself. And certainly, she was not pleased to see Mabel. But she could not dismiss Beatrice's maid out of hand, much as she would like to, so she nodded her head and walked on into the house, her arm around William's shoulders. She would not need to see much of Mabel, after all. And when Beatrice left, Mabel would leave with her. One sigh escaped Annie, however, as the house closed around her. The idyll of the honeymoon was most definitely over.

Indoors, she showed William up to the small bedroom next to the schoolroom. 'These rooms are for you.'

William gaped at her. 'Two rooms!'

'Yes. You'll dine with us in the evenings, except when we have guests or we're out, in which case you'll eat up here. So I thought you'd like one room as a sort of sitting room, where you can entertain your friends.'

He hadn't heard the last bit. 'Eat by myself?' He had never done such a thing in his life.

'I'm afraid so. That's how the gentry do things.'

'Why can't I eat in the kitchen?'

'The servants would hate that. They wouldn't be able to talk freely in front of you.'

'Oh.'

'Shall you mind very much?' She knew he would. William was the most gregarious of creatures.

He shrugged. 'It won't be much fun, but Mark says rich folk behave differently. I remember they sent us children up here to eat at Christmas, instead of all eating together like we do at Grandad's. Don't rich folk like to be with their children?'

'Some don't.' She gave him a hug. 'But I do. And I shan't change about that. It'll just be sometimes that you'll be on your own, William. And I daresay you'll find a few things to keep yourself busy with, or you can have Mark and Luke to stay the night every now and then.'

He brightened up. 'Yes, I can, can't I? That'll be fun. Will Brutus be allowed up here?' To his disappointment, the dog had been left outside in the capable hands of Robert, who had promised to find him a bed in the stables.

She hesitated. 'We'll have to see. The other dogs aren't allowed into the house.'

His face brightened. 'There are other dogs?'

'One or two.' It had surprised Annie how many worlds within worlds there were here at Ridge House. A plump cat to keep the mice down in the kitchens area, a lean cat stalking the outhouses, a terrier to keep the rats down in the stables. The gardener and his lad, the coachman and the under-coachman, for Frederick Hallam kept two carriages, as well as a stable lad to do the menial work. And indoors, a chambermaid who didn't deal with downstairs matters and a parlourmaid who considered herself superior to the chambermaids and didn't 'do' upstairs. Here Annie would be leading the sort of life Annabelle Lewis had always aspired to, but never quite gained. The only problem was that Annie had no patience with all the fuss and formality.

'I shall ask Mr Hallam if Brutus can stay up here with me in my rooms,' William decided. 'I've trained him to behave himself indoors, after all. If I hadn't, Kathy wouldn't have let him come inside. And I give him a bath every month, so he doesn't smell. He's a very intelligent dog, Brutus is. He'll soon learn his way around.'

'In the meantime, let me show you the attics.' Frederick had told Mrs Jarred to sort out his sons' old toys and things, which were stored in the attics and William was to be allowed to use any of them he chose. Annie led the way up to the big shadowed spaces under the roof, with their sloping ceilings and dormer windows. They were piled with heaps of lumber of all sorts. Another thing on her list to sort out once Beatrice had left. Did all the gentry collect attics full of rubbish like this? A smile tugged at her lips. Once she had finished sorting through this stuff, Tom and her father could take it away for her. They might as well keep the benefit in the family.

'What a grand place this house will be to play hide and seek in!' William exclaimed, rushing to and fro, poking at the piles of old furniture and sending up clouds of dust as he lifted and let drop the lids of trunks full of old clothes and other items.

'Be careful! We don't want anything damaging.' Annie knew how his eagerness sometimes made him careless. She led him over to one of the small dormer windows. 'This pile of stuff is for you, if you want it. There are all sorts of interesting toys and things which used to belong to Frederick's sons.'

William gave her a big hug. 'You're the best of mothers!'

She hugged him back. 'What made you say that, love?'

'You just are. I listen to the other fellows at school, you know, and their parents don't seem to spend much time with them at all, or talk to them. But you and I do lots of things together.' He looked up at her, suddenly very serious. 'You – you'll still have time for me, won't you? We'll still go for our walks and – and things.'

'I'll always have time for you, love.'

He gave her another hug. 'That's all right, then. And I don't mind if Mr Hallam comes with us sometimes.'

She hid her smile. 'He'll be pleased to hear that.' She left William in his room, chattering away and helping Peggy to unpack, and went downstairs to see Mrs Jarred. As she passed, she heard Beatrice in the small parlour, giving orders about the evening meal as if she were still in charge of the housekeeping. Annoyed, Annie stopped to listen at the door.

Mrs Jarred was looking uncomfortable. 'But Miss Beatrice, Mrs Hallam has already—'

'Are you refusing to obey my orders?' demanded Beatrice.

'No, but—'

'And am I to have no say in my own home?'

'But—'

Annie pushed the door open. There was no avoiding this confrontation. She did not intend to let her stepdaughter take over again. 'Ah, Beatrice. I saw you were back. Did you have a good journey?' She nodded dismissal to the housekeeper.

'Don't leave yet, Mrs Jarred! I haven't finished.' Beatrice ordered and turned towards Annie. 'I was just discussing the evening meal with Mrs Jarred.'

The housekeeper looked from one woman to the other with a most unhappy expression on her face.

'We'll definitely not need you, Mrs Jarred,' said Annie, and moved to hold the door open, ignoring Beatrice's scowl. She waited till the housekeeper had left the room and then closed the door firmly before speaking. 'There's no need for you to get involved in the housekeeping any more, Beatrice. That's my duty now.'

'I think there is a need.'

'Oh?'

'After all, I'm much more aware than you are of how a gentleman's household should be run.' She did not trouble to hide her scorn for her stepmother.

Annie spoke slowly, determined to control her own anger. 'Oh, I do have some small idea of what's needed.'

The sarcasm was lost on Beatrice. 'As a *servant*, perhaps, but not—'

Annie lost patience abruptly. 'You've obviously come home prepared to stir up trouble, Beatrice.'

'I've come home determined to ensure that our standards

are not lowered. While I'm still here, it's my duty to do that for my father.'

'In what way have standards been lowered?'

'The meals, for a start. You've ordered the number of dishes offered at dinner to be reduced. You don't seem to realise that gentlefolk are always offered a range of dishes. They have no need to economise on such things. Perhaps by the time I leave, you may have a little more idea of what to do.' She had had several long discussions with James's wife, who had agreed with her that Annie might need some guidance. Judith had, however, advised Beatrice to do this tactfully, or even to leave matters as they were.

'If it's customary to waste good food and money in a gentleman's household, then the changes I've made were more than necessary.' Annie was not surprised at how plump Beatrice was. Mrs Jarred had told her that Miss Beatrice was fond of sweetmeats and always had at least three desserts offered with a meal, though her father rarely touched them.

'Well, you shan't bring your nasty common ways into this house while I'm here!' Beatrice forgot all about being tactful in her fury. 'My mother would turn in her grave to hear of what you're doing.'

Annie abandoned restraint and self-control. 'What I'm doing and what I intend to continue doing, Beatrice, is running my husband's household as I see fit. He's made no complaints so far about my changes.'

Beatrice blew out a disdainful puff of air. 'Pah! You may get away with things for a time, while Father's still besotted with you. Old men get these infatuations, I'm told. But he'll soon tire of you – *very soon*, if you set him a poor man's table and make his life uncomfortable – and then see how you like it! He can be ruthless when he wants to. You haven't seen that side of him yet, but he treated my mother abominably.' Her voice was rising hysterically and was loud enough to be heard all over the house. 'He was a fool even to consider marrying you!'

Horrified to think that her son or any of the servants might be listening to this, Annie stepped forward until she was almost nose to nose with Beatrice, put her hands on the girl's shoulders and gave her a quick shake. 'That's enough!'

Beatrice gaped at her, but forgot the hysterics. 'Don't you dare lay your hands on me!'

'If you *ever* speak to me like that again, Beatrice, I'll not only lay my hands on you, I'll give you the spanking you deserve and then have you confined to your room until you learn better manners.'

'You wouldn't dare! And my father wouldn't let you!'

'On the contrary, your father has given me carte blanche to change the way this house is run and to act as a step-mother should towards you. I'm quite sure he'll support me in anything I do.' Annie paused for a moment, then said in a calmer voice, 'Why can we not try to live together amicably, Beatrice? You'll be getting married soon, but until then—'

'Until then, I want as little to do with you as possible and I won't put up with shoddy behaviour in my own home. I know what you're really like, you see. Mabel's told me all about you, about the way you carried on with Dr Lewis – everything!'

This time Annie did not hesitate to slap Beatrice across the face. 'If you ever repeat such lies again, I'll throw you out of this house myself, and that liar of a maid with you.'

Beatrice clutched her cheek and screamed, then flinched back and ran behind a chair as Annie moved forward again. 'How dare you!' she gasped.

'Oh, we common creatures from the Rows dare do a lot of things. In fact, you may be surprised at what I'll dare do if you push me too far.'

Fear flickered in Beatrice's bulbous blue eyes. She sobbed

and tried to run out of the room, but Annie grabbed hold of her arm and swung her round, shaking her like a rat. 'If you say one more word, or utter one more slander about me, I promise you that you'll be out on your ear, young lady! And I'm not sure that I oughtn't to dismiss Mabel immediately for the lies she's obviously been telling you about me.'

She let go and watched Beatrice stumble upstairs, sobbing.

In her bedroom Beatrice nearly fell into her maid's arms. Mabel smiled to herself as she soothed and petted and flattered her young mistress, then fed her with more lies about her new stepmother. Mabel intended to get her own back on Annie Gibson in any way she could. She had waited for it long enough.

In the parlour, Annie marched up and down, taking deep breaths and muttering to herself. Not often did anything make her lose her temper, and already she was regretting that she had struck Beatrice. When she had calmed down a little, she rang for the housekeeper. 'Any changes Miss Beatrice wishes to make are to be referred to me first, Mrs Jarred.' She paused, then added, 'I know it'll be difficult for you, but Mr Hallam has given the running of this house entirely into my charge now. Fortunately, Beatrice will not be with us for much longer.'

Mrs Jarred nodded, relieved to have things spelled out. 'I do understand, ma'am.'

Annie hesitated again. 'And if Mabel tries to spread any – any lies about me below stairs, I would appreciate it if you'd put a stop to it and let me know. I knew Mabel when I was in service myself. She can be very spiteful and she doesn't always tell the truth. She's already told Beatrice some dreadful untruths about me.'

Mrs Jarred nodded again. 'I'm well aware of what Mabel's like, ma'am. I said at the time that it was a mistake to take her on, but there was no one else suitable and Miss Beatrice was so taken with her that I had no choice. I'll certainly let you know if anything out of place is said, ma'am. In fact, I'll have a word with Mabel myself to ensure that it isn't, if you like.'

'Thank you. That would probably be best.' Annie watched the housekeeper leave, then went to sit down by the fire. In spite of its warmth she felt chilled and unhappy. The honeymoon was definitely over. All peace was at an end, and probably would be for the next two months. But, she vowed, as she stared sightlessly into the flames, she would not go running to Frederick with complaints and she would not allow that silly girl to spoil her life. Just over two months. That was all she had to put up with it for. After that, Beatrice would be safely married and living a long way away from Bilsden. And Mabel Clegg with her.

7

Ridge House: January to March 1849

When Frederick came home from the mill that same day, earlier than usual, his daughter, who had been watching out of the window for his carriage, met him in the hall and threw herself into his arms, sobbing.

Annie, who was, with William's help, clearing out and rearranging an upstairs sitting room for her painting studio, heard the sound of the carriage, but continued to push a chaise longue into place near the hearth.

'Isn't that Mr Hallam?' William asked, peering out of the window. 'I'll just go and—'

Annie grabbed the back of his jacket. 'No! Stay here.'

'But I want to ask him about—' William had already been exploring the pile of things in the attic.

'Not now. I – er – had words with Beatrice and she'll be with her father now.' Even as she spoke, the sound of Beatrice's voice, raised hysterically, echoed up the stairs. The girl did not seem to care who heard her.

William looked at her sideways. 'Is she telling him about your quarrel? I tried not to listen, but I couldn't help hearing her earlier, she screamed so loudly.'

'She probably is.'

'Telling tales is very babyish, isn't it?'

'I think so.'

He watched her carefully from under his thick sooty lashes, his blue eyes sparkling with scorn. 'Beatrice is very silly, isn't she?'

Annie smiled grimly. 'Very. But you're not to say so to anyone but me. She's Frederick's daughter and this is her home, so we must try not to let her provoke us.' She had already failed signally in that this afternoon, but now, at the thought of the damage Mabel's lies could do to William's happiness, the anger boiled up inside her again.

'Why does she hate you so much, Mother?'

'Because I've married her father.'

'But that's his business, surely?' William was fiddling with the handle of a drawer. 'I mean, he's old enough to do as he likes.'

Annie chose her words carefully. She always tried to tell William the truth. But this time, the truth was difficult. 'Rich families are often concerned about money, love. Beatrice is probably worried that her father and I will have children and that he'll have less money to leave to her.'

His eyes lit up. 'If you had more children, I'd have some brothers and sisters, wouldn't I?'

'Well – yes. Half-brothers and sisters, anyway.'

'Oh, I do hope you will have some. Married people usually do, don't they? I love Mark and Luke and Rebecca, and Joanie's all right, for a little girl, but it's not the same as having brothers and sisters of your very own.'

She hugged him, glad to have distracted him from Beatrice's spite and foolishness. 'We'll just have to see what happens.'

'"Man proposes, God disposes."' William quoted one of Saul Hinchcliffe's favourite sayings in a solemn voice, but pulled a laughing face afterwards. The minister's sermons had grown very long-winded recently and even his grandfather said it was getting to be a bit much and Mr Hinchcliffe should let the lay preachers speak the Lord's word more often. William hugged his mother, then pulled away and smoothed down his hair, which had become ruffled. 'Aren't you going to go downstairs now?'

'I'll give her time to—'

Frederick appeared in the doorway. 'Hello, William. Welcome to Ridge House.'

'Thank you, sir.'

'Are your rooms all right?'

'Oh, yes. I've never had *two* rooms to myself before. It'll be great fun when Mark and Luke come to stay. We can play games in the schoolroom without upsetting anyone. And those toy soldiers you let me have are splendid.' He studied the expression on Frederick's face and decided not to mention his dog just yet.

'Good. I hope you'll be happy here. Er – could you just leave your mother and me alone for a moment or two?'

'Yes, sir.' William went away, puzzling over the ways of the gentry. He had thought that being rich must make you happy, but Mr Hallam's family didn't seem at all happy. And as for Beatrice Hallam, well, she was the silliest creature William had ever met. He would just have to avoid her as much as he could. But whatever anyone said, he would not allow Beatrice to insult his mother. He would never allow anyone to do that.

Annie smiled across at Frederick, her arms full of books. 'Did you have a busy day?'

He had expected her to pour her troubles out, as Beatrice had just done, and as Christine had always done. 'Fairly busy, but Matt Peters had taken care of things well enough in my absence. That young man is proving to be worth his weight in gold. There was just one thing he hadn't settled.'

'What was that?'

'Oh, a group of workers wanted to discuss having a regular wakes week, like other towns do. Apparently in Burnley the workers have two free days beyond the weekend at the summer fair in July. My lot have gone one further. They want a whole week off in the summer.'

'And what did you say to them?'

'I told them to form a committee and put some written proposals to me.' He smiled. 'That shocked them rigid. They didn't expect me to agree.'

'And do you agree?'

'It seems only reasonable that they have annual holidays, the same as other towns do. Just because Bilsden is too new to have such traditions, there's no reason to deprive people of a holiday. Besides,' he grinned, 'I can use the time to whitewash the inside of the mill. I need to do that every year.' He paused, but she still showed no sign of making any complaints about his daughter.

'I'm glad you're going to agree. Operatives get very tired working in that mill of yours, even though you're the most considerate employer in town. I'm surprised there haven't been riots and mayhem with Jonas Dawton, the way he treats his workers. Have things quietened down there now?'

'For the moment, yes. But Dawton's a short-sighted fool, and so I've told him. His little economies and penalties lose him money in the long run – not to mention injuring his operatives when he skimps on safety.' He did not mention that Dawton was in serious trouble and had asked Frederick if he'd be interested in going into partnership. Frederick was tempted and had set Matt Peters to investigate. But he would do nothing unless Dawton promised to change his ways. Frederick, like his father before him, had always prided himself on treating his workpeople fairly. As long as they did their job properly, of course. You didn't make money from lazy workers.

He looked at the room with interest, studying the changes Annie had made. 'You look as if you've been busy.'

She gestured around her. 'I've been getting my studio ready, or rather, William and I have. What do you think of my arrangements? It's going to be a lovely room to work in with those big windows.'

He went across to draw her into his arms. 'To hell with the room. To hell with business, too. I've missed you today, Annie mine.'

She put her arms round his neck. 'I've missed you, too, Frederick.' More than she had expected to.

He sighed against her head. 'I'm apparently behaving like a lovesick, besotted youth.'

'Good. I like it. Keep doing it.' She leaned her head against his chest, nestling the top of her head against his chin. 'Beatrice said that, I suppose?'

'Yes. She met me in the hallway.'

'I heard her. Is she always so – er – volatile?'

'Hysterical, do you mean?'

Annie smiled against his chest. 'Yes. Hysterical.'

'Quite often, I'm afraid. Don't you want to tell me your side of it, Annie? Did you really slap her face?'

'Yes. I'm afraid I did.'

'What did she say to make you so angry?'

'I don't want to discuss that.'

'Are you sure. Shouldn't I—?'

She shook her head and leaned away from him, her whole body radiating determination. 'You gave me full control of the house, love. What happens here is my business now, don't you think?'

He pulled her towards him and bent to kiss her. 'Annie, you're a pearl among women. But don't let her—'

'I'll manage Beatrice.' She stopped his words with a kiss.

At dinner that night, Beatrice sat and sulked, but did not let her mood affect her appetite. Annie and Frederick conversed quietly, and William joined in from time to time, but devoted himself mainly to his food, being ravenous as usual.

When the meal was over, he went to kiss his mother. 'I think I'll go up and continue sorting out my things now, if that's all right. Good night, Mother.' He turned to Beatrice and hesitated for a moment before saying, 'Good night, Miss Hallam.' Beatrice made no attempt to answer him. He pulled a wry face at his mother and turned to the silent figure at the end of the table. 'Good night, Miss Ramsby.'

Jane smiled at him. 'Good night, William. I hope you find your new bed comfortable.'

'I had a good bounce on it and it seemed all right, thank you.' He turned to Frederick, thinking how stupid it was to behave so formally with your own family. Back at Netherleigh Cottage, he'd have hugged his grandparents, and then gone off for a natter with Luke before he went to sleep. 'Good night, sir.'

Frederick held out his hand and shook William's, clasping it in both his for a moment. 'Good night, lad. I hope you sleep well on your first night in a strange house.'

William grinned. 'I daresay I shall, sir. I usually do.'

When the boy had left the room, Beatrice stood up. 'I shall retire, as well.'

'I'd prefer you to come and sit with us in the drawing room for a while,' her father said, and his tone was not that of someone making a request.

'But I'm—'

'Just for half an hour or so. You never used to retire so early.'

'I never used to have reason to.'

Frederick glared at her. 'I shall put that unhandsome remark down to your tiredness. This time. As well as your rudeness to William.'

Beatrice glared back at him briefly, then her eyes dropped.

Frederick offered his arm to Annie and they led the way into the drawing room. The other women followed, but

Beatrice sat as far away from them as possible and added nothing to the conversation. After exactly half an hour she stood up.

Frederick stood up, too. 'Good night, Beatrice.'

'Good night, Father.'

As she turned to leave, his voice cracked out like a whip, bringing her to a sudden halt. 'You're forgetting your manners again, girl. Say good night to your stepmother.'

Beatrice breathed deeply and half-turned round, staring in the air above Annie's head. 'Good night, Stepmother.'

'Good night, Beatrice.'

'And to Jane,' he said.

Beatrice looked amazed, but complied. 'Good night, Jane.'

Jane nodded. She had hardly said a word since they entered the drawing room.

When the door had closed behind her, Annie let out her breath in a whoosh, forgetting Jane was there. 'It's going to be a long two and a half months, Frederick, love.'

'Very long. But,' he took her in his arms, 'you and I will have certain consolations.'

Jane slipped out of the room. They did not notice.

The question of a lady's maid for Annie took nearly three weeks to resolve, during which time Peggy helped her mistress out when necessary, and a newly hired general maid helped both upstairs and downstairs as needed. Mrs Jarred made enquiries locally and discovered no one suitable for a lady's maid, so she wrote to an employment bureau in Manchester which had found staff for her before. Two of the candidates they put forward seemed possible, so she arranged for them to come to Bilsden to be interviewed.

Annie, who was still not resigned to having a maid to look after her, left most of the arrangements to Mrs Jarred, and insisted that the housekeeper share the task of interviewing the candidates with her. 'Who is to be the first? Tell me about her.'

'Her name is Grimson. She's been working in the south.'

'Not Cora Grimson?'

'Yes. Do you know her?'

'There was a Cora Grimson who used to work for the Lewises! She left Bilsden with Mrs Lewis, when the doctor's wife went to live in Brighton. Surely it can't be the same one!'

But it was. Though Cora was looking much older. Something about her – perhaps it was the look in her eyes – made Annie feel uneasy. She left most of the questioning to Mrs Jarred, but when the references were produced, she saw to her surprise that there were none from Annabelle Lewis, or even from Jeremy. They were from some unknown lady in Brighton, though.

'Didn't you work for Mrs Lewis?' Annie asked just before she dismissed the woman.

'Yes, ma'am. At one time I did.'

'Were you not with her when she died?'

'No, ma'am. I'd moved on to Mrs Beattie by then.' A fictional lady, Mrs Beattie. Cora had paid good money for that reference, which came from an accommodation address which supplied references to servants who'd been dismissed – for a price.

The explanation didn't ring true. Annie didn't know why, but it was just one more thing that made her feel uneasy about Cora.

Cora, who had intended to open her own business after Annabelle Lewis died, a little shop, perhaps, for she'd saved up a decent sum of money, found that she'd lost the heart for it. She still had nightmares about that terrible night, nightmares about the blood Annabelle had lost after the baby's birth. Cora had been staying with her family since then, but when she came back to the north, she didn't let on that she had all that money saved in the bank. They were beginning to wonder about her nightmares, though, and she'd decided to leave soon. Getting a position as a lady's maid seemed like a good thing to do for a year or so, until she'd recovered her spirits and made a few plans.

'I'll let you know my decision shortly, if you care to wait in the kitchen,' Annie said.

When Cora had left, Mrs Jarred looked at Annie and pulled a face. 'She's a hard one, that. I didn't take to her at all. I don't know why. Do you know her?'

'Only slightly. And I didn't take to her either.'

The next applicant was an older woman with a worn face, who jumped nervously every time a question was asked; and whose voice had a whining edge to it. Annie didn't take to her, either. She looked at Mrs Jarred when the woman had left. 'She won't do. That voice would drive me mad within an hour. What are we to do? Wait for other candidates? I'm afraid Mr Hallam is pressing me to find a maid.'

'Well . . .' Mrs Jarred hesitated.

'Go on!'

'I do have a niece who's looking for a position. She came home to look after her mother, but my sister-in-law died recently. Laura used to be a chambermaid, but she helped her mistress from time to time as well. She loves clothes and she's good with hair. She'd need training, but,' she broke off, then said hastily, 'I will understand if you prefer not to—'

'If she's your niece, I'm very willing to talk to her. Tell her to come and see me tomorrow. I'm not promising anything, but she can't be any worse than those two. Will you tell them they've not got the position?'

Cora smiled wryly to herself as she walked back down Ridge Hill to wait for the afternoon coach to Manchester.

That settled it. She definitely couldn't work as a lady's maid again. She might try London – or even – she paused, wondering if she dared do it, then shrugged her shoulders. Why not? She'd go back to Brighton. She'd been thinking for a while of setting up as a madam, after all she'd learned from Annabelle Lewis. She couldn't do it on her own, but maybe Thomas Minton would help. You were always better off in that business with a man to protect you. And if he wouldn't help her, if things didn't look promising in Brighton, then she might go to London and see what she could pick up there. She should never have come back to Bilsden. She'd go mad from boredom in a place like this.

Laura Jarred proved to be much better than the first two applicants. She was a rosy-faced girl, well turned out and with an open friendly expression.

'Let's give her a try-out, shall we, Mrs Jarred? A month, say?'

Mrs Jarred beamed at her. 'That would be fine, ma'am. I'll let her know.'

And so Annie got her maid, to Frederick's relief. He didn't at all like to see her mending or brushing her own clothes. He would have preferred her to find a more experienced woman, but Annie seemed happy with Laura, so he didn't interfere. He had enough on his plate at home with Beatrice, who was continuing to behave in a spiteful and often childish way. And more than enough on his plate at work, for he'd decided to go into partnership with Dawton – with a few conditions, of course – and there was a lot to sort out.

Annie had expected Beatrice to accompany her as she started to go about and learn the ways of the town's ladies, but Beatrice flatly refused to go with her, indeed, refused even to speak to her stepmother when her father was not there. Annie did not intend to ask Frederick to bring the girl to heel about this, and did not really care, so Beatrice stayed at home sulking and Annie went out on her own.

She made a particular point of calling on Eva Bagley, wife of the town's chief haulage contractor. Annie never forgot those who had done her a kindness.

'How did your calls go today, my love?' Frederick asked over dinner that night.

'Very well. I found Mrs Bagley particularly kind and welcoming.'

Frederick could not fail to notice the sour expression on his daughter's face. 'Did you not enjoy your outing today, Beatrice?'

'I didn't go.' She saw his expression tighten and said hastily, 'I had a headache.'

'I see. It doesn't seem to have impaired your appetite tonight.'

'The headache's gone now.'

He did not try to include his daughter in the conversation for the rest of the meal, but when it was over, he turned to Annie. 'I'll join you presently, love. Jane, would you mind? I'd like a word with Beatrice.'

His voice was soft, but his expression was grim as he closed the door behind the others and turned to his daughter. 'In future, Beatrice, you will accompany your stepmother on her calls and you will sit with her to receive visitors when she's at home. And I shall make it my business to find out exactly how you behave in public, believe me. Is that understood?'

Beatrice concentrated on the thought of the dowry. Dear Reginald had been very apologetic that he had to concern himself with such mundane things, but as a younger son he hadn't enough money to take an undowered wife. 'Yes, Father.' Her knuckles were white as she clutched her table napkin.

'Beatrice, can we not stop this bickering and live comfortably together until you marry?'

'I'm not the one who's bickering. My stepmother is the one who's causing trouble.'

'You know she isn't.'

Beatrice told herself that it was foolish to antagonise the one who held the purse strings and just stared down at her plate.

He sighed. 'Very well. If you will not co-operate, I've decided not to pay your dowry until the day before your wedding, and payment will be conditional upon your good behaviour.' He paused, but she said nothing, only clenched her fists tightly in her lap. 'I think Annie and I can dispense with your company this evening.'

Beatrice ran upstairs and threw herself on the bed, sobbing wildly.

Mabel moved across to take her mistress in her arms and pet her like a child. 'There, there. Never mind,' she murmured, stroking the flushed face and smoothing back the dark tear-damp hair as she listened to Beatrice's diatribe against her stepmother. 'We'll think of some way to get back at her,' she said when the torrent of abuse ended.

'But how? My father says now that he won't pay my dowry until the day before the wedding. And he won't pay it at all if I upset his precious little wife.'

'Then we shall have to wait until you're married before we do something, shan't we?' Every time Mabel saw Annie queening it as mistress of this household, every time another servant spoke well of the new mistress, she felt physically sick with envy. By now, she had lost any sense of reason about her dealings with one whom she regarded as an old enemy.

Beatrice lay there for a moment, then sniffed and asked, 'But what can we do, Mabel? We'll be moving to London after my wedding.'

Mabel smiled, the smile of a hungry cat contemplating a juicy fishhead. 'Oh, I'll think of something. You leave it to me. When I care about someone, I don't let anyone hurt them.'

'D-do you care about me, Mabel?'

'Oh, yes, miss. I care very greatly. I love looking after you.' And that at least was the truth. Mabel might not have Annie's instinct for style, but she was meticulous in her duties, loving to handle the rich fabrics and to brush and fix her young mistress's hair. She had wanted to be a proper lady's maid for so very long before she got this position. And it was Annie Gibson who had prevented her from achieving her ambition before, when she had been working for Mrs Lewis. For that Annie deserved all she got.

8

March to April 1849

In later years, Annie always thought of the last few weeks before Beatrice's wedding as the lull before the storm. For every one of those weeks she had a feeling that something was looming, something unpleasant, and when Frederick noticed her abstraction, about a month before the wedding, and tried to joke her out of it, she burst into tears, to her own surprise and to his consternation. Yet she could not explain what was wrong.

And indeed, except for the annoyance of putting up with Beatrice and her sulky behaviour, things were going well for her and for most of the people she knew. She was beginning to find her feet as Frederick's wife, and no longer felt strange when addressed as 'Mrs Hallam' or 'ma'am'. She had grown quite used to ordering a large household, though in truth, Mrs Jarred was so capable that Annie felt superfluous. She had even grown used to having her own maid, and was quite enjoying teaching Laura the finer points of sewing, mending and caring for clothes.

Even the salon was functioning smoothly and Mary Benworth had now gained the confidence not only to manage it properly, but to suggest improvements and extensions to the services provided there. And if Hardy in the draper's shop next door was as ill as he looked, maybe they would be able to extend the salon one day soon, as Annie and Tom had often discussed, for Hardy had no son to follow him, only three married daughters, none of whom lived in Bilsden.

So why she should have this niggling worry at the back of her mind, she could not think. And when she went out in town, she had started to feel as though someone was following her, which was plain ridiculous. She had caught sight once or twice of the cadaverous man she had seen on the way to her wedding, but when she began to wonder if he was following her, he seemed to vanish from the face of the earth for a while. And yet, she still felt as if she were being watched.

'I think I'll go and visit Kathy this afternoon,' she said idly to Frederick one day as he was getting ready to go into Manchester to the Exchange.

'Give her my regards,' Frederick said, coming across to plant a farewell kiss on her cheek. 'You know, I greatly envy you the closeness of the Gibson family.'

She looked at him in surprise. 'Well, you're part of the family now.'

'So I am. But maybe I'll feel more like I belong to it when your father stops calling me "Mester Hallam" and when Kathy stops jumping every time I address a remark to her.'

'Give them time.'

As he sat alone in his carriage being driven to Manchester to meet the other cotton men and deal in the staple of the industry, Frederick thought with wry amusement how strange it was that he should envy John and Tom Gibson, two of his former operatives. The other thing he envied was Annie's closeness to her son, who was a fine lad and whose love for his mother shone in his eyes.

Frederick was finding that it was one thing to vow to be a better father this time round, but quite another to build up a close relationship with a lad of ten who was clearly jealous of the amount of time Frederick spent with his mother, and who went back to see his grandfather every time he had a problem. It was even more difficult to form a relationship with the boy when Beatrice sat at the table every night scowling impartially at everyone, even poor Cousin Jane, who had surely never hurt anyone in her life, and putting a distinct damper on the conversation. It irritated him a little that Jane always hovered on the fringes of their life like a sad ghost. He'd tell Beatrice to take Jane to London with her when she was married. He'd continue to pay Jane's allowance, of course, but the fewer people living at Ridge House the better. He wanted Annie to himself.

During the daytime, the other ladies of the town called on Annie regularly and some of them, at least, genuinely welcomed her into their homes. But none of them, not even Eva Bagley, formed a truly close friendship with her. They were a little afraid of her sharp tongue and her intelligence, and they never quite knew what to expect from someone with her background, however ladylike she appeared. Many of them had risen in the world, and some were still rising as their husbands made money, but none of them had started from such a lowly role as maidservant to Mrs Lewis, and none of them had grown up in the Rows.

Unfortunately, Pauline Hinchcliffe was away for several weeks after the wedding, staying with a cousin in Scotland. She was not to return to Bilsden until the middle of March and Annie missed her greatly. Only with Pauline and with her own family, did she feel relaxed nowadays and able just to be herself.

So when Pauline came bustling into her sitting room one afternoon in early March without giving the indignant Winnie a chance to find out if her mistress were at home, Annie's face lit up. She flew across the room to hug her friend. 'Pauline, how lovely to see you! I didn't know you were back.'

'I returned a little early. I'd had enough of my cousins. I only stayed this long because Stephen was getting on well with them.' She hugged Annie in return, then held her at arm's length and studied her face. 'How are you, my dear? I haven't seen you since the wedding. You look well, but there's a shadow in your eyes. What's wrong?'

Annie, who had just had an icy interchange with Beatrice, wished her friend were not quite so shrewd. She tried to avoid answering that question. 'It's lovely to see you again. Do come and sit down.'

Pauline pulled off her fur-lined gloves and cloak, noticed that the parlourmaid was still hovering to take them away, and said cheerfully, 'I hope you're going to give me more than a cup of tea. I'm famished after visiting some of the poorer members of Saul's flock this afternoon. Really, some of those women are so foolish! They spend their money wildly when they have it, then their families go hungry when it runs out. They have no thought for the morrow.'

Annie dismissed Winnie and hid a smile as she turned back to Pauline. 'I'm sure you told the women you visited that.'

'I certainly did.'

'And then you helped them.' Annie chuckled, knowing the answer already. Pauline had helped her, too, when she was first pregnant and newly dismissed by Annabelle Lewis, and Pauline had been very brusque, but practical in the help offered. The Collett family had always helped the nearby villagers, but the poor of a bustling industrial town were a different breed, with different needs and a sturdy independence that made them accept help only grudgingly. Whenever they could, they preferred to help one another.

But since Pauline's marriage to Saul Hinchcliffe, Annie had watched her mentor and benefactress develop a genuine interest in the lives of the poorer members of the small Methodist congregation. She knew that Pauline had now begun to help townsfolk who weren't in the congregation, and that Pauline had once or twice had sharp words with Jonas Dawton about the way he treated his workers. Frederick usually managed to find some other work for his employees in the slack times or remitted their rents and provided food for them, but Dawton either could not or would not help his people in any way, and simply laid them off till times were better.

Annie had found out recently that Frederick had bought a share in Dawton's mill and had been furious. 'I don't like even associating with that man! He makes my flesh crawl. How could you go into business with him, Frederick?'

'He has a good business there if he will only manage it properly and stop taking profit out without putting money in. But if he's going to go to the wall, I want to be the one who takes the business over. He has some choice property near the town centre, you know, as well as the mill.'

'You'll never persuade that one to look after his people,' Annie retorted.

'Oh, we're making some progress,' Frederick replied, and since then had not mentioned the matter again, though he had entertained Jonas Dawton and his wife to dinner. Annie realised that Pauline was speaking and dragged her attention back to the present. No need to spoil this visit by pouring out her troubles and worries.

Pauline shrugged. 'Well, *someone* must help our poorer brethren. We can't sit and watch folk starve, can we?'

'Of course not. And you do wonders in this town.'

'I mean to involve you in helping people from now on.'

Annie gaped. 'Me? Oh no! I'm *not* going to join the Ladies' Society for the Relief of the Deserving Poor. I'd feel an absolute fool trying to play Lady Bountiful.'

A most unladylike grin creased Pauline's pale features. 'Fool or not, there's want and improvidence among the poorer folk, and it's your duty as Frederick Hallam's wife to do something about that.'

'Our people are well looked after,' Annie protested.

'And Dawton's people? I believe Frederick is taking an interest there.'

Annie flushed. 'No. They're not well looked after. But Matt Peters is starting to change things now.'

'Well, that will take time and until then, I've one or two schemes in mind and you needn't think you're going to escape involvement But you needn't worry. I shan't be doing it through that silly society.'

Annie sighed. When Pauline got that look on her face, you were just wasting your time trying to go against her wishes. 'I'll think about it.'

'You'll do more than think about it, my girl.'

A sudden memory of herself at seventeen, pregnant and facing ruin, needing all the help she could get, made Annie capitulate. 'Well, start slowly then, and give me time to get used to it. I really shall feel a fool at first.'

Pauline nodded, but her expression did not settle into its usual calm assurance that all was right with her world, and a frown was still wrinkling her brow.

'How are things at home, Pauline? My father says Mr Hinchcliffe hasn't been looking well lately.' Annie now went to St Mark's Parish Church with her husband – when they went at all – as even her father acknowledged to be her wifely duty. John Gibson had just assumed that a wife would follow her husband's lead in religion and made no fuss about Annie's defection from the chapel.

Pauline hesitated. She was not used to confiding in people. But she needed to talk to someone, and Annie had a good head on her. 'Saul's well enough in body, but not in spirit. I tell you frankly, Annie, that if it weren't for him, I would never have joined the Methodists. They're a rigid lot, even more rigid than the Established Church which they deride for its immutability.'

'Has something happened to upset Saul?'

'The local Circuit Council *has* decided that my husband should move on to another chapel. They say he's been here in Bilsden far too long. And they're complaining about the way he conducts his services, saying he should allow more lay preaching and hold more meetings to call sinners to redemption. And some of them are even complaining about the flowers I send to the chapel every week, saying that such decoration smacks of the Established Church.'

'Dad says Mr Hinchcliffe's sermons are getting very long.'

'Far too long. And far too abstruse for the congregation. I think – I'm beginning to wonder whether he's trying to convince himself that he still cares as deeply as he used to about Methodism.'

'My father also says—' Annie broke off, not sure whether this comment would be wise.

'Tell me what your father says. He's become a very influential figure in the chapel, in his quiet way.' Pauline saw that Annie was still hesitating and added, 'I'd rather know. Truly I would. How else am I to help Saul?'

'Dad says folk need to find their own way to God, not have it all spelled out for them by a minister. And he agrees with the Circuit Council. He'd like to let the lay preachers speak in chapel more often. I think sometimes that he'd like to become a lay preacher himself, though he's not yet dared to stand up and preach.'

Pauline was fiddling with her skirt. 'Between you and me, Annie, I think Saul is going through a period of doubting his calling. And I can't seem to find a way to help him.'

'Perhaps he really does need some time away from Bilsden, then.'

'My dear, how can we move? I can't and won't leave

Collett House. It's been my family's home for generations. And I don't think Saul really wants to leave, either. He loves his library and our quiet life there.'

'I always did think that he enjoyed the teaching and studying side of his ministry more than the preaching.'

Pauline stared at Annie as if she had said something of vast import. 'Yes. Yes, he does. I wonder . . .' Then she changed the subject firmly. 'That's enough of that. I came here to see how you were. Is everything all right?' She saw Annie's expression. 'There *is* something wrong. I knew it. Is there a problem with Frederick? Surely he's treating you well? He seemed quite besotted with you at the wedding.'

There was a knock on the door and Winnie entered, carrying a tray loaded with sandwiches and cakes, followed by Jen from the kitchen with the tea things on another tray.

Annie waited until the door had closed behind the two maids, then realised that Pauline, tenacious as ever, was still waiting for an answer. 'No, of course there's no problem with Frederick.'

'Then what is it?'

'It's Beatrice, I'm afraid.'

'I might have known. Christine didn't just spoil that girl; she ruined her.'

'Yes. Beatrice bitterly resents me taking her mother's place.'

'She should have been spanked regularly as a child.'

'She's a bit too old for spanking now.' Annie's hands had itched to smack Beatrice's sneering face several times in the past few weeks.

'More's the pity.'

'Never mind. She's getting married next month. And I doubt she'll come back to visit.' Beatrice had made that very plain. She and Reginald were to buy a house in London and she hoped never to see Bilsden again as long as she lived. 'So it's just a question of endurance.'

'Endurance can be very wearing.'

'Yes.' And Annie hadn't been feeling in the best of health, either, to cope with it. She suspected that she might be pregnant, and knew that Frederick could count the weeks as well as she could, but she had not brought the subject out into the open. She felt embarrassed to think of bearing a child so soon after the wedding – and if it came early, it would give the gossips more ammunition. And she was a little afraid, too. Still, it was early days yet. She would wait until she was more certain before she voiced her suspicions or went to consult Jeremy Lewis.

Pauline changed the subject and began to talk about her visit to Scotland.

Annie was relieved that the confidences were at an end. She didn't think it helped to talk of her problems with Beatrice, and Frederick would hate to have his daughter's spiteful behaviour known in the town. She had endured the girl for two months already. She could and would endure one month more.

Tom told his partner at the Shepherd's Rest to give Rosie her job back when she recovered from her lying-in.

Seth nodded. 'All right. She's a good lass, Rosie is. Draws a nice pint.' He was very fussy about how his beer was treated.

Tom always had to rein in his impatience with Seth, who doled out words as if each one cost him a guinea. Their partnership was still quite recent and Tom had found that Seth, a conservative man at heart, could only cope with one change at a time. 'You know we said we'd get someone in to sing to the customers in the new room,' he said.

Seth nodded.

'Well, Rosie can do that.'

Seth thought this over, then nodded again. 'She used to

do a bit of singing here afore she fell for the bairn. Yes, all right.'

'Well, this won't be like before. This time I'm going to get a piano and put it in the big room. We'll need to find someone to play it. An' we're not going to let folk behave roughly in there from now on. After all, we don't want the piano damaging, do we?'

Seth shuddered at the thought, then shook his head, grinned and flexed his big muscular arms. 'I'll make sure no one does that.'

'So you give Rosie her job back. An' pay her double what we were payin' her.'

'What!' If there was one thing Seth disliked it was paying out money.

'You heard me. She'll more than earn it. I'll make sure of that.'

Seth heaved a great sigh.

Tom walked across the bar room to stare into the large room at the back. 'An' get this place whitewashed. It's filthy, with all that smoking. I don't know how folks can enjoy tobacco. It tastes and smells foul to me. And get the floor scrubbed every morning, too.'

'Folk don't mind a dirty floor,' protested Seth, for whom cleanliness in anything but the making of his precious beer was not a high priority. 'They'll only spit on it an' spill beer on it if we clean it up.'

'Then we'll keep cleaning it up,' said Tom, striving for patience. 'An' we'll give them spittoons.'

'They won't use them.'

Tom gave a wolflike smile. 'Oh, I'll make sure they do. Leave that to me.' He stared at the room through narrowed eyes. 'And you're not to dismiss Rosie without my say-so.' He knew that Rosie had an impulsive nature and a quick tongue.

Seth winked. 'I understand.'

Tom stared at him coldly. 'No, you don't. You don't understand a bloody thing. Any help I give Rosie is out of past friendship, *long past*. She got herself in trouble after I stopped seein' her an' I don't want to see her starve. You should have told me she was expecting, by the way.'

Seth shrugged. 'Barmaids are allus having bairns. It didn't seem owt special. I knew you'd stopped seeing her.'

'Aye, well, I'll not be seeing anyone again like that. I'm a happily married man nowadays, an' I don't even fancy any other women. Not with a wife like mine.'

He looked so fierce as he said it that Seth swallowed hard and nodded. 'I can see that, Tom lad.'

'We're getting Rosie back here because when we open our free-and-easy in the better part of town, we want her to sing for us there. She can practise doing it here.'

'She's got a right nice voice,' Seth allowed.

'She's got more than a nice voice. She's got a bloody lovely voice. So we're going to pay for singing lessons for her, too.'

Seth gaped at him. 'Whaffor?'

'So she can sing better. So she can learn new songs.'

'But—'

'So we can make more money.'

'Ah.' Seth still didn't understand why singing lessons were necessary for someone who could already sing like a skylark, but if Tom Gibson said they'd make more money out of Rosie by doing that, then Seth was willing to go along with it and see what happened. Since Tom had taken a hand in the business, Seth had been making more money than he had ever expected to see in his life. Not just making it, but keeping it, though Tom insisted on them putting it in the bank when Seth would have preferred to keep his savings at home where he could count them.

Tom said Seth had a rare hand with the beer an' if he didn't drink too much of his own stuff, Tom would see he got rich. Seth wouldn't mind being rich. He was getting older now and he wanted to make sure he didn't starve when he got too old to work. Of course, he had a bit saved. He was a careful man. But you could never have enough money. 'All right,' he said again. 'Whatever you say, Tom lad.'

Tom nodded. 'You just keep makin' the beer. Is that warehouse I rented for you to brew it in all right?'

'Aye. I've got the first brew mashing nicely.'

'Good. So you'll see Rosie an' offer her a job, eh?'

'Me?'

'Yes, you.'

'Why can't you see her?'

'Because I'm a married man an' because it's you as runs this place.'

'Oh.'

'So go and see her today.'

'All right.' Eyes narrowed in thought, Seth watched Tom leave. There was more to this than just business. Whoever heard of Tom Gibson increasing someone's wages like that? Well, whatever was going on, that was Tom's secret. Seth just hoped this business with Rosie wouldn't set a precedent for the other employees. The less you could pay folk the more money you could make out of what they did for you.

When Annie moved out of Netherleigh Cottage and William followed, she left a hole in the lives of her family which was not nearly filled by her visits, frequent though these were. Kathy, urged on by the maid, Lally, whom Annie had chosen because of her native shrewdness, found herself entertaining other women from chapel to tea, and found herself enjoying these small social events. She also began to help her less fortunate brethren from the chapel, in a shy hesitant way that gave offence to no one, because she was now rich – rich meant you had everything you needed and something to spare. It did to Kathy, and the Bible said you should share your wealth with those in need.

Young Samuel John grew and thrived, his rosy face so like his half-brother Tom's that everyone remarked on it. The baby and her husband were the centre of Kathy's universe, the treasures she had never expected to win on earth, and she thanked the Lord most fervently every day for the blessings he had heaped upon her. She was well aware that her thin frame and nondescript features displayed no hint of beauty, but John didn't seem to mind that, and continued to demonstrate his love for her as often as a man half his age. When she found she was expecting a baby for a second time, they were both delighted.

Tom was not delighted when he found out. His father had eight children living now, and that was enough for anyone. Tom still felt embarrassed at his father starting a third family in his fifties. And young Samuel John looked so much like Tom's unwanted son by Rosie that he could hardly bear to look at the child nowadays. He was starting to worry that other folk in the town might notice the resemblance and wondering whether he should pay Rosie to move elsewhere. He saw his father and half-brothers every day at the yard, of course, but he called less frequently at Netherleigh Cottage, leaving that to Marianne, and pleading a rush of business.

Rebecca was not interested in babies, either Kathy's or Marianne's coming event. She was sorry that Annie had left the salon, but was still enjoying her life as an apprentice seamstress there, and was secretly trying to design gowns like Annie did. At thirteen Rebecca had not yet started getting her figure, but she wore her clothes with style and behaved as if she were a woman grown, ordering her brothers and sisters round imperiously and quarrelling with Mark when he did not do as she bade him. You couldn't quarrel with Luke. He just wouldn't let you.

Mark was not at all interested in his baby half-brother, or in whether Kathy had any more children. What he was interested in, obsessed with even, was the business and making money. He had now become a member of the fledgling Working Men's Institute started by Frederick Hallam, which was temporarily housed in St Mark's church hall until Frederick could persuade the businessmen of the town that it was to their interest to pay for a building where they could extend the skills of the young men who worked for them.

John was not sure that he approved of his son spending time at St Mark's church hall, for whatever reason, but when he voiced his concerns, Mark became angry.

'I'm trying to improve myself, Dad! What's wrong with that?'

'But you're going to St Marks. We're Methodists.'

'I'm only going to the church hall to borrow books and talk to folk. I'm not going to the services. There's nothing wrong with the 'Stute an' what we do at the hall has no connection with religion, as I keep tellin' you.'

'Those others are all older than you. I don't want you getting into mischief, not with drink or with girls, mind.'

'Honestly, Dad! I'm not interested in girls.' Which was not quite true. Mark had begun to notice girls, but he had not dared do anything about it so far other than look. 'Anyway, the other fellows don't know I'm younger than them, so don't you go telling anyone.' He flung out of the house before his father could answer and went down to the church hall.

At first he hovered shyly on the fringes of groups there, doing more listening than talking. Most of the other fellows were arrogant with all the vigour of young manhood, whatever their station in life, and none of them realised that Mark was still only fifteen, partly because he was working in a man's job at the yard. It pleased him that he looked older than his years, and that already he was the tallest in his family.

He knew he was a solemn fellow, and he could not remember ever feeling as young and carefree as some of the men he met at the 'Stute. That was his mother's fault, he reckoned. He had learned early about the harsh realities of life from her feckless ways, yes, and learned about hunger, too.

But as he gained in confidence, Mark decided that most of the other fellows were rather stupid. They used the 'Stute more like a social club, not thinking of what they could learn there and not bothering to borrow the books Frederick and Saul Hinchcliffe had provided. They attended the lantern shows for entertainment and frequently interrupted the speakers to shout ribald comments instead of listening and learning. And they often teased Mark about his studiousness and his refusal to go out with them for a beer. He would have gone with them if he could have seen any benefit in it, whatever his dad said about the evils of drink, but he couldn't see any benefit in boozing yourself silly, and he didn't really like the taste of beer, so he continued to save his money and concentrate on improving his skills and knowledge. And when the other young men discussed women, Mark just listened. Women, everyone agreed, only wanted to marry you and saddle you with children.

He wasn't going to get wed, he decided, not till he was at least thirty, anyway. He was going to make something of himself first.

At the end of February, Jeremy Lewis asked his housekeeper to come and see him in the parlour after dinner. 'I need to talk to you about Catherine,' he said by way of an excuse.

He was finding it increasingly difficult to get a moment alone with Ellie, who was observing the proprieties with the utmost care, and who usually spent her evenings with Hetty in the nursery.

When Ellie knocked, he went to open the door himself. 'Come in, love.'

She looked round, afraid someone would hear. 'Shh!'

He closed the door and pulled her into his arms, and though she resisted at first, after a moment she sighed and allowed him to kiss her then cuddle her against him. 'Ellie Peters,' he said in her ear, 'I don't intend to wait any longer to make you my wife.'

She jerked in his arms. 'Jeremy, you know it won't look well if we marry so soon after Mrs Lewis's death.'

'Marianne and I've been discussing that.' The soft warmth of Ellie's plump body against his only reinforced his desire for her and it was an effort to speak calmly. He certainly needed her body, for he had always had a healthy sexual appetite and he had not wanted to visit the houses in Manchester since he had declared his love for Ellie. But he had realised recently that he also needed the sheer comfort of her presence beside him, in bed, at his table, sympathising when he lost a patient who should have lived, something to which he had never grown accustomed. He drew her over to the sofa and sat down, holding her hands in his and staring at her earnestly. 'You do love me, don't you, Ellie? You do still want to marry me?'

'You know I do, Jeremy.'

'Then let me have the banns called. No, listen to me, love. Marianne and I've been discussing this. She thinks that if we tell folk that I'm marrying you to give Catherine a mother, they'll accept our marriage without too much trouble.'

'They'd accept it if I weren't your housekeeper,' she said bluntly. 'As it is, they'll talk. You know how folk can be.'

'Ellie, I don't care about things like that.'

'Well, you should care. First Frederick Hallam marrying a woman from the Rows, then you marrying your house-keeper. And doing it so soon after your wife's death, too. The gossips will have a feast. A doctor's got to think of his good name, you know.'

He pulled her to him and silenced her protests with a kiss. 'I need you, Ellie. Desperately. Please marry me soon.'

He looked so wistful as he spoke that she hesitated.

'People will talk whenever we marry,' he said in her ear. 'You know they will.'

She stared at him, for once unable to hide her own longing. 'I – I – oh, very well.'

He held her away from him and shook her gently in mock dismay. 'Never did a woman accept a proposal so reluctantly. I'm dismayed, demoralised, distressed—'

She put her hand over his mouth. 'This is nothing to joke about. Jeremy, are you sure? Are you really sure?'

'Of course I'm sure. I love you, Ellie Peters, and have done for a long time.'

Three weeks later they were married at a simple service in St Mark's Parish Church. Ralph Hemmerson, the curate, officiated. Theophilus Kenderby had not appeared in public since his daughter ran away with Daniel Connor. Gossip said that Kenderby had become morose, and when a strong manservant suddenly appeared at the parsonage, they said that the old parson had lost his wits and had to be confined for his own safety. Only Jeremy knew that Kenderby was suffering from a growth of the stomach and had sunk into a depression, confronted at last by his own mortality, and having to face this on his own, without the daughter upon whom he had leaned and whom he had tyrannised for so long.

Although Sam Peters, the father of the bride and the man

who had brought Methodism to Bilsden, disapproved of his daughter getting married in the parish church, like John Gibson, he acknowledged that it was a wife's duty to follow her husband's lead in worship, so he agreed to attend and to give away the bride. Mrs Peters was brought to the wedding, the first time she had appeared in public for a long time. Jeremy gave Sam something to calm her down and the woman who looked after Elizabeth stayed close beside her all the time.

Although folk nodded to Mrs Peters, they had been asked to leave her to herself, told only that she was suffering from nervous debility. Perhaps because Elizabeth had wanted to see her eldest daughter married for so long that it had become one of her many obsessions, and also because her new son-in-law looked so much the gentleman, she sat and smiled throughout the proceedings. She seemed to have forgotten that she had once hated Jeremy Lewis. She had also forgotten her hatred for Annie Gibson, and smiled at her, too, mouthing her maiden name as she passed.

Elizabeth's rate of decline seemed to be accelerating. This was the last time she was able to go out, the last hint of sanity, which soon slipped away, leaving her an angry woman, not knowing why she was so angry, only knowing that she had lost something – if only she could remember what – and striking out against those who tried to restrain her from wandering away to seek it.

Matt Peters was a pillar of strength to his father on that wedding day, for Sam felt as ill at ease with a daughter marrying into the gentry as John Gibson had done. But Matt looked very much the gentleman himself, in a fine new suit of dark brown worsted and a brilliant white stock. And if his eyes dwelled upon Annie rather often, well, only he knew how much he regretted his behaviour all those years ago, and he admitted, to himself at least, how foolish he had been to lose her. As Hallam's wife, she was as far distant from him now as the stars in the sky. He knew that. And it was more than time he got wed. He was beginning to look around for a wife, but it was not easy, for there was no one to equal Annie, and anyway, most women of his age were wed already. Still, a man in his position needed a wife, needed children, too, else why strive so hard to better yourself?

The other Peters children, all grown up now, came back to see their sister wed, bringing their families with them. They seemed like strangers to Ellie, all except Lily, who had stayed on in Bilsden and still lived with her parents. Seeing them all together brought a tinge of sadness to Ellie's face, as did the sight of her mother's vacant expression.

'Are you all right, my love?' Jeremy whispered afterwards, as they drove away from the church.

She nodded.

'Are you sure? You looked so sad just then.'

She smiled at him. 'I was just thinking about my brothers and sisters. How far apart we've grown! I haven't seen our Patty for years, and yet she could hardly be bothered to talk to me yesterday. She treated me like a stranger. Life's funny, isn't it? You never know what's round the next corner.'

He nodded. 'Very funny.' And for a moment his own expression grew sad, as he thought of how unhappy he had been with his first wife. Her death had released him from a nearly intolerable bondage, but he still shuddered when he thought of how she had looked in death, so bitter, so worn, old before her time, with all her beauty destroyed. Then he squeezed Ellie's hand and the warmth of her touch made him smile again. He knew for certain that he wouldn't be unhappy with his second wife.

After the wedding, a reception was held at the Three Feathers Inn, which had been partly refurbished a few years ago. It had a room where parties might be held, though it was getting a bit shabby nowadays. Bill Odhall, the landlord, was as obsequious as ever, but he seemed to have lost his grip on business matters and his catering arrangements were not as good as they should have been. Still, no one let that worry them. They were here to celebrate a wedding, not fuss about details.

Frederick stood at the side of the room with Annie, watching the crowd and feeling happy and relaxed. Beatrice had been invited to the wedding, out of courtesy, but Frederick had not insisted she attend, not wanting to spoil Jeremy Lewis's day. So the pleasure of the celebrations was unalloyed. He grinned as he bent to murmur in Annie's ear, 'Does your son never run out of energy?'

She leaned against him briefly and smiled at the sight of William talking and gesticulating furiously to Luke and Rebecca. 'No. Not unless he's ill.'

Beaming with pride, Jeremy was escorting his new wife round the room to speak to all the guests.

'Do you think they'll be happy?' Frederick wondered aloud.

Annie caught Ellie's eyes and smiled across the room. 'I'm sure they will.'

'Not as happy as we shall be once Beatrice has left,' he said confidently.

Annie could not understand why a shiver ran down her spine as he mentioned Beatrice's name. 'Don't tempt Providence, talking like that,' she said lightly. 'No one is guaranteed happiness.'

'I'm tempting nothing, Annie, my love. I shall work in every way I can for your happiness. And for that of our children.' He picked up a glass of wine and raised it to her in a silent toast. 'You're everything a man could want in a wife.'

They clinked glasses, but afterwards she frowned, feeling

uneasy about his confidence in the future, she knew not why. He let the subject drop, content just to be with her and to share in Jeremy Lewis's special day. She tried to forget the hungry women waiting at the back of the inn for the scraps from the feast. Progress at Dawton's was very slow, and she was beginning to wonder whether Frederick regretted going into partnership with that man.

9

April 1849

The day of Beatrice's wedding came round at last. Annie woke early and watched the rising sun poke shafts of light through the heavy brocade curtains on to the edge of the new carpet. As the sun's rays grew stronger and fanned across the bedroom ceiling near the window, she smiled. She was glad this day had arrived, glad, too, that the winter was over, even though the weather hadn't exactly been warm lately. Sunshine, however weak and fitful, always cheered you up. She hoped it wouldn't rain today. Nat Jervis had said it might just hold off until after the wedding and he was usually right about the weather.

Frederick was still asleep, having been up late entertaining their gentlemen guests, so she blew him a silent kiss, then lay there for a while, lost in her own thoughts. She was in no hurry to get up in a house full of guests, and besides, rising the minute she awoke made her feel sick lately.

She was not looking forward to her day's duties as hostess. Frederick's family were a stiff-necked bunch in her opinion. To her surprise, Beatrice was as spiteful and sulky with her brother and sister, and in company generally, as she was in private, and far from being upset by this, Reginald Barrence seemed to regard it as a source of entertainment. He remained rather detached from everything and everyone around him, even his fiancée, as if he felt himself superior to them. Well, just let him patronise me once more, Annie decided. I've had as much as I can take of him patronising me.

But she knew she would do nothing to spoil this day. Surely even Beatrice would be happy on her wedding day? And pigs might fly over the moors, Annie thought, still frowning. None of Frederick's children seemed to know how to be happy. Or if they did, they didn't show it. But Frederick had made no secret of his happiness in his second marriage, almost brandishing it in his children's faces.

Her thoughts drifted back to Reginald. The bridegroom was a strange man. Annie could not understand what Beatrice saw in him. She had tried to work out just why he made her feel uncomfortable, but could find no real reason. He was always exquisitely polite to her, and indeed to everyone, but there was something about him, a mocking air, that set her teeth on edge.

When he had arrived the previous day, he had barely greeted his hostess or even his fiancée before declaring himself prostrated by the journey and going upstairs to lie down for an hour. Later, he had been closeted with Frederick and Jonas Pennybody for a while, emerging from that session with a smug smile on his face, presumably because the dowry was now his. After dinner he had adjourned to the library with the other gentlemen of the party to celebrate what his elder brother, Lawrence, called his 'last night of freedom'. Since Annie had heard Reginald leading the singing that issued forth from that room in his soaring tenor voice, it was clear that he did not lack energy for the evening's pursuits, however languid he had been in the daytime.

Lawrence, the heir to the Barrence family estate, was here to stand as groomsman and the only other person present from Reginald's side was his best friend, Wilfred, another spindly young man, to whom Annie had taken an immediate and unjustified dislike. Something about him made her hackles rise. This was strange, because Wilfred was far more polite than Reginald and, apart from a few incomprehensible speeches about Literature and Art (which he always pronounced as if they had capital letters), was mindful of his duty to converse with his hostess and fellow guests.

How could Beatrice not see that Reginald was marrying her purely for her money? Annie wondered. But Beatrice could see nothing clearly where her betrothed was concerned. She hung upon his arm at every opportunity and agreed with every remark he made, her eyes glowing with admiration as they dwelled upon him. And he was quite good-looking, Annie had to admit, in a slender youthful sort of way. It was hard to believe that he was twenty-seven, just a year younger than Annie herself. She felt so much older than him.

She lay in bed for a few minutes, then, as the nausea started to subside, decided she could bear to stay there no longer. She got up and tiptoed through into her dressing room, where she did not summon Laura to bring some hot water, but washed quickly in cold before donning a simple but elegant gown which she would change before going to church. That was one of the annoying things about her new life, the need to change her clothes so frequently. She had to admit, though reluctantly, that Frederick had been right to insist that she needed a personal maid, and luckily Laura was shaping up quite well.

When Annie went downstairs, there were no guests to be seen, and the servants were still bustling around finishing the housework and lighting the fires. She smiled as she listened to Winnie scolding the new general maid in a low voice for spilling ash on the carpet, then she went through to the kitchen which was situated at the rear of the house. It was a hive of activity and already redolent with the smells of cooking, for the extra staff brought in for the occasion had started work at five o'clock.

Mrs Lumbley stepped forward to greet her mistress, but her eyes kept flickering towards a pan that was simmering on the big closed stove and she frowned at the maid who was stirring it. 'Can I help you, ma'am?'

Annie shook her head. 'No. I just came to check that everything was all right.'

Mrs Lumbley stiffened. 'I do know my job, ma'am.'

'I wasn't implying that you didn't, merely satisfying myself that you had everything you needed.'

The cook inclined her head, 'Thank you, ma'am. It's very kind of you to concern yourself.' But it was obvious that she was offended rather than pleased by Annie's presence in her kitchen.

'When someone has a moment, perhaps they could bring up a tea tray to my sitting room?' Annie could easily have made the tea herself, but knew better than to try that in Mrs Lumbley's domain, so she nodded to everyone and left the kitchen.

'What's *she* doing down here so early?' asked the temporary kitchen maid, brought in from the Three Feathers for the day to help out.

'She allus gets up early,' Jen replied.

'It don't seem right, one of *them* coming in here.'

'Oh, she goes everywhere, she does. Not to pick at us, mind, just to keep her eyes on things. She's strict, but fair enough. You've got to allow her that. An' she's give us some better beds an' a sitting room of our own, too, as well as a bathroom.' That bathroom was a point of pride for the servants at Ridge House. No other servants in town had their own bathroom.

'Enough chattering, Jen Firby!' commanded the cook, who was as glad as her subordinates to see the mistress leave, though she would have died at the stake before she admitted that to them. No matter how pleasant a mistress was, you didn't want her breathing down your neck at a time like this.

In the hallway, Annie met Mrs Jarred, with whom she had become as friendly as the housekeeper's views on their different situations in life would allow. 'I've just been hinted out of the kitchen,' she said cheerfully.

'Mrs Lumbley does prefer to be left to get on with things when we have an event to cater for.'

'Yes. And she's very capable. William tells everyone that she's the best cook in the world. She's certainly the best in Bilsden. But I don't like feeling so useless.' Annie shrugged. 'I don't think I'll ever settle down to being waited on hand and foot, if truth be told, Mrs Jarred.'

The housekeeper watched her mistress walk along the hallway to her own room with her usual brisk step and frowned. Mrs Hallam had seemed very restless during the past week or two, as if something were worrying her. Mrs Jarred suspected that her mistress might be expecting, for there had been no monthly clouts to wash for a while now. In addition, Mrs Hallam had seemed a little pale lately in the mornings, though her skin had taken on a sort of glow, once she got over that first hour or two.

Mrs Lumbley agreed with Mrs Jarred's prognosis. She prided herself on being able to tell such things, though she had never borne a child herself, since the 'Mrs' was a courtesy title only. In fact, the staff were all hoping their new mistress would have some children and they had discussed the possibility at length, but Mrs Jarred had threatened Peggy, the chambermaid, with instant dismissal if she said anything about the mistress's condition to outsiders before an announcement was made. Children made a house much happier, even if they did cause a lot of extra work. Look at how Master William had won all hearts. Well, all except Miss Beatrice's.

Mr Hallam was a different man since his second marriage, but it seemed to gall Miss Beatrice to see her father so happy. Not as much as it galled her maid, Mabel, though. Goodness, they'd be well rid of Miss Spiteful when she and Miss Beatrice left today. Mrs Jarred and the cook always called Mabel that between themselves. The woman could cause an atmosphere more quickly than anyone Ruth Jarred had ever met. Without Mabel, the servants' sitting room would be a cheerful place, for it was very comfortable now, thanks to the new mistress's generosity; with Mabel present, however, there were always moods and nasty remarks, and nothing would shut her up, for she knew herself to be secure in Miss Beatrice's affection and traded on that.

Mrs Jarred shook off these thoughts and continued her preparations for this momentous day. She had been up since four o'clock and she did not expect to get to bed until well past midnight. But it would all be worth it to get rid of Miss Beatrice at last.

Two hours later, Annie took her place at the head of the breakfast table and prepared to make polite conversation to her guests. The meal was a stiff affair, though. She remembered the noisy happy family breakfasts at Netherleigh Cottage, with half the children trying to talk at once, and she suppressed a sigh. How she missed them all! And thank goodness Beatrice had not come down today! Annie was still feeling slightly queasy and had a headache. She was relieved to be spared the irritation of her stepdaughter's presence!

Mildred was there at the table, however, and that was a trial, too, for Mildred was waxing sentimental about weddings, and it was hard to agree with her that dear Beatrice would make a lovely bride.

Judith Hallam contributed little to the conversation, except to say grace, at Annie's request. The grace lasted long enough to have most of the other visitors fidgeting. Lawrence and Wilfred were rather pale and looked as if they had drunk too deeply the previous night, though Frederick, grinning at Annie from the other end of the table, was his usual urbane self. As he had said to her last night, today spelled freedom for them, and he would be glad to see the back of Beatrice, by hell he would!

The wedding was to take place at noon and Annie was one of the last to leave Ridge House, sharing a carriage with Mildred and Jane Ramsby. The latter was to accompany Beatrice to London and make her home with the newlyweds, at Frederick's suggestion. Annie wondered why Beatrice had agreed to that, but supposed that Beatrice would have agreed to anything to get hold of her dowry. Jane would presumably be expected to act as unpaid housekeeper and later, look after any Barrence children who arrived on the scene. You couldn't imagine Beatrice in a maternal role. Frederick had just shrugged when Annie worried aloud that this arrangement would sentence poor Jane to a life of unpaid servitude, so Annie had taken Jane aside and assured her that if she ever needed a home or help, she would find it at Ridge House.

The wedding went off perfectly. Beatrice had complained about having a mere curate officiating, but with the parson so ill, there was nothing to be done about that. She seemed to have forgotten most of her worries today, for once, and sailed down the aisle of the crowded church with a smug expression. She was clad in a cloud of white silk and veiling, and exuded a strong odour of rose water.

Annie sucked in an angry breath when she realised that the wedding gown she had designed so carefully to minimise Beatrice's plumpness had had several more lace frills attached to the bottom of the skirt, and was being worn over extra petticoats which distorted its lines. However, there was nothing to be done about that now.

'She looks very fat today,' William whispered in his mother's ear.

'She's altered the gown I made her,' Annie whispered back.

'That was silly. You always know best what suits someone.' He smiled up at her. 'But then, she is silly, isn't she?'

'Shh!' But Annie could not help smiling.

The ceremony continued very smoothly. When Frederick joined Annie in the pew after giving his daughter away, he smiled conspiratorially at her in much the same way as William had, then clasped her hand in his as he waited for it to end.

Afterwards, the guests were driven back to Ridge House for a reception, where Beatrice queened it, undisputed centre of attention. For once, her father did not reprimand her for usurping some of Annie's duties and ordering the servants to make last-minute changes, though his lips became a thin line as Beatrice drew back when Annie would have given her the traditional kiss of congratulation. 'If it were any other day but her wedding day, I'd have that young madam over my knee,' he growled at Annie afterwards.

She shrugged and went to tell her family not to attempt to congratulate Beatrice. She had a feeling that Beatrice would say or do something outrageous if any of the Gibsons approached her today.

The reception seemed interminable to Annie, whose headache was growing worse by the hour. She smiled and nodded and agreed that the bride had looked charming, but when people asked if the dress had been made at the Bilsden Ladies' Salon, she shook her head. 'Oh, no. Dear Beatrice wished to have her gown made by the same people who made for her friend. She knows Miss Benworth likes fussy styling.'

That brought her a few stares, but it was better that than

people thinking the salon which they knew she and Frederick still owned would be involved in the design of such a lumpy garment.

At length, the bride simpered her way upstairs, accompanied by her sister, to change her gown. The newlyweds were to take a train from Manchester and spend the night in London before going on to Reginald's ancestral home in the country, which Beatrice had never visited. As the estate would go to Lawrence, the elder son, Annie could not understand why Beatrice was making such a fuss about the place.

The children of the family were outside by this time, promenading up and down the lawns in their best clothes, not daring to play with balls or get themselves dirty after threats by their various parents and governesses about the dire consequences if they misbehaved in any way. The sky had clouded over, but the rain was still holding off.

William and Rosemary Jemmings had a short quarrel, which both enjoyed enormously, but after it she went off to play with her sister, turning her nose up at him.

He stood there for a moment on his own and was surprised when Beatrice's maid, Mabel, approached him.

'Miss Beatrice wants to see you,' she said unceremoniously. 'She has some things she forgot to give to your mother.'

Being William, he did not stop to wonder why the things could not simply be given to his mother's maid, but cheerfully accompanied Mabel indoors.

Once upstairs, she pushed him suddenly into one of the spare bedrooms.

'Hey, what are you doing?' He tried to shake her hand off his shoulder, but her fingers were digging in and although he could have kicked her and got away, he felt his mother would not like him to kick a servant.

'There's something you need to know,' Mabel said, drawing out this moment. She had longed to get her revenge on Annie for years, and she intended to make the most of it now her moment had come.

He looked at her in puzzlement.

'Your mam never told you, but I reckon you ought to know.'

'I don't think—'

She pushed him into a corner and stood there, trapping him as much by her gloating expression as by her heavy body, then she said, 'Barmy Charlie wasn't your father.'

He opened his mouth to protest, but something in her face made him close it again and swallow hard. He had never seen such malevolence in anyone's eyes and it made a shiver run down his spine. He had never realised how large Mabel was, or how strong her hands were.

'I reckon a lad ought to know his own father. Don't you?'

He found his voice, but it was shrill and unhappy. 'I don't believe you.'

'Well, just listen an' then you can think whether what I say's true or not. Your mother, your precious mother, used to knock around with men a lot – afore she was married to Charlie.'

He was old enough to realise what she was implying. 'She did not!' He shoved at her, but she slammed him back against the wall and jammed her face closer to his, so that he could see the pores on her skin and the hairs inside her nose.

Mabel gave a slow smile. 'Oh, yes she did. I worked with her, an' she couldn't hide it from me.'

His eyes were bulging with horror, but his voice was faint and uncertain as he said, 'I don't believe you. I don't.'

'Then why did Mrs Lewis dismiss your mother?' She didn't wait for him to answer, but poured out words like a floodtide of acid. 'I'll tell you why. It was because she was expecting *you*. An' your father, your real father, was called Fred Coxton. He was a bully as lived in Claters End an' he had a way with women. As your mother found out. She was engaged to marry young Matt Peters then – oh, yes, she was! – but she betrayed him with Fred and then, when Matt found she was expecting, he wouldn't have nothing to do with her. An' I don't blame him. What man wants a bastard foisted on him?'

William tried again to push past her, but Mabel was a burly woman and her hands were grasping his shoulders like vices. 'I'm not finished yet.' She thumped him against the wall.

'I don't want to hear any more of your lies. Let me go!' He tried to kick out at her, but the force of his kick was lost in her thick petticoats and skirts, and she just laughed at him.

'They're not lies.' That was the beauty of it all. Mabel had only had to embroider the truth a little. She smiled now, utter certainty on her face. 'I'll swear it on the Bible, if you like.' She dragged him over to the bedside table. 'Here.' She let go of the boy for a moment to flourish a big leather-bound Bible in his face and then lay one palm dramatically upon it. 'I solemnly swear on this Holy Bible that your real father is Fred Coxton, an' that your mother was already gone with his child when she married Barmy Charlie.'

She dropped the Bible on the table and patted William's shaking shoulder. 'There. I know it's harsh, but it's the truth.' She walked towards the door, where she turned to toss a parting shot at him. 'A lad ought to know his own father, don't you think? So if you want to meet him, he's back in town at the moment.'

William could only stand there, horror-struck, shuddering.

'Fred Coxton went away when he found your mother was expectin', 'cos he never marries 'em, but he's come back now. You've only got to go down to the Shepherd's Rest in

Claters End any evening an' you'll see him there. He's fond of his ale, Fred is. Allus was. Only he calls himself Frank now, Frank Black. An' you'll enjoy meetin' your little brother, too, won't you? You look a lot like each other, you an' young Jemmy do.' She threw back her head and laughed, then closed the door with a bang, but opened it a few seconds later to add, 'Don't forget to tell your mother. She'll be delighted to see old Fred again.'

Laughing even more loudly, she went up to the servants' quarters to pick up her luggage. It had been a nice touch, swearing on the Bible. She only wished she could see Annie's face when William told her about his real father. But you couldn't have everything in this life, so she'd just have to imagine the scene.

Miss Beatrice would be pleased to hear how things had gone. It was just sheer luck that Mabel had seen Coxton's boy in town and noticed his strong resemblance to William. She had followed him, puzzled, seen him go into a house in Claters End, then come out again with a man. She hadn't recognised the man at first, but something about him had made her continue to follow them. When he moved into a patch of sunlight and held his head in a certain way, it had suddenly come to her who he was. Fred Coxton.

How Miss Beatrice had laughed when Mabel had told her that Coxton was back in town. The perfect weapon for their mutual revenge. But just to make sure Annie found out, just in case the boy kept it from her, Miss Beatrice wrote her stepmother a note, to be delivered by Peggy after the Barrences had left for London.

William could not move for a long time after Mabel left him. He leaned against the wall, sick with horror. Mabel had sworn on the Bible that what she had told him was the truth. On the Bible! And something in her tone of voice had shaken his certainty that she was lying, that his mother would do no wrong. Suddenly, he was retching with the horror of it, and had to stagger across to the toilet stand to be sick into the big flowered bowl. He vomited till long after his stomach was empty, but it didn't seem to make him feel better. The words 'Fred Coxton is your father' kept ringing in his ears. 'Fred Coxton. Fred Coxton.'

He heard someone coming and went to hide under the bed, but the footsteps went past the door. That particular bedroom was small and rarely used. Mabel had chosen her place well.

A little later there were more footsteps going downstairs and then a lot of noise from outside. William dragged himself out from under the bed and crept along the corridor, intent only on escaping. He knew that the house would be full of people until the next day, and he could not, *he just could not*, face them until he had found out the truth of what Mabel had told him. 'Oh, Dad,' he moaned under his breath, and it was Charlie he was thinking about. 'Make her be lying, Dad. It can't be true. Make her be lying.'

Luck was with him as he crept down the back stairs, but at the bottom he bumped into Peggy, the chambermaid.

'Eh, Master William, what's wrong?'

'I've just been sick,' he managed. 'In the little bedroom. I'm sorry for the mess. I need some fresh air.' And he pushed past her, running as fast as he had ever run in his life, pursued by all the devils in hell, who had come out specially to torment him that day.

When the newlyweds had departed for Manchester and the other guests had left, the adults of the Hallam family went back into the house. They were to stay in Bilsden until the next day, so Annie gritted her teeth and prepared to do her duty as hostess. She assumed that William was with the other children, but Miss Mimms, who had her hands full, with the older girls to see to as well as her young charge because the nurserymaid was feeling poorly, never even thought to question where he was.

Rosemary Jemmings missed him, but assumed that he had gone back home with the Gibsons. She liked the Gibsons. They were all so kind to each other and they had such fun. And William's mother was lovely, too. Mrs Hallam actually played with William and talked to him often. Rosemary had seen the two of them laughing together at the wedding. Her own mother was dead, her father never talked to her and her stepmother never played with any of the children. There was just Miss Mimms, the governess, who didn't believe in having fun, only in learning the Kings of England and the capitals of Europe.

It was not until just before dinner that Beatrice's note was brought to Annie. She was in the drawing room at the time, but Winnie whispered that Peggy said it was urgent, so she excused herself to read it. She turned so white that Judith asked if she was all right.

Annie stared at her stepdaughter as if she had spoken in a foreign language, then realised where she was. 'Bad news,' she managed to say, though the words had to be forced through chattering teeth. 'Please – excuse me.'

She ran from the room, leaving the others to speculate about what the news could be. Annie's only thought was to find William, who must be desperately shocked and unhappy, if Mabel had really done what Beatrice boasted about in the note. But William was not in his room, not in the schoolroom, not in any of his usual haunts. And no one had seen him for hours, not since before Beatrice left with her new husband. Even Mrs Lumbley, still grimly upright on aching feet as she produced yet another meal for the family, had not seen hide nor hair of him.

'Are you all right, ma'am?'

'What?' Annie managed to focus on the speaker and realised that Winnie was staring at her. 'Send Mr Hallam up to our bedroom, please. At once.' She sucked in enough breath to fuel her body up the stairs, then collapsed on the bed, sitting there huddled up like a battered rag doll.

When Frederick came up to the bedroom, urged by Winnie, who had said that she thought the mistress had took a 'real bad turn', he could not at first get Annie to answer him. Then she blinked her eyes and realised who was there. 'Frederick! Oh, Frederick!' She threw herself against his chest sobbing wildly, as he had only once seen her sob before.

He held her for a few moments, rocking her to and fro, and murmuring soothing words in her ear, then, as she quietened a little, he said, 'Tell me what's happened, love.'

She opened her hand and a crumpled piece of paper fell out. The sight of it made her sob again.

He picked it up and smoothed it out, his lips tightening into a thin angry line as he recognised his daughter's handwriting.

> Annie
>
> I've made sure Mabel told William about his real father. It was about time he knew about you and Fred Coxton, don't you think? Especially as Coxton's back in town at the moment.
>
> Beatrice Barrence

Frederick cursed aloud, then screwed the note up and threw it into the fireplace. He gathered Annie into his arms again. 'Oh, my love, what can I do? I can't believe that even Beatrice would be so cruel.'

'I t-tried to f-find William. I looked everywhere. I can't f-find him. He'll be so,' she had to stop to wipe her eyes and gulp back the hysteria that was threatening, 'so *hurt*.'

'How could Beatrice have known about Fred Coxton?'

'Mabel.'

'The maid?'

'Yes. She – she used to work for Mrs Lewis. She always hated me. It was she who told Mrs Lewis I was pregnant.'

'But why didn't you dismiss her at once, then? Why did you allow her to go on working here.'

Annie caught her breath on a sob. 'I thought – I thought it didn't matter. She'd be going away with Beatrice. I d-didn't want to make things worse than they were.'

His arms were still around her. 'I'm ashamed,' he said, his voice low and tears of sympathy shining in his eyes. He knew all about Annie's past, knew, too, that her only full sister, Lizzie, was a prostitute in Manchester, and even that had not shaken his desire to marry Annie. 'I'm so bitterly ashamed that a daughter of mine could do such a thing.' His voice became harsh. 'But she's no daughter of mine from now on. I shall never speak to her again. Never.'

There was a knocking on the door. 'Sir! Sir! Can you come quickly, sir?'

'Can't it wait, Peggy?'

'It's Miss Ramsby, sir. She's just come back an' she's in a terrible state. She's sittin' in the kitchen, sobbin' her heart out.'

He put Annie from him. 'But Jane was supposed to go with Beatrice.' They stared at each other. 'What's she done now?' he whispered, then stood up. 'I'll have to go down and see what's happened, Annie, love. I'll be back as soon as I can.' He strode out of the room, only half-opening the door, so that Peggy wouldn't see the state Annie was in.

'Send for Laura at once to attend her mistress!' he ordered. 'Mrs Hallam's not well.'

Downstairs, Jane Ramsby was slumped in a chair in the servants' sitting room, sobbing as wildly as Annie had.

Mildred was standing helplessly by her side patting her shoulder. She looked up at her father in relief. 'I can't think what's wrong with Jane. She won't stop sobbing and she won't tell me why she's come back.' She lowered her voice and whispered, 'She came back on foot, too. What can have happened?'

Frederick put his arm around Jane and looked at his daughter. 'Will you go and look after the guests for me, Mildred? I know I can rely on you to act as my hostess and do the right thing. I'm afraid Annie's been taken ill.'

Mildred's face showed only satisfaction at his trust in her as she said, 'Poor Annie. Yes, of course I'll see to things, Father.'

'I doubt either of us will be down to dinner. Can you and Peter take charge?'

Mildred nodded. 'Yes, of course. But what's—'

'I can't talk now. Just help me out and stop people asking questions. I'm relying upon you, Mildred.'

She nodded again, and was surprised when he came across to give her a quick hug before he led Jane away. He had rarely ever done that.

Frederick took Jane automatically to the library, so long his refuge from his first wife. When he sat Jane down, he found that her hands were as cold as ice and her clothing soaked. He stared down in puzzlement at her shoes, which were caked with mud, as was the hem of her dress. What in heaven's name had happened to her? He poured out a glass of brandy and forced some of it through her chattering teeth. 'Don't try to tell me what's happened until you've calmed down, my dear Jane. Here, come closer to the fire.'

After a moment, she had recovered enough to clutch his arm and gasp, 'You – you won't throw me out into the street, will you, Frederick? You'll let me stay until I can find myself employment? Please. I won't be any trouble, I promise you.'

This made no sense and his first thought was that she had run mad. 'Of course you can stay. But what's happened to Beatrice? Has there been an accident?'

She shook her head and buried her face in her hands, sobbing more loudly, her whole body shaking with the violence of her weeping.

'Jane, you must tell me what's happened. I thought you were going to live in London with Beatrice.'

'She – she never wanted me. I knew that. But I thought – I thought if I could make myself useful, she wouldn't mind too much. And then, as we were driving across the moors, she – she suddenly said—' Jane broke off and mopped her eyes with her handkerchief, then looked sideways at him, as if she didn't dare to continue.

'Tell me exactly what she said. I promise you I won't throw you out on to the street and I won't get angry with you for anything Beatrice has done.' The doubtful way she looked at him hurt. 'I mean that, Jane. You're welcome to make your home here permanently. I'd never let a relative of mine want for anything. You should know that.'

'Beatrice said you were sick of me, you w-were all s-sick of me. That you'd told her to find me other employment in London. B-but she'd changed her mind and didn't want me hanging around on her h-honeymoon journey. So I could just get out and w-walk. I asked her what I was to do and where I was to go, and she said she didn't care, but I wasn't to come back here.'

He stared at her in horror, unable to believe what he was hearing.

She whimpered in her throat. 'And Mr Barrence just laughed when she said it. He l-laughed.' She took a deep breath and forced more words out. 'Then Beatrice told the coachman to throw my baggage down on to the road. Everything I own in the world. It's still lying there. I could only carry one s-small case back with me.'

Frederick closed his eyes and wondered if his daughter had gone mad. Then he realised that Jane was rocking to and fro like a hurt child, sobbing quietly and desperately into her sodden handkerchief. He pulled himself together and patted her shoulder tentatively, then put his arm round her and drew her towards him. 'I'm relieved that you had the sense to come back here, Jane. I'd never have forgiven myself if you'd taken Beatrice at her word. It's not true what she said, it's not true at all.'

She hiccupped to a halt and stared at him, fear still writ large upon her face and tension radiating from her body, so thin and bony under his arm. 'I w-wasn't going to come back, only – only I remembered Mrs Hallam. She s-said if I was ever in n-need, I was to – to come to her. I thought – I thought she might let me stay in the servants' quarters so as not to anger you.'

He pulled her to him again and held her close. 'Jane, Jane, do you know me so little that you'd think me such an ogre?'

Her voice was muffled and halting. 'I don't feel to know you very well at all, F-Frederick. I'm s-sorry if I've done something wrong, something to upset Beatrice.'

'You've done nothing wrong.'

She wasn't really listening to him. 'I had to walk for such a long way, then a farmer gave me a lift on his cart, and then I had to walk again. And – and then it started raining.'

He held her at arm's length. 'Look at me, Jane.'

She raised a face whose features were blurred with tears, whose eyes were red and puffy. She was almost beyond understanding what he was saying, but he had to try to make her understand. He spoke slowly, choosing his words with great care. 'Jane, I'm glad you came back. You can make your home with us here for as long as you choose. Never, ever doubt that you're welcome here. Never.'

'But I'm not your relative, really. I'm Christine's cousin, and only her second cousin at that.'

'It doesn't matter. I was married to Christine, so I now consider you my relative and I shall not let you want.'

She stared at him and slowly understanding dawned in her eyes. 'Oh, thank God!' Then she collapsed against him again, sobbing in relief this time. The words, 'so grateful' were the only ones he could distinguish.

When the library door opened, he looked round and found Judith staring at him, her eyes bulging in shock.

'Come in and help me,' he begged. 'Jane's had a dreadful experience. She needs comforting, but I want to get back to Annie.'

Judith came across the room and put her arm around Jane, relieved that it was not what she had first suspected when she saw the woman in her father-in-law's arms.

'Will you take Jane upstairs to her old room, please, Judith? And find her some clothes to wear. Hers are soaked. Oh, and send the coachman out to look for the rest of her luggage. It's lying on the Manchester road where Beatrice tipped it.'

She gaped at him for a moment, then she pulled herself together and stepped forward to take his place on the sofa and put an arm round the sobbing woman. 'Yes, of course I'll help her, Father-in-law.' Judith always insisted on his full title, though she knew he disliked it.

He forced himself to stay there for long enough to explain, though he was aching to get back to Annie. 'Beatrice threw Jane out of the carriage on the way to Manchester.' His family would have to know what had happened, but he was sure they would keep the information to themselves.

Even Judith's monumental calm was shaken. 'But why?'

'I don't know why. I think she must have run mad. She

told Jane none of the family wanted anything more to do with her. Let Jane tell you herself exactly what happened, see if you can make sense of it all, then do what you can to help her. And make her understand that we'll take care of her. It's our Christian duty, as far as I'm concerned.'

That struck the right note with Judith, as he had known it would. 'Indeed it is. And anyway, she's your first wife's cousin, is she not? Family.'

'Indeed she is.' He strode across the room, turning at the door. 'I'll tell Annie about this, of course, but she won't be able to do anything at the moment. She's not at all well.'

But when he went back to the bedroom, Annie was not just unwell. She was doubled up in pain on the bed, losing the baby so newly planted in her womb. It was a few days before she even found out about Jane.

And it was left to Frederick to organise a hunt for William, who seemed to have disappeared off the face of the earth.

10

William: Late April 1849

When he fled the house, William had no idea where he was going. He was fleeing partly from the idea that Charlie Ashworth had not been his father, but also from the thought that his mother, his wonderful mother, could ever have behaved immorally. He knew what was right and wrong. Both his mother and his grandfather had seen to that. And for as long as he could remember, his mother had answered all his questions about life and its puzzlements – truthfully he had believed – even those questions his grandfather said should not be thought of by a lad his age. But now he knew that she had lied to him. Lied about his father.

As William fled across the moors, choking on sobs that seemed as solid as pebbles in his throat, the rain that had been threatening all day suddenly pelted down, half-blinding him. Only a bad fall that left him winded and gasping stopped the headlong flight. He lay there on the muddy ground then, with the rain lashing down unheeded on his back, and he sobbed until he could sob no more. Mabel had sworn on the Bible, *on the Holy Bible*, so the dreadful things she had said must be true. His grandfather said you couldn't tell a lie if you were touching the Bible. You couldn't, even if you wanted to.

After a while, the racking sobs subsided and William began to shiver violently, his teeth chattering, his whole body shaking. He moaned in his throat as he became aware that the rain was running in icy trickles down his neck. The dampness seemed to have penetrated everywhere in his body to match the chill in his soul. He heaved himself to his feet and stood there alone in the vastness of the rain-swept moors, bewildered by a world turned suddenly upside-down, a world become harsh and terrifying. *His mother had lied to him!*

Mabel had said his real father would be at the Shepherd's Rest that night. Someone called Fred Coxton. The words were burned into William's brain and he had to find out about this man. Another bout of mingled sobs and shivering shook his body, but he ignored it. Mabel had said that he had a half-brother, too. Jemmy, she'd called him. He didn't want a strange half-brother intruding in his life. And he didn't want a stranger for a father, either. But he had to find out about them. He had to.

Shivering intermittently, William began to tramp back towards the town, choosing his path carefully so as to avoid Ridge House. He could not bear to face anyone he knew just yet. Especially not his mother. He knew it would upset her, him running away, but he couldn't face her with what he knew. Not until, he gulped back a sob, not until he'd seen this man. But why had she lied to him? Why? And could she really have been – immoral? His mother!

In the town centre he paused, wondering where to hide until evening. At first he turned automatically towards the yard, then he stopped in his tracks and shook his head. No. Not the yard. They'd look for him there. And if they found him, they'd stop him going to look for that man. He could not even think the word 'father' in connection with this stranger.

As he stumbled along the streets, he met very few people, and those he did meet were warmly wrapped against the rain, unlike him. The better dressed folk were carrying umbrellas, and everyone was hurrying to get back indoors again. He saw no one that he knew, and if he had seen them, they would not have recognised him, for he looked a sodden ragamuffin figure. His hair was plastered to his head and the rain had darkened the rich auburn colour to brown. His new clothes, specially made for the wedding, were torn where he had forced his way through the shrubbery then climbed over the walls that surrounded Ridge House. His clothes had been further dirtied and damaged by his fall.

When a carriage passed him in the street and threw up a sheet of dirty mud and water, he hardly noticed the vehicle or the drenching, for he was already soaked to the skin. He was too engrossed with his personal anguish even to brush the mud off his face.

In the end, he stood for a moment beneath the lych gate of St Mark's churchyard, where he had been a few hours earlier for the wedding, then he stumbled inside and found shelter under a marble monument erected, ironically enough, to the memory of Thomas Hallam. It had been Frederick's whim to give his father the largest tombstone in Bilsden, and spanning the carved white marble walls just in front of the headstone there was a ledge, with a dry space beneath it just large enough to fit a boy's shivering body.

Not until the world was safely dark did William crawl out of his hiding place, and by that time he was so stiff and cold that he had trouble walking properly at first. He was beyond noticing that, however, for Mabel's revelations had filled him with such horror that they were still churning round in his brain.

He stumbled on through the town, avoiding the centre where the modern gas lighting made the streets too bright. He knew, in a hazy sort of way, that people would be looking for him, but his mother and his family seemed like actors on a distant stage at the moment, actors mouthing words which he could not quite hear. He hid once or twice when he heard people approaching, shrinking into doorways or creeping round corners, but it was still raining and the streets were almost deserted, so mostly he just pressed on.

When he reached Claters End, he paused and steadied himself against a wall. He felt so dizzy and feverish that for a moment the world spun around him. Then, with the last of his strength, he pulled himself together and made his way towards the noise and warmth of the Shepherd's Rest. He had never been inside it before, because neither his mother nor his grandfather approved of such places, but he knew where it was, for he had grown up in the Rows. Light shone out from the windows of the public house that had grown bigger over the past year or two, and noise beat through the big double doors as William slipped inside behind a couple of men.

He paused for a moment to sigh with relief at the warmth, then made instinctively for the shadows at the side of the room. He looked round and saw that most people were going into the big room at the back, so he followed them. No one seemed to be paying any attention to him. They were all watching a lady on a small stage in the corner who was singing about 'My Irish Lad'. When she finished there was loud applause from the Irish folk in the audience and friendly jeers from the rest of the people there.

On the stage, Rosie sighed and looked around the smoke-filled room. It was a way to make a living, but she wanted more than this from life now. If she couldn't have her Tom, she'd have to find something else to give her life meaning. On a whim, she whispered to the pianist and then began to sing 'The Dream', a song she loved, but which she had never tried to sing here before, where folk liked jolly songs to which they could join in the choruses. Her lovely voice soared up into a room fallen silent at first in surprise, then in pleasure:

I dreamt that I dwelt in marble halls,
With vassals and serfs at my side,
And of all who assembled within those walls
That I was the hope and the pride.

William was the only person in the room not watching or listening to Rosie. He was standing in shock in front of a lad who was like a poor copy of the face he saw in the mirror each morning. 'Are you – Jemmy?' His words came out as a croak, too quiet to disturb the room, though the people nearby frowned at him.

The lad nodded. He seemed as stunned by the sight of William as William was by the sight of him.

'Is your – your father here?'

The lad nodded again and pointed. A man who must have been large once, but who was shrunken now so that his clothes hung loosely upon him, was sitting watching Rosie, a half-empty glass of ale in his hand. As she finished, he applauded with the rest, but clapping and cheering made him start coughing and the cough went on for long after the applause had died down, so that those sitting near him moved back. They had all heard that sort of cough before.

William crept forward and stood there staring at the man. 'Is your name Fred? Fred Coxton?'

The man blinked and tried to focus on the speaker. 'Shh, you silly bugger! What did I tell you?' Then he realised that this wasn't his son Jim, but a boy who looked remarkably like him. 'Wassit t'you who I am, lad?'

William shook his head and took a step backward, suddenly afraid. 'Nothing.'

But Fred, always alert, grabbed him before he could move away. 'I asked what it was t'you?' He shook William with the remains of a once great strength.

Too frightened to move, William stared at this horrible

man, as if all his worst nightmares had come to life in front of him.

'Worra y'starin' at me like that for?' Fred's eyes narrowed. Drunk he might be, but there was something about this lad, something— As Jim moved forward, Fred's breath hissed out in a foul stream of surprise. This was more than a chance resemblance. 'Dammit if you ain't the spitt'n image of my Jim. Older. But the spitt'n image. Who's y'mother, boy?' He grinned and pawed at William. 'I reckon you're my get. Yes, I reckon y'are that.'

William gave an inarticulate cry, but seemed frozen, unable to move, even when Fred's hand fell off his shoulder and picked up the glass of ale.

Rosie, who was passing through the crowd on her way back to the bar, stopped next to their table, sensing trouble. 'Another drink?' she asked, but it was the boy in sodden clothing she was looking at. 'Aren't you William? William Ashworth?'

'Mmm.' William tried to nod, but the effort made him sway on his feet. The room started spinning around him, the voices rising and falling, and the air suddenly lacking oxygen. He gave a low moan, his eyes rolled upwards and he crumpled to the ground.

'I don't know no Ashworths,' Fred said. 'Who was his mother before she wed?'

Rosie drew in a deep breath. 'What's it to you?'

'Look at my son.' He pointed to Jim, standing puzzled but obedient next to him. 'And then look at that one.' He nudged William's body with his toe.

Rosie looked and gasped. She didn't need to look down to see the resemblance to Tom's nephew in Jim's face. She was just surprised that she hadn't noticed it before, because she knew William by sight, and this man had been coming to the Shepherd's Rest with his son for a few weeks now.

She wasn't going to agree with him, however. Tom wouldn't want this fellow claiming any sort of relationship with him. 'So what? You surely don't want to find his mother an' get asked for money, do you?'

'Eh?' It took a while for this idea to sink into Fred's booze-soaked brain, then he scowled. If the mother complained to the parish, they'd be on him like a ton of bricks for maintenance. That was why he'd left the town in the first place. 'No one can prove anythin',' he said, draining the last of the ale from his glass. He choked as it went down the wrong way.

When he stopped choking, he found Rosie there, smiling and setting another full glass in front of him, and as she didn't seem to expect payment for it, he didn't offer. Perhaps she fancied him. He'd always been a one for the women. He blinked at her. Nice looker, too. He winked and sucked the froth off the ale. Good stuff they served here. The best.

'I'll see to the lad,' she said briskly. 'An' I won't tell anyone about you, neither. A fellow like you don't want some woman comin' askin' him for money.'

He was still suspicious. 'Why should y'help me?'

She shrugged. 'Why not? You're a good customer. Better the Shepherd's Rest gets your money from you than some woman who'll only spend it at the corner shop.'

He nodded and pretended to be satisfied with that, but he continued to watch her carefully through narrowed eyes.

Rosie turned to the other boy. 'Give us a hand with him, young fellow, an' I'll give you a penny for your trouble.'

Always ready to earn money, Jim moved forward and took William's feet, while Rosie put her hands under his shoulders, clearing a way through the crowd with a good-humoured jest or two.

Seth bustled forward. 'We need you behind the bar now, Rosie.'

'Wait a minute, Seth. This lad's fainted on us.'

'You're paid to serve at the bar, not look after stupid lads who shouldn't be in here in the first place.'

She glared at him. 'This stupid lad happens to be your partner's nephew.'

'What?' He gaped at William. 'Nay, I don't believe it!'

'Believe it or not, it's true. I'm going to call a cab an' send him home, so you just pull up the bar top an' let us through to the back room with him.'

Seth muttered something to himself and lifted William's unconscious body out of her hands, nodding dismissal to the other lad.

'She promised me a penny for helpin'.' Jim remained where he was. He'd learnt to be tenacious where money was concerned.

Rosie fumbled in her pocket and found only a sixpence. 'Here. It's your lucky day, lad. Now get back to your father an' forget what you've just seen.'

Jim put one hand on her arm. 'Is it true, though?'

'Is what true?'

'That he's my brother.'

She shrugged. 'How would I know? What's your dad's name?'

'Er – Frank Black.'

She stared for a moment. 'His real name?'

Jim jerked away from her, fear on his face.

'I won't tell anyone. Go on. I know he isn't called Frank Black. He looks familiar, but I can't place him.'

Jim looked over his shoulder and whispered, 'Fred Coxton.'

'Bloody hell!' Then she saw that the lad was looking terrified, and repeated, 'I won't tell anyone.'

'Is that boy my brother, though?'

'I doubt it. I know his mam. She wouldn't have anything to do with Fred Coxton.' Which was a lie, because Tom had told her what had happened. 'He don't really look like you. It's just the bad light in here.'

But Jim was not convinced by her airy words. If there was nothing in it, why had she been so keen to find out his father's real name?

When he got back, Fred growled, 'What have they done with the lad?'

'Put him in the back room. They're sending for a cab to take him home.'

'You go an' find out where he lives, then. There's more here than meets the eye.' He gave Jim a shove. 'Go on! And don't lose them!'

Jim slipped outside, huddling in the doorway and trying to keep out of the way of the rain that was still beating down. When the cab arrived, he heard the words 'Ridge House' and said them to himself two or three times so that he'd remember, then he went back to tell his father.

'Ridge House,' Fred said slowly. 'That's where the bloody Hallams live. Maybe—' He broke off and then said, 'You can go there tomorrow, an' find out who's living there now.'

Jim nodded, then, as his father ordered another pint of beer, he went off to spend some of the sixpence Rosie had given him on hot food before his dad could take it off him. Afterwards he hid the rest of the money in the rags stuffed into the toes of his overlarge boots. Later still, at chucking out time, he returned to help his father back to the cellar they were renting in a sagging house round the corner.

When the cab arrived at Ridge House with its semiconscious and feverish passenger, Winnie once again went running for her master. Frederick breathed a sigh of relief at the news that William was safe and set the servants' bells pealing. He carried the boy upstairs himself, and left him in his bedroom in Peggy's charge for the moment. He then went down to pay the driver and ask a few questions about how Annie's son came to be in the cab.

'Rosie sent him, Mester Hallam.'

'Who the hell is Rosie? Rosie who?'

'She sings at the Shepherd's Rest an' serves behind the bar, too. I don't know her other name.'

'How would she know to send him here?'

The man shrugged. 'I dunno, sir. She said he'd collapsed in the street outside. Nice lass, Rosie is. Wouldn't let a sick lad just lie there in the rain catching his death of cold.'

'Then I owe her my thanks.' Frederick made a mental note to go and see this Rosie as soon as Annie was better.

Message delivered, and more than satisfied with the generous tip, the cab driver returned to town, where he forgot about his unusual passenger as he stabled his horse and took a swig or two from a bottle he kept there to warm his chilled bones, before going home early for once. It was a bugger of a night outside.

As soon as he'd got rid of the man, Frederick ran back upstairs to William's room where Peggy had stripped the sodden clothes from the lad's shivering body and was wrapping him in a blanket.

'Best we get him into a hot bath, sir. Jen's in the bathroom filling it now.'

'Good. I'll send Robert to fetch Dr Lewis, then I'll come and help you.'

'Mrs Hallam's awake again, sir, and asking for you.'

'I'll go to her as soon as we've got this young fellow warmed up.'

When he tiptoed into their bedchamber, Frederick found Annie restless and only semiconscious after the sleeping draught Jeremy Lewis had given her.

'Frederick?' Her voice was husky, a mere thread of sound.

He sat on the edge of her bed and took her hand. 'Yes. I'm here, love.'

'I heard someone at the door. Have you found him?'

'Yes, he's back.' She tried to raise herself up, but he pushed her gently down again. 'Stay still, my love.'

'I want to see him.'

'You can't at the moment. He's having a nice hot bath. He was chilled through.'

'Is he – all right?' She was having trouble thinking clearly, but she knew something was wrong with William, very wrong, so she was clinging on to consciousness.

'He's not hurt.' Frederick bent to press a kiss on her forehead. 'If you promise to stay quietly here, I'll go and check that he's had his bath.'

'Send for Jeremy Lewis.'

'I have done already.'

'Stay – with – him. For me.' The words came out very slowly and her eyes closed again.

Frederick stood up and nodded to Laura. 'Fetch me at once if she wakes up again, or if she needs anything.'

'Yes, sir.' Laura turned to the bed, an expression of both determination and compassion on her face. She had thought that rich people lived a charmed life, wanting for nothing, but in the two months she'd been at Ridge House, she'd seen that they could have nearly as many troubles as poorer folk.

When Frederick tiptoed into the lad's bedroom, William was lying with a couple of earthenware hot water bottles wrapped in flannel tucked in beside him. His face had regained some colour, but intermittent shivers still shook his thin frame and when his eyes flickered open, they seemed too large for his face, too large and too anguished.

Frederick, who had rarely touched his own children, found himself clasping the hand of Annie's son, found himself hurting at the pain he saw in those eyes. *I'll never speak to Beatrice again,* he thought, renewing the vow he had made earlier. *Never.* It sickened and shamed him that his own daughter had stirred up this trouble and had hurt someone so young and tender. And poor Jane, too.

It seemed a long time before Jeremy Lewis arrived, and William said not a word as they waited. But he clung to his stepfather's hand. When Frederick heard the noise of the carriage returning, he whispered, 'I'll be back in a minute, lad' and left Peggy to keep an eye on William. He intercepted the doctor in the hallway. Drawing Jeremy Lewis into the library, he explained briefly what had happened. 'So if the lad rambles on—'

Jeremy nodded. 'I'll understand what he's talking about. And don't worry – I'll say nothing. I knew about Annie's past, anyway. I was the one who tended her after Fred Coxton's attack. But I still couldn't persuade my wife that she really had been raped.'

'It was that obvious?' Frederick wouldn't have been human if he hadn't had some curiosity about this.

'Very obvious. She'd been beaten and there were rope marks on her wrists. And she'd clearly been a virgin before it happened.' He realised that they were wasting time. 'Take me to see the boy now.'

Frederick did so, then came down to his library, where he stood for a few minutes, fists clenched, lost in sorrow for his wife. 'No,' he said aloud. 'I'll not have Beatrice near me again. And I'll let the others know why before they go to bed.' Distasteful, but it must be done. He didn't want his other two living children alienated by thinking he was treating Beatrice unfairly. He wanted to mend his fences with them, if he could. If it wasn't too late. If they believed him.

Only then did Frederick remember Annie's family, also waiting for news. He sat down to write a quick note to them, saying that the boy had returned, and reassuring them that Annie was all right, even though she had lost the baby.

The following morning Fred woke up early and poked the lad. 'Go an' get us a loaf an' a jug of tea.' When he had eaten, tearing off great chunks of crust and chewing them noisily instead of just picking at things as he usually did, he hawked a gob of phlegm into the corner and asked, 'You're sure they said that lad lived at Ridge House?'

'Yes, Dad.'

'Right, then. You go an' find out what you can there, an' I'll ask around in Claters End, see if I can find something about him.' For on none of the times he'd followed Annie Gibson had he seen her son with her. He had not asked about her, just been content to follow her, to make her uneasy. He still fancied her, but it was too much trouble to waylay her and take her, as he had done before. He could see she'd done well, though, by the clothes she'd been wearing and he'd decided now that there might be some money in it for him.

He grinned. He'd enjoyed seeing the puzzlement in her face when he let her see him following her, the way she turned her head and frowned. When he'd had a bad patch of health, he'd told Jim to follow her. Today, although he didn't realise it, Fred looked more like his old self.

Jim strolled along the street, as usual looking for a chance to earn a penny or two as he went. The four pennies he had left from Rosie's sixpence were digging into his toes, but he left them in his boots. It was the safest place he knew. He had a few shillings saved in there now, wrapped up in the strips of cloth he used to pad out the boots. His dad didn't know about them.

Just as Jim was giving up hope and deciding to pull out a penny for a piece of bread and butter and a nice hot cup of tea, another lad grabbed a woman's shopping bag right in front of him. Always quick to seize an opportunity, Jim was able to grab it back and return it. He didn't try to keep hold of the other lad, though, for he knew the town constables would lock him up if they caught him and he didn't want to get anyone locked up.

The woman whose bag he had saved stared at him, taking in the thinness of his body and the gaunt look of his face. 'Thanks for that.'

'It's all right, missus. It's wrong to steal.' He shivered and hugged himself, trying to look as small and pathetic as possible, though he was growing fast lately.

'You hungry?'

He nodded. 'Yes, missus. I'm allus hungry.'

'Then come back home with me an' I'll find you a butty.'

The butty translated into two thick slices of bread and butter with a chunk of cheese and a glass of buttermilk, not Jim's favourite drink, but it'd do to fill the great hole that always gaped inside him. He'd been lucky last night with the sixpence, and this morning, too, with his dad in a mood to buy them breakfast, but he could always eat more. Most mornings, his dad said Jim had better learn to take care of himself, because he wouldn't be around much longer to look after him. But his dad was in a good mood today for some reason.

Jim got the woman talking and by careful questioning, found out who this William Ashworth was. He heard all about the boy's mother and the miracle of a woman from the Rows marrying the richest man in town. It didn't seem possible to him that a woman like that would have had anything to do with his father, let alone borne him a child, but you never could tell with women. Jim was under no illusions about his father. Fred was a brute, but for some reason, the women seemed to like him – or they had done before he got so ill. Now he looked old and withered, and no woman had come near him for months. Nor had Fred sought anyone.

Jim strolled along the street after he'd finished, whistling as he enjoyed the weak sunshine that had followed last night's rain. He found the walls of Ridge House easily enough, but he couldn't see the house itself. If the other lad lived here, he was a lucky sod. Jim crept closer to the gates but the gatekeeper came out to chase him away.

'Get back where you belong, you scruffy little devil!'

'Please, sir, who lives in that house?'

'What's it to you?'

'I saw that boy last night in town when he fainted. I helped carry him. They said he was called William Ashworth and he lived in Ridge House, so I come to see if he was all right.'

The gatekeeper relented. 'Well, he's a bit poorly, they tell me, but the doctor's been to see him, so he'll be all right.'

Jim opened his eyes wide and played the young innocent he had never been. 'I'm glad of that, sir. Right glad.'

'Well, now you know, you'd best be getting about your business. That lad is the stepson of Mr Frederick Hallam, who owns half this town.'

Jim let his mouth drop open. 'Ooh.'

The gatekeeper nodded. 'Right, then. Off you go.'

'Yes, sir.'

Jim ran off, but slowed down again once he was out of sight where the wall curved round. He found a tree he could climb to look over the wall, curious to see where the boy lived. What he saw made him whistle under his breath. These folk were real nobs. Rich. Filthy rich. As he walked back into town, his expression was thoughtful. Perhaps, for once, his dad's schemes might come to something. It'd be nice not to be hungry.

*

Tom received another missive from Rosie that morning, this time asking him to go and see her immediately, not to wait even an hour. 'Desprit urgent' was the phrase she used, underlined twice.

He stormed along to Claters End, furious at her for calling on him for help again. He'd given her the help she'd demanded for young Albert and he'd made sure she had a good job, singing as well as serving. She had nothing to complain or worry about, so what did she want now? She was just playing tricks, hoping that he'd keep coming round to see her, that she'd get him back. Well, she wouldn't. Marianne was all he needed in a woman. All he'd ever need.

He veered into Bobbin Lane, making an old woman who was just tottering round the corner, yelp with surprise. Tom didn't even notice her. He pushed open the door of Rosie's rooms without knocking and strode inside. 'Well?'

Rosie was sitting by the fire in the downstairs room, nursing the baby. She looked up and smiled. 'Hello, Tom lad.'

'What the hell do you mean by sending for me like that? What did I tell you about keeping away from me?'

She put the baby down, fastened the front of her dress and glared at him. 'You arrogant bastard! Did you think I couldn't live without you, or summat?'

He stood very still, eyes narrowed.

She stood up, hands on hips, almost as tall as him, her dark curls bouncing aggressively, so angry was she. 'I've a good mind not to tell you anything, Tom Gibson.' She shut her mouth for a moment, then continued more quietly, 'Only I don't want your Annie worried.'

'Annie?'

She nodded. 'Mmm. Sit down, Tom. There's trouble brewing an' I thought you'd be the best one to deal with it.'

He sat down. 'Trouble for Annie?'

'Yes. And her son.'

'But Frederick sent word that William had been found.'

Rosie snorted. 'Aye, an' I'm the one as found him. She grinned at his surprised expression. 'Your Mr Hallam can be very generous. Sent me round a guinea this morning for my troubles, he did.' The grin faded. 'But I reckon Annie's troubles are only just starting.'

Tom leaned forward. 'Tell me.'

'Fred Coxton's back in town. I hadn't realised before. He'd changed his name, an' he's not a well man. Looks like the grandfather of the chap we used to know. But last night I found out who he was.'

Tom's breath hissed inwards in shock. 'I thought he was dead. I'll kill the bastard if I lay my hands on him.'

'Everyone thought he was dead. I reckon he must've put that rumour round himself. He allus was a sly one. There were a few folk as had a grudge against him when he disappeared. An' a few bills left unpaid, too, if I remember right.'

'Well, he'll not be staying in Bilsden for long.' The expression on Tom's face was one Rosie hadn't seen there for a while, not since he'd been a lad, knocking around with a rough crowd.

'There's more, Tom.'

'What?'

'Your William came into t'Shepherd last night an' met Fred. Someone must have told him that Fred were his father.' Her voice softened for a moment as she added, 'He looked bad, your William did, soaked through an' shiverin'. I fair felt for the lad. An' he met Fred's son Jim there, too. Anyone with half an eye could see they were brothers. William's not stupid.'

'Hell an' damnation!' Tom started walking to and fro, too angry to sit still.

'Your William was fair done in. When he fainted, I got

him away from Fred an' sent him back to Ridge House in a cab.' She was picking at the hem of her pinafore, not enjoying relating this tale. 'Fred found out William's name, but he didn't connect it with Mr Hallam. I told him if he went lookin' for the mother, she'd likely try to get money out of him. He didn't seem happy at that thought.'

'He'll be even more unhappy if he tries to go near our Annie!'

'Yes, well, he's a sick man, so maybe he won't.'

'How sick?'

'Coughing sickness. Lost a lot of weight, he has, an' when he starts coughing, it nearly tears him apart. I reckon he's not got long to live. I've seen that look on folk's faces before. His son's not a bad lad, though. Sharp as a tack. Jemmy, he says his name is, but I've heard Fred call him Jim sometimes. The lad looks a lot like your William, though. A lot. Folks'll start talkin' if you don't get him an' Fred away from here.'

'The two of them will be out of this town so fast their feet won't touch the cobblestones. I'll find out where Coxton's stayin' then I'll go to see him myself to send him away. I'll enjoy doing that.' Tom would actually like it best if Fred gave him some trouble. He'd really enjoy smashing Fred's face to pulp. He hadn't felt this angry with anyone for years. He felt guilty, too. He hadn't been as sympathetic towards Annie as he might have been when she was in trouble. Well, he'd make that up to her now.

Rosie grinned at him. 'Still mad at me for sendin' for you today, Tom Gibson?'

He grinned back. 'No. I should have trusted you. You always were a good lass, Rosie.'

When he'd gone she sat there for a while, and picked up the baby again, for comfort. As she sat rocking little Albert, her eyes filled with tears. 'An' you're a good lad, Tom Gibson.' She drew in a breath that seemed like broken glass in her throat, so painful was it. 'Ah, what's the use?' she said aloud. 'I've lost him now. It's about time I faced up to that an' got on with me life.'

When Jim got back with his information about this William Ashworth, Fred pieced the puzzle together slowly, nodding from time to time. There must be some way to get a bit of money out of the bitch for a poor orphaned lad who was the half-brother of her son. He grinned at the idea.

That night he got even drunker than usual, so that when he woke up next morning, he felt dreadful. 'I'm going, Jim, lad,' he said when he'd recovered from a long bout of coughing. 'It won't be long now.' A tear wound its way down his face. 'You'll miss your poor old dad, then, that you will. No one to look after you. No one to love you.'

Jim said nothing. When his dad was in this sort of maudlin mood, there was nothing you could say that would please him. Although Fred talked about dying, and was obviously well on his way to the grave, he didn't like you to agree with him and he seemed to believe that he would last for many years yet.

In the late afternoon, someone knocked on the door.

'Tell 'em to piss off,' Fred grunted, annoyed at being woken from a nap in which he'd been dreaming of the old days when he was young and strong.

Jim went to unbolt the door. A firm hand pushed it open as soon as the bolt was off and that same hand caught the startled Jim by the shoulder and propelled him quickly to one side. The intruder then slid the bolt on the door again, before turning back to stare round the dim cellar room, lit only by a window that looked out into a brick-lined well with a grating above it.

Fred, who was sinking into sleep again, grunted in shock as a foot kicked the pile of sacks aside and then connected with his ribs.

'I've been wantin' to meet you for a good few years,' Tom roared.

Fred rolled over, bewildered, and then cried out as Tom pulled him to his feet and shook him like a rat. By this time, Fred was starting to cough again.

Jim darted forward and tried to shove Tom out of the way. 'You leave my dad alone! He's sick.'

Tom thrust Fred away from him as soon as he realised what sort of cough it was. 'He bloody deserves to be sick, that one does.'

Jim helped his dad into the only chair and went to fetch him a drink of water from the bucket.

It was several minutes before Fred had recovered enough to stare at his attacker. 'Tom Gibson,' he grunted.

'I've been lookin' for you for years.' Tom's expression spelled danger.

'Whaffor?'

'For what you did to my sister.'

Fred shrugged. 'Thass a long time ago.' His face was white as chalk and he kept giving little spluttering coughs.

The lad was standing between Fred and Tom. 'You leave him alone,' he said shrilly. 'He's sick.'

'I can see that.' Tom could also see the shadow of death on Fred's face. Suddenly all thoughts of beating the fellow senseless left him, but he still didn't intend to let Fred upset Annie again. 'I want you two out of town today.'

Jim took it upon himself to answer, because his dad seemed only half there today. He'd never seen his dad so bad before. 'We 'aven't nowhere to go. An' no money. An' he's sick.'

Tom stood thinking for a moment or two. He was unnerved by Jim's resemblance to William, but even more so by Fred's present appearance. He remembered Fred as a vigorous man, glorying in his brute strength, making sparks fly from his clogs on the cobblestones as he confronted an opponent.

Somehow, seeing him now, Tom could not summon up the raging anger that had brought him racing round here once he'd found out where Fred was staying. And there was this lad to think of, too. What the father had done wasn't Jim's fault, and he'd be on his own when Fred died. It seemed wrong that a lad who looked so like William, hell, let's face it, a lad who was William's half-brother, should lack food and the necessities of life.

'Right then,' he said briskly, coming to a sudden decision. 'I'll find a cart an' send you two over to Manchester. You can find yourselves a room in Little Ireland, an' I'll send you the rent money for it as long as you stay there an' don't come back to Bilsden. If either of you set one foot in this town again, the money will stop.'

Jim brightened. This looked promising. 'All right.'

Fred looked up. 'In the old days, I'd have done as I pleased.' His voice was a hoarse growl, the cough still rasping in his throat.

Tom shook his head. 'No, you wouldn't. In the old days, I'd have killed you myself for what you did to our Annie.' He turned back to the lad. 'Get your things together an' get that sod ready to leave. I'll be back with a cart.'

When Tom had left the room, Fred nudged his son. 'Thass a bit of luck, eh? Him payin' us to stay away. Saves me botherin' his sister.'

'Why is he so mad at you?' Jim asked, curious to fit the pieces of the puzzle together.

Fred's expression broadened into a grin. 'I had 'er. One night. Met her in the street an' dragged her back home with me. Nice tasty piece, she was. I'd fancied her for a while. An' I was the first to have her, too.' He liked it when women screamed and fought as Annie had. It made everything that much more exciting.

Jim nodded and started gathering their things together.

His dad seemed to have forgotten the other boy now. But Jim hadn't. If that boy was this Annie person's son, then he was Jim's half-brother. That might be useful one day.

Maybe when his dad died – for young as he was, Jim had no illusions about his father's state of health – he'd come back here to Bilsden an' see what he could get for himself out of that relationship. Maybe they'd pay him to stay away, too, and help him keep out of the workhouse. He nodded. He wasn't soft like that other boy. He'd find some way of profiting from this. You had to look after yourself in this world; because no one else would.

II

April to May 1849

Physically, William suffered no more harm from his soaking than a severe chill that kept him in bed for a few days. Frederick went to have a talk to him before he let the boy see his mother, wanting to spare Annie as much anxiety as he could. But the talk did no good. William just could not lie to his mother and within half an hour she had got the whole story from him.

There was a long silence after he had finished. William sat at the end of Annie's bed, well wrapped in a blanket, his eyes avoiding hers.

'It didn't happen like that, William,' she said at last, her heart breaking to see the stiffness of his body. She did not dare try to cuddle him, afraid that he would push her away.

'Oh?'

'What Mabel and Beatrice told you – it was twisted, deliberately twisted.'

'But Mabel swore on the Bible.'

'She was lying, then.'

He just stared at her, as if he were beyond believing anything.

She steeled herself to explain. 'I was seventeen when it happened. Courting M— someone from the Rows. We were saving up to get married. I was working for Dr Lewis, as maid to his wife.'

He was still staring at her, solemn and distant, but at least he hadn't run away or refused to listen to her.

She hated even trying to remember it. 'It was my Sunday off. I was going back to Park House in the evening after visiting Dad and Emily in Salem Street. It was snowing, dark, freezing cold. And on the way back,' she sucked in a breath for to talk about it sickened her, 'I bumped into Fred Coxton.' How did you tell your son something like this? She could think of no way to soften it, so she said baldly, 'He grabbed me and dragged me back to his lodgings. He was big and strong. I fought, but he – he was stronger. Afterwards,' no, she mustn't reveal that Alice had been involved, because Alice's past was her own secret, 'someone who lived in the same house untied me while he was asleep, and I escaped. I went back to Park House – it was midnight by then. Dr Lewis was still awake. He – he looked after me.'

William's eyes were full of tears, but his mouth was a thin closed line.

'A few weeks later I found I was expecting a child. You.'

William sniffed and his mouth wobbled as he tried desperately not to cry.

'I wasn't pleased at the time, William, but from the minute you were born and Widow Clegg put me in your arms, I couldn't help loving you. I promise you that's the truth, love.'

In a tight raw voice, not the voice of the carefree child he'd been a few days previously, William said. 'Why did you marry my f— why did you marry Charlie Ashworth?'

'It was he who asked me to marry him. He'd been injured, you see, and he couldn't have children of his own. But he knew about me and he was happy to give a name to my child. He loved you even before you were born. You were the son he'd never been able to have.' Tears were rolling down her face now. 'William, in every way that matters, *every possible way*, Charlie was your father, your real father.'

William shook his head, unable to accept that now.

'Yes, he was, William. He loved you dearly and thought

of you as his son. He was so proud of you. You couldn't
have had a better father. Charlie,' her voice faltered for a
minute, 'Charlie was a very special man, for all that he was
a bit slow-thinking.'

William stood up, but he didn't go near his mother.
'Thank you for telling me.' He might have been a stranger,
a very polite stranger. 'I feel rather tired now. I think I'll go
and have a lie down again.' Without another look at her, he
left the room, the blanket trailing along the floor behind
him.

When Frederick came back from the mill at noon, he
found Annie lying there staring blankly at the ceiling with
a swollen, tear-stained face. As he pulled her into his arms,
she burst out sobbing against his chest. 'I had to tell William
the t-truth about how he was conceived. Oh, Frederick! He
was so *hurt*!' She could not speak, only sob against him.

'What did he say, my love?'

'N-nothing.'

'Nothing at all?'

She shook her head. 'He just s-sat there on the edge of
the bed and listened. He was polite, but – but not like my
son.'

Frederick stayed with her until she fell asleep, then went
to find William.

The boy was sitting hunched up in the bed, his arms
round his knees, his face bleak. Every now and then he
coughed or sneezed, but otherwise, his body was still, almost
rigid. And the pain on his face cut straight to Frederick's
heart, for it was as sharp as that on Annie's face. He had
never before seen so strong a resemblance between the two
of them.

'Want to talk about it, lad?' He sat down on the bed and
put one arm around William.

His question was answered only by a shake of the head.

'You should talk.'

William shot him an angry look. 'Why? What's the point? I don't even want to *think* about it.'

'Because if you don't talk, it'll eat away at you, turn you sour like Beatrice.' Frederick continued to hug William to him and for a minute felt a response, then the thin body stiffened again and pulled away from him. 'Well, I need to talk about it, even if you don't.'

William turned to look at him, frowning in puzzlement. 'Why?'

'Because Beatrice is my daughter, and I feel ashamed, deeply ashamed of what she's done.'

William shrugged. 'That's not your fault. I don't blame you. And it was Mabel, not Beatrice, who told me.'

'She was doing it for Beatrice. They must have planned it together. I don't intend to speak to my daughter or have her visit us here ever again,' Frederick said. 'I'm too disgusted with her.'

'Someone would have told me about it – one day.'

'But they wouldn't have lied about your mother when they did so.'

William's voice broke as he tried to speak. 'It makes me feel sick. That man, that horrible man, is my *father*.'

'Not in any way that matters.'

'"Bone of my bones, and flesh of my flesh".' William quoted a phrase from the Bible that his grandfather was fond of using. Only now it didn't illustrate why members of the same family should care for one another. It only illustrated the fact that a terrible man was his father, and that nothing could change that. Nothing.

'Does that mean that you can never regard me as your father?' Frederick asked.

'What?' William looked at him blankly.

'I promised Annie that after we were married, I'd treat

you as my own son. And I do think of you as my son now. Will you deny me that right?'

A sigh and a shrug were the only answer he got.

Frederick persevered. 'Especially now that I've disowned my daughter.'

'She's still your daughter, whatever you do.' Like Fred Coxton was still William's father. 'Flesh of your flesh.'

'She doesn't feel like my daughter any more.'

William slipped down under the blankets, his face white and his eyes still staring in that dreadful agonised way that had so upset his mother, and which was upsetting Frederick almost as much.

'I need to sleep now, sir, if you don't mind.'

Frederick stood up, unable to think of any other words that might bridge the gap between them. 'Then sleep. We'll talk again when you're feeling better.'

And so it continued for the next few days. William spoke to his mother, politely, like a stranger. When his cold was better, he moved around the house like an automaton. The servants whispered about it. Frederick tried several times to reason with him. But even Mark and Luke, who were as close to him as brothers; could not break through the ice that seemed to encase him.

It was John Gibson who finally made that chill carapace crack, though nothing would ever turn William back into the bright, utterly carefree boy he had been when he moved to Ridge House. John came up the hill once or twice to see his daughter and to visit his grandson in their time of trouble, braving the huge house and the servants who spoke more elegantly than he did. In the end, he spoke out from the heart. 'It won't do, lad.'

William looked at him warily. 'What won't do?'

'The way you're treating your mother. And Mester Hallam, too, come to that.'

'He says you should call him Frederick.'

But John was not to be diverted. He put his gnarled, work-worn hand on top of William's and said gently. 'Do you believe in our Lord, lad?'

'Y-yes.'

'So do I. I believe he loves us all, every last one of us, and works for our soul's good, though we may not always understand what he's doing.'

William was silent, then he burst out, 'But how could God have let that man hurt my mother so? And how could he have given me a father like that?'

'I've been puzzling on that. An' I think I've got it worked out.' John was silent for a moment, gathering his thoughts together, and mentally begging his Lord to help him, then he said with such quiet confidence that William could not help believing his words. 'It was through being hurt that your mother got you. If it had been another man as fathered you, he would have got a different lad on my Annie.'

William frowned. This view had clearly not occurred to him before.

'It were only that fellow, that Fred Coxton, as could make you, our William, the lad you are. For all his evil ways, he must have good inside him somewhere, for you're a fine lad.'

'How can a man like him have good inside him?'

'There's no sinner as can't be redeemed, William. No sinner as the Lord can't love if he only repents. That's why he gave his life for us on the cross. An' although our dear Lord gave your mother a hard burden to shoulder, he gave her you as well, someone to love. An' the hard times is what have made her into a strong woman. An' it took a strong woman to save our Tom, for a start.'

'I don't understand what you mean.' But William's hand had crept into his grandfather's.

'Our Tom were a wild lad, allus in trouble. I used t'wonder what'd become of him. It were Annie as made him think on, made him stop his wild ways and take up honest toil. An' when my Em'ly died, it were Annie as saved us, me an' my childer. I shouldn't have known what to do without Annie's help, an' that's the truth. She saved Kathy, too, when she were nobbut a lass. So you see, out of that evil came great good.'

'But I thought Charlie was my dad! I want him to be my dad!' It was a wail of pure agony.

John spoke sternly. 'An' he were your dad. It's a wicked thing to deny that he's been a father to you. Downright wicked. It's time for you to stop bein' so selfish, our William. You've had things easy in your life so far. Your mother's looked after you well, an' so did Charlie. But life nearly allus gives you hard blows. That's how things are in this world. But our dear Lord can give you the strength to bear them, an' he can bring you through to better times.'

'You don't understand!' It was the age-old cry of the young to the old.

'I've lost two wives as I loved dearly. Two lovely lasses. An' I've lost childer, too. If anyone should understand, it's me, don't you think?'

William stared, gulped, then threw himself into his grandad's arms, sobbing bitterly.

John let him sob for a while, then said gently, 'You've had a hard blow, lad, I'm not denyin' that, but you've still got your mam an' a new father as care for you. An' you've got all your family, too. That other lad, your brother, what has he got? Or the man who fathered you, come to that?'

The words came out muffled. 'I don't want a brother like him.'

'Nay, why ever not? Our Tom said he seemed a likely enough lad, lookin' after his sick father, as is only proper.

Fred Coxton is dyin', you know. Then that lad will have no one to care for him.' He pushed William away from him and looked him in the eyes. 'You're a Gibson, our William, for all your name's Ashworth. Us Gibsons don't give in to trouble like that. We face up to it an' then we carry on with our lives. An' so must you, if I'm to keep thinkin' well of you.'

William drew in a long shaky breath.

'So I want you to go an' see your mother again. She's lyin' there weepin' an' frettin' about you. What has she done to deserve that?' He looked sternly at the boy, then gave him a hug. 'Trust in the Lord, dear lad, as I do. He'll see you through this. An' look after your mother. Did you know she just lost a babby because of all this trouble?' He saw the amazement in William's face and nodded to reinforce his words. 'Yes, she were carrying Mester Hallam's child, but it weren't to be. You're not the only one with troubles, think on. Don't add to our Annie's. Or to Mester Hallam's. He's sorely 'shamed of that daughter of his, you know.'

'I'll have to – to think about it.'

'Aye. You do that. An' pray, too. There's help for us all in our hour of need if we seek the Lord in prayer. Think on that.'

Later that day, William appeared in the doorway to Annie's bedroom, where she was lying on a day couch staring listlessly into the fire.

'Hello, love,' she said, in a voice made husky by much weeping.

He ran across the room and threw himself into her arms. 'I'm sorry, Mother.'

She stroked the hair from his flushed forehead. 'Whatever have you to be sorry for?'

'For troubling you.'

'We all have troubles to bear.'

He leaned against her. 'Yes. That's what Grandad said,

but – he told me you'd lost a baby because of all this. It's all my fault.'

'Rubbish!'

'But it is!'

'No. It's Beatrice's fault, if it's anyone's. And Mabel's. They're a nasty pair. I'm sorry Frederick's disowned Beatrice, though. I don't think you should ever disown a child, whatever it does.' She sighed and held William to her and they sat there quietly for a while, not speaking, but close again.

A little later, he said, 'Grandad explained it all to me. About life, and how the Lord makes you stronger through adversity. And I do see that my father – Charlie Ashworth, not *that man* – really loved me like a son.'

'Of course he did.'

'But – it still hurts, Mother!'

She could only nod against him and say shakily, 'I know.'

After a while, he said, 'I do love you, Mother.'

'And I love you, darling.'

And there they left it. Gradually, as the weeks passed, William regained something of his old energy and enthusiasm, especially when he was playing with Brutus. But he also had quiet times, times when his face was sad, when he was withdrawn.

John Gibson told his daughter, when she worried about that, 'Only time can heal a wound like that. But in any case, the lad's growing up. You can't keep him a carefree child for ever, lass. You can't protect him from life.'

But she would have done, if she could have found a way.

Once he knew that Annie was on the mend, Frederick remembered that he hadn't been to see this Rosie woman, to thank her personally, which he thought someone from the family ought to do. He went to the Shepherd's Rest, causing the daytime regulars to crane round to stare at him.

They had never expected to see Mester Hallam in a place like this.

Seth gave him Rosie's address and Frederick walked round to Claters End. He'd left the carriage at the mill, not wanting the servants to gossip about where he'd been. 'Damned place!' he muttered, staring around him. 'I hadn't realised how bad it'd got down here.' By the time he reached Bobbin Close, his nose was wrinkled in disgust at the strong smell that emanated from the muddy stream of garbage and filth that ran down its middle.

Rosie opened the door to him herself, with little Albert on her hip. The smile died on her face as she saw who her guest was and her mouth fell open in surprise.

'May I come in?' But Frederick's prepared speech died on his lips as he looked at Albert. His breath whistled inwards in shock, for the resemblance between Albert and young Samuel John was quite astounding. Apart from the age difference, the two of them could have been twins.

'Oh, hell!' Rosie jerked her head in an invitation to enter and slammed the door shut on the curiosity of her neighbours. 'Won't you sit down, Mr Hallam?'

'Thank you.'

'What can I do for you?'

'I came to ask you that same question. We're very grateful to you for sending William safely back to us.' But his eyes kept flickering towards the laughing child.

'You've noticed the resemblance,' she said dryly.

'It's – quite amazing.'

'Yes. So Tom tells me.'

A knowing look came into his face. 'Ah. The child is Tom's, then?'

'Whose did you think it was? His father's?' She grinned. 'No. It's Tom's. Me an' Tom have known each other for a good many years. But,' her grin faded, 'we haven't been seeing one another since he started going with the doctor's daughter.'

'How old is the child, then?' His question was pointed.

She flushed. 'A few months. It was just the once I saw Tom. When he was upset about something.' The truth showed clearly in the bitter way she added, 'I wish to God he would get upset more often!'

He looked at her quietly. A pretty woman, a bit plump and with an expressive sort of face, especially her fine dark eyes. 'You love him,' he said, and it was not a question.

She nodded. 'Aye. More fool me, eh? Tom thinks the sun shines out of his Marianne's backside. An' you needn't think I'll be pestering him, or any of your wife's family. He gives me money for Albert here regular, an' that's all I ask of him.' She sighed. 'But if I had some way of leaving Bilsden, I'd be gone tomorrow, that's for sure.'

'What would you do?'

'Get myself some better singing lessons. I've learned all that the singing teacher here knows.'

'To what purpose?'

'To find a job singing for my supper,' she mocked. 'But somewhere better than the Shepherd's Rest. Maybe even in a theatre.'

He raised his eyebrows. This was the last thing he would have expected. Rosie had a lush look about her which might once have attracted him if he had not met Annie. He would have expected her ambition to be to set up as a high-class whore or even a madam.

She stared at him and gave a short bark of laughter. 'That surprised you, didn't it? Eeh, Mr Hallam, I've known Tom since we was both seventeen, an' he's been the only one for me ever since then. But he don't want me no more. So,' she blinked furiously to clear the tears from her eyes, 'I've made up my mind to make something of meself. I hear there's good money to be made from singing. An' if there's one thing I can do, it's sing.'

'Show me.'

'What?'

'Sing something to me now.'

A smile transformed her face, making it pretty, showing the innate generous nature of Rosie Liddelow, daughter of a whore and a passing half-gypsy drover, but no whore herself. She put Albert down, then turned, threw back her head and launched into 'The Dream' again, singing it with all her heart. She followed that by a lullaby, then by a wickedly raucous ditty that always made the patrons of the Shepherd's Rest curl up with laughter.

Frederick laughed, too, then held up his hand. 'Enough. You have a beautiful voice, Miss Liddelow. If you'll permit me to, I should like to help you, not only to get away from Bilsden for all our sakes,' he looked meaningfully at the child, 'but also to make your way in the world as a singer. A voice like that can give pleasure to a lot of people.'

Forgetting who he was, she threw her arms round him and smacked a kiss on his cheek, then she picked up her son and waltzed him round the room till he was breathless with laughter and excitement. 'You're a real gentleman, Mr Hallam, a real gentleman.'

Then she saw his quizzical expression and added challengingly. 'An' I'm goin' t'stay respectable from now on, too. I'm not risking another little interruption like this one, fond as I am of my bonny lad.' She gestured towards Albert.

Frederick nodded. 'I'll let you know the details, then, when I've made some arrangements. I think you'll do well in your new life, Miss Liddelow.'

She grimaced. 'Not Miss Liddelow. That's no name for a posh singer, is it? I'm goin' t'call meself somethin' different from now on.'

'What?'

She put her head on one side to consider that. 'Somethin' foreign, I think.' She grinned. 'I'll tell folk that me mam, God rest her soul, was Italian.'

'Then Rosa might be a better first name.'

She nodded approvingly. 'Yes. That's near enough so I won't forget who I am. An' for a second name?'

'Rosa Lidoni.'

She burst out laughing. 'So near an' yet so far. That's it, Mr Hallam. I'm Rosa Lidoni from now on.' She shook the child on her hip gently. 'You hear that, young fellow. Your new name is Albert Lidoni.'

Frederick was still smiling as he walked back down the street, but his expression became thoughtful as he debated whether to tell Annie about this. On the whole, he rather thought not. She'd only worry. Or decide to take an interest in the child herself. She was ferociously loyal to her family, his Annie was.

12

June to July 1849

When Marianne's pains started, late one Friday evening in June during the first warm spell of the season, Tom sent immediately for Widow Clegg. He also sent word to Jeremy Lewis, who came round to keep his son-in-law company through the long night hours, though he was not normally called in on a birthing unless there was trouble. Women preferred other women to tend them at such times.

Dr Spelling had been the one to deal with young Mrs Gibson throughout her pregnancy, for propriety's sake, but Jeremy had kept an eye on his daughter from a distance. He had worried a little at how large she had become, but otherwise been satisfied to see how well she looked. Tonight Dr Spelling was away at one of the outlying farms, so Jeremy preferred to be within call – just in case.

'It won't be fast, with a first baby,' he warned Tom, who was pacing up and down the living room like a wild animal trapped in a cage.

But it was fast. Even Widow Clegg was taken aback at the speed with which the baby was born, a little girl. But afterwards Marianne didn't lie back and rest, as the Widow had expected. She continued to push and strain, and soon a second baby's head appeared.

'Nay, there's another babby comin'!' the Widow exclaimed. 'Now where's that been hiding?'

'Twins!' gasped Marianne, trying to raise her head to see.

'Thee lie back an' push!' ordered the Widow. She wrapped

the squalling baby deftly in a soft blanket and turned to Megan. 'Fetch Dr Lewis up. Best be on the safe side with twins,' she said in a low voice. She laid the first baby in the nearby cradle and turned to help the next child into the world.

Megan rushed downstairs to fetch Dr Lewis. 'It's twins,' she gasped. 'Widow Clegg says can you come up.'

Tom was on his way upstairs before she had finished speaking, followed closely by Jeremy. He threw open the bedroom door just as the newly born Master Gibson opened his pink rosebud of a mouth and wailed a protest against the harsh world into which he had just been thrust. The new father stopped dead in the doorway, clutching the door frame in relief that his wife was still alive, and although the baby continued to wail, Tom's eyes were fixed on Marianne.

Jeremy thrust his son-in-law aside and strode over to the foot of the bed, throwing off his jacket and rolling up his sleeves. 'What's wrong?'

Widow Clegg threw him a quick glance and turned back to wrap up the second baby. 'There's nowt wrong. I should've sent for thee afore now if there'd been owt wrong.' She cast a disapproving glance at Tom, who was hovering in the doorway, watching Megan wipe her mistress's brow. 'Tha shouldn't be here, Tom Gibson.'

'I'm not leaving till I find out how my wife is.'

At the sound of her husband's name, Marianne opened her eyes and immediately held out her hand to him.

She looked utterly exhausted, poor love, he thought, as he moved forward in a little rush and knelt to clasp the hand. 'Clever Marianne!' he said softly, his love shining from his face.

Jeremy moved to stand close to Widow Clegg. 'Why did you send for me, then, Mrs Clegg?'

'Just to be on t'safe side, Dr Lewis. Tha can never tell what'll happen with twins.'

'Twins!' Tom turned white. '*Twins!*'

'Ah. I did wonder about that.' Jeremy walked to the head of the bed and laid one expert hand on his daughter's brow. 'How are you feeling, darling?'

Marianne rolled her head over to smile at him. 'Tired. You didn't tell me it was such hard work, Father.' Her eyes moved back to Tom, who was still kneeling at her side, clasping her hand. 'Have you seen them, Tom, love? Have you seen our children?'

He shook his head. 'No. It's you I'm concerned with.'

She had a teasing expression on her face, tired as she was. 'Do you mean I've done all that hard work and you aren't even interested in looking at your son and daughter?'

He smoothed the hair back from her forehead. 'Not as much as I am in looking at you, love.'

'Well, I want to see them and I want you to see them, too.' Her voice was tired, but held a note of triumph. 'And oh, I want so much to hold my babies. So we'll examine them together, if you please, Mr Gibson.'

Tom stood up as Widow Clegg moved forward. She thrust one bundle into the crook of Marianne's arm, the other into the new father's arms. An expression of alarm replaced the tenderness on Tom's face. 'Hey!'

'They don't break. They're a lot tougher nor they look, babbies are,' she informed him. Gesturing to Megan to hold up the sheet to preserve modesty, she began to clean up the mother.

When she had finished her ministrations, the Widow turned her attention back to the babies and clicked her teeth in exasperation, for neither Tom nor Marianne had moved, and Dr Lewis was looking fondly down at his new grandson and granddaughter, making no attempt to examine either mother or children. Within the minute, the Widow had a protesting Tom out of the bedroom and the babies lying uncovered on the bed for the doctor's inspection.

Jeremy was filled with a sense of wonderment as he examined his grandchildren. Something he had longed for, dreamed about. 'They're beautiful, darling,' he said to Marianne, in a voice thickened with emotion. 'Absolutely beautiful.'

'Have you done lookin' at them?' the Widow demanded, nudging him back into awareness. 'Then let me wrap them up again. Megan, open the door for the doctor.'

Jeremy took the hint. 'I'll see you later, darling,' he said to Marianne, then went outside, where he lingered on the landing to blow his nose and get his emotions under control again.

He had hardly set foot on the stairs than Tom darted out of the parlour. 'Is she all right?'

'Yes, of course.'

'And the babies?'

'Perfect.'

Tom grabbed Jeremy's arm as he took the last step down into the narrow hallway. 'Are you sure?'

'Of course I'm sure.' Jeremy steered Tom back into the parlour and sat him down in the big wing chair. The first rays of the sun were just gilding the leaves of the bushes outside the window. Jeremy yawned. He found these sleepless nights more tiring nowadays. He was getting older. Ellie had pointed out a whole tuft of grey hairs at his temple the other day. Dear Ellie. She was a wonderful wife.

Tom's voice broke into his reverie. 'And you're sure that Marianne's taken no harm?'

'As sure as I can be at this stage. But she needs to sleep now. Have you thought about names for your children?'

'What? Oh, yes, names.' Tom shrugged. 'Marianne thought

of Lucy if it was a girl – after my mother, you know – and perhaps David for a boy.'

'After my father,' said Jeremy, pleased. 'Well, there you are then. Now that you've got one of each, you can use both the names.'

Tom bounced up, unable to sit still, and grasped Jeremy's arm so hard that it hurt. 'Are you absolutely *sure* she's all right?'

Jeremy put his arm round Tom's shoulders. He had never realised quite how much Tom loved his daughter till he had watched him pace this night away, raw with anxiety for his wife. He frowned. He'd expected Tom to take much more pride in his children. 'Yes. I told you. She's fine. Tired, but fine. You'll have to look after her for a week or two, till we're sure she hasn't developed puerperal fever, but with Widow Clegg, that happens less often than it does with other midwives.'

Tom nodded, managing a half-smile. 'She's a terror, the Widow is.'

'A real terror. But a wonderful nurse. When I get my hospital, I mean to put her in charge of the nursing and housekeeping side of things.'

But Tom wasn't interested in the prospect of a hospital for Bilsden. All Tom was interested in was his wife. Even his children came a long way behind Marianne who was the absolute centre of Tom's universe nowadays.

Not only did Marianne not develop puerperal fever, she made such a rapid recovery that she was up and about within a couple of days, scandalising her neighbours, who had very firm views about how long a woman should take for her lying-in. Marianne scandalised Tom, too, who wanted to wrap her in cotton wool and wait on her hand and foot.

'I'm *not* ill!' she stormed, when he tried to persuade her to go back to bed. 'And I'm not going to lie up there bored to tears when I could be down here minding my babies. Most women in the Rows get up the day after the birth, you know.'

'Well, you don't live in the Rows and you don't have to get up.'

'I *want* to get up!'

'But there's no need. I can afford to hire extra help—'

'You've already asked Megan to live in without so much as consulting me. That's the last time you do that sort of thing, Tom Gibson! The house is my concern.'

He ran a hand through his crinkly brown hair. 'But for someone like you, a gentleman's daughter—'

'Oh, pooh! What do you want me to do? Sit on a cushion and sew a fine seam?'

'Yes!'

'Well, I'm not cut out for that. And I won't lie around idly in bed, either! It bores me. And don't call me a girl. I'm not a girl now. I'm a woman, a mother of two babies.'

As if they knew they were being spoken about, the babies began to wail, in unison as usual.

'There, see what you've done, Tom Gibson, with your fussing!'

He raised his eyebrows to heaven and growled inarticulately through clenched teeth.

She just laughed at him. 'Pass me David and get back to the yard, Tom. I'm fine, really I am.'

'Women!' But it was said fondly.

But when Tom had gone, Marianne shed a few tears over the wonder of it all as she looked down at the two cradles. And she found that by the time she'd fed the babies, she did feel exhausted. Especially when they continued to cry, Lucy setting David off again, for he was the more placid of the two.

Hearing the babies yelling, Megan came in and caught her mistress sniffling into her handkerchief.

'I don't know what's wrong with me,' Marianne sobbed. 'And I don't know what's wrong with them, either. I've just fed them.'

'They probably need changing. Or they've got wind.' Megan smiled, feeling much more experienced than her mistress where babies were concerned. Hadn't she helped her mother with eight of them, and helped bury three of them, too? But those poor little things had been sickly at birth, not like the twins, who were a fine lusty pair. 'There's nothing wrong with you havin' a cry, ma'am. That always happens afterwards. My mam used to get all weepy, too. An' when she wasn't weepin', she was shoutin' at us.' Megan hesitated. 'Mind you, it's harder rearing twins.' In the Rows, even the more respectable end where she came from, it was hard rearing any child.

Marianne nodded. 'I can see that. While I'm feeding one, the other cries, and then that upsets the one I'm feeding.' She looked down at her depleted breasts. 'At least I seem to have enough milk for two.'

Megan cleared her throat and decided to take a risk. 'I was just havin' a think in the kitchen, ma'am, an' I think Mr Gibson's right. You do need extra help now.'

'Other women manage.'

'Yes, but they wish they didn't have to manage. They wish they had the chance of some help. An' maybe if they didn't have to work so hard, women could rear more of their babies an' live longer themselves.'

Marianne sighed. What Megan was saying made sense. 'I wanted it to be just me and Tom living here.'

Megan's dismay showed in her face. 'Don't you want me to live in?'

'I do and I don't.' She reached out to pat her maid's hand.

Marianne could never stand on her dignity with servants, and she had always treated them more like friends who were helping her than menials. The babies were settling down now. After being expertly burped by Megan, they snuffled gradually into sleep.

Marianne let out a breath of relief at the blessed silence. The lusty yelling of her son and daughter was very wearing in her present state. 'You're right, really, Megan. We are going to need some more help, because,' Marianne's face lit up, 'I intend to have a large family. And,' she stared round thoughtfully, 'much as I like this house, it isn't going to be big enough for us all. We'll have to think about moving somewhere larger.'

By the time Tom came home, Megan's sister Bronwen, who was just fourteen to Megan's seventeen, had been hired as nursemaid, and Marianne was lying on the sofa, tired but satisfied with her day's efforts. In the kitchen Megan was instructing Bronwen, newly washed all over and clad in one of Megan's print frocks, about how to go on in a gentleman's household. Tom might not consider himself a gentleman, but Megan did, and woe betide anyone who hinted differently to her.

Tom couldn't bring himself to complain about Marianne being downstairs, for the house seemed to echo around him when he dined in solitary state.

'I've hired a new maid, Tom,' she declared, holding her cheek out for a kiss.

He gaped at her. 'After all the fuss you made when I suggested it!'

She grinned. 'Well, I got to thinking. Then Megan and I discussed how we would manage, and with two babies, we decided that we needed more help.'

'And you've hired someone already? How did you find her?'

'It's Megan's sister, Bronwen. She's been practising for years on her brothers and sisters, so she knows what she's doing.' She gave him a challenging stare. 'It's my job to hire servants, Tom, and my job to run the house. I meant what I said about that.'

He sat down on the edge of the sofa and put his arms round her, planting another kiss on her smooth white forehead and smoothing back the blond hair he loved so much. 'Well, that's fine by me, Mrs Gibson.' He never tired of using that name.

'And what's more,' she added wickedly, 'I think we're going to have to move house before our next child is born.'

He jerked against her. '*Next child*!'

'Yes.' Her smile was warm and dreamy. 'I want a very large family. Don't you?'

'Well, I never thought of it, actually.' And he didn't want a large family. He just wanted a couple of children, which he'd got now, and his wife. But he didn't like to say that to Marianne in her present fragile state.

'Then you'd better think about it, Tom, for I want more children, and soon, too.'

She looked so beautiful as she lay there on the sofa that she could have asked him for the moon and he'd have flown off to get it for her. 'If that's what you really want, love, it's all right by me.'

'Good.' She yawned and snuggled down.

In the corner, two infants sucked their thumbs and smacked their lips a few times, then relaxed into sleep, lying in the cradles Marianne had insisted Megan bring down to the parlour. Tears blurred Tom's eyes as he stared at his dozing wife, then he got up and tiptoed across to look down into the cradles. It was the first time the babies had had his undivided attention. He brushed away a trail of moisture from his cheek as he stared down at the two small bodies.

The babies were well wrapped in shawls and covered with blankets, for all the mildness of the evening. His children, his and Marianne's.

A fringe of fine light brown hair showed on each forehead, but the babies' features were indistinguishable as yet. They certainly had good lungs, though. He reached out a tentative finger and stroked one soft cheek, marvelling that this was his son, then moving on to stare down at his daughter, who had managed to get one fist out of her shawl. He touched the tiny pink fingers wonderingly. So small and yet so perfectly formed. And with such a strong grasp. Two babies. He'd have to make sure he worked hard and provided for them as they deserved.

He turned back to look at Marianne and chuckled to himself. A new house, she'd said. A bigger house. Three days after having the twins, she'd come downstairs, hired a maid and started planning for the future. And he had wanted to lap her up in cotton wool and protect her from all harm when they got married. Nay, you couldn't coddle a woman like Marianne. She was too busy and active, too full of life. He didn't realise that that was the first time he'd really thought of her as a woman, not a girl.

He went back to his chair and sat there quietly as his wife dozed, content just to look at her rosy sleeping face. When she awoke, he rang for a tea tray, and later watched as she fed the babies again, with Bronwen in attendance. For all her youth, Bronwen seemed very experienced, holding one child in her scrawny arms and shushing it as it waited its turn at the breast.

When it was all over, and Bronwen had taken the babies upstairs, Tom and Marianne had their own meal, of which Marianne ate so heartily that he could not but believe in her good health. Soon afterwards, however, Tom complained about feeling tired, so that he could get Marianne to bed early, before the next feed. And he was tired, too. He hadn't had much sleep lately.

One month later, Tom decided that Marianne was right. They did need a bigger house, and they needed it now, not later. A house where he could go and sleep in the spare bedroom, if necessary, while his wife attended to the babies. He started looking and found one in Church Road, larger than Throstle Lane, with attics and a landlord who was prepared to put in a proper bathroom for a long-term tenant, although it'd mean a slightly higher rent. Tom could have bought a house himself, but he didn't want to tie up his capital at this stage. He had too many business plans bubbling away.

Best of all, the new house had four bedrooms and two attics, so he could use one of the spare bedrooms when the babies, whom his wife insisted on having by her side of the bed, were sleeping badly, as children do sometimes. He'd never expected to feel like this, never thought he'd want to sleep away from Marianne, but then, he'd never felt so exhausted before. He wished they didn't have to wait to move into the new house. The children were thriving. His wife had not succumbed to any post-natal infection. He was the one who was suffering, he thought indignantly as he sat and yawned in front of the fire.

He was so desperate for sleep that he went round to his father's one afternoon and took a nap on the sofa there, to Kathy's amusement. It was no easy task being the father of lusty twins, he told her when he awoke. She had it easy with just Samuel John to look after.

'Aye, well, there'll be another to join him soon.'

He forced a smile and left. Wherever he turned he seemed to be surrounded by pregnant women, or by women who wanted to get pregnant. And no one understood how hard it was for him. No one.

13

July 1849

When Seth Holden sent a message round one evening, to say that there were a few matters that needed discussing, Tom grumbled about never getting a minute to rest, and let the note wait.

It wasn't until the next evening that he decided a walk in the fresh air would do him no harm. It had rained earlier, but a glorious sunset was glowing above the rooftops now, lending a brief beauty even to the smoky Bilsden skyline.

Before the babies' birth, he thought gloomily as he walked along, he might have taken Marianne walking with him. They had often enjoyed a stroll together, especially up on the moors, but now she didn't want to be parted from David and Lucy, not even for half-an-hour. Apart from going to work, he'd hardly left the house since the twins had been born, and to tell the truth, the first flush of pride in watching his wife and babies was giving way to a sneaking boredom with the processes of looking after them and the lack of response from the infants, who always seemed to be either crying or sleeping.

It seemed, he thought as he walked along, as if he were locked out of a feminine conspiracy that even the two young maids were part of, and he admitted to himself that he was dissatisfied with that. He wanted Marianne to himself and deep down he wished they had not started a family quite so soon. Still, the fact that it was twins seemed to have satisfied the gossips about the birth taking place so soon after

the marriage. Twins had a habit of coming early. There was
that to be glad for, at least. He didn't want a breath of gossip
blackening Marianne's name.

Ellie had already visited Marianne several times. 'Folk will
never believe that these two came early,' she said one afternoon, cuddling little David and smiling down at him fondly.
It still amazed her that she had become a grandmother before
she was even a mother.

'I don't really care what people in the town believe,'
Marianne retorted. 'I'm happy in my own home, with my
own family and friends, and that's all I want out of life.'

'At one time, you wished you could be a doctor, like your
father,' Ellie reminded her.

'Chance would be a fine thing! I can't see men ever letting
us women become doctors.'

'Jeremy says there's one woman training to be a doctor
in New York. He heard about it from a friend in London.
Just imagine that!'

'Well,' Marianne's gaze softened as she watched her
daughter suck hard on her breast, 'I've changed my mind
lately about women becoming doctors, or lawyers, or
anything else that men do. Quite honestly, I don't see how
women could cope with a life outside the home, not when
they have children to care for. Becoming a doctor would
mean giving up so much, not getting married, not having
children. It wouldn't be worth it.'

'I wouldn't want to be a doctor, anyway,' said Ellie with
a shudder.

'Maybe not. But that doesn't mean women can't make
themselves useful in the world. I shall go back to help in my
father's free clinic in Claters End after the children are
weaned. I can still help people who're in need, I hope. I'll
certainly find a way to do that.' She looked thoughtful and
added, 'You really must read *Mary Barton*, Ellie. It's quite

harrowing, but it makes you think about how other people have to struggle just to live. I wept and wept as I read it. I'm sure the author must be a woman. Only a woman could so understand how other women feel. And morally, I don't think it's fair that a woman should be penalised for ever just for an indiscretion in her youth, like Mary's aunt was. Or that poorer people should die of starvation while others have far more to eat than they need.'

Ellie shook her head. 'I grew up in the Rows an' that's taught me as much as I need to know about poorer people's lives, thank you. I don't want to read about trouble. There's enough around without inventing more.'

They'd had discussions like this before, so Marianne just smiled and let the matter drop.

'And anyway, I've no time for reading. I'm too busy.' As Jeremy's wife, Ellie had a lot to learn. Even the way she dressed was changing. Jeremy had insisted she buy herself a whole new wardrobe in keeping with her status as the doctor's wife. It had seemed a waste of money to Ellie, but she had done as he asked. And now Annie was insisting that the new Mrs Lewis take tea with her regularly and meet the other ladies of the town. To Ellie, that was a huge ordeal, and she found that she was glad to have the fashionable clothes to boost her morale. Besides, any clothes produced at the Bilsden Ladies' Salon were bound to be beautiful, for all that Annie didn't run it herself any more. Mary Benworth was a very capable woman.

They chatted on comfortably for a while, then Ellie looked at the clock on the mantelpiece. 'Well, I suppose I'd better be going,' she said, reluctant to leave.

Marianne stood up and came over to hug her. 'Give Catherine a kiss for me, then. I've missed seeing her. I'll be round to call on you in a week or so.'

'You should take things easy, love, while you can.'

'Oh, pooh!' Marianne grinned at her as she led the way to the door. 'It's boring taking things easy. I'm really looking forward to moving into a larger house next month. There'll be a lot to sort out there.'

As Ellie told Jeremy in bed that night, his daughter seemed to be turning into a universal mother. 'I'm proud of her, though, proud of the way she cares about other folk as well as her own family. Aren't you, love?'

'Indeed I am.'

'And the extra weight she's gained since she had the children suits her, I think.'

'I agree. Absolutely.' It made Marianne look less like Annabelle, and Jeremy never liked being reminded of his first wife. Young Catherine resembled her mother greatly, and he wished she didn't. There seemed to be no sign of the unknown father in her, though, thank goodness. He'd grown very fond of the child he'd acknowledged as his own. How could you not, when a creature so small and soft was totally dependent upon you?

'You're downright soppy about your grandchildren, and about Catherine, too,' Ellie teased. Even in the dark she could sense that Jeremy was smiling.

'Well, it makes up for the fact that I was denied other children for so long. Marianne's like me, I think. She wants a large family.' He paused, waiting for Ellie to speak, then, when she didn't, he decided to raise the matter himself. 'You didn't get your monthly courses, love.'

Ellie burrowed against him. 'It's early days yet. Anything can happen.'

'Mmm. But I hope we do have some children. And the sooner the better, as far as I'm concerned. I'm not getting any younger.'

She did not echo his words, as he had expected and he stiffened. 'Don't you want a family, Ellie?'

She tried to find tactful phrases to explain her feelings. If the truth were told, she had never hankered after children, as some women did. In her mind, children were linked with trouble and hard work. She had known days when her mother was hard put to find food for her family, and had never forgotten the feeling of gnawing hunger from the bad times. 'I don't want a large family,' she said slowly. 'Two or three children, perhaps. That'd be all right. But seven or eight – no, I'd hate it.'

She lay there against his tense body. 'Jeremy, is there some way to keep our family small?' She blushed, even in the darkness, as she added, 'apart from abstaining, I mean.' Her own joy in their lovemaking shocked her still, raised, as she had been, by a mother who considered that side of marriage a grudging concession to men's sinful natures.

At last he said slowly, 'Yes. There is a way.' But he'd rather not have thought of that. He'd rather have had a house full of children. Which was unfair of him, he knew, since it was the women who put their lives at risk every time they bore a child.

'That's good. I'd like to have a child every two or three years, not be pregnant all the time.' Ellie could sense that he was a bit disappointed, so she hugged him to her. 'Stop worrying, Jeremy Lewis,' she said softly in his ear. 'I'm not like Annabelle was. I shan't deny you children, my love. Not if we're able to have them – as seems likely now. But let's have them one at a time, so that we can care for them properly and still have time for one another.'

'Your wish is my command, Ellie Lewis,' he said lightly.

She knew he was not fully in agreement, but she knew also that she would have her way, in this as in most things. Jeremy Lewis was not a dominating sort of man. In fact, in some ways, he was downright weak, especially where women were concerned. Look how his first wife had ruled the roost.

'But I have been feeling a bit queasy in the mornings,' she added, to cheer him up.

His voice was eager and boyish in the warm darkness, not the voice of a middle-aged doctor at all. 'You're sure of that?'

'Oh, yes. More than sure. Actually, I've been sick a couple of times.'

He covered her face with kisses, then hugged her to him as he said huskily, 'Ellie, you don't know how happy that makes me.'

I do, she thought, as she hugged him in return. I know more about how you feel than you'll ever realise, Jeremy Lewis, for I've been watching you since I was a little lass of twelve. And I've lived and worked in your house all that time.

When Tom arrived at the Shepherd's Rest the evening after Seth's message, the big room which folk now called the singing saloon seemed very quiet and Seth had that gloomy look on his face that usually meant the takings were down. 'Where's Rosie?' Tom asked, noticing the silence from the little stage area, not to mention a new woman serving behind the bar.

'She's gone.'

Tom stopped dead. '*What?*'

'Gone.' Seth waved a piece of paper at him. 'She sent round a note to tell me she weren't comin' here any more an' she sent round this other note for you. It's been waiting here for you since yesterday. You should ha' come then, when I sent word.'

Tom shrugged. 'I was goin' to come round last night, but I fell asleep after my tea. Those bloody babies have the loudest voices in Bilsden. I haven't had a proper night's sleep since they were born.'

Seth grinned. 'Ah. I thought the delight at bein' a father 'ud soon wear off. Welcome to the real world, partner. Us fathers count for nothin' with the womenfolk once the babies start arriving. Take my wife, now . . .'

Tom let Seth natter on while he read Rosie's letter, then he said, 'Shush!' and reread it intently.

Dear Tom

Just to let you no that I'm leavin Bilsden. I've got a chanse at a good job singin so I've took it. It pays a lot more than servin behind the bar does.

Don't worry about us. I'll be abel to look after Albert proper, like you want, and I'll see he gets his schoolin.

Tom, it was real good between us, but I can see its over now, so dont try to find me, love. And dont worry about me or Albert. If I'm ever in need I'll come to you for help.

Rosie

PS You can pay Alberts money into the Bilsden Savings Bank. I've got an account there. It'll give him a start in life later.

It was the longest letter Rosie had ever written. She had had to copy it out twice, because tears would keep rolling down her cheeks, dropping on to the page and smudging the ink. In the end, she managed something that half-satisfied her, with only one teardrop stain, and she left it at that. How did you tell someone that if he ever wanted you, you'd come running back? In this case, you didn't, because he wouldn't want her, Tom wouldn't. Not when he had his Marianne. She'd never seen anyone as besotted as Tom was with his wife.

Tom stared down at the crumpled piece of paper and touched a fingertip to the tear stain. Had Rosie found herself a gentleman friend? What was she doing with herself? Was she all right? 'I wish I knew where she's gone,' he said, before he could think.

Seth stared. 'Whatever for?'

'Oh, me an' Rosie go back a long way.' Tom was surprised to realise that he was going to miss her, not being with her, of course, but seeing her around and knowing she was all right. And he'd miss Albert, too. He was a fine lad, young Albert was. Big and healthy looking, with a smile for all the world. Tom's legitimate son, David, looked much frailer, and much less like Tom, which didn't seem fair at all.

'Well, more to the point, what are we goin' to do about gettin' oursen another singer?' Seth demanded. 'I've got a new lass in to serve the ale – that's no problem – but singers don't grow on every tree, not singers like Rosie, any road. She had a rare fine voice, Rosie did, an' a good way with the customers, too. She could stop a fight afore it even started an' get the lads laughin' together in two minutes.'

Tom made a sudden decision. 'We'll do without the singing for a while. I'll keep Gerry to play the piano an' he can get folk going on a sing-song, or them as wants can stand up an' sing for the rest.'

'They'd rather have Rosie.'

'Well, they can't have her.' Tom's mind was racing ahead, as it always did when he was working out business schemes. 'We'll offer a prize each night for the best singer. A shilling and a free drink. That'll make 'em feel better.'

Seth frowned. 'I don't know about that. It's just giving money away.'

'I'm right. You'll soon see.' Tom waved a hand airily and added in a falsely refined tone, 'Manchester may have its Gentlemen's Concerts, but we've got the Bilsden Sore

Throats Club.' The singing in the Shepherd's Rest was loud, if not tuneful, and it sometimes made Tom's throat ache in sympathy to hear the way folk tried to sing louder than each other.

Seth chuckled. 'Sore Throats Club! Get on with you, you daft sod. Seriously, though, wouldn't it be better to get another singer in?'

'Not yet. It's time to make a start on that new place I've been thinking about, Seth. I want a real posh place, not just a free and easy singing room, like we've got here.' Tom could not help smirking as he said, 'And I've got an option to buy the Three Feathers, now that Bill Odhall's died. I'm going to call it the Prince of Wales, though. It sounds better, don't you think?'

'That'll cost a fortune!' yelped Seth, who hated to see any of his precious money paid out once he had garnered it in.

'Worth it. Well worth it. You have to spend money to make money, Seth lad, as I keep telling you. There's enough land behind the Three Feathers to build a big room for music – in fact, we'll call it a hall, a music hall, like they do in Bolton, and we'll have assemblies there, too, where the gentry can go and dance. Bilsden being such a new town, we haven't got an Assembly Room, but as my esteemed brother-in-law says, "If we haven't got something, we must provide it for ourselves."'

Seth shook his head.

Tom ignored that. His words were tripping over one another to escape in his enthusiasm. 'We can serve food an' drink in there, Seth, but we're not encouraging any rough types, not even to the music nights or concerts. We want to attract a better class of person than we get here.'

He waited for some response from Seth, some sign of approval or pleasure, but none was forthcoming. 'Well?' He nudged Seth in the ribs.

'Am I included in all that fancy stuff, then?' Seth demanded, making patterns in the spilled beer on the counter.

Tom pursed his lips, trying not to smile, but the grin would not be kept at bay. 'Of course you are, you dozy bugger! Who else is going to manage the place for me? Who makes the best ale in town? An' besides, if you've a bit of money to spare, you may care to invest some of it in my music hall. We've gone well as partners here.' He knew that Seth provided a necessary brake on some of his wilder ideas, as did Annie.

Seth let out a long, low breath of relief. 'All right. Partners, it is. But whatever are you goin' t'think of next, Tom Gibson?'

'All sorts of things,' said Tom, with a fierce look on his face. 'I'm going to get rich, Seth Holden, as rich as Frederick Hallam, if I can manage it.'

'Nay, lad! That's a tall order.' A sly look crossed Seth's face and he nudged Tom. 'It's a far cry from Ma Corry's boozer. Remember that place? An' poor Billy Pardy? He didn't make old bones, did he?'

'I don't want to remember those days,' said Tom, his voice harsh, 'and I don't want you remembering them, either. Billy Pardy died in jail. An' a few others we knew got into bad trouble, too. You an' me had the sense to keep out of it. Or the luck. And that sort of thing's over an' done with for good. We've both changed a lot, learned a bit of sense.'

Seth chuckled. 'Aye. Honest Seth, that's me now.' He looked round fondly. 'I like this place, though. I feel comfortable here. I'm not sure I'll feel comfortable in a great posh place. An' I don't know as I need much more from life than summat as brings in enough money to feed an' clothe me an' mine, an' gives me summat to save for my old age.'

'Well, I do. I need a lot more, an' I'm goin' to get it, too. See if I don't. My wife,' Tom thumped his fist on the counter, 'is going to live like a lady before I'm through, and my children will be brought up as gentry.' There was a moment's silence, then he clapped his companion on the back. 'So are you with me in this, my friend, or are you not?'

Like Rosie, he and Seth went back a long way. In fact, Seth was the only one of the friends of Tom's youth who had made anything of himself. And even then, Tom hadn't asked how Seth got the money to buy into the Shepherd's Rest. His partner's past morals were no concern of his. But Tom had made it plain from the start that the business would be run honestly and had explained why very carefully.

Seth said reflectively now, 'Aye, I suppose I am with you, lad. I might as well. Eh, it's nice nowadays not t'have to worry about whether those bloody constables are going to be knocking on the door, isn't it?'

Tom shuddered involuntarily at the memory of the one time the constables had come knocking on his door in Salem Street, when he'd let his cart be used to move some stolen stuff. Annie had saved him and then had told him to get out of her home and her life, though she'd relented after a while. Hell, he hadn't thought about that in years. He'd nearly cooked his own goose that time. Annie had always been ferociously respectable and honest, and he supposed she always would be.

'There's more than that to it,' he repeated patiently now, dinning in the lesson to Seth. 'We'll earn a lot more money over the years if we build up a reputation for honesty, the best ale in town, good clean rooms and quality food, even the stuff we serve in our pie shops. Dr Lewis was telling me about the fuss some doctors are starting to make about adulteration of food, not to mention the poisons some folk put into food an' drink to make it look nice. I wouldn't want my wife and children eating stuff like that.'

And, he realised with surprise, he genuinely didn't want

to sell rubbish to other folk. Eh, Seth was right. How the two of them had changed!

Another partnership in the town was not going as well as Tom and Seth's. Frederick Hallam stalked into Jonas Dawton's office and glared at his partner. 'What's this I hear about you fining your operatives again?'

'I don't know what you mean. Do sit down, Frederick old chap, and we'll discuss things in a civilised way. Let me ring for a tea tray.'

Frederick thumped his hand on the desk and remained standing. 'Damn the tea! Just you answer my question. Why are you fining folk again?'

Dawton's smile faded. 'It's the only way to make them be careful. You're the one who doesn't want any more accidents. Well, if we don't force them to be more careful, there'll continue to be accidents. Make up your mind what you want. You can't have it both ways.'

'What I want is for the operatives in this mill to be able to do their work safely and without harassment, and then at the end of the week to take home enough money to feed their families.'

'I've told you before, Hallam – you're too soft with your operatives. If you pay them more money, they just go along to the nearest boozer and drink themselves stupid. Since you insist on making all these *improvements to safety*,' his tone was very mocking, 'then that money's better coming back to me, I mean, to us, in fines.'

Frederick continued to look down at him, then said very emphatically, 'If you ever refuse to let Matt Peters into this mill again, I'll ruin you.'

Dawton took a long slow breath before replying. 'You'll not escape unsinged if you ruin me, Hallam. You'll waste all the money you've been investing.'

'That's the only reason I'm hesitating. Though I can afford the losses and you can't.' Frederick had castigated himself several times already for forming a partnership with Dawton. But Dawton's property was very close to his own, and if Dawton went under, Frederick wanted to be the one who got the land. A leopard couldn't change its spots, though. He should have known that. Dawton had made many protestations about adopting new ways of managing the mill, once the money was available, but he clearly hadn't meant it, and he still needed bodyguards when he went out.

Well, for Frederick, it was merely a question of making the best of a bad job and getting rid of Dawton as soon as he could. 'I have several people who can let me know what's happening inside this mill,' he said, 'not just Matt Peters. So don't think to hide things from me. No more fines. And maintain that equipment properly.'

On his way out of Dawton's yard, people standing near the gate shouted abuse at him, as some people now did when he passed them in the street. Frederick found that that upset him a great deal. Annie hadn't said anything, but Robert said they'd shouted things at her, too, once or twice. If things didn't start to improve, he'd have to do something more drastic about Dawton. He didn't intend to go on like this for much longer.

14

July to September 1849

E llie found her husband becoming more and more preoc-
cupied with his work. He had a finger in so many pies
in the town that it seemed as if there were never enough
hours in the day.

Her father was still Dr Lewis's assistant. Dr Lewis sometimes said that Sam Peters knew as much as many men who
practised as doctors, especially those trained under the old
system. Ellie only knew that she and her father were on good
terms again, and that made her feel happy. Her mother was
like a violent animal nowadays, but Jeremy said they were
better looking after her at home. The county asylum in
Lancaster was overcrowded and the patients there were kept
more like animals in a zoo than like sick folk who needed
help.

During the long hours she spent waiting for him to come
back from meetings, she tried to remember how he was
helping folk, and she did the same during the equally long
hours he spent reading *The Lancet* or corresponding with
other doctors. But sometimes it was hard for a wife to see
so little of her husband, especially when she loved him so
much. For the first time she had some understanding of why
Annabelle Lewis had been so very unhappy in the marriage.
But Ellie did not intend to be unhappy. She would accept
her Jeremy as he was, for she was sure that nothing was ever
going to change him.

Not content with caring for his patients, Jeremy was now

involved in the new thrust towards sanitary health, a movement that had sprung up all over the country, he said. This had been given an added impulse in southeast Lancashire in June and July by the death from cholera of more than twenty navvies on the Woodhead Tunnel workings. That was a bit close to home for people who had lost loved ones in various epidemics of one sort or another. There had been minor outbreaks of cholera in Bilsden from time to time, but not recently, not in the parts which had access to the new water supply, anyway. Jeremy said there must be some connection, though he had found no one among his medical acquaintances who knew exactly what that connection might be.

He became very angry when he heard about the deaths of the navvies. Indeed, the only time Ellie ever saw her kindly husband fly into a rage was over avoidable deaths and injuries. When an employer or a landlord's neglect of simple sanitary precautions led to employees or tenants dying unnecessarily, or when a husband's defiance of the doctor's edict that a wife was not to have any more children led to a woman's premature death, then Jeremy would search out the guilty person and harangue him, not caring who else heard the interchange. Bystanders would linger, grinning and nudging each other, and these incidents only added to the legend that was growing up around 'the doctor'.

In the end, she decided to get him to take a holiday. And the obvious place for them to go was Blackpool. Everyone said it was a wonderful place. Why, John and Kathy Gibson had never stopped talking about their honeymoon there. They said that the air was so strong and bracing it made you feel on top of the world. Blackpool wouldn't be like Brighton, of course, which was Ellie's idea of paradise, but going there would get Jeremy away from Bilsden and his work for a while.

Mind you, she'd heard that even Brighton had suffered a decline the previous year. Fewer folk had visited it because they were apparently frightened the French might try to invade the south coast of England. Silly, that was, just plain silly. It wouldn't have put Ellie off going there. As if anyone would ever manage to invade England! They never had and they never would. And anyway, the fuss in France had all blown over, hadn't it? The older generation might talk about bloody revolutions, but they were a thing of the past to Ellie's generation.

In pursuance of her aim, Ellie began to complain gently about tiredness, hinting that she needed a change, reminiscing wistfully about her visit to Brighton and how much she'd loved paddling in the sea. She smiled to herself when Jeremy became thoughtful after her hints.

She smiled even more, in early August, when he came bouncing into Park House like a lad who'd won a prize at the fair, grabbed her by the shoulders and waltzed her up and down the hall. Dot, the new general maid, giggled to herself at the sight of them, then eavesdropped on their conversation quite shamelessly before returning to the kitchen area to tell Mrs Cosden what was being planned.

'How would you like a holiday by the sea?' Jeremy asked, leading Ellie into her small parlour and pulling her down on his knee for a thorough kissing.

'Holiday?' She buried her face in his shoulder to hide the smile of triumph that she could not prevent from creeping across her face. 'What do you mean, holiday by the sea?'

'I've found another young doctor to help me out – there's too much work for Jonathon Spelling on his own – and anyway, Frederick wants me to become the new Medical Officer for the Bilsden Board of Health—'

She squealed and hugged him again. 'It's going to happen? It's really going to happen?' She knew that one of Jeremy's greatest ambitions was to set up a Board of Health in the town, as last year's Act of Parliament permitted.

'Frederick's pushed the Town Council into it. And that new Bilsden Improvement Society he's founded has been demanding it, too.' He chuckled. 'Folk are joining the Improvers to get on good terms with him, and then they're finding they'll benefit from the changes he's pushing them towards – no, not pushing, *manoeuvering* – so they're staying with the Improvers.' His body shook with gentle laughter against Ellie's soft curves. 'I've learned now to watch for a certain expression on Frederick's face. His eyes start to twinkle and he gets a kind of bland, harmless smile, but he's at his most dangerous then.' Jeremy's smile faded for a moment. 'He has the same smile when he looks at Dawton now. I think he's planning something.'

'Never mind Jonas Dawton. Will the Town Council agree to you being the new Medical Officer?'

'Will they dare to disagree? And anyway, who else is there?'

'Oh, Jeremy, that must make you so happy!'

'Very. I'll really be able to clear up Claters End. You know how long I've wanted to do that. Becoming Medical Officer will give me my start. But,' he ran a fingertip down her plump cheek, 'we were talking about a holiday. Would you like one or not, Mrs Lewis?'

'I'd love one. As long as you're coming with me. I'm not going off anywhere on my own.'

'And I'm not letting you. We'll go together.'

'What about young Catherine?'

'Marianne's going to keep an eye on things here, but Hetty and the rest of the staff are very reliable, especially with Mrs Cosden to manage them. Besides, we shall only be away for a week. I'm afraid I can't afford to take longer, love. Let's just hope the weather stays fine.'

'When can we leave?'

'Could you be ready by next week? Our new doctor – and yes, I did choose Douglas Macbain from Inverness – has agreed to accept the position and will be able to start here on Friday. Spelling will keep an eye on him for me.'

'What shall we need to take with us?'

He threw up his hands. 'That, my love, I can't tell you. I've never actually been to Blackpool. I believe things are very different to your beloved Brighton there, much less elegant and full of common working folk.'

'Oh, pooh, who cares about elegant?'

'Not me. But maybe you can see Kathy Gibson and ask her what you'll need to take? She and John went there last year, didn't they?'

'You leave it to me.'

Kathy Gibson was happy to explain how things were done. It was still a wonder to her when folk came to her for advice. 'Well, you'll need to take your food with you, which the lodging-house keeper will cook for you. Mind you, some of them make a real hash-up of that, but you don't seem to care as much when you're away on holiday. You just laugh and make do.'

'And how do you pass the time there? We can't spend all day walking round, after all.' Ellie flushed and added softly, 'Not in my condition, anyway.'

Kathy hugged her at once. 'Oh, Ellie, I'm so pleased for you! But there's plenty to do. You can go out in fishing boats, if it's fine. One of the fishermen was telling us that he makes more money by taking the visitors out in summer than by his old trade since the railway branch line went through. Just fancy that.'

'And whereabouts should we stay?'

'Somewhere in the north part of town. It's much nicer there. Folk can get a little rowdy in the central and southern streets. We didn't realise that when we went an' it was quite noisy where we were. Well, you know what the operatives are like on Saturday nights here, and they're worse when they're away on holiday.'

'Don't I just know! When I used to work in the mill, the other girls were very rough and cheeky, and they haven't improved since. But they mean no harm. It's all high spirits.'

The week in Blackpool was a golden interlude for Jeremy and Ellie. The weather was kind, being fine every day but one. They walked along the beach, sat and talked for hours and explored all the attractions of the fast-growing town. Everywhere, it seemed, buildings were going up, rows of larger terraced houses with enough bedrooms to accommodate visitors. Shops and cafés. Public houses. It was a wonder just to see it all, so full of life and bustle.

As Kathy had said, the operatives enjoyed themselves in a very noisy way in Blackpool. They were there either for the wakes weeks that many towns now held yearly, or for the weekend breaks which some folk took off work by pretending to be ill. Ellie just smiled to see them calling out to passers-by and holding impromptu sing-songs on the beach. 'I remember the days when no one I knew had been further than Manchester,' she said one day, 'and now, even ordinary folk think nothing of going down to London or spending the weekend by the sea. Things have changed a lot, haven't they, love? And so quickly.'

'Yes. And they'll continue to change. Wait until we get our branch line to Bilsden. You'll think nothing then of going shopping in Manchester for the morning.'

'I can't see why I'd need to. We have everything I need in Bilsden. Oh!' She clasped Jeremy's arm suddenly. 'Surely that's—' She broke off to stare at a pair of young women, who were leaning against a wall, exchanging pleasantries with a group of young men.

One of the young women turned and saw Ellie staring, then grinned and nudged her companion. The two of them abandoned the young men abruptly and strolled across to the Lewises.

The shorter of the two women stuck a hand out, a challenging expression on her face. 'Eh, it's Ellie Peters. Fancy meetin' you here.'

Ellie automatically took the hand that was offered to her, but she could see Jeremy frowning. He obviously hadn't recognised the young woman and was annoyed that someone like her had dared to accost his wife. 'This is Annie's sister, Lizzie,' she explained before he could say anything. 'And May, isn't it? Annie's stepsister, love.'

'Ah.'

'Lizzie, you remember Dr Lewis, don't you? He's – er – well, we're married now.'

Jeremy shook hands, but he still looked very stiff and disapproving.

No wonder, thought Ellie. The way Lizzie was dressed made her look anything but respectable. Her skirts were too short and her neckline too low. Her face was rouged as well, her lips coloured a particularly vivid red. No respectable woman every painted herself. Lizzie looked, well, like a woman of the streets. Or what Ellie imagined a woman of the streets would look like.

'I didn't know you'd got married,' Lizzie said in a low throaty voice, her pale eyes glittering with malicious enjoyment of the situation. She nudged her companion. 'Our Annie's not the only one who's done well for herself, eh, May? Congratulations, I'm sure, *Mrs Lewis*.'

'And what are you doing with yourself?' Ellie asked, then gasped as she realised that this might not be a tactful question to ask.

Lizzie smiled in a knowing way. 'Takin' a holiday here, what else?'

'Yes. Of course. What else do people come to Blackpool for?'

May put her arm round Lizzie's shoulders. 'Why don't we all go and 'ave a cup of tea together, then you can tell us all about our Annie and her new husband. We 'aven't seen her for ages. How does she like bein' rich?'

Jeremy did not look best pleased, but there was no way they could refuse this offer without giving offence. Lizzie was Annie and Tom's full sister, after all. But he had seen women dressed like these two in the less reputable streets of Manchester, and indeed, had used better-class whores himself during his marriage to Annabelle, so he had more than a suspicion of how Lizzie and May were earning their living nowadays.

They found a café with a free table in the corner and ordered a pot of tea and some cakes.

'Soon be the end of the season,' said Lizzie regretfully. 'Sad, that. The town half-closes down then.'

'There's a nip in the air already,' agreed Ellie, sipping her tea. The silence lengthened and she began to wonder what on earth they could talk about. 'Have you been here long?'

'We come to Blackpool for the summer, actually,' Lizzie volunteered, with one of her sly smiles. 'A sort of workin' holiday. The air here allus does May's chest good. Nice, it's been.'

May gave a snort of laughter and crammed a piece of cake into her mouth.

'We shall 'ave to go back to Manchester soon, though,' Lizzie continued. 'There's not much work around in Blackpool when the season ends. Pity, that. If I was rich, like our Annie an' Tom are, I'd live here all the time.' Another silence, then she asked, 'So go on, tell us about our Annie. How's she gettin' on with Mr Hallam? I can't imagine her wed to him, you know. He were a right tough sod to work for in the mill.'

Ellie smiled and put down her cup. 'They're very happy together. He's devoted to her. And William lives with them up at Ridge House now, of course.'

'An' our Tom? I heard he'd got married, too.'

'He married my daughter, actually,' said Jeremy, his voice chill. 'They now have twins, a boy and a girl.'

'So I'm an auntie again.' Lizzie's eyes challenged him to deny that.

'They've named the girl Lucy after your mother,' Ellie put in. Jeremy was looking as if he had smelled something rotten and she was terrified that he was going to say something that would upset Lizzie and May.

'Lucy, eh?' Lizzie's expression became unfathomable. 'Ah. That's nice. She were all right, our mam were.'

After a few minutes more of stilted conversation, Lizzie stood up abruptly. 'Well, we must get back to work.' She winked at Jeremy. 'Money doesn't earn itself, does it? Give our Annie my love. I might write her a letter sometime. I might just do that.'

Lizzie linked her arm in May's and they left the café, pausing by the door to exchange some remarks with two men sitting at a table there and shriek with laughter at the men's responses. The latter got up, paid their bill hurriedly and followed the two women out.

Ellie sat there with tears in her eyes. 'Surely she can't have—?' She broke off and looked pleadingly at her husband.

'Can't have gone on the streets?' he finished for her.

Ellie nodded.

'It looks like it, I'm afraid.'

'Do you think Annie and Tom know?'

He shrugged. 'If they do, they're not likely to have told anyone, are they?'

'I don't think we should say anything about meeting Lizzie,' Ellie said later, as they walked back to their lodgings.

'Not to Annie, anyway. I might have a word with Tom, though.'

'Yes, that would be best,' she said in relief.

And that encounter was the only thing that marred the holiday. By the time they returned to Bilsden, the Lewises both looked well and happy, and Ellie was satisfied that for once her husband had been persuaded to rest.

While Ellie and Jeremy were still away, matters came to a head at Jonas Dawton's mill. This time it was a man who was injured when the belt broke from the flywheel, the belt he had been telling his master to replace for the past month.

The first Frederick knew of it was when a group of operatives waylaid his carriage on the way home one evening. Their mood was clearly desperate and their faces filled with anger.

'Get down, Mester Hallam!' one of them ordered gruffly.

He stared at the face, noting its determination and the fact that the man was not carrying any weapons, not even a stick. He opened the carriage door.

'Don't get out, Mr Hallam!' the coachman yelled, fear in his voice.

'I'll be all right, Robert. They won't harm me.' He stepped down, to stand on a level with them. He was the tallest there. Mill operatives were not usually big men, not those who had hungered in their youth, anyway.

One of them stepped forward, but made no threatening gesture. 'It's about Dawton's. They say you've got a share in it now.'

Frederick nodded. 'Not the major share, but some interest, yes.'

'Then, mester, if you don't do something about the way things are run, we s'll have to.'

The coachman fingered his whip and the horses twitched to and fro, catching his mood, but Frederick stood still, one man against a dozen. 'Tell me.'

'Phil Medlock's just lost an arm in th'engine room,' one said. 'Master's fault, not Phil's, though Dawton claims otherwise.'

'An' now Dawton's told Phil's wife there'll be no work for him once he recovers.'

'*If* he recovers,' another said savagely. 'That new doctor tended him. How do we know what he's like?'

'Shut up, will you, Ted, an' let me tell the tale, as we agreed.' The leader turned back to Frederick. 'And if that's not bad enough, Mester Hallam, Dawton won't pay Phil's wages, either. Says his carelessness cost the mill running time, an' he's fined for it.'

They were all looking at him, not as he was used to operatives looking at him, with respect and trust, but with anger and hostility and blame. 'Take me to see this Phil,' he said abruptly. 'Two of you get into the carriage, then the rest can go home and leave us to deal with it.'

'Nay, I'll not do that,' said the man who'd been addressed as Ted. 'I've seen it happen afore. "Go home!" "Do as you're told!" An' nowt gets done. Bairns are still killed in that mill, an' mothers an' fathers too, Mester Hallam. I'll not rest till summat's done.'

'It were his niece as were killed last time,' the leader explained to Frederick, his eyes begging for understanding.

Frederick nodded, a lump in his throat. There had been accidents at his mill – there were accidents in all the mills – but it was years since anyone had been killed at Hallam's. If the men blamed Dawton for this, there was a good chance that they were right. He had thought that Dawton was mending his ways, not as quickly as Frederick would have liked, but mending them. Hell, Matt Peters had thought so, too, and Matt was no fool. 'Then suppose you get into the carriage with me as well,' he offered. 'Then you shall see for yourself what I do about your complaints.'

The man looked at him, a dour look, as if he were still expecting to be cheated, then he shrugged and moved towards the carriage. 'You other lads go an' wait for us at t'mill.'

'Ted—' it was a warning tone from the leader, 'we agreed that there'd be no violence.'

'George Tomkins, we agreed to try to do something this time. An' if we must use force to do it, then I s'll not flinch from that. Do you *want* other little lasses to be killed like our Julie was?'

George shook his head and moved towards the carriage, then paused. 'We're in all our muck, mester. We've just come off work. We s'll dirty the seats.'

Robert coughed, reassured a little by this mundane concern. 'I have a rug here, Mr Hallam. They could sit on that.'

'I'll sit up there with him,' said another of the group suddenly. 'We don't want him losing his way, do we?' He gave a wolf's smile and was up beside a startled Robert before anyone could say a word. 'I've allus wanted to ride like a gentleman!' he yelled down to his mates, and though they laughed, the anger was only lightened for a moment.

Frederick turned to the waiting trio. 'Well, lads?'

Silently they clambered inside, their eyes darting here and there as they studied the carriage. A new experience for them, to ride inside in comfort. One fingered the upholstery. Another ran a fingertip over the oil lamp with its etched glass shade.

As Frederick took his place, he guessed that none of them had even seen inside a gentleman's carriage before. Unlike some of the other masters, he didn't make the mistake of thinking them stupid because of that. The carriage jerked into motion and he clasped the hand strap. One of the men imitated him; the two others just relied on the tight fit of their bodies.

Frederick had never thought to experience such a drive. He and his father had kept violence away from Hallam's by treating their workforce fairly. He had prided himself on that – not being soft with them, you didn't win respect that way – but always being fair. He found now that he didn't like the thought that he had been found wanting, and he admitted, to himself at least, that perhaps his obsession with Annie had led him to neglect the very details that made such a difference to the operatives in his own mill. He should have kept a closer check on Dawton himself, since their last confrontation, not left it to Matt.

The three men were silent, but their presence filled the carriage. Hard-working men, their faces and hands showed it, as did the sweaty smell they gave off. Angry men, too, even the leader. They were angry with a world which denied them safety and then, when they were injured, denied them justice too, unless they took it into their own hands.

Frederick had never subscribed to the view that the lower classes needed to be kept under for fear of riots and mayhem. He'd worked too closely with them all his life, for his father had started him off in the mill at the age of twelve, three days a week, to get the feel of it. The other two days studying, doing a week's lessons in those two days, because he was too proud to let the other lads get ahead of him. He'd seen how these same lower classes that others despised welcomed the setting up of the 'Stute, formed Friendly Societies to help one another, were generous in misfortune, raucously happy in the good times.

He'd also seen one or two of the men study the flora on the moors until they became as expert as the visiting botanists who drifted through the town from time to time, though the latter were usually the ones who took the credit for the discoveries the working men shared with them. In fact, in his opinion, operatives generally behaved like normal human beings, if only they were allowed. Oh, there were occasional troublemakers, and Frederick gave them short shrift – he was *not* a soft touch – but on the whole, folk just wanted to earn their daily bread and to enjoy themselves a little when they could. He gave them the work and he profited from what they did, as Tom Gibson was profiting from their desire to enjoy themselves.

When the carriage arrived at Dawton's, people were still loitering nearby and the gates were barred. As it stopped and the men piled out, followed by one whom all recognised immediately as Mester Hallam, folk began to move closer.

'Ho, there!' yelled Robert, conscious of his master's dignity. 'Open up!'

One of Dawton's bully boys came out and stood behind the wrought-iron barrier. 'Mr Dawton said not to open the gates, not for anything.'

Frederick moved forward. 'Is he inside?'

The man hesitated, looking sideways at the crowd of folk, listening to the conversation. The expressions on their faces were not friendly.

'Take the carriage to the end of the street and wait for me there, Robert,' Frederick said.

'Sir?' There was an unspoken question in Robert's eyes.

'Just wait! Nothing else,' Frederick insisted. 'They won't harm me.'

Robert looked unconvinced, but at a sign from the leader, the crowd stepped aside to let the carriage through, and the coachman did as he was told.

Frederick rattled the gate. 'Well, fellow, aren't you going to let me in?'

'Mr Dawton said no one was to enter. No one.' The voice was surly and the man was holding a gun openly in his hand.

'I'm not no one,' Frederick said loudly. 'I'm part owner of this mill, and if you don't let me enter, I'll fetch the constables to force a way in for me. Owners have rights of entry and you'd be wise to remember that.'

'Let him in, you fool!' called a voice from behind the watchman's shelter.

At the sound of that voice, the crowd started to yell and shout, cries of 'Shame!' and 'Murderer!' and 'Justice!' echoing around Frederick.

'Do it quickly,' Dawton hissed and disappeared inside the mill offices again.

The bully opened the small gate within the larger one. It was barely big enough to let one person through. 'Just you, Mr Hallam.' He brandished the gun needlessly at the nearest men.

Frederick stepped through into the yard, but instead of moving aside to allow the bully to lock the small gate behind him again, he shoved the man hard in the guts, taking him by surprise. 'Just you three!' he yelled.

The three men who had ridden in the carriage with him ran forward and were through by the time the bully had shoved Frederick aside. For a moment all hung in the balance, then Frederick said gently. 'Close the gate now, if you please. This is just a deputation. The others will wait outside.'

Ted rumbled in his throat, but George nudged him and he subsided.

Outside, folk had fallen silent, watching. 'Mester Hallam will do summat,' they told one another. 'He's going in to see Dawton.'

As Frederick walked into the offices, followed by the three operatives, Dawton gasped loudly and fumbled for a gun that lay beside him on the desk.

'Put that damned thing away!' snapped Frederick. 'We're here simply to talk and your little friends are the only ones who're armed.'

Dawton shoved the gun to one side, but it was still within reach.

'I hear you've had a bad injury here,' Frederick went on. 'How did it happen?'

'Carelessness.'

'Show me.'

Dawton stared at him for a moment. 'Show you what?'

'The belt that broke.'

'Are you calling me a liar?'

Frederick leaned forward, hands resting lightly on the desk. 'Not yet,' he said, very softly.

The three men watched and when Ted would have opened his mouth to join in the conversation, George jabbed him hard with one finger and shook his head.

Dawton looked at the second bully who was lounging in a corner of the room. He nodded at his master, patting his pocket.

'I'll find my way myself, then,' Frederick said, keeping his voice calm, though he was feeling more and more angry, and the emotions raging in his companions were almost tangible.

'I'll show you.' Dawton came round the desk. 'But these three can stay here.'

The bully pulled out his gun.

'These three come with us,' said Frederick, moving to stand between them and the gun.

'There's no need,' Dawton blustered.

'I think there's need,' that quiet implacable voice told him.

Dawton snatched up the gun from the desk and for a moment, violence seethed beneath the surface.

'You won't need that, but if it makes you feel more comfortable, put it in your pocket,' Frederick said scornfully and turned towards the door.

The three operatives stood back to let Dawton pass, then filed out behind him. Not one of them paid any attention to the armed bully who brought up the rear. As they walked, George nodded in satisfaction. He'd told the others, 'We'll take it to Mester Hallam,' he'd said, when they were all for breaking into the mill and smashing up every dangerous piece of machinery so that no one else could be hurt. And he'd been proved right.

The broken belt was nowhere to be seen. A brand new belt had been fixed to the flywheel and the dour mechanic who was in charge of the machinery was wielding his oil can and polishing up the brass.

'Got it fixed, Reuben?' Dawton demanded.

'Aye, master.'

Dawton turned to Hallam. 'You can see the quality of the belts I use.'

'But I can't see the broken belt.'

'Reuben probably threw it out.' Dawton's voice was scornful. 'Look around you. My equipment is well maintained.'

Ted moved towards the door.

'Where are you going?' The bully's voice was sharp. 'Get back with the others.'

Ted turned to Frederick. 'I know where they'll have thrown it, mester.'

'Go and get it then.'

'I'm not having him loose in my mill,' Dawton protested. 'He's a born troublemaker. In fact, I'm not having any of these fellows in my mill again. You hear that? You're all dismissed. It's troublemakers like you who get the rest a bad name.'

Frederick saw the anger burn higher in the men's eyes. 'We'll all go and look at the belt,' he said mildly. 'You'll stay with us, won't you, Ted?'

Ted grinned, not a nice grin. 'Aye, mester.'

George sighed in relief.

They found the belt round the back on a pile of rubbish that Frederick was sure would be harbouring rats and other vermin. 'For heaven's sake, man, why don't you get this lot carted away?' he snapped. 'Do you want to bring disease into your mill?'

'I get it carted away when there's a full load for the dray,' said Dawton.

'There are two drayloads there, at least.' Frederick had worked his turn in the loading bays in his youth and could estimate loads nearly as well as his own draymen.

'There it is, mester!' Ted's triumphant voice interrupted them and his pointing hand directed their eyes towards a scrap of belting that had been pushed under a pile of debris.

'Get it out for me, would you, Ted?' Frederick asked.

The bully looked at his master for guidance, but Dawton was chewing his lip and fidgeting beside Frederick.

The belt was worn, frayed and well beyond the time it should have been changed.

'It's another belt,' said Dawton suddenly. 'They've planted that old thing there to incriminate me, but I won't have it. I know their ploys. The man lost his arm through his own carelessness. Reuben's been complaining about him for weeks, but I was giving him another chance. He deserves all he got! It's always the same.'

'And what about the little lass as died,' Ted growled. 'Did she deserve all she got, too?'

'She was a careless child. The overlooker will tell you . . .'

With an inarticulate cry, Ted lurched towards him, unable to bear any more. 'Lies!' he roared. 'All lies! And folk's blood shed because of them.'

Dawton raised his gun.

'No!' roared Frederick. 'Don't fire.' He stepped forward between Ted and Dawton, but too late. The crack of the shot was followed by a searing pain in Frederick's side. As he staggered, Ted reached Dawton and smacked the gun from his trembling hand. The other two men leaped across to club the bully to the ground.

'No more violence!' yelled Frederick, clutching his side, feeling the dampness as blood seeped through his fingers. He watched as the two men knocked the bully to the ground and started kicking him. 'That's enough!' he yelled. 'Just hold him. I'll bear witness for you with the magistrate.'

George dragged his fellows off the bully, picked up the gun and moved towards Frederick with it.

Before anyone could stop him, Ted moved across and punched Dawton in the face, then he turned round. 'You'll change things, mester?'

Frederick nodded, trying to ignore the stabbing pain in his side. 'Yes, I'll change things.'

'You saw what he did—' began Dawton.

'Shut up!' replied Frederick. He accepted Dawton's gun from Ted, and George handed him the one they'd taken from the bully. He hated the feel of the gun in his hand, but he levelled it at the bully. 'Get up, you. Stand beside your master.'

'Look, Hallam,' Dawton began. 'It was all a dreadful mistake. Send for someone to tend you, man, for heaven's sake.'

'Stay where you are, Jonas Dawton,' Frederick said. 'I'm taking you before the magistrate and charging you with attempted murder.'

'Against them?' Dawton's voice was a squeak of dismay.

'Against them and me. The four of us were together.'

Only when the constables arrived did Frederick lower the gun and allow them to take over. Only then did he allow Dr Macbain, who had also been summoned, to tend his injury, fortunately only a flesh wound.

15

Bilsden: September to October 1849

When the Lewises called on Tom and Marianne, as they did the first day back, Jeremy took Tom on one side. 'If you have a moment, there's something I need to talk to you about.'

Tom looked sideways at him, eyes narrowed. 'Oh? That sounds as if it's not something pleasant.'

'It's not,' Jeremy said quietly.

'Come into the dining room, then.' He went across to his wife and kissed her cheek. 'We've just got a spot of business to discuss, love.'

Marianne pulled a face at him. 'Do you ever talk about anything else, Tom Gibson? Well, don't be too long. Father wants to see his grandchildren. And I want to see my father.'

In the dining room, Jeremy stared at Tom, uncertain how to start. He could think of no easy way to say it. 'We met Lizzie and May in Blackpool.'

'Ah.'

'They sent their regards.'

'Oh. Nice.'

There was silence, then Jeremy added, 'Er – did you know what they were doing, how they were earning their living?'

Tom let out his breath in a long slow exhalation. 'Yes. We had a little visit from them last year, when they were down on their luck and needed money.' The silence lay heavy between them for a moment, then Tom added, 'Did Ellie realise they were whores?'

'She could hardly miss it, the way they were dressed, and the way they were carrying on. Apparently, they've spent the summer working in Blackpool.'

Tom's voice was low and bitter. 'And if they continue to do that, they're bound to run into other folk who know them. Especially after the Bilsden branch line's built and people from here start going away on holiday more often. And then the fat will really be in the fire.' He thumped one fist into the other. 'The stupid bitches!'

'What shall you do about it?'

'I don't know yet. I'll have to have a think.'

'Shall you tell Annie?'

Tom shrugged. 'I don't know.' But he did. He had no intention of telling Annie, who had already proved herself a soft touch in dealing with their younger sister. But he would have to do something about Lizzie and May. He was not going to let them mess up his life. And no hint of scandal was going to touch his wife.

'If I can be of any help . . . ?'

Tom shook his head. 'No. You've got enough on your plate with your new job. Er – Lizzie and May didn't happen to give you an address, did they?'

'No. But they said they weren't going back to Manchester for a couple of weeks, so you might still have a chance of finding them if you go to Blackpool straightaway. It's not that big a place, hardly more than a big village when there are no holiday visitors.'

'Leave it with me.'

'How's Frederick? Macbain said it was only a flesh wound.'

'He's fine. You heard about the fuss at Dawton's, then?'

Jeremy smiled. 'I'd hardly got through the door before Mrs Cosden was puffing upstairs to tell me about the trouble. How bad was it really?'

'Could have been bad, if Frederick hadn't been there.

He's a brave man, my brother-in-law. And George Polditt did well, too, holding the men back.'

'And is Jonas Dawton really locked up?'

Tom nodded. 'For his own protection as much as anything. Folk are still angry about the deaths his greed caused. Frederick's offered to buy him out, so that Mrs Dawton and the children will be provided for, and he's agreed to drop the murder charges as long as Dawton leaves Bilsden – provided no charges are brought against the men, that is.'

Jeremy nodded. 'The town will be better off without that man. I've had a trail of injuries to deal with from his mill over the years.'

Tom grinned. 'Mind you, Annie wasn't best pleased with Frederick for risking his life, nor for the way he's refused to rest. He's put Matt Peters in complete charge at Dawton's, and George Polditt with him. He says if the man could stop violence erupting, then he's got the skill to help manage the changes now. I think Polditt's a bit stunned by the responsibility, but he's good at picking men, our Frederick is.'

Jeremy nodded, satisfied to have a straight tale instead of the wild rumours Mrs Cosden had fed him.

In the end, Tom didn't go to Blackpool to sort out Lizzie on his own. It was the question of money that decided Tom to confide in Frederick. Tom was fully stretched with the purchase of the Three Feathers and the subsequent renovations and extensions. If he had to buy Lizzie and May off, as he suspected he might, they wouldn't be satisfied with a few guineas this time. And besides, not only would Frederick be as eager to keep the pair of them quiet and out of sight as Tom was, but he was a figure of some importance to anyone who had grown up in Bilsden, so Lizzie and May might listen to him. Frederick wouldn't want anything bothering Annie. Since she had lost the child, he'd been very protective towards her.

★

Frederick grunted and pulled a face when Tom told him about the problem the next day. 'I've been half-expecting her and May to turn up in Bilsden ever since you and Annie told me about them. They're only human and they'll want to dip their fingers into my money pot if they can.'

'Aye, that's what I thought. So before they come back flaunting themselves in Bilsden, I think we should go and find them and sort this out. If you're well enough, that is? How's the side?'

'Healing nicely, thank you. I've had worse gashes when I was a lad. It just bled a lot at the time.'

Tom nodded. 'Good. So you'll be fit to lend a hand to sort out Lizzie. And mind, I don't want our Annie told about it.'

Frederick raised his eyebrows.

'She's too soft, our Annie is. Gave Lizzie her shawl last time, as well as some money. Said Mam would want her to see that her sister didn't want for anything.'

'Yes, well, family ties, you know.' But Frederick's family ties were a bit different. He had completely severed his relationship with Beatrice. Her vicious treatment of young William sickened him still. The lad hadn't fully recovered from that and sometimes his eyes betrayed a sadness that hadn't been there before. He and the dog had been inseparable lately, taking long walks on the moors or just sitting cuddled up together in the schoolroom.

'I don't want our dad told about Lizzie, either,' Tom went on. 'It'd break his bloody heart if he knew what those two were doing.'

'How will you explain our little trip to the womenfolk, then?' How would *he* explain? Annie'd go through the roof when she heard he was planning a trip. She was still trying to make him rest more.

'I'll say it's business.'

'Marianne might accept that, but Annie won't. She knows I mostly leave that sort of thing to other people nowadays.'

'Except where Dawton's is concerned,' Tom teased.

'Yes, well, that turned out all right in the end. And Matt's dealing with things now.'

'Is Peters still a sanctimonious prig?'

Frederick shrugged. 'His religious beliefs are his own business, but no, he doesn't seem overzealous nowadays. It wouldn't matter to me if he was. All I ask from him is that he manage the mill efficiently and honestly. And he does that.' In fact, Matt was doing far better than Frederick had ever expected, perhaps because work seemed to be his only interest in life. There was silence for a moment as Frederick tapped his fingers on the chair arm, a habit he had when he was thinking, then he said slowly, 'In fact, Annie will be very suspicious, whatever we do. I don't really want to lie to her. Tom, I think we should tell her about your sister, I really do.'

'No! Not this time. She'll be too soft. I want to settle Lizzie's hash once and for all.'

A frown creased Frederick's brow. 'Then we shall have to work something out to explain our absence, something convincing.' There was a moment's silence, broken only by the continuing drumming of Frederick's fingers and the soft sigh of a piece of coal settling lower in the fire. Then Frederick stopped tapping and grinned at Tom. 'Of course, we could say we're going over to look at some business possibilities in Blackpool.'

'She'd want to come, too, if I know our Annie.' Tom grunted in exasperation. His sister had never been easy to fob off.

'Then we'll say we're looking at properties. Thinking of investing in a few.'

'She'd still want to come with us. She's got a good eye

for an investment. And anyway, she knows I've no money to invest in anything else. The Prince of Wales is taking everything I have.' Which was nearly true.

'Give me a day or so. I'll think of something.'

But here fate took a hand, for William came down with a streaming cold and Annie, remembering his illness earlier in the year, would not leave his side.

When Frederick, feigning boredom, tried to persuade her to leave her son and go off for a business trip to Blackpool, she refused point blank.

'We can go to Blackpool later.'

'Well, yes, of course we can, but I've got a sniff of a little proposition that won't wait.'

'You shouldn't even be thinking of business trips, Frederick Hallam. Your side—'

'Is nearly better now. And William will be all right. You fuss over that lad too much, you know.'

She glared at him, her anger roused by this callous remark, as he had intended it to be. 'And I'll continue to fuss over him, thank you very much – over William and over any other children we may have. You'll have to go without me this time, Frederick, if you need to make a quick decision.'

He pulled a face. 'Not as much fun, my dear.'

She relented and went over to kiss his cheek. 'It'll only take you one night, won't it?'

She was looking at him so trustingly that he felt guilty, but he reminded himself that he was doing this for her. 'Probably.' He turned, then paused. 'I wonder if Tom's free?'

'Tom?'

'Yes. Your brother. Remember him?'

She nodded, her thoughts more on William than anything else.

Frederick said slyly, 'He's got a good eye for a business

deal and I'd enjoy his company. Besides, I think he's getting just a little bored with fatherhood.'

That made her smile. 'More than a little bored. Who'd have thought that Marianne would turn into such a besotted mother?'

'Not me. I remember Annabelle Lewis. She hadn't a maternal bone in her whole body.'

'Marianne takes after her father.' Annie's face lit up. 'Isn't it wonderful news about Ellie expecting a baby?'

'Wonderful. So do you think I should invite Tom to come with me?'

Annie glanced at the clock and mentally dismissed Blackpool. 'Do what you want. It's time for William to take his cough medicine. If I'm not there to insist, he forgets – on purpose.'

'It probably tastes vile.'

'It does, but if Dr Lewis says it'll do William good, then he's taking it.'

When she had whisked upstairs, Frederick sighed with relief and went to write a note to Tom. He was losing his touch. It had been very easy to lie to Christine, but he found that he didn't even want to lie to Annie. For a moment, he wished that Tom hadn't involved him in this affair, then he shook his head. No. Something needed to be done about Lizzie and May. Permanently. For all their sakes.

The journey to Blackpool from Manchester was as rapid as usual, but the state of the train carriages roused Frederick's ire. 'I've a good mind to write a letter of complaint,' he said, prodding a piece of crumpled sticky paper with the ferrule of his black silk umbrella and brushing some crumbs off the seat. 'You'd think they could keep things cleaner than this! What's the use of all these railway mergers if the standards drop?'

'Ah, the Lanky's never been noted for its high standards,' said Tom easily. 'What does it matter? We won't be in it for more than an hour or two. All it needs to do is get us there.'

But it seemed a long journey to two men facing a distasteful task.

In Blackpool it was raining, water sluicing down from every rooftop and gurgling along the gutters. Even from the station, the two men could hear the sea pounding on the shore, and when their cab got closer to the sea front, they could see great roaring walls of dirty brown water crashing on to the empty beach. Grey skies. Muddy streets. An icy and malicious wind that tugged at garments and blew moisture into every gap that it could find. The few holiday-makers were huddled behind windows, staring out glumly at the hostile weather, or sitting inside 'tea shops' which sprouted like mushrooms in people's front rooms during the holiday season.

After they'd booked into the hotel – Frederick had not even considered staying in anything but the most luxurious accommodation available – and had a cup of tea, the two men braved the weather and started searching the centre of the town.

'We'll never find our Lizzie in weather like this,' said Tom gloomily. 'She'll be tucked up snug and warm somewhere. Like we should be. I'm soaked to the skin already.'

'We have to try,' said Frederick, holding his hat down with one hand and not bothering to open his umbrella. It was a battle even to walk against such a howling gale. 'Let's try the tea room that Jeremy Lewis told us about again. She might have gone in there for a rest.'

The tea room was even more crowded than it had been earlier. Its steamy atmosphere smelled pungently of strong cheap tea, sweat, sugar buns and none-too-clean bodies. And it was filled with noise, shrieks of laughter, conversation, arguments. Young people mostly, making the best of things. But there was no sign of Lizzie and May there. Nor could the two women be found anywhere else. By the time the grey day started fading into night, Frederick and Tom were damp, chilled and more than ready for their evening meal in the hotel.

'I'll just go and have a look round the boozers,' said Tom after they had eaten.

'I'll come with you.'

'You sure?'

Frederick nodded. 'We have to try everything.'

Grimly the two men donned their wet overcoats and went out into the rain again, making their way from one cheap drinking house to another.

'These places make the Shepherd's Rest look like a palace, don't they?' Tom commented, standing in the doorway of one brightly lit public house filled with drunken merriment and a strong smell of pipe smoke and unwashed bodies.

It was not until they were leaving a sleazy one-room boozer in a shadowy side street, that Tom suddenly grabbed Frederick's arm and hissed, 'Over there!' He pointed to two figures huddled in a doorway.

Hearing footsteps, the two women turned round. 'Need a little company, gentlemen?' Lizzie called, moving forward, pulling the short skirt that advertised her calling even higher to reveal a plump ankle and calf.

'What the hell do you mean by coming to Blackpool, you stupid bitch?' roared Tom, furious to see his sister behaving like that.

Lizzie dropped her skirt and set her hands on her hips. 'Oh, hell, it's you!'

'Aye. I've come here specially to find you.'

'Fancy that. The perfect way to end a lousy night, a bloody family reunion.' She turned to look at the taller man standing next to Tom and her mouth opened in surprise, then twisted into an unpleasant sneering smile. 'Well, I do believe it's the almighty Mr Hallam. Still, I suppose you're family as well, now, aren't you? Shall I call you Freddy?'

'Is there somewhere comfortable where we can go to talk?' asked Frederick, his voice curt. 'It's freezing out here. Amazing how quickly the weather can change, isn't it?'

Something in his tone stopped Lizzie from making another provocative remark.

May nudged her stepsister. 'If you have two shillin' to spare, Mr Hallam, we can go into a house I know. It's not far.'

'I presume it's a house of assignation?' he queried.

She looked puzzled at the term.

'A whorehouse,' said Tom crudely.

May's face cleared. 'Yes. Well, sort of. But it has a side entrance, so you won't be seen going in, if that's what you're worried about.'

Taking the men's agreement for granted, Lizzie flounced off down the street, yelling over her shoulder, 'Come on, then. I could murder a gin. You're not the only ones as are cold.'

Inside the house, where the two women were clearly well known, a quiet conversation and an exchange of coins bought them a gaudily decorated bedroom and a bottle of gin. No questions were asked about the four of them using the same room, and the muscular fellow on the door looked bored more than anything else.

'Busy, Frank?' Lizzie asked him as she took the key.

'No. Weather like this allus puts folk off.'

Upstairs Tom refused a seat and stood leaning against the door, scowling at his sister, loathing her tawdry finery and the paint on her face. No amount of make-up would ever make her pretty, but somehow the full over-red lips hinted at sensuality in a way that angered him.

Frederick refused any refreshments and sat down on the only chair in the room, turning it round and sitting astride it, hands resting lightly on the high back. Lizzie and May sprawled on the bed side by side, propped against the pillows, shoes kicked off and cold feet in damp stockings tucked under the quilt. They sipped at their gin with sighs of appreciation. Both looked pale and chilled to the bone.

Lizzie took the initiative. 'So why were you looking for us, then, our Tom? It must be important to bring you so far.' She raised her glass in a mocking toast. 'Here's to family reunions.'

'To hell with family reunions!' snapped Tom. 'If I never saw you two again, I'd die happy.'

Lizzie's grin faded and she began to look angry. 'You're a fine one to talk. You've cut a few corners yourself in your time, Tom Gibson. An' dabbled in a few shady deals.'

'Not since I was a stupid young lad,' retorted Tom, nettled that she should say this in front of Hallam. 'I'm a respectable married man now. An' honest. I've made a good name for myself, an' I intend to keep it.'

'An' you're the father of twins, too, so Dr Lewis said,' put in May, in a more conciliatory tone. 'Congratulations.' As Lizzie opened her mouth again, May dug her in the side and said, 'Shut up, love. Let's hear what they want first.'

Lizzie snorted, muttered that it was all right for some and took another gulp of gin. In the face of Frederick's calm assessing gaze, she was not nearly as confident as she made out.

'We want you two out of the way,' Tom said. 'As far out of the way as possible.'

Frederick sighed. 'Tom, you're too angry. Let me handle it, hmm?'

Tom shrugged and stuffed his cold hands into his pockets. 'Just as long as you get them off the streets and away from

me.' He glared at his sister, disgusted with her blowsy appearance. She looked old and raddled tonight, years older than
Annie. But he had no intention of feeling sorry for her. No
intention at all. She had chosen her own path. She had had
no need to go on the streets. Annie had found a way to earn
an honest living, even when she was pregnant. Lizzie should
have done the same.

Lizzie toasted Tom again in her gin, silently this time,
then turned her attention to Frederick. 'Let's hear your offer,
then, Mr H. An' it'd better be a good one. I'm not goin'
back to work in no mills.'

'How would you like to stay in Blackpool?' Frederick
began persuasively.

In October, Tom received word that Fred Coxton had died,
but when he went over to Manchester, there was no sign of
the boy, Jim. He came back to report to Frederick and the
two of them decided to keep an eye open for the lad.

'It's my guess that he'll come back here if he's in trouble.
He'll probably try to contact William.'

And that was exactly what happened. In late October,
William was accosted on his way home from school. Just as
he was passing the graveyard, someone said, 'Sst! William
Ashworth.' When he turned he found himself looking at a
face he recognised instantly, for it was a flawed image of
himself.

Jim tugged at William's sleeve and looked round anxiously.
'I need to talk to you.'

William hesitated. Somehow, he knew his mother would
not want him to associate with this boy. But Jim was also
his half-brother and William had been brought up to think
family mattered, so could not turn away. 'All right. Just for
a minute, then.'

They went into the graveyard and Jim indicated that they

should sit down on the smoothly shaven grass behind Thomas Hallam's grave with its fine memorial monument. William shivered, remembering that dreadful day, and shook his head. 'No. Let's go and sit over there.'

Jim shrugged and followed him.

William sat down, careful that no one passing in the street would be able to see him. 'What do you want?'

'To talk to you. We're brothers, aren't we?'

'Half-brothers.'

Jim shrugged. 'Not much difference.'

William looked at him steadily, waiting for the other boy to say something. Jim Coxton might be younger than him, but the look in his eyes was too knowing for a child his age. It worried William, that look did.

Jim cleared his throat, wondering how best to start. 'He died, you know.'

William knew exactly who he meant. 'Oh?'

'I thought you'd like to know.'

'No. I don't want to know anything about him, actually.' But that was a lie. William would love to have heard something good about his real father. The little he did know was all bad, whatever his grandfather said.

'He got a chill on the chest an' went fast. I looked after him.' Jim paused, surprised to find that he had a tear in his eye. He swiped it away with a very grubby hand. 'He was all right, you know. In his way. He looked after me when me mam died, anyway.'

There was no answer, but Jim must have seen something in the other boy's expression that encouraged him to continue. 'Your uncle paid him to stay away from Bilsden.'

William looked surprised. 'My Uncle Tom?'

'Yeah. The one as runs the junk yard. Hard fellow, isn't he?'

'I don't think so. Not to me, anyway.'

'Well, I wouldn't like to cross him.' But he had already crossed Tom Gibson, and he was a bit worried about it. Tom had told him that when Fred died he was not, under any circumstances, to return to Bilsden, and most especially he was not to contact William. But somehow Jim felt he had to. He had no one in the world now except this half-brother. And his half-brother was rich. So there must be something to be gained from him. He knew that there was little to be gained from Tom Gibson.

'What are you going to do now?' William asked, when the other boy remained silent.

Jim shrugged. 'Try to stay out of the poorhouse. I dunno. That's why I came to see you.'

'Oh?'

'Yes.' Jim was tracing circles with his toe in the raked gravel pathway that circled the better part of the graveyard. 'I thought – if you asked him – he might do summat for me. Your uncle.'

'Do summat?'

'Yeah, get me taken on somewhere. Give me a job. In that junk yard, maybe.'

'I don't think he'd do that.'

'Why not?'

William put his chin up. He knew he was the older of the two of them, but somehow he felt at a disadvantage next to this hard-faced lad. 'Because of my mother.'

'Huh?'

'You look like me. If other people in Bilsden saw you, they might – they might say things about my mother.' Suddenly William lost all his diffidence. He turned to seize Jim by the front of his filthy jacket. 'And if you do anything, *anything at all*, that hurts my mother, I'll kill you myself.'

Jim blinked. He'd judged this rich brother of his to be a softie, but when he spoke about his mother, William looked so fierce that you knew he meant exactly what he said. 'I don't wanna do anythin' to hurt your mam,' he said placatingly. 'Why should I? I've never met her. I just wanna get meself somewhere to live an' a way of earnin' me livin'.' He shuddered. 'An' I don't wanna wind up in Little Ireland again. It's bad there, William. Real bad. Once me dad died, I got out quick, or they'd have took all my money off of me.'

'Who would?'

'Anyone. They'd have come lookin' to see if there were any pickin's. So I told the carter to tell your uncle, like he'd arranged, an' I got out. I've been travellin' around a bit since then, lookin' at the countryside. But I don't like it. It's nearly as bad as Little Ireland.'

William wrinkled his brow in puzzlement.

'I got a few odd jobs here an' there, an' they work you hard on those farms – they treat the bloody animals better than they treat the lads who work there. An' anyway, it's too quiet. So I ain't goin' to work in the country. An' I ain't goin' back to Little Ireland.'

'Oh. Well, what do you want me to do now?'

'Give me some money first. I'm hungry. I haven't had anythin' to eat today.'

A look of horror crossed William's face. 'Nothing at all?'

'No. An' I only got a bit of stale bread yesterday.'

William fumbled in his pocket and produced two half-pennies. 'That's all I've got, I'm afraid.'

Jim snatched it off him. 'It'll do. Can you get some more money?'

William nodded. He had quite a lot of money saved up. But he wasn't going to give that to anyone. He was saving to buy his mother a really good present at Christmas. And his grandfather, too. It was expensive having so many relatives, but nice. 'I can get another sixpence,' he volunteered, testing the water.

'That'll help. I'll see if I can find some work. Till you talk to your uncle.' He fixed William with a look that belonged to a much older man's face. 'You're my best hope. An' you're my half-brother, so I reckon you owe it to me.'

William stared down at the ground, then nodded. This stranger was family, even if he didn't like him. 'All right. I'll talk to my uncle about you.'

'I'll wait for you here tomorrow morning. You can give me the other money then.'

'Yes. On my way to school.' William hesitated, then took him round to Thomas Hallam's grave, braving the demons that had made him shy away from that place ever since the day he found out about his real father. 'And if you've nowhere to sleep, this place is sheltered. I hid here once. See. Under the shelf.'

Jim nodded. 'Right. Thanks.' He watched William stride away, then tensed as William stopped dead and turned round again. 'What's the matter?'

'Can you try to stay out of sight? Someone might recognise you.'

Jim nodded. 'I'll do my best.'

'Right.' This time William did not stop.

When his rich brother had disappeared from sight, Jim went to find a bakehouse and buy a bag of broken bits. Mindful of the need not to antagonise anyone, he stuffed his hair under his ragged cap, pulled it down over his forehead and kept as inconspicuous as possible.

William went round to the junk yard the next day after school, knowing he'd likely find his uncle there. Mark was minding the front buying area, but he pointed to the wood store when William said he had a message from his mother.

Tom, who had been sorting out the reusable timbers from the firewood, looked round as the door opened. He usually left this task to others, but he'd tackled it today because he needed some physical exercise. And some time to think. 'William? What are you doing here, lad?'

'I need to talk to you, Uncle Tom. Privately. It's rather important.'

'Oh? That sounds ominous? Come in, then. Stop hovering in the bloody doorway. I can't see what I'm doing.' He indicated a stack of old planks and threw a ragged blanket over them. 'It's not a comfy chair, but it's better than standing up.'

William hesitated, then came over to perch on one end of the planks. He tried desperately to think how to start.

Tom waited a minute, then prompted, 'What's wrong?'

'There's nothing wrong, well, not exactly. It's just that – I need some help for – for a friend.'

'Oh? Why can't your friend's family help him?'

William gulped, then took the plunge. 'I am his family, his only family.' He stared down at the ground.

'Aah! That little bastard came looking for you, didn't he? Coxton's son.'

A nod was his only answer.

'I told him not to come near you again. And not to come to Bilsden, either.'

'He's keeping out of sight,' William said hurriedly. 'He knows we don't want anyone recognising him.'

'Oh, is he? Why didn't he wait for me in Manchester? He didn't even stay to bury his own father, that's what sort of a person he is, William.'

'He didn't stay because the people who lived nearby would have taken his money away and put him in the poorhouse. He said it was really bad there.'

Tom frowned. There could be some truth in this. He regarded himself as tough, but even he wouldn't like to go into some parts of Little Ireland on his own.

'Uncle, he – he wants us to help him find work.'

'I'll find him work, the little devil! Where is he?'

William's bottom lip became a straight line of determination. 'I'm not telling you where he is till you've promised to look after him.'

'And why the hell should I do that?'

'Because he's my half-brother.'

'You don't even know him. And we owe him nothing.'

'Grandad says we should all help one another. Look after our poorer brethren. And he says family is the most important of all. Jim's family, Uncle Tom. My family, anyway. I thought about it last night, thought and thought. We can't let him starve. Even if he doesn't stay in Bilsden, we have to help him.'

Tom scowled. Jim had judged right in coming to William. 'Oh, hell! All right, we'll arrange something.'

William's jaw still had that firm square look to it. 'What?'

'How the hell do I know what? Something. And he'd better be grateful for it, too, and stay away from here from now on. Tell me where he is.'

William hesitated, then shook his head. 'Not yet.'

Tom grabbed his nephew's sleeve and shook it. 'Every minute that little bugger is loose puts your mother in danger. If we don't get him out of sight, he'll undo everything your stepfather and I . . .' He broke off.

'Does Mr Hallam know about him, too?

'Yes.'

'Then we'll have to speak to him as well, won't we?' And from that William would in no way be moved.

That evening, Tom strode up the hill and pounded on the door of Ridge House. 'Mr Hallam, please.' He caught hold of Winnie's arm. 'I want to see him alone, on business. I'll talk to my sister afterwards. I'll wait in the library.'

Within the minute, Frederick had walked into the library and shut the door. 'Mysteries? Why didn't you come and say hello to Annie first? She'll be suspicious, think we're keeping something from her.'

'I was too bloody mad to see her till I'd talked to you.' In a few choice phrases, he explained about William's involvement with Jim Coxton.

Frederick nodded. 'Then I'd better see William myself. You stay here and I'll go up to his room quietly. He went up to bed half an hour ago.'

William sat bolt upright in bed as his door opened. He immediately recognised Frederick's silhouette.

'You don't mind if we speak in the darkness? I don't want your mother to know about this.'

'No.' William didn't want her to know, either. 'All right.'

'Where is he?'

'What are you going to do with him?'

Frederick laid one hand on William's tense shoulder. 'If I promise that I'll see he's all right, will you just trust me, lad?'

'You won't put him in the poorhouse?'

'No.'

'And you won't make him work in the country?'

The condition intrigued Frederick and he couldn't help asking, 'Why not?'

'He hates it. Too quiet. I wouldn't like to work on a farm myself.'

Frederick could not help smiling, in spite of the seriousness of the situation. 'No. I won't make him work in the country.'

'What are you going to do with him, then?'

'As I said, lad, you'll just have to trust me there. I've got a lot of contacts. I'll make sure he's all right, I promise you.'

William had a final condition. 'I want to see him again one day, when I'm older. I'll go somewhere where it won't hurt my mother to do it. But I want to see him.'

Frederick stared at him, then shrugged. 'I'll arrange it. But not till you're eighteen, though.' When he rejoined Tom, he grinned. 'Clever little sod, isn't he, young Coxton?'

'Yes. What the hell are we going to do with him?'

Frederick's grin broadened to make him look about twenty years old. 'We're going to give him to Lizzie to bring up. She owes us.'

An answering grin slowly softened the grim lines on Tom's face, was followed by a chuckle, then both men roared with laughter.

'I don't know who I pity most,' Tom said to Frederick as he left, after chatting to Annie, 'Jim or Lizzie.'

'I think it'll be the making of your Lizzie,' said Frederick thoughtfully. 'And I'd back her against young Coxton any day. She's learnt some lessons in a hard school.'

'Her own fault.' Tom would not hear a good word about Lizzie and May, and had bound Frederick to absolute secrecy about them.

16

November 1849

One chill misty day in November, Frederick came home from Manchester jubilant. 'It's all settled,' he told Annie, whirling her round in his arms.

She was laughing helplessly. 'Put me down, you fool! Don't you know that grandfathers should behave in a more dignified manner?'

The gleam in his eyes said that this was one grandfather who had no interest in dignity, and the crushing kiss left her in no doubt about how he felt.

Jane Ramsby, who had been about to enter the room, took a step backwards. At times like this it was hard not to feel bitter. Annie had everything a woman could possibly want, while she, Jane, had nothing, not even her independence. Then she took a deep breath and scolded herself. That wasn't Annie's fault, and Annie had been more than kind to her since Beatrice's wedding day. Kinder than Beatrice or Christine had ever been.

She cast a quick glance round to make sure that no servants were nearby, then she moved closer to the door. It wasn't right to listen to other people's conversations, she thought with a wry smile, but it had become a habit with her now. She knew far more about the people in the house, both servants and family, than people realised. And she relished the knowledge. It filled her with a secret feeling of power. What things she could tell if she chose to!

Inside the room, Annie had forgotten for a moment that

Frederick had some news for her. She stood in his arms, her breathing deepened, then realised that a servant could come in at any moment and pulled away. 'What's settled, then?'

He guided her across to the sofa and sat down, one arm still round her shoulders. 'The railway is settled, that's what.'

'Oh, how wonderful! I can't believe it! We've wanted a branch line for so long. It'll be wonderful just to step on a train and be whisked off to Manchester. And from there, we'll be able to catch a connecting train to anywhere in England.'

'We'll have to start keeping Railway Time, if you want to do that. Do you know, the church clock in Bilsden is several minutes slower than the clocks in Manchester? And those fools on the Council refuse to have it changed.'

'Does it matter that much?'

'It will when the railway opens. Several minutes could mean missing a connection. Most towns set their clocks by Greenwich time now.'

She nodded thoughtfully. 'The whole country will be keeping the same time eventually. We change in small things as well as large, don't we? But the main thing is that we'll be getting the Bilsden Branch Line.'

'Not quite.' He paused to heighten the effect of his next announcement, 'It's actually going to be called the Bilsden and South Pennine Branch Line.'

She stared at him for a full minute, then burst out laughing. 'But the line's only going to serve Bilsden and it'll only connect us to Manchester. Why South Pennine?'

He chuckled. 'The Board of Directors in their almighty wisdom have decided that just in case the line should ever be extended, there ought to be scope for that in the name.'

'Extended to where?'

He shrugged. 'Anywhere. After all, there are about twenty

people living out at Clough Knowle. Maybe they'll want *their* own line next.' There was a rumble of irritation in his throat. 'I sometimes think that the mere thought of railways drives half the sense out of some people's heads. Look at how much money Mildred's husband has lost on railway investments in the past few years. Even you would have enough sense not to invest in small branch lines.'

'Even me?' she asked provocatively, pretending to be offended.

'You know what I mean. Although you're a woman, you have a far better business head on you than most men I know.' He stared at her, eyes narrowed, then added thoughtfully, 'When I change my will, I'm going to leave everything in your hands.' He made a mental note to see Jonas Pennybody soon. He should have dealt with that as soon as he married. If anything happened to him, he wanted to make sure Annie was absolutely secure.

She shivered and put a finger on his lips. 'Don't say things like that, love.'

He kissed the finger, then held her hand away from his lips and kissed it in an old-fashioned courtier's way. 'One has to face facts, Annie. I'm older than you. It's very likely I'll die first. And I mean to leave you and any children we have well protected.'

Jane heard the door of the servants' quarters bang open and Winnie's voice calling something. She didn't want to be caught eavesdropping. She tiptoed up the last few steps of the staircase, then came down them again, clearing her throat rather loudly as she did so. But when she entered the room, Frederick was still sitting close to his wife on the sofa and neither of them noticed her at first. Jealousy shot through Jane. Had the man no sense of what was proper? But she suppressed her feelings and hovered by the door, giving them her usual half-smile.

Annie saw her first. 'Jane, do come in and hear the news!'

'Am I interrupting?'

'No, of course not. Frederick was just telling me about the new railway line.'

He rose and waited until Jane had sat down again before resuming his place close to Annie.

You couldn't fault either of them for manners, thought Jane, as she smoothed her skirts and looked at Frederick, waiting for him to take the lead in choosing a subject of conversation. They treat me as if I'm a valued member of the family. Only I have nothing to contribute, and no one really needs me. I'm here on sufferance, that's all, just sufferance. Beatrice was right about that. Jane had accepted her position for a long time, but since Beatrice's ill treatment of her, the feeling of helplessness was eating away at her. She looked enquiringly across the space that separated her from the other two, realising that they were waiting for her to speak. 'It must be good news, from the expressions on your faces.' Her voice was as calm as always, no indicator of the turmoil raging within her.

'Excellent news,' said Annie and told her about the branch line. Then she turned to Frederick. 'We must let Tom know.'

'Invite him and Marianne to dine with us tonight. We'll tell him then.'

But as Annie had half expected, only Tom came. Marianne could rarely bear to leave the babies, whom she was still feeding herself, much to the disgust of some of the town's matrons, who felt that that sort of thing should be left to the lower classes.

William joined them for the meal, as he always did when it was only family. He was an accomplished young gentleman nowadays, able to hold a polite conversation and handle his cutlery with aplomb.

As he sat down in the drawing room, Tom cleared his

throat and looked at his host and hostess. 'Er – Marianne sends her apologies. She's,' he took a deep breath as he forced the words out, 'she's feeling a little queasy.'

'Not—?' Annie broke off.

'Yes, she's expecting another child.' Tom tried to look pleased as he said that, but in fact he had not grown used to the idea himself yet, and was furious that Marianne had got pregnant so soon. But she had been insatiable in bed, seeming to take more satisfaction from the prospect of conceiving another child than in the physical pleasure he tried to give her. And now that she knew she was pregnant, she had completely lost interest in her husband again. He was beginning to feel somewhat superfluous.

William cheered loudly. 'So I'm going to have another cousin. Or cousins. Do you think Aunt Marianne will have twins again, Uncle Tom?'

Tom shuddered visibly.

'I thought people didn't get pregnant while they were still feeding a child,' Annie said.

Frederick smiled to see Jane's glance of disapproval at this open admission of the facts of life, but Annie was always open with William.

'So did I.' Tom realised that his voice had given away his feelings and tried to summon up a smile, but failed woefully. 'We Gibsons produce too many children,' he added without thinking.

Annie murmured suitable congratulations and glanced sideways. Frederick had that stony expression on his face now, a barrier even against her. She was one Gibson who didn't produce too many children. She knew how much he wanted another child, how upset he'd been when she lost theirs in April. And since then, there had been no sign, no sign at all, of another.

She changed the subject deftly and they began to discuss

the building of the railway and what it would mean for Bilsden, both during and after construction. Nothing had come of the business trip to Blackpool, though Frederick was toying with the idea of buying his family a holiday home there. Annie wasn't sure about that. She didn't like to go too far from her business. The salon was thriving and she continued to keep the accounts and design gowns for it, in the face of Frederick's continued mild disapproval. It was one of the few things upon which they did not agree wholeheartedly.

From that they went on to discuss Tom's new business venture at the newly renamed Prince of Wales, which was causing a great deal of interest in the town.

William listened to all the discussions with great interest. He and Mark often talked about what they would do with their lives. Mark wanted to become rich, but William wasn't sure what he wanted. Since his long talk with his grandfather, his thoughts kept drifting back to religion and God, rather than to making money. His grandfather had explained it all so well. He understood now exactly why his mother had been tested like that. He understood the Lord's purpose. And he admired the way his grandfather could explain such things. Far better than Mr Hinchcliffe did. One day, William hoped earnestly, he too would understand life well enough to help other people.

His thoughts drifted away for a moment as he wondered yet again where his half-brother Jim was. All his stepfather would tell him was that Jim was being looked after, had been found both a home and employment and that it would upset William's mother to talk about him. William rather wished Jim lived nearby. It'd be nice to have a relative of his own age to talk to. Since coming to live at Ridge House, he'd spent an awful lot of time with grown-ups. Not that he didn't love being with his mother, and his stepfather was not too bad, but he missed Mark and the others more than he had expected.

Some of the lads from school, who had once scorned a seamstress's son, had tried to get more friendly with William since his mother married Mr Hallam. Several had hinted for invitation to Ridge House, but William knew exactly why they were now seeking his company, and he had discussed that with his grandfather, too, as he discussed everything that puzzled him. Such friendships were worth nothing. But he wished Mark were not always so busy nowadays, and that when Luke did come to Ridge House, he did not spend half his time talking to the head gardener, going on for ever about boring stuff to do with plants.

'Could I be excused?' he asked, yawning, as the business talk continued. 'I'm rather tired today.'

'Yes, love.' Annie held out her cheek for a kiss, then gave William a hug. 'Sleep well.'

'I usually do.'

'Good night, lad.' Frederick shook William's hand, as he always did, then turned back to Tom. 'Got enough finance for your Prince of Wales?' he asked idly, as the door shut behind the boy. 'Or would you like another partner?'

Tom shrugged. 'I've already got one partner. Seth Holden.'

'Does he have enough capital?'

'A reasonable amount. He's got more money than you'd believe, our Seth has. He lives very – er – modestly.' Actually, Seth lived like a miser at home, and his wife and children, while adequately fed and clothed, had no luxuries at all in their everyday life and no idea of their worth. 'And besides, he's the best brewer in town, Seth is. That's as good as money invested. Even our fussy Dr Lewis approves of the beer, ale and porter that Seth brews. Says it's very wholesome stuff.' He grinned. 'The customers don't care about that; they're just interested in the taste of it.'

'I prefer wine myself,' said Frederick, draining his glass. 'Jane, would you like another glass?' He always asked her that when he served himself and his guests, but she rarely took more than one glass.

He was already turning back to Tom, when Jane said suddenly, 'Yes. I think I would tonight. If you don't mind, Frederick.'

'Why should I mind? It's your choice to drink only one glass, Jane, not mine.'

She sat sipping the ruby fluid, admiring it in the light of the gasoliers, unaware that Annie was eyeing her curiously.

What had got into Jane lately? Annie wondered. She seemed very twitchy. Surely she wasn't still brooding about the way Beatrice had treated her? I'll have a talk to her soon, Annie decided. She looks so unhappy. Her mouth has quite a droop to it when she thinks no one is looking at her. I should have noticed that before. But Annie had been too engrossed in Frederick to notice much about anyone else – except William, of course. She always had time for him.

From then on, the railway became the main topic of conversation in Bilsden. Everyone who was anyone had ridden on a train and had bemoaned the fact that Bilsden was not connected to the Lanky, as the Lancashire and Yorkshire line was more commonly known. And those humbler folk who had not yet ridden the rails were longing to do so from the safety and comfort of their own town. The railways were the wonder of the age, opening up new horizons to people whose parents had never gone further than ten miles from the town or village in which they had been born.

It wasn't only in the better houses that the proposed railway was being discussed. The operatives in the mills often talked about the changes the railway might make to their lives and seized upon each new titbit of information with fascination. Holidays. Trips to Manchester. And who knew what else? Some braver souls even nourished a desire to visit London and see the Queen and her children.

And the young men discussed the coming railway with great vigour down at the Bilsden Institute, which was still meeting in the church hall, but without the constricting presence of Parson Kenderby, who had been knocking on death's door for a while, it was now known.

Even the members of the congregation of the Bilsden Methodist Chapel spoke in glowing terms of Sunday School picnics and temperance excursions. The railways made so much possible and they took folk away from the temptations of drunkenness and public houses.

John Gibson had to bite his tongue sometimes when the temperance group at chapel spoke so disapprovingly of drinking. He still enjoyed the odd glass of ale himself and could see no harm in that. Not if you only drank in moderation. And Seth Holden's ale was the best he had ever tasted. He was proud of what his Tom was doing. Proud of all his children. All the ones who lived in Bilsden, anyway. He didn't know what had happened to Lizzie. Or May. He felt he had let poor Em'ly down, not keeping a better eye on her daughter.

Tom had snapped his head off when he suggested going to look for Lizzie in Manchester. John intended to do that one day, but now wasn't the time for going away, not with Kathy expecting another child any day now. Eh, the Lord had blessed him, giving him so many children. Eleven of them, he'd fathered, and only two had died, if you didn't count those poor little still-born mites that Lucy had had. John sometimes thought he must be the luckiest man on earth.

He felt even luckier when his second son was born, but

there were a few anxious moments during the birth and Widow Clegg insisted they call Doctor Lewis in, just to be on the safe side. That had made John sick with anxiety for a few dark hours, for he had never forgotten the death of his first wife in childbed.

But Kathy came through it safely, tired but glowing with happiness when she cradled her second son in her arms.

Jeremy Lewis took John on one side afterwards. 'No more children, John. Your wife's not a strong woman. It's the result of poor feeding as a child. It's a good job the baby wasn't any bigger.'

John's face turned white. 'But she's all right now, isn't she?'

Jeremy patted his arm. 'Yes. She's all right this time. But don't risk it again.'

John nodded. 'I won't. But it's hard on a man.'

'Not nowadays. We know a bit more about how to prevent babies.' He gave John a thorough lecture on modern contraceptive methods which made John's face brighten up again.

'Don't fear, doctor. I'll be careful. I shan't risk my lass.' He had done that once with Annie's mother and lost her. He wouldn't do it again.

The excitement heightened to fever pitch in Bilsden when the first group of surveyors arrived to start marking out the actual route for the rail tracks. Folk who had land on the proposed route began to think gleefully about selling it to the railway company – you got huge sums for small patches of land, it was said, whether it was good land or not. Folk who had land elsewhere bemoaned the fact that they were likely to miss out on the chance of a nice little nest egg to safeguard their children's future.

Tom changed his plans about the Prince of Wales almost overnight and began to think in terms of providing accommodation for rail travellers visiting Bilsden.

Accommodation both for the gentry and for ordinary working folk. After some careful thought, he went back to discuss a partnership with his brother-in-law. 'If you're still interested, that is,' he added with feigned casualness.

'I am interested. But not for the same reasons as you.'

'Oh? What better reason could there be than making money?'

'I've made as much money as I'm likely to need,' Frederick said, with an indifference to money that made Tom shudder, 'even after the purchase of Dawton's, but I'm determined that the new buildings everyone's planning to erect won't spoil the town centre.'

Tom leaned back in his chair, a bit puzzled by this reaction. 'Oh?'

'I mean that. I'm more than willing to join in your redevelopment plans for the Prince of Wales, but I want a big say in how the new part of the building looks from outside.'

'Suits me.'

It didn't suit Seth, though. He was in awe of Hallam and was already worrying about working with him. And when Hallam started talking about more elaborate buildings, and using stone instead of brick, Seth really started to fret about what he had got himself into. 'Nay, I'm in this to make money,' he protested at one of their initial meetings. 'We shall make nowt if we put up a real fancy place like you're talking about. And there's no *need* for it.'

'That's my condition for joining you, take it or leave it.' Frederick smiled, knowing full well that Tom would ensure they took it. He'd have to ask his acquaintances in Manchester about suitable architects and builders. Bilsden wasn't the only town that was looking to spruce itself up. Pity Daniel Connor had proved such a fly-by-night. The few things he had built were quite sound. He knew his trade, but he was a poor money manager. He would probably have been all right if he had had someone like Matt Peters to take care of the details for him. Or if he'd had more capital behind him. Annie said Daniel was another one who had lost money on the railways. Funny that a man who knew how to build them had not known how to invest in them wisely.

Then the surveyors came back into town with long faces and the Board of Directors had to convene an emergency meeting at the half-refurbished Prince of Wales. Not only had the surveyors been forbidden entry to Darrington land by two keepers carrying guns, but a curt note from His Lordship's London lawyer had been handed to them by the grinning men: it begged to inform the Board of Directors that His Lordship would not sell any of his land, and would take it amiss if the railway were even visible from his estate.

'The man's a fool,' Frederick declared to Annie at dinner that night, still fuming. 'Not visible from his estate! Does he think we're still living in the Middle Ages, and that he can dictate how we all act.'

'What shall you do about it? Is there anything you can do?'

'We'll have to hope that the surveyors can find another route. I'm sure Darrington waited to tell us of his opposition on purpose. He wanted to make sure we'd invest our money and then fail to get our branch line built. I suppose he thought that would prevent us from trying again. He's as bad as Kenderby, his precious Lordship is. Utterly reactionary. And a fool, to boot.'

'His second wife is much younger than him. Very attractive. She never came back to the salon, though, after I made her the ball gown.' Annie was regretful about that, but she hadn't really expected Her Ladyship's ongoing custom.

But before the surveyors had time to reconsider their plans and search out another route, a second letter to the

Board of Directors had them rushing to convene a further meeting.

Like the other directors, Frederick sat up in shock as the letter was read out.

> Mr Daniel Connor, at present resident in London, begs to offer the benefit of his expertise and understanding of the building of railways to the Directors of the Bilsden and South Pennine Branch Line. In return for a Directorship and an honorarium of £1,000, he will demonstrate how another route can be found for the proposed railway, one where there will be no difficulty about acquiring land, and will then oversee its construction.

There was instant uproar.

'Isn't he the one who set up as a builder here?'

'Yes, and went broke within the year.'

'The fellow's a fraud.'

'Why should we pay him anything?'

'The surveyors will find us another route without this chap's help.'

Frederick caught the Chairman's eye and the latter thumped his hand on the table.

'Gentlemen, please!'

When there was silence, Frederick said thoughtfully, 'Gentlemen, before we decide anything, I propose that we ask Connor to come to Bilsden and explain his plan to us. I'm not fond of the fellow,' not after what he'd tried to do to Annie, 'but he undoubtedly has expertise in the building of railways and it cannot hurt to listen to his proposal. After all, we do have a problem.'

And so it was decided. But not till they'd argued the point for a further hour.

'You're surely not going to deal with him!' Annie snapped, when Frederick told her what had happened.

'I'd deal with the devil himself if it would benefit Bilsden, my love.'

She leaned across the table, absolutely glaring at him. 'Even when you know how he tried to ruin me?'

'My love, in the world of business, it can be costly and catastrophic to hold grudges.'

'But it'll mean – it'll mean that Daniel Connor will be coming back to Bilsden.'

'Presumably.'

'I won't receive him in my house! I won't even acknowledge him in the street.'

Frederick glanced meaningfully at William and Jane and changed the subject.

Annie closed her mouth with a snap on whatever she had been going to say and began to push the rest of her food around her plate.

In their bedroom that night, however, she confronted her husband again. 'Frederick, you can't do business with *that man*!'

'We may have to.'

'I meant what I said. I won't have him in my house.' She was a blaze of anger.

'You're magnificent when you're in a rage,' he said, reaching for her.

She avoided his arms and moved to the other side of a chair. 'Did you hear me?'

He nodded. 'Yes. But it's my house, too, you know, love. And although I shall not expect you to treat the fellow like a long-lost friend, I see no harm in allowing him to help us with this impasse. If he really can point us to a solution – which has yet to be proved.'

'He's not to be trusted.'

'Indeed, he isn't. I shall make very sure that he can deliver what he's promised before I allow him to join the Board. And we shall not pay him anything until the railway line is finished.'

That night, for the first time, she turned her back on him in bed, too upset to feel amorous. 'Don't. I'm tired.'

He caught her shoulder and pulled her round to face him. 'You'll be tireder still before you sleep.'

She struggled desperately not to respond, but he was skilful enough to overcome her resistance. She was still angry when she woke in the morning, though, and she snapped at everyone in the house all day, from her son to the chambermaid.

When Annie heard that the Directors were to hold their next meeting at Ridge House, to ensure full secrecy until they'd found a way around Lord Darrington's opposition, she and Frederick quarrelled again. But she found him implacable. For the first time she was reminded of how people used to say that he was a hard master, fair but hard. But that didn't stop her trying to change his mind.

'You're wasting your time, my love. Business is business, and we need to keep emotions out of it. I didn't get rich by holding grudges.' He had said this already, several times, and he could see that he would have to continue repeating it until Annie realised that he meant it. It was the first thing they had really disagreed about since they married.

She clutched his arm, unaware that her fingers were digging in. 'Don't you *care* what he tried to do to me, Frederick? Don't you care?'

He loosened her fingers and retained her hand in his. 'Of course I care, love. But I'm not intending to make a friend of the man, only do business with him. And Connor didn't actually do anything to you in the end, thanks to your friend Helen. He's her problem now.' He paused and added, 'Surely you'll be glad to see her again? She was a good friend to you.'

'She's *his* wife now,' Annie muttered, pulling her hand away from him. 'So she's on his side.'

'She's also Kenderby's daughter. She was bound to come back to Bilsden, you know, with her father so ill.'

For some reason, Annie had not even considered this possibility. 'Well, I bear her no malice, but I'll not be glad to see her if it means seeing Danny O'Connor as well.' After that, she gave up trying to convince Frederick. You might as well try to convince the Tower of London to jump across the River Thames as change Frederick Hallam's mind when it was set on something. He never shouted or stormed at you, but he usually found a quiet path to getting his own way if he really considered it important. She'd found that out already in some of the smaller things. And she'd watched him influence the Town Councillors. Not overtly, but pushing them in his direction.

On the morning of the meeting, Annie left the house and went to spend the day with Pauline, still furious. But her friend didn't agree with her, either, for Pauline kept insisting that Frederick was right. Business was business. And you didn't let your feelings about people get in the way of it.

'You're only saying that because the railway won't be coming anywhere near Collett Hall.'

Pauline smiled. 'If dealing with Mr Connor meant the difference between you losing your salon and all your money, and retaining the salon, what would you do, Annie?'

'But it doesn't! And there's no *need* for Frederick to deal with him. Someone else could sort out the railway.'

'Who?'

Annie sniffed and huffed her shoulders. 'How should I know? I'm only an emotional woman.'

Pauline actually chuckled at that. 'Well, woman or not,

you understand as well as anyone else how big a difference the railway will make to some of the other businesses in town. Your brother's, for one. He'll be able to send fresh produce into the Manchester markets at a fraction of the cost once the railway is built. You really can't blame the Directors for finding out what Mr Connor has to suggest.'

'Yes, I can.' But Annie's voice had lost its fire. Even Tom had not understood her feelings. But she knew, she absolutely knew, that once Daniel Connor got a foot back in the door, he'd not rest till he'd charmed his way into Bilsden social circles again. After all, his family still lived here. Whenever she saw Bridie in town, which was not often, thank goodness, Annie had to bite her tongue not to say something sharp when Bridie started telling her about Daniel and how well he was doing. And how kind his new wife was, writing to them regularly and sending them presents.

And, Annie thought glumly, with Helen as Daniel's wife connecting him to the Kenderby family who had lived in Bilsden since the dark ages, there would be many people in the town who would not hesitate to receive him, whatever he had done in the past.

17

December 1849

A few mornings after the meeting, Annie jerked upright in bed, gasped and clapped her hand to her mouth. By the time Frederick had realised something was wrong and thrown the covers aside, she had rushed across to the hand basin in the corner of her dressing room and was retching into it. She had felt sick for a couple of mornings now, but it had soon passed.

When she had finished, Frederick helped her back to the bed and tucked the covers warmly around her shivering body. 'I hope this means that you're pregnant again, my love,' he said, smiling down at her. 'You've looked a little pale for the past few mornings and I have been wondering.' He went across the room, dipped a cloth in the ewer of icy water and came back to wipe her face. 'We need to get a fire lit in here.'

She didn't even attempt to respond, just lay breathing in the chill air of the bedroom and trying to control the sickness that still threatened to overcome her.

Frederick put the wet cloth down by the bed and hovered next to her. 'Shall I ring for Laura to help you? Would you rather I left you alone?'

She started to shake her head, but the room began to waver around her and she could only mutter, 'No!' through teeth clenched to keep back a new wave of nausea. She didn't want to be left alone just now. She clutched Frederick's hand and pulled him towards her.

He sat down on the edge of the bed and stayed there, holding her hand till she sighed and relaxed a little. When she opened her eyes again and tried to smile at him, he asked gently, 'Better?'

'Yes. A bit. Thank you.'

'Would you like a cup of tea?'

She shuddered.

He stroked the damp hair from her forehead. 'I think we'll call in Dr Lewis today, Annie. After last time, I don't want to risk anything with you or the child.'

'Yes. I suppose so.' It was still an effort to speak and even lying down, she felt so dizzy that she could not think straight.

'I'll see to it, then.' Frederick hid his surprise at her acquiescence, for he'd expected her to protest. She usually hated to be fussed over. 'Will you be all right while I get dressed?'

'Yes.' She closed her eyes and lay there, her lips pressed together. When he didn't move away, she opened her eyes again. 'It takes nine months.' She managed a ghost of a smile. 'You'll have time to get dressed before you do anything.'

He saw that the smile faded almost immediately and that her body was very still in the huge bed. Normally she would be talking, gesticulating, her eyes sparkling, words tumbling out of her mouth. That vitality was one of the things that he loved most about her. His stomach clenched as he looked down at her. What would he do if anything happened to Annie? He did not think he would be able to bear that.

As Frederick fumbled through his cupboards in search of a shirt, he clicked his tongue in annoyance. Dressing was a task for which he had always refused help other than what the chambermaid could give him to care for his clothes and keep them tidy. Now, hunting for something to don in a hurry, he had left a trail of disorder behind that was most unlike him. As he was pulling on the first shirt that had come to hand, he decided suddenly that, like Annie, he needed more help with his clothes. 'You're getting vain in your old age,' he told his reflection as he kicked aside the nightshirt and studied the tall lean body in the mirror.

It was cold in the dressing room and his stiff fingers seemed to take far too long to fasten the buttons. Annie had mentioned that they needed another chambermaid. Well, they would get a valet as well. He had too many things on his mind lately to bother about what he should wear each day. He wanted someone who would select things for him and leave them ready, tidy things away after him and tell him when he needed to buy new clothes. 'Aping the gentry,' he mocked his reflection as he tied his stock and studied the effect. Since his marriage, he had grown more fastidious, wanting to appear his best at all times. He had laughed at himself many times for that, but when you had a wife so much younger than yourself, you needed all the help you could get to maintain your attractions.

But most important of all just now was Annie. The minute he was dressed, he went back into the bedroom to see her. She seemed to be sleeping, so he tiptoed out and down to the library where he scribbled a quick note. He set the bell pealing for Winnie almost before the ink was dry and when she came bustling in, clearly surprised to see him at his desk before breakfast, he looked up and frowned as if she had been slow to answer. 'Have this note sent round to Dr Lewis immediately, please, Winnie.'

'Yes, sir.'

He watched her leave and sat on in the library for a few moments. He had said in his note that he would like Jeremy himself to attend Annie, not one of the two younger doctors who now worked with him. He wanted only the best for Annie, and the best in Bilsden was Jeremy Lewis. It might take nine months for a baby to grow inside a woman's body, but Annie had looked dreadful this morning. He had never seen Christine as ill as that in the early stages, for all her protestations and vapours. He was not even aware that he was speaking aloud when he murmured, 'Please don't let her lose it. Not again.'

At last he stood up and made his way into the small room in which the family ate when there were no visitors. William looked up and smiled at him. 'Isn't Mother coming down?'

'Your mother's not well.'

William looked alarmed and hastily swallowed the food in his mouth. 'What's the matter? She hasn't caught a cold, has she?' His mother was never ill.

'Er – we're not sure. But no, I don't think it's a cold.'

Jane looked at him sharply across the table. When Frederick shook his head slightly to warn her not to ask anything, she bent her eyes to her plate, wondering if Annie was with child again. Annie had been looking a bit pale these last few days. Jane always noticed things like that. Well, a child would please Frederick. He had made no secret of the fact that he wanted children by Annie.

'I do hope Mother hasn't caught a cold,' William said, attacking with gusto a plate piled high with food. He was growing again, and often made extra trips down to the kitchen between meals for snacks to 'put him on', as his grandfather called it. 'It's miserable when you're sneezing and sniffling,' he added. 'And Dr Lewis's cough medicine is *awful*! Ugh! I hope I never need to take any of that again.'

There was silence while he demolished another few mouthfuls, then, 'Can I go and see Mother when I've finished my breakfast?' He had soon learned to ask before invading the rooms that his mother shared with his stepfather. He had been embarrassed once or twice to catch the two of them kissing and had backed out hurriedly with a scarlet face. He had gone to discuss this with his grandfather as he did everything that puzzled him.

John had smiled. 'Nay, lad. Married couples usually do quite a bit of kissing.'

'Oh.' There was silence, then, 'Do you kiss my Grandma Kathy a lot?' William stared across the table at Kathy as if she were a strange beast that had crept in from the garden.

'I certainly do,' John assured him. He blew Kathy a kiss and she blew one back at him.

Another silence, then William pulled a face. 'In that case, I don't think I'll ever get married. I wouldn't want to have to start kissing girls like that. I don't know how people can breathe when they're kissing each other like my mother kisses my stepfather. It's just silly, that sort of stuff is.'

'You learn the trick of it with a bit of practice,' John declared, keeping his face straight.

Kathy was not able to hide her smile.

William was still staring across the table at her. 'I think girls are silly. Not you, Grandma. But young girls. You should meet Rosemary Jemmings. She's always arguing with me. I couldn't kiss someone like her.' He shuddered at the mere idea.

'You'll change, lad,' John said, with a wink at Kathy.

'No, I won't.'

Now, when Frederick did not immediately reply to his question, William repeated patiently, 'Can I go and see my mother when I've finished my breakfast, please, sir?'

'What? Oh, no. Not just now, lad.'

William's fork paused halfway to his mouth.

'I'm sure it's nothing much,' Frederick said hastily, 'but your mother's gone back to sleep and I don't want you waking her up.' The last thing Annie needed at the moment was William clattering upstairs to chat to her in his loud cheerful voice.

The boy shovelled the rest of his poached egg into his mouth and loaded his fork again with ham. 'All right. I won't.

I'll take Brutus for a little walk instead. But I'll write Mother a quick note before I leave for school, shall I? She'll like that.'

'She'll love that.' Once again, Frederick envied Annie her closeness to her son and wished he could get to know the boy better. But he was so busy with the extra work from Dawton's and it was as much as he could do to keep the evening hours free for his family.

Jane, as usual, said nothing, but saw all. She had noticed Frederick's tentative efforts to get closer to his stepson, but the boy had not responded with anything but careful politeness. He was probably a bit jealous of how much his mother loved her husband, and you couldn't blame him. She was jealous herself. No one had ever loved her like that.

Jeremy arrived to examine Annie within the hour, having given her priority over all his other patients. 'It's too early to be sure,' he said afterwards, 'but all the signs indicate a distinct possibility that you're pregnant. Are your breasts tender?'

She nodded.

'Let's bring your husband in and discuss this,' he said.

'Discuss what?'

'How you're going to look after yourself.' Jeremy patted her hand. 'You do want to carry this baby safely to term, don't you?'

Her heart constricted at the mere thought of losing a second child of Frederick's. 'Yes, of course I do.'

Frederick was hovering outside and was through the door almost before Jeremy had opened it. 'Well? How is she?'

'She's all right. Sit down, Frederick. We need to discuss a few things.'

Frederick sat on the bed, clasping his wife's hand without realising what he was doing. He looked down at her searchingly before staring back at Jeremy. 'There's nothing seriously wrong with Annie, is there?'

'No. Of course not.'

'Is she—?'

'I've just been saying that it's too soon to tell for sure. But it's likely that she's with child, given the signs.' He turned to look directly at Annie. 'And with your history, my dear, that means you'll need to take things easy for the next few months.'

She sighed and leaned her head back. Her cheeks were almost as white as the fine linen pillowcase. 'I thought you'd say that.'

'What do you mean by "with your history", Jeremy?' Frederick demanded.

'Annie was quite ill when she was carrying William. She had to stay in bed for the final few weeks and would have been better if she'd been able to rest for the last few months. Some women just don't carry children easily.' He looked at the two anxious faces in front of him, the clasped hands, the concern in Frederick's eyes. He had to make sure they understood, even if what he said worried Frederick. 'And since you've lost one baby this year, we must be especially careful now, my dear.'

'I'll make sure of that,' Frederick promised. 'She shan't lift a finger.'

Jeremy laughed. 'I didn't quite mean that. It would be as bad to take no exercise as to overdo things. I see wealthy women regularly who spend their entire pregnancies lying down and who seem worse, not better, for that. No, we must think in terms of moderation and a tranquil life.'

'How tranquil?' demanded Annie.

'Light exercise. Keep yourself quietly busy. Do some sketching, perhaps.' Ellie had told him about Annie still designing for the salon and he thought it would be a good way of occupying herself now. 'No upsets. No getting too tired. Definitely no late nights or travel.'

'I'll make sure she keeps to that,' said Frederick. 'This is one time, my love, when I'm going to insist.'

Annie felt so wretched that she could only lie back and sigh her agreement. She hadn't felt this bad in the early stages with William. And she desperately wanted another child, Frederick's child. She wanted it just as much as he did, perhaps more.

By Christmas, Daniel Connor had convinced the Board of Management of the projected Bilsden and South Pennine Line that he knew what he was talking about and had been put in charge of the railway, though the £1,000 was not to be paid to him until completion of the line. The Board had, however, agreed to his suggestion of paying the navvies weekly, to stop the randies and drunken binges that characterised irregular payments, and Connor said he was quite happy to wait for his money.

Daniel and his wife were living temporarily at the parsonage, where Theophilous Kenderby was fading fast. Jeremy Lewis told Helen that it was a miracle her father had hung on for so long. The parson was an emaciated shadow of his former self, all his bluster lost, and he was pathetically grateful that his daughter had returned to care for him in his final days. He nodded vaguely to Daniel when reintroduced, but seemed not at all interested in his daughter's husband. It was as if he had completely forgotten that the two of them had run away to get married in London and that he had disowned Helen because of it. All his talk now was of death and repentance and of the Lord who was waiting to welcome him into the kingdom of heaven. He was as confident that he was destined for heaven as he had been confident of the opinions he had trumpeted loudly from the pulpit for the last forty years.

Helen made no attempt to contact Annie, because she was uncertain of her reception, though she would have dearly loved to see her friend again. She still thought of Annie as a friend, the best friend she had ever had next to her Aunt Isabel in London. In the meantime, Helen prepared for a quiet Christmas, listened to her husband's plans and celebrated with him when he won the chance to oversee the construction of the new railway line along the track that he had mentally marked out years before when he bought the land his parents now farmed, the land that would be so valuable, for it was essential to the railway.

'You should have told your parents that half of their land was likely to be sold one day,' she said thoughtfully. 'You can't put off telling them for much longer now that the Directors have agreed to your plan.'

'They'll still have enough land left to serve their own needs.'

'Are you sure? Your father loves that farm of his.'

Daniel looked her squarely in the eyes. 'It's my farm, though. I own it.'

'You told them you'd bought it for them.'

'I bought it for all of us. A good investment. Putting them in to farm the land stopped folk linking it with the railways. I gambled that any branch line from Bilsden was likely to go by that route, and it will. Rich sods like Darrington don't often allow railways to be built over their land. I've seen them stop lines going through time after time. So this is one gamble that's paid off.'

She nestled against him. 'You're a clever man, Daniel Connor.'

He grinned. 'Not stupid.' He had married Helen for her money, but had found to his surprise that she was great fun to live with, and even more fun in bed. Parson's daughter or not, she wasn't the slightest bit straight-laced. In fact, she was a cosy and willing armful. He'd been lucky so far that she'd not got pregnant, but she hadn't hesitated to use the sponge he'd provided, thank goodness.

Still, if things went well in Bilsden, they'd probably settle here. He always thought of it as home. Only when everything was sorted out would they think about having children. He'd build them a fine house and they'd raise a family. A couple of sons, a daughter perhaps, but not a large family. Large families dragged you down and dissipated your fortune. He frowned as he thought about the future. The only blot on the horizon was that Helen's lawyer had tied up her fortune in a trust before she got married, so that she had the final say in how her husband accessed and used her money.

'What are you frowning at?' she asked, running a fingertip along the creases in his forehead.

'I was thinking about your money.'

'Oh?'

He grinned and playfully bit the end of her finger. 'You're a cunning bitch, tying it up like that. Are you going to loosen the purse strings a little now and let me build you a house?'

She took a slow deep breath before replying. 'Not till I see how we go on in Bilsden. When my father dies, we can rent a house here for a while till you've finished the railway. It'll be time then to make a decision.'

The grin faded. 'I'm not sure I like that, Helen.'

She looked at him squarely. 'I love you and I lust after you, Daniel Connor, but I don't trust you where money's concerned.' She held her breath as she waited for his reaction. The need for this conversation had been brewing between them for quite a while.

He was glaring at her now, his body stiff with anger against hers.

She didn't yield an inch. If she once gave him the upper hand with her money, he'd be impossible. 'I like dealing with my money myself, Daniel. And I don't see why that should worry you. I'm good with figures and you're not.' She laid a finger on his lips to prevent him replying. 'Shh. Let me speak. When I invest in your business, when we're sure that you can set up again here as a builder, that you'll be well enough received in the town, you're going to need someone to help you with the money side of things. And who can you trust more than your own wife?' Her hand strayed down his body in a casual caress.

The frown still lingered for a moment, then he pulled her into his arms and gave her a bruising kiss. 'Your father would expire on the spot if he knew what you were really like, woman.'

She pulled his head down for another kiss. 'Who cares about my father? It's you and me, Daniel my lad. And if you want to be rich, then you'll make good use of my gift for figures.' She framed his face in her hands. 'Don't worry, love. I won't hold the money back. You just concentrate on building that railway line. That's what'll get Bilsden folk trusting you again.'

It was a day or two before they returned to the topic of the farm and Daniel's parents, and it was Helen who raised the matter. 'We could always buy Mick another farm, you know.'

'We?'

She shrugged. 'Well, I could.'

'Why should you do that when you won't give your money to me?'

'I haven't said I won't give you my money, only that I intend to be involved in deciding how it's used.' She linked her arm in his. 'You can't do everything, Daniel Connor. You'll be in charge of the building. Why do you resent my wanting to manage the accounts?'

'Because it'll make me look a fool.'

'No, it won't. And anyway, no one need know.'

'You'd better make bloody sure they don't. And why should we spend more money on my parents? We'll need a lot of capital to set up as builders, much more than I had last time. So we're not going to waste any of what we've got.' He amended sarcastically, 'Or rather, of what *you* have got!'

'We have enough to do both. Anyway, I like your parents, Danny and I don't want them hurt.' She hesitated, then said slowly, 'If we don't buy them another farm, we could help them set up a little business on what's left of the land. I've been thinking about that.'

'Oh? What sort of business? All my father knows about is farming and getting children.'

'Looking after convalescents.'

He gaped at her. 'What the hell do you mean by that?'

'Didn't you tell me that young Aidan was not expected to live when he came over here from Ireland? Just look at how Bridie's nursed him back to health. And Annie once said that she went out to the farm to recover after her friend Sally died and that she was absolutely spoiled.' She let that sink in for a moment before saying, 'I think Bridie would enjoy looking after people.'

'But is there money to be made in that?' His voice had lost some of its anger. 'Would that be worth doing?'

'Oh, yes.' She smiled. 'At least, there would be money if I were running things.'

His tone was still grudging. 'You're a devil, Helen Connor. Do you know that? If you'd been a man you'd have made yourself a fortune by now.'

She didn't tell him that she'd already increased her money considerably by careful investment. He'd need time to think about her suggestion and then to come back to her. She was learning how to manage him. Subtly, but very firmly. And she was learning how to keep him happy, too. He was a sensual man. And that suited her very well.

But Daniel didn't raise the matter again, so Helen started discussing it one evening almost casually. 'You know, if we do follow my plan for your parents, there'll be enough left of the farm to keep your father busy, but there won't be enough work to support your brother Rory as well.'

'Mmm. Especially if he decides to marry young as the others did. They're fools, my brothers and sisters are, absolute fools. And as prolific as my parents. The less I have to do with them from now on, the better, or they'll be tapping us for money. And as for my mother's cousin Finola, it's more than time that old hag stopped scrounging off my mother and stood on her own feet.'

'And Aidan? And little Caitlin? Are they to earn their own livings, too?'

'They should do as soon as they're old enough.' He scowled. Against all the odds, Finola's grandson Aidan had not only survived, but seemed to have recovered completely from the consumption since he had come to live in the bracing moorland air. At ten he was still slender, with red hair, freckled skin and grey-green eyes, but he was no longer frail-looking. Bridie said proudly that you couldn't beat fresh air and good farm food. Mick said it was Bridie's cooking as much as anything else. He was very proud of her skill in the kitchen.

The parents of Finola's granddaughter, Caitlin, had died in the Great Hunger that followed the potato famine. The child was eight now, a cheeky little madam, in Danny's opinion, with curly blue-black hair and vivid blue eyes that stared at you as if they could see into your very soul. Bridie said she had the second sight like her poor mother. Whatever it was that Caitlin had, it made Daniel feel uneasy and he had said several times to Helen that he would be glad to get the brat out of his mother's house.

'You might think of taking Rory into the business with you, you know, and training him up as a builder,' Helen suggested gently.

'Why the hell should I do that?'

'Because you can trust your own family more than you can trust other folk. Because if we get as rich as I think we shall, given your skills and my way with money, then you'll need someone like that to help you. Even the great Frederick Hallam has his Matt Peters to depend on. No one can do everything, love. So you leave the money side to me and start planning for your building company. You can offer Rory a job when you tell your family about the farm.'

Mick and Bridie stared at Daniel in horror when he made his announcement the following Sunday.

There was complete silence for a few minutes, then Mick burst out, 'You're going to sell us out! Why, you're no better than the bloody landlords were back home.'

Tears were running down Bridie's face. 'Oh, Danny, son, why did you do it?'

He tried to explain, to make them understand. 'I always knew this was on the cards. That's why I bought the farm in the first place. It was a good investment.'

Mick got up abruptly and stalked out of the door.

Bridie bowed her head and wept.

'Look after your mother,' Helen said, and followed Mick without waiting for Daniel's agreement.

Outside she met Finola and Caitlin coming back from the henhouse with a basket of eggs. 'What's wrong with our Mick?' Finola asked, staring at the figure stalking away across the field.'

'He's just had a bit of a shock.' Helen picked up her skirts and ran after him, heedless of her dainty shoes. 'Mick! Mick, wait for me!'

She had to call out twice more before his innate courtesy made him stop. He stood glowering at her. 'Leave me alone, will you, woman!'

Helen went up to him and put her arm in his, feeling how rigid his body was and seeing the trails of moisture on his cheeks. 'Your son is an idiot.'

'What?' It was the last thing he would have expected her to say.

'I said that your son, your eldest son, Mr Daniel Connor, is a great stupid idiot.' She shook Mick's arm. 'He shouldn't have broken it to you like that.'

'How else can you tell a man that you're taking his land away from him?' demanded Mick, body still stiff with both anger and despair.

'And you're another idiot.' She shook his arm again. 'Couldn't you have waited to see what we'd planned for you? Did you really think we'd just turn you off the farm?'

'There isn't going to be a farm any more! There's barely enough land now to make a living.' He looked down at her, so small and determined. He liked this wife of Danny's, though it had been a shock when Danny married her after courting Annie for so long.

'Well there's something else you could do here, instead, something that'd bring in a better living and do a bit of good in this world into the bargain.'

'Now what are you getting at, woman? What else can you do with half a bloody farm?'

'I've travelled abroad and I've seen places where sick people go to recuperate. I think you could do something like that here. Look at how well Aidan's recovered, with Bridie's good food inside him and this clean air blowing around him.'

She had caught his attention now, though his frown had more of puzzlement in it than anger. 'Go on.'

'Bridie loves looking after people. And I've seen you with

children. You're good with them.' She smiled. 'And you love playing with them. I think you should set up a convalescent home here on the edge of the moors, Mick O'Connor. Keep a few farm animals still to provide fresh milk and eggs and cheese. Goats' milk is particularly good for invalids, you know. And you could charge rich folk for looking after their children.'

There was a long pause, then he asked dubiously, 'Would they pay us for that? Would they trust folk like us?'

'Oh, yes. At least, they would if you let Dr Lewis help you set it up and got him to recommend you. Think of all the folk in Manchester breathing in that smoky air. I think they'd pay you well to look after their sick children. Not while they're still sick, of course, but when they're starting to recover.'

He was standing utterly motionless, his mouth half open, surprise and hope warring on his face. 'And they'd pay for it?' he repeated, needing desperately to be reassured that he could still earn his family's bread.

'Oh, yes. Of course, we'd have to build on a few more rooms, but with a builder for a son, that'd be no problem.' She gave him a sudden hug, wishing she had had a father like this big gentle man, not a selfish, sharp-tongued old bigot like her own. 'You don't think your Danny would just take the farm away from you and not work out first how you could go on earning your living, do you? And running a convalescent home would be a lot easier on a man of your age.' She let that sink in, not hurrying him.

'Sure, you've fair thrown me mind in a tizzy,' Mick said at last. 'I don't know what to think now, and that's a fact.' Then his face clouded over again. 'But what about our Rory? There's him to think of, too, you know. I'd expected to pass the farm on to him.'

'We've thought of that as well. Daniel will give Rory a

job. Once he's built the railway, he'll be starting up as a builder again. He'll teach Rory a good trade and pay him well. He'll be needing an assistant he can trust. Who better than his own brother? And Rory's a practical lad, good with his hands.' She turned round to head back to the farm, chatting quietly to Mick as they walked slowly along about the changes they would all have to make.

When Helen and Daniel left the farm, Mick and Bridie stood waving to them until they were out of sight, then he turned to Bridie and asked, 'Do you think it'll work, lover?'

Bridie nodded. 'It will if she says so. She's got a man's head on her, that one has. She's the best thing that's ever happened to our Danny. Better than Annie would have been. Helen will keep him in line. Eh, wasn't our Rory excited, then?'

'Aye, he was that. And you're excited, too.'

She nodded. 'I like lookin' after people, especially children.'

'That's all right, then.' As long as he could live the rest of his life here in the good fresh air and earn his living honestly, he didn't mind too much about the changes. He could never get enough of the bracing moorland air after the years he'd had to spend penned inside the stuffy mill.

They turned to walk back into the house, arm in arm, his grey head bent possessively over hers, her eyes smiling up at him. To Mick, they were still the eyes of the young girl she had been when he first met her. To Bridie, he was the handsome fellow she had fallen in love with over thirty years before.

'We'll go in to morning mass tomorrow,' she said as they reached the door, 'and say a special prayer for our Helen. She'll be the making of my Danny, so she will. You see if I'm not right.' And maybe, if Bridie prayed hard enough, Helen would see the light and convert. That was the only thing now worrying Bridie about her eldest son's marriage.

18

January to July 1850

That Christmas Frederick did not invite his children to visit him, and he allowed only a quiet celebration with Annie's family on the afternoon of Christmas Day. He asked John, who was now more at ease with his rich son-in-law, to explain the reason to them all when Annie was not there. 'She's a bit down about the way she's feeling.'

'Aye, I'll do that, never fear,' John replied. 'You'll look after her, won't you, Frederick? I lost her mother in childbed. You allus worry about them you love.'

'I shall do everything humanly possible,' Frederick assured him. 'And how's young Master Benjamin going on?'

John beamed. 'Eh, he's as lusty as his brother, that one is. But he favours Kathy's family. Dark hair like her father had. He and Samuel John will be good friends for each other, born so close. Not much more nor a year between 'em.'

Frederick let John tell him all about young Ben, and he was smiling as the carriage drove away from Netherleigh Cottage. He had never met anyone who cared about his children as much as John did. Nine living now, he had, and loved them all dearly. He even spoke fondly of Lizzie, whom he hadn't seen for years, and who was not the nicest of people, as Frederick had found out over the past few months. Yes, John would make a fine grandfather for Frederick and Annie's child, and John looked so well that Frederick could see no reason for him not to live long enough to see the child grow up. Anyway, John was Frederick's own age, though he always seemed older, and Frederick intended to live to a ripe old age. Marrying Kathy seemed to have rejuvenated John. As marrying Annie had made Frederick feel young and hopeful again.

Back at Ridge House, Frederick went to tell Jane about the limited festivities himself, then hesitated and asked, 'Would you mind taking charge of organising things for us? I don't want Annie to tire herself in any way,' he smiled as he added, 'but William is clearly expecting something special for Christmas.'

She looked at him in surprise, realised he meant it and nodded briskly. 'I'd be happy to do that.'

'You're sure you don't mind?'

'No, I don't mind at all. I like to feel useful.' She had helped out at Christmas before, but only to put Beatrice's plans into operation. It would be good to make her own plans this time.

He hesitated. 'Then – if you truly don't mind helping out – Annie and I were wondering how you'd feel about taking charge of the housekeeping from now on. I've spoken to Mrs Jarred and she perfectly understands the situation. Only if you wish to, of course.'

Jane gaped at him. 'Do you really mean that?'

'Of course I do.'

'And Annie – she won't be offended?'

'On the contrary. She's not at all fond of domestic duties. And just now, she doesn't want to waste her good moments on organising the household.' For Annie continued to be poorly a lot of the time.

Jane allowed her face to slip into a smile that somehow became a beam of sheer delight. 'Well, in that case, I shall be very happy to help you both in any way I can. And Frederick – I shall enjoy being useful.'

'Thank you.' He put his arm round her and gave her a

hug, unaware that it was the first time he'd ever hugged her like that. 'I'll feel a lot better having you here to rely on, Jane. Annie's still not at all well, though she never complains.' He wished she would complain. This listless sleepy Annie was beginning to worry him, though Jeremy insisted it was nature slowing her down, to give the baby a chance.

'I shall not let you down, Frederick.' Jane went away, eyes still gleaming with pleasure, and lips curved upwards into a happy smile. She discussed the coming festivities with Mrs Jarred and the cook, and afterwards, sitting in the small parlour at the rear of the house which she had chosen as her headquarters, she admitted to herself how much she would enjoy the feeling of being in control of something. Her life had been so useless and unsatisfying these past few years.

Even in her present state, Annie could not help noticing how much happier Jane started looking, once she had something real to occupy her days, and she felt a great sense of relief about that. Although Annie had taken over the reins of Ridge House with her usual efficiency when she married Frederick, the everyday details of managing a large household were beginning to bore her. As was the necessity to call regularly and ceremonially upon the other wives of Bilsden's dignitaries. They were such an uninspiring bunch. The only woman whose company she really enjoyed nowadays was Pauline Hinchcliffe. But Pauline had been rather busy lately, helping her husband to set up the small school for coaching young gentlemen wishing to go to university which she had funded to keep him happy now that he had left the ministry. There was to be an assistant master to take charge of the everyday matters, but it was Saul who would make the major intellectual input.

It had been a great shock to the congregation of the Methodist chapel when their minister resigned. Saul Hinchcliffe had explained his reasons briefly from the pulpit, and then had left as soon as a replacement was nominated. A younger man had taken his place, an earnest and dedicated fellow, who welcomed lay preachers and who had started off a lot of new activities and study groups for the growing congregation. Annie would have gone along to the chapel the first time her father stood up as a lay preacher, but her illness prevented her. Luke told her all about it on one of his regular visits, however, before disappearing into the garden to discuss cuttings with Nat Jervis, the head gardener. She sometimes wondered who Luke came to see, herself or Nat.

Annie admitted, to herself at least, that she still missed Helen Kenderby. No, Helen Connor now, she reminded herself. She had found Helen's company even more stimulating than Pauline's, because Helen had an unconventional and rather mischievous mind. The trips the two of them had made to London had been wonderful. Ellie was a dear friend, and always would be, but she had no interests beyond her home and her family.

But even if Annie had resented Jane taking over at Ridge House, it would have been too much trouble to get upset about it at the moment. Her anger against Daniel Connor had faded as well. It took too much energy to get upset about anything. Otherwise she would have started to worry about Frederick who had made two further trips to Blackpool – 'just keeping an eye on developments there,' he said without any real reason that she could see. What was he up to? He knew she wasn't in the least interested in buying a holiday home in Blackpool. As William grew up, not to mention any other children she might have, she would prefer to take them further afield for holidays, to broaden their understanding of the world. When she was better, she would have to find out exactly what was going on in Blackpool. But not till she was better. Not till she had lost this overwhelming desire to sleep.

Once she was over the first three months, Annie found that she usually felt well enough by the afternoon to sketch a little, to stroll around the grounds with Frederick, who often popped home from the mill on purpose to see her now that Dawton's was on its feet again and a manager brought in. She spent time with William when he came home from school, but by the evening, she would be fading rapidly again, and she usually had to go to bed long before her husband. She had never in her whole life needed so much sleep. But the thought of the baby made her feel so protective that she just followed the dictates of her own body. She was, she thought sometimes, simply dreaming away the months, marking time until the baby was born. But it would all be worth it, for she wanted Frederick's child every bit as much as he did.

Jeremy Lewis, who came to see her each week, professed himself more than satisfied with her progress. 'I wish all my patients would obey my instructions so faithfully.'

Annie shrugged. 'I'm too lazy to do anything else but obey at the moment.' She hesitated, then asked, 'You're sure everything is going all right, Jeremy?' She clasped one hand protectively over her belly as she spoke.

'As sure as one can be.'

She nodded. 'And how's Ellie keeping? I haven't seen her for ages.'

'She's blooming.' He smiled as he spoke, the proud smile of a happily married man. Jeremy looked a different person nowadays and had even put on a little weight, not much, but enough to take away that gaunt cavernous look that had shadowed his face for years and made his body seem all bones and angles.

'Good. I must call on her one of these days.' But Annie

hadn't called on anyone since she started feeling ill, and it was Ellie who came to see her occasionally, looking so fit and cheerful in her more advanced pregnancy that Annie felt jealous afterwards and snapped at everyone.

Frederick took to going upstairs with his wife after dinner, staying to chat to her till she fell asleep, then going down to the library again to read or drink a glass of port. He would reflect wryly on the turn of fate that had thrown him back into the solitary evenings he had endured before. But this time it was only temporary. This time he would get Annie back again.

If she survived the childbirth, said a chill little voice inside his skull. If you don't get her pregnant next year and make her ill again. You'd be a fool to risk it. He could not quieten that voice. Annie was obviously not like Christine, bearing children easily. Strange, that. For Christine had insisted that she was delicate and had fussed and fretted her way through each pregnancy, while Annie, sick as a dog most mornings, did not complain, just endured what she must stoically.

When Annie was awake and well, she still liked to design clothes, however, and the salon was the only thing which interested her nowadays outside her family. Even the progress of the railway seemed irrelevant, though she was glad that the navvies were not causing too much trouble in the town. She felt disinclined to go into the salon herself, so she recruited Jane to help her with that as well as the house. She often discussed the designs with Jane, too, soliciting her opinion of a sketch made for some lady they both knew.

One day she asked idly, 'How old are you, Jane?'

Jane stared.

'Oh. I didn't mean to offend you.'

'I'm not offended. I'm thirty-two, actually.'

'Is that all?' The words were out before Annie could prevent herself. 'Oh, Jane, I'm sorry! I didn't mean—'

'It doesn't matter.' Jane had that gruff tone in her voice, which only came when she was trying to hide her upset.

Annie grabbed hold of Jane's hand and refused to let go. 'It does matter. I've hurt you, and I didn't mean to.' She paused, looking at her companion in puzzlement. 'But why do you – I don't mean to offend you, but why do you dress so dowdily? And pull your hair back like that? You obviously have a strong sense of fashion, from the comments you've made on my sketches.'

'When I came here, Beatrice said it would be more suitable if I dressed quietly. She said,' Jane gulped, 'she said that poor relations were like governesses and should not – should not put themselves forward.' Tears were rolling down her face now, and she was gulping to try to prevent herself sobbing. 'And – and she bought the clothes for me. I don't have much m-money of my own, so I didn't waste it on – on buying others.' She tried to save as much as possible of the allowance Frederick made her, just in case something untoward happened. You never knew.

'Oh, my dear!' Annie drew Jane into her arms, patted her back and shushed her like a child until the sobs had subsided. When Jane pulled away, Annie said softly, 'The harm that wicked girl did! She's left a trail of pain behind her!' She didn't need to tell Jane that William still had patches when he was obviously brooding about his real parentage. They both knew what brought the sad look into his eyes, and they both knew that there was nothing anyone could do about that. The harm had been done now.

'I really am grateful for all Frederick's help. I don't know what's got into me today.' Jane wiped her eyes and blew her nose, still fighting not to weep.

'The same thing's got into you as would get into any

woman forced to play a role which doesn't suit her. Especially one forced to dress so dowdily. Stand up, would you? Hmm.' Annie studied Jane as she would have studied a new customer at the salon, and then nodded briskly. 'Right, we'll have to change a few things.'

'There's no need to – to—' Jane hated being obligated to them.

'There's every need. I can't have one of my relatives looking less than elegant, especially one who is helping me with the salon.' Annie nodded as Jane gave a reluctant smile. 'And also, my dear, I need something to keep Laura occupied. The poor girl's bored to tears acting as lady's maid to an invalid. Why don't the two of you try out some new hair styles? And I'll design some new gowns for you. Oh, my dear, don't start crying again! My treat.'

'It's only – because I'm happy.' Jane mopped her face and in a sudden fit of rebellion, pulled out the pins that held her hair back in a severe bun. 'There. I've hated wearing my hair like that.' The hair cascaded out of its confinement, waves of shining chestnut reaching nearly to Jane's waist

'But your hair's quite lovely!'

Jane flushed. 'My father always said I should hide it. He – he said it was whore's hair.'

'He must have been mad!' Annie clapped a hand to her mouth. 'Oh, I beg your pardon. I shouldn't have said that about your father. I'm not being very tactful today, am I?'

'I'm not offended. It's quite true. He was a hard man, my father, and he only cared about his religion. I think my mother was glad to die in the end, because it was the only way she could get away from him. He seemed to cast gloom around him wherever he went.'

After that conversation, the two women grew much closer. Annie started replacing Jane's dowdy clothes by more fashionable gowns and altering the ones she had. No need to waste them. Annie might be a wealthy man's wife now, but she still could not abide waste. The new gowns were simple in styling, for Jane was tall and her angular frame would not look well in fussy designs, but they had the usual cachet of all Annie's clothes.

The clothes which Mary Benworth was now designing for the salon were the same. Elegance personified. They suited and flattered the wearer, and were original and fashionable without becoming too fussy. This was, Annie sometimes thought, an age of fussy clothes. And fussy buildings, too. As far as she was concerned, Gothic styling in architecture was the equivalent to excessive flounces and embellishments on a gown.

With Laura's help, Jane developed several new ways of dressing her hair, ways that had Frederick calling Annie a witch in private, and had William saying openly how much nicer Jane's hair looked like that.

Jane loved her expeditions to the salon. She found Mary Benworth a charming woman and she revelled in being part of the bustle there, able to go behind the scenes and influence what went on. She had never been so happy in her whole life, and it showed in her face, which seemed to soften and grow younger looking. Her chestnut eyes sparkled with enthusiasm nowadays and her cheeks were rosy with colour.

When Mary asked her to tea one Sunday, Jane realised that she had found a friend, an independent friend, and that she did not need Annie's help in everything. That, too, was a joyful realisation and added to her new-found confidence.

And finally, to make Jane's cup of happiness overflow, there was William. He had only Jane to chat to after meals and he was an inveterate talker, so the two of them soon became close friends. Few people could have resisted William's charm, and Jane was certainly not one of them.

'I'm glad you're here,' he said one evening, pushing the

remains of his dessert around his plate and scowling at the dining-room door as it closed on Annie and Frederick. 'If you weren't, I'd have no one to talk to at all. Shall we play a game tonight?' His mother had often played board or card games with him in the evenings before she grew ill, and he missed the fun of that, even though Mark said it was a bit childish to play games. William grumbled about the situation at times, but he had accepted what was happening to his mother with a fairly good grace, for she had explained exactly why she was so ill, and had told him about the days when she was carrying him, when she had also had to rest.

'So you do understand, William, don't you,' Annie had said, clasping his hand in hers, 'that I must give this child a chance? As I did you.'

He nodded. 'Yes. I understand, now you've explained it all. But I do miss you, Mother.'

'I know, love. And I miss you.' She could not help sighing as she added, almost to herself, 'I miss a lot of things at the moment. But we have no choice. Not if I want to give you a brother or sister. We'll have to start thinking about names for the child, won't we?'

And William had been thinking about names ever since, discussing them with Jane, and making a joke of finding outlandish names. 'Jephthah. Elfleda. Lambertus. Mariabella. Marmaduke. Tamsin. Zephaniah.' He would chant them aloud and laugh as he walked around the house. But tonight he didn't want to think or talk about the baby. 'Shall we play a game, then?' he repeated when Jane didn't respond immediately. 'Or are you too busy?'

'No. I'm not too busy. But you'll have to show me what to do.' Jane spoke calmly, hiding her deep pleasure at the invitation.

'Oh, we can play a game that you know. I don't mind what we play.'

'I don't know any of your games.'

His face reflected utter amazement. 'Didn't you ever play games when you were a child?'

'No. My father didn't believe in them.' Her father had not allowed idle hands in his house. Once the cleaning and washing were finished, then there was always mending to do, or there were shirts to make, or chapters from the Bible to learn. More rarely, there were clothes to make for herself, but never the sort of clothes she wanted, always plain dark colours and unfashionable styles. When her mother died, Jane had been only fifteen, but that was old enough to keep house for her father, with the aid of one maidservant, as best she could.

On the day of her mother's funeral Jane's childhood, what little she had been able to snatch, ended completely. There had been no time then to go for walks on the moors, and even less time after her father fell ill and stopped bringing in money. They had had to let the maidservant go and eventually had had to ask their relatives for help. The Ogsden branch of the family had prospered, as the Ramsby branch had not, and Christine Ogsden had done extremely well for herself by marrying young Frederick Hallam of nearby Bilsden. No Ramsby had ever known how to make or keep money. They had only known how to endure their privations, accept the grudging charity of their richer relatives and pray to a God who did not seem to Jane to answer any of their pleas.

Until now. Lately, Jane had suddenly been granted most of what she had ever wanted from life. Power to make decisions, albeit power delegated from Annie. The pretty clothes she had always hungered for. And even affection. For Frederick had hugged her several times now, and William simply assumed she would love him and treated her accordingly, scattering kisses and hugs around him with indiscriminate generosity. Jane was family, wasn't she? And all his family loved one another. So Jane must love him. As he had grown fond of her.

Even the dog, Brutus, she thought, which was now firmly entrenched inside the house and slept each night on a rug beside William's bed, would come over to lean against her and ask for her attention. There was something almost hypnotic about a dog's soft fur and melting eyes. She loved to pet Brutus.

It seemed to Annie afterwards that 1850 was a year of babies. Kathy's son, Benjamin, had been born in November, so the year started with a new member of the family yelling and screaming at Netherleigh Cottage.

Ellie Lewis bore a daughter, Penelope, in late February.

Annie's own daughter arrived in May, a little earlier than expected.

And finally, Marianne's second son, Richard, was born on the first of July, a little late. And within the hour, Marianne was sitting up triumphantly in bed, cradling him and paying more attention to him than to her husband.

The birth of Annie's baby was relatively easy, because unlike William, the baby was very small. Frederick paced the landing outside the bedroom all night and would not move away in case he was needed. Jane sat in the school-room with William, who had, of course, been woken by the fuss. He was trying desperately to hide his fear that something might happen to his beloved mother. But he could hide nothing from Jane, and so she sat close to him, speaking quietly of this and that, and hugging him when he fell silent and fought to hide his terror.

Little Tamsin was born just as dawn was breaking over the smoky valley of the Bil. Afterwards, when Frederick came in to see his wife and marvel at his tiny daughter, Annie insisted that William be brought into the bedroom as well to meet his new sister. Frederick demurred, but she enlisted the midwife's support in this and it was done before he could prevent it.

Widow Clegg simply nudged Laura, who had been helping on the periphery of things and said, 'Fetch the lad.'

'But Mr Hallam said—'

The Widow gave her a look of utter scorn. 'It's thy mistress who's done t'work tonight and if she wants to see her lad, then thou can just go an' fetch him. An' if Mester Hallam says owt different, I'll have a word with him mysen.'

She was a firm believer in people holding their babbies, so while she was waiting for William to appear, she gave Tamsin first to Frederick, saying briskly, 'Here's thy daughter, Mester Hallam. Nay, keep a hold of her neck. She can't hold her head up herself yet.'

'I've never held a baby before,' he said meekly, adjusting his hold under her direction.

'And thee with four childer. Shame on thee, mester, shame on thee!'

Frederick stared down at the tiny wrinkled face and found that he had tears in his eyes. 'She's like you,' he told Annie. 'She's even got your hair.'

'Poor thing!' Annie was tired, but happy that it was all over. 'Ah, here's William.'

He ran over to the bed to kiss her cheek, then stand by her side, studying her anxiously. 'You don't look any different.'

'I'm a bit thinner now.' She patted her stomach.

'Here's your little sister.' Frederick held the child out for inspection.

The Widow intervened. 'Nay, mester, let William hold his sister hissen.'

William gulped and took a step backwards. 'I'll just look at her, thank you.'

'Nay, lad, tha mun hold her. Thou art th'only big brother she's got, so tha'll have to get used to lookin' after her. An' she'll want some lookin' after if she's owt like her mother.' She pulled him forward, took the baby from a reluctant Frederick, pretended not to see when the mester dashed a hand across his eyes, and handed Tamsin to the boy, all with such practised economy of action that it was done before they knew it. 'There. What's t'a think of her, lad?'

'She's so tiny!' breathed William, awe-struck at the lightness of the bundle in his arms. 'I didn't realise how *small* babies were.' He stared down at the crumpled red features, then blinked across at his mother, a very solemn expression on his face. 'I'll always look after her, Mother,' he promised. 'Always.'

'We'll all look after her,' Frederick said, putting his arm around William's shoulder, and for once the boy looked up at him with a trusting smile. 'That's what families are for. And don't you think it's about time you started calling me Father? Stepfather, if you prefer it, but I'm getting sick of Mr Hallam and "sir" in my own house.'

William looked sideways for a moment, then nodded. 'All right. I'd prefer to say Father. I don't think my – my first father would mind, do you, Mother?'

'No.' Annie spoke gently, not wanting to spoil this moment 'Charlie would want you to have another father to look after you.'

'And after all, it'd be silly for me to say "Stepfather" when Tamsin is calling you Father.' William nodded, quite satisfied now at this solution. If Frederick had pushed the point when he first arrived at Ridge House, he would have protested, but now he'd grown to like Frederick for his own sake, so it seemed all right to call him Father.

He bent his head for a final look at his sister and smiled. 'It's me who found your name, you know,' he told the infant proudly.

Widow Clegg took the baby from the boy's arms, then shooed the two males from the birth chamber. 'The mother needs some rest now.' She looked around as she followed them to the door. 'Not that she'll have any trouble resting in this great palace of thine, Mester Hallam.' At the door, she seized Frederick's sleeve and held him back for a moment 'When's that hospital going to get started, mester?'

'Soon.'

'It can't be soon enough, think on. There's Bilsden women dying in childbirth all the time as could be saved, if we could only look after them properly. An' it's about time the rest of Claters End were cleared up, too.'

'I'll start setting things in operation,' he promised. Somehow, it seemed right to give practical thanks that he still had his lovely young wife.

Tamsin gave them a few anxious weeks, but by July, the tiny baby was thriving and putting on weight.

'She'll be a little 'un, like her mother,' said the Widow, brought back, on Jeremy Lewis's suggestion, to judge the progress of Miss Tamsin Hallam.

'Perfect,' said Frederick, smiling at both his women.

Everyone in the town was surprised at the name they had chosen, which was one of the obscure ones which William had found in a book of names in the library. But Frederick had taken a fancy to it, especially as it was a feminine version of Thomas, his father's name.

'If we have a daughter, I'd like to call her Tamsin. Do you mind?' he'd asked Annie a few weeks before the birth. 'It's not only a female version of Thomas, my father's name, but it's pretty and unusual. I'm glad William found it. If we have a son, I'd like to call him Thomas.' Because there would be no other children. He'd decided that already.

Frederick didn't seem to care whether the child was a boy or a girl, to Annie's relief, and he insisted on taking precautions afterwards when they started to share a bed again. 'I'm not sure that I want to go through that again,' he said, folding Annie in his arms the first night. 'If anything had happened to you, my love, I'd have been lost. I haven't had a single good night's sleep since I moved into another room.'

She nestled against him. 'Well, I wouldn't like to have another baby just yet, but I would like to have one more a bit later, if we can manage that, Frederick, and this time I'd like another son.'

'We'll see.' His voice was soothing, but his mind was already made up. He was not risking her life again. And he would start building the hospital, whether the other businessmen of the town contributed money to it or not. Somehow, it seemed like a payment due to fate, which had been so good to him. And Hallams always paid their debts.

19

August 1850

With Tamsin still small enough to cause them some concern, Frederick did not dare leave it too long to christen her. He did not say this to Annie, whose face glowed with love each time she held her tiny daughter in her arms; he just went ahead and arranged a private ceremony with only the family invited.

James and Judith came over from Leeds, stiff but dutiful. Judith was expecting a child, but was keeping well and making no concessions to her condition. They stayed only the one night, to everyone's relief. Mildred sent her apologies, then spent the rest of the letter begging her father not to continue to exclude Beatrice from the family. He did not even reply to that part of her letter. He did not feel that he could ever forgive Beatrice.

The christening was Annie's first outing since the birth, but it was a very short one, merely a drive down the hill to St Mark's and then a drive back to Ridge House for a ceremonial family tea, with all the Gibsons assembled, even Marianne there for once.

But that didn't feel like a real outing to Annie. What she was longing to do, now that she was feeling more herself again, was to go striding over the tops with the wind in her hair and clean crisp air in her lungs. She would prefer to go with Frederick, but even going walking on her own would be wonderful. However, as she was feeding the baby herself, a longer outing would have to wait. She started pacing around the garden in between feeds and became quite friendly with Nat Jervis. It still seemed amazing to her that all this walled space belonged exclusively to Frederick, and that the people labouring in it were his to command.

What she considered her first real outing did not take place until the end of August. One day, when she was sure that Tamsin, now three months old, was out of danger – well, as out of danger as any child could be – Annie stared out of the window at the sunshine and gave in to temptation. She finished feeding her daughter, then left her in the hands of the nursemaid whom Frederick had hired, at first against Annie's wishes.

'I think she'll sleep now, don't you, Ellen?'

'Oh, yes, ma'am, bless her.' Ellen was a solid young woman whom Tom had found for them on one of the nearby farms. Having helped her mother with several younger brothers and sisters, Ellen was an expert on caring for babies. She considered herself to have landed unexpectedly in paradise, with only one to care for, no meals to cook and other servants to chat to from time to time.

Annie went down from the nursery to her own bedroom and set the bell pealing for her maid. 'Laura, I'm going out. Find my spotted muslin. I'm sure it'll fit me again.'

'Don't you think something smarter, ma'am?'

'No. I'm not going visiting. And the muslin's quite full around the bust, with a fichu that'll hide any leakages.' For her breasts were overflowing with milk this time.

Laura was disappointed. She had been looking forward to turning out her mistress in style once more. 'Very well, ma'am,' she said, face wooden. 'I'll send a message down to the stables while you're dressing, shall I?'

'No. I'm going to walk into town. It's a beautiful day outside.'

'Shall I come with you, then, ma'am?'

'No, thank you.'

Tight-lipped, Laura did as she was ordered. She knew she should be glad to have found this place as a lady's maid, but she had expected more from Mr Hallam's wife, much more. One day, she vowed to herself, she would find herself a mistress in London, one who really cared about how she looked.

Unaware that she had scandalised all the servants by leaving the house on foot and alone, Annie strolled through the grounds, feeling suddenly carefree. On the way she stopped to chat to Nat, praising the display of flowers. 'Luke says it's been a good year at Netherleigh Cottage, too.'

'Aye. It'll allus be a good year for Master Luke. He has green fingers, that one. Not often you get a young lad so interested in plants – beggin' your pardon for expressing an opinion, Mrs Hallam, ma'am.'

'Why should you beg my pardon? Who knows about plants and gardening better than you, Mr Jervis?'

He flushed with pleasure. 'Well, I'm glad I give satisfaction, I am that.'

'More than satisfaction. Your gardens are the prettiest in town, far prettier than Lord Darrington's, and everyone knows it. Mr Hallam says His Lordship has tried to poach your services from us several times for his estate.'

'Well, I do have a green thumb, that I will admit. I like to see things bloom and flourish. But I wouldn't go and work for His Lordship – not if he paid me double, I wouldn't. Especially now.'

'Why not?'

It's young Mr Jonathon Darrington as is in charge at the Hall just now, and he's a chancy young fellow, meaning no offence, ma'am. He'd ride his horse through a flowerbed and not even notice, that one would. Well, I know for a fact that he's done it several times now. I couldn't thole that sort of thing. I've got my pride.'

Annie wrinkled her brow. 'I don't think I've ever seen him.'

'Mr Jonathon usually lives in London, that's why. You'll be seeing a bit of him now, though. He came up while the little lass were still a bit delicate, so I don't suppose you heard.' For the whole household had revolved round Annie and Tamsin for the first two months of the latter's life. 'They say Mr Jonathon's gotten hissen into trouble down south and been sent up here to Lancashire till it blows over. Fair thrown the servants at the Hall into a turmoil, it has. They'd been having it easy since the old madam died, with His Lordship only visiting once or twice a year. An' now there's Mr Jonathon, pestering the maids an' getting drunk of a night.'

Nat realised that he was gossiping a little too freely and blew his nose loudly to end the conversation. He nodded to his mistress and went back to check that the two garden boys were watering the vegetables thoroughly. There'd been no rain for several days now and he didn't want them skimping over his peas. Mrs Hallam was very partial to a dish of fresh peas.

'Frederick was right about hiring a nursemaid,' Annie said aloud as she strolled down the hill towards town, breathing in the warm air, pulling a face at a plume of dark smoke belching from her husband's mill, and admiring the flowers in the gardens as she passed. 'It is nice to have some free time. And I couldn't have that without Ellen.'

She was a little saddened to see that some of the flowers were already past their best. She seemed to have missed most of summer this year. Oh, well, it was worth it. She smiled involuntarily at the thought of Tamsin, who had stolen everyone's heart. Even William spoke of his little sister in a very proprietary way, and was happy to take her in his arms and jiggle her around till she chuckled at him.

Annie hadn't realised quite how much he'd wanted brothers and sisters of his own. Her expression became very determined. Whatever Frederick said or did, she fully intended to have another child. Just one more. She didn't want Tamsin feeling like an only child. After all, Jeremy Lewis hadn't forbidden her to have any more children, as he had forbidden Kathy. She'd asked him straight out about that and he'd hummed and hawed for a bit, then told her to wait a couple of years and be very careful with herself if she got pregnant again. Poor Kathy was upset about not having any more children, Annie's father too. How he loved children! But there were ways to prevent that now that her father hadn't known of when her mother was alive, and she knew he wouldn't put Kathy's life at risk.

By the time she got to town, Annie was feeling more tired than she had expected. She went into the salon, and had a chat to Mary. Alice popped in while she was there, to deliver some more items. Alice was now fully in charge of the second-hand clothes business, running it from Salem Street with Hilda James's help, but she still delighted in producing little caps, aprons and other smaller items for the salon, things so pretty and frivolous that the ladies who came there just couldn't resist them. Annie paid her a commission on them, and for the first time in her life, Alice was saving money.

As she was coming out of the salon, Annie saw a crowd gathered outside the next door premises. Young Dr Spelling come pounding down the street and rushed into the draper's shop without even noticing the people standing around.

Mary, standing on the doorstep of the salon, exchanged glances with Annie. 'It'll be Mr Hardy, I should think. He's been looking dreadful for the last few months, a sort of pale yellowish colour, like cream that's gone off. And he's been even more bad-tempered than before. His wife does most of the serving in the shop now. No one can stand him to serve them, he's so sharp-spoken. Downright rude, he is, sometimes, the old misery.'

Two ladies left the shop, saw Annie and came across to speak to her. 'My dear Mrs Hallam! Are you quite recovered now?'

'Yes, I'm feeling well again.'

'And your dear little daughter?' Eva Bagley paused delicately.

'Tamsin is putting on weight nicely now, thank you.'

Eva's face relaxed from its tight careful expression. She had lost two babies herself. 'I'm so glad for you, my dear Mrs Hallam. The first few months are always worrying, aren't they? Still,' she beamed, 'if you're out and about, the dear little baby must be better.' She looked around and lowered her voice, though no one was near. 'Poor Mr Hardy collapsed while he was serving us. Fell down as if he'd been struck by lightning. It's a seizure, I'm afraid. My father went the same way. You can't mistake that dreadful staring look.' She glanced back at the shop. 'They sent for Dr Spelling, but he won't be able to do any good. You can always tell when death is near, don't you think?'

Annie shivered. Death could come so swiftly. Suddenly she was anxious to get back home, to check that Tamsin really was all right, and she wished that she had brought the carriage, for in spite of her brave words to Mary and Alice, she was feeling tired and reluctant to face the climb up the hill. She bade farewell to the two ladies and made her way along to the Prince of Wales. She wanted to see Tom, and afterwards he could send one of his staff out to fetch her a cab.

She stopped for a moment to stare at the hotel building

before she went inside. It was still surrounded by builders' debris, but the new wing was looking good. On Frederick's advice, the builder from Manchester had designed it in a simple elegant style to match the Georgian facade of the old inn. Tom hadn't been pleased about that, and had wanted to put in some Gothic touches, but Frederick had insisted on simplicity. And he was right. The hall for music and festivities was just beginning to rise at the rear from the black flattened earth, with men calling cheerfully to one another as they set the bricks one upon the other and mixed the mortar.

'Why, Annie, how nice to see you!'

She spun round. The last person she would have wished to see, the very last. But it had to happen one day and she did not intend to flinch from him. She had done nothing wrong, after all. 'Daniel,' she said, nodding coolly.

Helen let go of her husband's arm to step forward. 'I've been wanting to see you again, Annie.' She waved a hand at her husband in a gesture of dismissal. 'You go ahead, Daniel. I want to talk to Annie.'

Annie opened her mouth to say that there was nothing for them to talk about, then shut it again. She owed Helen gratitude, if nothing else, for rescuing her from Daniel's blackmail threats.

Helen was looking at her quizzically. 'You are going to talk to me, aren't you, Annie? I can understand you wanting to avoid Daniel. He deserves your scorn. But you and I were such good friends. I've missed you, you know.'

Annie suddenly remembered the doctor rushing into the draper's shop, his face grim. Life was too short, too uncertain, to hold grudges. She held her hand out. 'I've missed you, too, Helen. Why don't you come and call on me one day.'

Helen shook the hand, clasping it in hers for a moment

in silence, while both ladies remembered the dreadful days when Daniel Connor had threatened to blacken Annie's reputation if she didn't give him a large sum of money, almost all she owned, in fact.

'Don't bring Daniel with you, though,' Annie said, as if reading Helen's thoughts. 'Quite frankly, I wish I need never see him again as long as I live. But you and I can still be friends.' It wouldn't be the same as before, but she needed some mental stimulation. She loved her family dearly, but they were very limited in their outlook. Tom was engrossed in his own family and business interests, and Mark, the brightest of Emily's brood, was at that stage, peculiar to young men, where he seemed to think it beneath him to acknowledge that any woman had a brain. Annie had spoken sharply to him several times lately about his arrogance and condescension towards her.

Helen nodded. 'I quite understand. And thank you.'

Annie turned to go. 'I must find my brother now. I'm feeling more tired than I'd expected. It's my first real outing since Tamsin was born. Come at three o'clock on Friday, Helen, for tea. No one will disturb us and we'll have a long talk then. You can tell me about – oh, everything.'

With a nod, Helen turned and walked away. It was more than she had expected. Annie was still a bit stiff. But they had been such good friends before. Surely they could retrieve something from the wreck of their friendship?

Daniel was waiting for Helen round the corner. 'Well? Did Her Highness condescend to speak to you?' he mocked.

She gave him a thoughtful look. 'Considering how you behaved, Annie has every right to be offended. She doesn't want to see you again, but she'll receive me.'

'Well, it's a start, I suppose.'

Helen shook her head. 'I'm not doing it for you, Daniel. This is purely for me. I'll make no attempt to get Annie to receive you again. I wouldn't blame her if she cut you dead every time she saw you for the rest of her life.' Sometimes his lack of moral fibre irritated her; sometimes it just amused her. But always she enjoyed his handsome body and skilful lovemaking. Life had offered her a chance to marry him and she had seized it with both hands, knowing what he was like. But knowing what she herself needed as well.

She left him standing there, open-mouthed, and walked on towards the house they were renting just off High Street. When her father had died, they had had to leave the parsonage. And that had been more of a loss to her than her father's death, if truth be told, for she had a lot of happy memories of that house and of painting in her studio there. Memories of her mother were especially poignant. She had loved her mother dearly. With a sudden fierce surge of determination, Helen decided to get her paints out again. It was about time she did a few things for herself. She didn't regret marrying Daniel, but she was not blind to his faults and she intended to keep a very firm hand on the business and purse strings. Always.

Annie went inside the Prince of Wales, feeling exhausted now. Tom wasn't there, but she found Seth just coming up from the cellars and asked him if he could get her a cab. 'This is my first real outing and I'm afraid I've overdone things.'

'Of course I can. Come and sit down over here while you're waiting, Mrs Hallam.'

'Annie. We've known each other for a long time, Seth Holden.'

He grinned. 'Annie, then. As long as your husband doesn't object. I'll send the cellar lad out to find a cab at once. Would you like a tot of brandy while you're waiting?'

She shook her head. 'No. But this chair feels wonderfully

comfortable.' She leaned her head back and closed her eyes, hoping the lad would find a cab quickly. He did.

As she was going outside to it, a young man on a horse galloped towards them along the main street, causing the cab driver to mutter under his breath and move the cab along the street hurriedly to get out of the way. As if he had not noticed, the rider reined to a halt in front of the bright new sign saying *Prince of Wales* with a needless flourish of his riding crop. Annie stood watching him with a scornful curl to her lips. There was no need for that sort of behaviour in the centre of a town. Who did he think he was, showing off like that?

'Ho, there!' the young man shouted and a groom ran out of the stables at the left side of the inn. When he saw who was calling, the groom hesitated, then came forward looking apprehensive.

'You! Look after Jason here, while I get myself some refreshments.' The rider turned to stare at Annie quite openly, nodding as if he liked what he saw.

Seth looked from Annie to the newcomer. 'Would you mind if I left you now, Annie, love? Master Jonathon Darrington likes to be waited on by me personally. And if he has to wait, he can . . .' he paused and shrugged his shoulder, before finishing, 'annoy people.'

'Like that, is he?'

'Very. High in the instep, like all the Darringtons. But,' Seth winked, 'he'll take as much fuss and flattery as you care to dish out to him, so he's not too hard to handle once you've got the trick of it. It'll be a sad day when he inherits the Hall, though. He won't care for it, or the tenants; he'll just milk it for all he can get.' He guided Annie to one side of the entrance. 'Keep well out of the way of that four-legged devil Darrington rides till Heddy's taken it round the back. Not fit to be taken into town, that horse isn't. But that fellow likes to cause a stir. And none of his horses are what you might call well-trained.'

The groom was having a lot of trouble with the horse, which was rolling its eyes and rearing up. When offered a wizened apple, the animal promptly bit the hand that proffered it, and his master, who had been standing enjoying the spectacle, just roared with laughter.

Definitely not a nice young man, His Lordship's elder son, Annie decided. When he threw her another admiring glance, she turned her head aside without acknowledging that she'd even seen him and moved towards the cab which had drawn up further along the street at a prudent distance from the rearing animal. As they pulled away, she saw Jonathon Darrington still standing in the doorway watching her. He raised his hat, but she did not show by so much as a flicker of her eyelids that she had seen him. For some reason, she had taken him in dislike. Not because of his appalling manners, or even because of his stupidity in bringing a restive horse into the town centre, but because of something about his lean aristocratic face, something cruel, as well as arrogant.

She shook herself as the cab left High Street and began to climb Ridge Hill. She was just being fanciful. What did she have to do with sprigs of the nobility? Or they with her? She smiled. She had far better spend her time deciding how she was going to deal with Frederick, who was sure to make a fuss about her going out alone on foot.

Sometimes the restrictions placed upon ladies by their position and their husband's wealth irked her. Sometimes she just wanted to head for the moors and wander about alone. Then, when Frederick took her in his arms, she would know why she put up with things that other women would have sold their souls for, but which did not interest her, like exchanging calls with the other ladies and giving formal dinner parties where nobody said what they meant and where the men talked business exclusively to one another and left the ladies to their tittle-tattle.

She loved Frederick, loved him far more than she had expected to love anyone, but she cared very little about his money. It was much more fun to make your own. But Frederick Hallam was in her blood now. Her Frederick. And one day she was definitely going to have a son by him, whatever he said.

Cyril Hardy was dead before the doctor got to him, and he was lamented by no one but his grieving widow. This did not stop her from putting the business up for sale almost at once, but when Tom offered to buy it, she refused point-blank. 'I'm not letting you Gibsons have it.'

'Why not? My money's as good as anyone else's.' It would stretch his budget considerably to buy the shop, but he could not afford to miss this opportunity.

'Because I don't like you Gibsons, and my Cyril didn't like you, either. He'd turn in his grave to think of you having this shop.'

Tom grinned, a nasty smile. 'What about the lease, then?'

She jerked even more upright than before, her head thrown back to challenge him. 'What do you mean, what about the lease? It's got ten years to run, that lease has. Nothing wrong with our lease.'

'Better check it, then, because the lease on my sister's salon says it reverts to Hallam on the death of the lease holder. If your husband's name was on your lease . . .'

Mrs Hardy stared at him. 'I don't believe you.' She did not give him time to reply, but whisked into the back of the shop and did not come out again until he had left.

He looked round the serving area with a proprietorial air as he walked slowly outside. Dark and old-fashioned, but it had a lot of potential and it was in exactly the right location. 'I will get it, you know,' he declared, causing the young woman behind the counter to stare at him sideways, then exchange glances with the lad who fetched and carried.

Tom strode out into the High Street and up the hill to see his sister. Best strike while the iron was hot.

'Care for a little business proposition, Annie, love?'

She brightened. She'd been feeling bored all morning. 'What?'

'With Hardy dead, we might take over the drapery business. It'd fit in well with your salon. We could knock a door through the wall between them. We'd need to get someone to manage that part of the shop, of course, but it could still bring us in a useful coin or two, that drapery.'

She put her head on one side, considering, then nodded. 'Why not? As it happens, I have a bit of capital to spare. And we could do wonders there if we expanded the range of dress fabrics. Did you know *The World of Fashion* is going to carry paper dress patterns for readers from now on? And for only one shilling each. I'm sure we could find a way to take advantage of that. We don't want the women who make their own clothes going into Manchester to buy their materials. Perhaps we could offer an advisory service on home dressmaking to tempt them to shop with us.' Her mind was racing with ideas at the mere thought of taking over the drapery. Such an old-fashioned business. So much you could do with it.

'You'd better talk to Frederick about it then.'

'I don't need to talk to anyone about what I do with my own money, thank you very much, Tom Gibson. Frederick has complete faith in my ability to manage a business.'

'He might have faith, but as your husband, he'll still have to sign any papers for you, and anyway, the business is no good without the lease being renewed. And since he owns that whole row of shops, he'll be the one who has to approve a new tenant.'

She noticed an edge to his voice. 'Is there some problem about all this? You seem – well, a bit angry.'

He shrugged. 'I went to see Mrs Hardy today to make her an offer for the shop, and she refused point-blank to sell to a Gibson. Why does the woman hate us so? What have we ever done to her?'

'She hates me because her husband once tried to – to flirt with me.'

'That old sod! He didn't look as if he had any juices left in him.'

Annie shuddered. 'Even the touch of his hand when he was giving me my change used to make my flesh crawl. I always send Laura there nowadays when I want anything, or Rebecca, if I'm in the salon. That girl's got a good eye for a colour match and she's beginning to develop excellent cutting skills.'

'Never mind our Becky. It's the drapery we're discussing and why Mrs Hardy hates us Gibsons.'

'Well, there's nothing much to discuss. Mrs Hardy was the one who got up that petition to prevent me getting the lease on Number Twenty-Four because her husband—' she broke off, not knowing how to phrase it without seeming conceited. 'Oh, you know!' she said in exasperation.

'Yes, I know. He fancied you. And no wonder. Who'd have thought that scrawny redhead sister of mine would turn out so well?'

She shrugged. It embarrassed her when people drew attention to her looks. Looks weren't the only thing in life, or even the main thing. The people you loved were the most important – family. And the money you earned.

'Well,' said Tom gleefully, 'Frederick won't stand for any

nonsense from Mrs Bloody Hardy now. Not if it's you who wants the shop.'

'I don't know about that. I'll have to ask him. I daresay he'll turn the matter over to Matt Peters. Matt usually sees to that sort of thing nowadays.'

Frederick frowned when Annie spoke about the drapery that evening before dinner, and as her excitement at the prospect became obvious, his frown turned into a scowl. 'You don't need another business, Annie. I have more than enough money for the two of us.'

She didn't notice the scowl. 'It's a good opportunity, though.'

'Then leave that opportunity for someone who really needs it.'

She stared at him in surprise. 'I need it.'

'In heaven's name, why?'

'I've told you that before. For William. To give him a start in life.'

His voice was cold, and there was no warmth in his expression. 'And I've told *you* before, Annie, that I shall be happy to provide for William. I am his stepfather, after all.'

They glared at each other for a moment or two, then Annie sighed and put her hand on his arm. 'I need it for me, too, Frederick. I'm going mad sitting around playing the idle lady. I need something to do, some challenge, something to make me think.'

'You're still designing for the salon.'

She pulled a face. 'That's nothing. And anyway, Mary does more and more of it nowadays.'

'And there's Tamsin. You do have a daughter, remember?'

'Tamsin has a perfectly capable nursemaid to look after her.'

'But you're still feeding her yourself.'

'Only for a month or two more.'

He took a deep breath. He had to make her see how unnecessary all this was. 'Annie, my love,' he took her in his arms, 'leave business matters to other people. My wife doesn't need to dabble in—'

She stiffened and pulled away, setting her hands against his chest to keep him back. '*Dabble!* Thank you very much, Frederick Hallam! So all I do is *dabble* in business, is it? I didn't earn my living from it for all those years, I just *dabbled*. I didn't support my son and give my brother a job, and look after my father's family and—'

He was too irritated to consider his words as he cut into her torrent of speech. 'It is dabbling when you've no need to do it. Especially for a woman.' He had given her over a year to get used to her change in status, to get used to being his wife. He had expected her interest in business to wane gradually and die a natural death. 'To be frank, I'd rather you weren't involved in any business matters, Annie.'

Her voice was dangerously quiet. 'Are you forbidding me to get involved in the drapery, then, Frederick?'

He hesitated, then decided it must be done. 'Yes.'

She glared at him, then got up and walked out of the room, slamming the door behind her. He let her go, thinking it best to give her time to grow used to his edict.

She did not appear for dinner and when he went to look for her, it took him a while to find her, sitting in the dark in her studio, staring blindly out of the window.

'Didn't you hear the dinner gong, love?'

'What? Oh. No. I'm not hungry. You go down without me.' Her voice was cool and she did not turn from the window. Her shoulder was hunched against him, her whole body tense.

'You're still angry with me.' It was not a question.

'Very angry. And hurt.'

'Annie—'

The words burst from her, low but furious. 'You make me feel like a – a slave.'

His voice was sharper than she'd ever heard it before. 'And you make me feel as if I don't count. As if you don't need a husband.' The words came out in a controlled way, far more controlled than hers, but there was passion and anger simmering behind them.

She waved one hand as if struggling for words, as if she was dragging her phrases from the air around her. 'I thought – I really thought, Frederick – that I'd found myself a husband who was different, one who would allow me some freedom. I thought that you and I could be truly happy together.'

'And we have been happy. Very happy.'

'Yes. Until now.'

'Do you intend to throw a tantrum, then, whenever your desires are frustrated?' But he knew it was unfair to call this a tantrum, knew it as soon as the words left his mouth. Christine had thrown the occasional tantrum. Beatrice had frequently thrown them. Annie was deep-down angry, but she had not lost control of herself. Even as he frowned at her, he had to admit to himself that he admired her self-control, as he admired so much about her.

There was silence for a few moments as she stared at him coolly. 'Well I shall not be happy unless I have something to occupy my mind, Frederick. Something more than a house – or a husband – or children. You knew that when you married me. We discussed it.'

'You have the salon.'

'Pff!' She dismissed the salon with a wave of her hand and a spurt of angry sound.

'And you also knew, Annie, that I had a position to uphold in this town.'

'You're rich enough to do as you please.'

'No one flouts society with impunity. Especially women. And if they do, it reflects on their children.'

'Well, this woman is going to be the exception then. And anyway, I won't be flouting society. What I want to do is perfectly respectable and I'll keep in the background.'

She had not moved from the window seat, not moved one inch towards him. It was he who moved over to her now. 'Come down to dinner, Annie. Let's talk about this in a day or two when you're calmer.'

'You mean, when I've grown used to the idea of being a nothing and have given in to my lord and master?' She nearly choked as she said the last words.

He took a step back again. 'You're being foolish. I've never wanted to dominate you.'

'Not till now.' She turned back to stare out of the window. 'I'm not hungry, Frederick. And even if I were, I'm too upset to sit at table and play the gracious lady.'

He spun on his heel and walked away, too angry to argue with her further. From the library he rang for Winnie and sent her to Jane with a message that neither he nor Annie would be taking dinner. Then he stayed in the library, alone with his anger. He was, he knew, being unfair in one sense, because he had indeed agreed that he would allow Annie to run her business – but he had not expected her to want to purchase new businesses. That would involve a lot more effort on her part. Planning and setting things up took time and energy.

Suddenly, he remembered how once, before they got married, she had told him that she enjoyed the challenge of setting up a business more than she enjoyed running an established concern. He got up and poured himself a glass of port, gulping down a mouthful, then setting the glass on the table without really tasting its contents. 'Damn you, Annie!' he said aloud. 'Do you have to be so *very* different to other women?' But he knew the answer. She just was different, innately different. That was why he loved her so much. And he did respect her business acumen. Why else would he have made a will leaving her in charge of everything if he died?

Much later, as he picked up the port again, he sighed. He couldn't have it both ways. The intelligence he loved was balanced by her need to use it.

When he went upstairs, she was sitting up in bed reading. She eyed him stonily without her usual expression of welcome, then her eyes went back to the page.

He nodded and went into his dressing room to change, still not ready to give in. When he got into bed, she put the book down and turned out the graceful oil lamp by the side of the bed, but she did not say anything, or look at him.

They lay there for several minutes, then, in the darkness, he sighed. 'Annie Hallam, what am I going to do with you?'

Still she did not reply. She would not, could not give in to him on this.

'Can you not be content with running the salon?' But he knew the answer even before she spoke.

'No.' There was silence again, then she too sighed and her hand reached out for his. 'I wish I could, Frederick. but – but since Tamsin was born, I've felt so restless, so caged in. Once she started thriving, anyway. I've nothing to challenge me. And I *need* something to make me think. I – I can't help it. That's the way I am.' Another pause, then, 'I'll go mad if I have to spend the rest of my life changing my clothes every hour or two, calling on other ladies and running this house. And Jane runs the house far better than I do anyway.'

He pulled her into his arms roughly. 'Yes. I do understand that. But it's one thing to run a business that you started years ago and quite another to set up a new business, because if I know you, you'll not be content to leave things at the drapery as they are.' Another pause, then, 'And I can't help sometimes wishing you were a more – more conformable wife.'

She chuckled softly in the darkness, sensing that she had won, in part, at least. 'You'd be bored to tears with me if I was. You'd go off and find other women, as you did with Christine.'

He framed her face in his hands, and suddenly he was kissing her furiously, no gentleness that night, just a wild coming together of equals and a joy in their union that bridged the gulf that had yawned for a time between them. But he still did not forget to take precautions.

The next morning, Frederick asked Annie to come into the library after breakfast. 'Tell me about your plans for the drapery then. I'll be your landlord there, after all, as well as your husband. And I'll have to sign all the papers – we can't change the law, even for you.'

They settled down on two separate chairs, which felt strange to Annie. Usually they sat close together on a sofa.

'The only conditions I'll make,' he continued, 'are that Tamsin is not to be neglected and that you're to keep me abreast of all you're doing.'

She nodded and immediately began to tell him what she and Tom were planning. Before she'd spoken half-a-dozen sentences, her eyes were sparkling and she was gesturing happily as she painted a picture of all the things they could do when they combined the drapery and the salon. When she'd finished, she added, without thinking, 'What a stupid law it is, though, making women the property of their husbands! I'm glad it's you I've married, not a – a dictatorial type of man.'

He pulled a wry face. 'Well, that's one thing to be thankful for, at least.' But he was still not sure he approved of this venture. The only thing he was sure of was that if he didn't agree, it would alienate Annie. And he couldn't bear to do that. Annie was a madness in his blood as well as a wonderful friend and companion. She was the very centre of his universe.

You're a besotted old man, Frederick Hallam, he thought, just as he was falling asleep that night. Or maybe he said the words aloud. But if he did, Annie didn't hear them. She had been breathing deeply and evenly next to him for the past few minutes. She was, he decided grumpily as he tossed and turned, probably dreaming about her new shop.

20

Early March 1851

In March 1851, the Bilsden and South Pennine Railway was opened formally by John Bright, the Member of Parliament for Manchester, a man with whom Frederick was acquainted and a figure of some importance in the region.

'I hope you're not going to be long, Annie,' Frederick called from the dressing room as his valet, Jimson, a taciturn man with an unexpectedly wry sense of humour, helped him to get ready for the ceremony. Outside it was a fine, but frosty March morning; inside a roaring fire had taken the chill off the bedroom and adjoining dressing rooms.

'Please hold still for a moment, sir.' Jimson made a fine adjustment to the cravat, then stepped back to give his master a thorough inspection from head to foot.

'Will I do?'

'Yes, sir. You will definitely do.' As his master nodded and strode out of the dressing room, Jimson began to tidy up quickly. All the servants, except Cook, who couldn't abide 'them puffing great monsters', were to be allowed to go and watch the first passenger train leave the station and head for Manchester, loaded with the town's dignitaries. Jimson's master had even presented him with a ticket for the journey, together with one for Laura, so he would be going on the train too. There were a lot of advantages to working for the most important man in Bilsden.

Those less important people who had had enough wit to rush to buy tickets on the first morning they were put up for sale at the station's brand new booking office would be following their richer fellows in second- and third-class carriages. Frederick Hallam had absolutely insisted that some tickets be reserved for the people of Bilsden, and that folk of all stations in life should be allowed to participate in this momentous occasion. He had bought tickets himself for John Gibson and family, to the delight of the four older children, though Luke, Mark and Rebecca were fast leaving their childhood behind them now, to John's softly voiced regret.

Frederick hovered in the doorway of Annie's dressing room. 'Aren't you ready yet, woman?'

Laura finished her mistress's hair, which was too curly to part in the middle and style in the smooth severe curves that most women wore. She settled the new drawn bonnet chosen specially for the occasion on to the sculptured mass of curls. Its soft green ribbons exactly matched the velvet of the warmly lined pardessus, which had a double frill around the bottom, cut on the cross to avoid bulk and edged in the same ribbon as the bonnet. The pardessus was buttoned to the waist but then curved open in a short skirt over the many-tiered dress.

'If skirts get any wider, we'll have to knock bigger doorways into our houses,' teased Frederick. 'Your petticoats must weigh a ton.'

Annie shrugged. 'It's the fashion. And on an occasion such as this, I want to do you justice.' She twirled round in front of him with a satisfied smirk, for she knew what his answer would be. 'How do you I look, Frederick?'

'Wonderful.' But his eyes were on her face, not the gown.

She rolled her eyes at Laura, mouthing the word, 'Men!' gave herself a final inspection in the full-length mirror, then swept her husband a curtsy. 'I'm ready.'

Frederick offered his arm and led his wife proudly downstairs. She was looking as lovely as he had ever seen her.

Motherhood only seemed to have enhanced her beauty, and starting up the new Bilsden drapery, which had now become known as Gibson's Drapery, had put a sparkle back into her eyes. He hadn't realised until then how much that sparkle had been dimmed during her pregnancy, and that realisation had only reinforced his determination not to have any more children. He had children enough; he had only the one Annie.

'Last year the Tyne Bridge was opened,' he said, in a mock-oratorial tone as they went down the last few steps into the hall, 'not to mention the bridge over the Menai Straits. But this year we have something far more important; this year the town of Bilsden comes on to the railway map. The businessmen of all England, nay, all Europe, can now rush here and queue up to use our services or buy our goods.'

Annie laughed up at her husband, and there was a warm gleam in her eyes as they rested on him. Maybe his hair had a little more silver in it than two years ago when she married him, but not much. And he still had a young man's body, not to mention a young man's ardour. Almost as important to her, he was an excellent influence on William and he was absolutely besotted with Tamsin. Like her father, Annie believed that family came first. You didn't just marry to find yourself a husband, but to provide a good father or mother for your children.

However, Frederick was already showing signs of spoiling his little daughter, so Annie was going to watch that very carefully. She disliked spoiled rich brats. They grew up into people like the Honourable Jonathon Darrington, who had returned to Bilsden again quite suddenly the previous month.

Rumour said that he was in a black mood, getting himself drunk most nights and having to be carried to bed by the footmen. Rumour also said that none of the young maids was safe with him and that one had already left in tears. Surely his parents knew what he was like? Didn't they care about their servants? Now that the elderly aunt was dead, the Darringtons seemed to treat the town that had given them both a fortune and a position in the county merely as a prison for the son and heir. Why did they never stay at the Hall themselves? And how could they possibly think their son and heir would learn to feel a sense of responsibility for his estates if he only came here as a punishment?

The Darringtons had had their day, Frederick said, and should sell their estate to someone who would care for it properly and care for the people whose livelihoods depended upon it, too. The Darringtons did not care nowadays. Annie knew that by that he meant they should sell it to him, but she hoped they never would. Ridge House was quite large enough for her, thank you very much. If she had to run a place as large as the Hall she'd have no time for anything but her household duties.

She saw that Frederick was looking at her and realised that she'd been standing there lost in thought. She grinned at him cheekily. 'Well, what are you keeping me waiting for? Surely we should be going now?'

He threw back his head and laughed, as only she could make him laugh, then led the way outside. Behind them, William gravely offered an arm to Jane, and the two of them followed.

'I have to confess something,' Frederick said as the carriage trundled down the hill into town.

'Oh, what?' Annie asked, not paying much attention.

'As you know, the Board of Directors felt themselves obliged to invite His Lordship and his family to the opening ceremony. Unfortunately, we had a late message that Jonathon Darrington has accepted that invitation on behalf of his father. I meant to tell you last night, but I forgot.'

'Oh, no!'

'I'm afraid so. I don't like that young man myself, but we can hardly turn him away, can we?'

'Well, I hope I don't have to speak to him.' Annie had not forgotten the unease he had inspired in her the previous year outside the Prince of Wales, or the way he had stood in the doorway staring after her. And the same unease had crept along her spine on the few occasions she had seen him in town since then. A wild young man – though not all that young, he must be thirty at least – and he rode a series of horses as brutal and ill-mannered as himself. It was a public scandal that he even brought such creatures into a crowded town centre, but no one could do anything about that. He was still a Darrington, Darringtons were nobility and the nobility seemed to expect and receive special treatment and special tolerances for their wayward offspring. There was a second Darrington son apparently, Christopher, but she hadn't met him and as he wouldn't be inheriting the estate, he did not matter to anyone round here as much as Jonathon Darrington did.

'Why do you say unfortunately, Father?' asked William. 'Don't you like Mr Darrington?'

Frederick shrugged. 'He's not – er – not a very nice young man, I'm afraid.'

'In what way?'

Annie knew this answer would have William poking and prying into the matter until he was satisfied. 'Never mind that.' She looked at her son sternly. 'And you're not to discuss Mr Darrington with anyone, not even Mark or Luke. Is that clear?'

'All right, Mother. But I still don't see—'

'We'll talk about it later, when we get back home. Just remember what I said.'

He sighed and dropped the matter, but she knew he would

raise it again later. He could never leave a question unanswered.

Frederick changed the subject. 'In May, I think we'll go down to London, my love, to see if this Great Exhibition is as great as people say it's going to be.' He reached across to ruffle William's hair. 'And if he's good, we may even take this scamp with us.'

William cheered loudly.

Annie looked at Frederick gratefully. Nothing could have distracted William quite so well.

'What about you, Jane?' Frederick turned to her. 'Do you fancy a trip to London?'

Jane stared at him in delight. 'I'd love it. I've never been there.'

'Haven't you? I thought—'

'No. Beatrice never took me with her when she went to visit Mildred.'

'Well, you must certainly come with us this time then. And afterwards, perhaps you can bring this young ruffian back to Bilsden for us while Annie and I go on to Paris.' He turned to his wife. 'What do you think of that for an idea, love?'

'I think that I don't want to leave Tamsin for so long, and I'm even more certain that I don't want to take her with us. Your daughter's company manners are still not at all good, my love.'

All four people grimaced. Tamsin was proving to be a very temperamental child, that much was evident even at the age of ten months. She had a loud and penetrating cry and a mind of her own. The nursemaid Ellen, who had been far too lenient with her young charge, had recently been reinforced by an older woman who styled herself a nursery governess. Annie had great hopes of Miss Rudd, who was kindly but firm. But she still intended to be there in person to supervise her daughter's upbringing. Foreign travel, which she had once hankered after, seemed much less important than that. Besides, she had a few more ideas to put in place at the drapery.

'Where's the woman I used to know, who longed to travel all over the world?' Frederick teased.

'She's turned into a mother and takes her responsibilities very seriously,' retorted Annie. Her voice lost its humorous tone as she added, 'I don't want to risk taking Tamsin anywhere just yet. She was very ill with that cold last month. We were up with her for several nights. Jeremy says she might have a weakness of the lungs and that we must guard against trouble.'

He nodded. 'We'll only go to London then. But you're not backing out of that. You need a holiday, too. And with Ellen and Miss Rudd to look after our young madam, not to mention uncles, aunts and grandparents just down the hill, Tamsin will come to no harm.'

Annie frowned.

'If you don't take care,' he added gently, 'you'll become as obsessive a mother as Marianne.'

'Oh heavens, I hope not. I don't know how poor Tom puts up with it.'

'Bravely.'

Annie nodded. 'It's a good thing he's so besotted with her still.' Then she realised that William was listening and said no more. But her thoughts ran on for a while. At least, since the birth of her son Richard the previous year, Marianne had not managed to get pregnant again, though it was not for lack of trying, the whole family knew that. 'Poor Tom', indeed. The lovely golden girl he idolised had become a plump young matron whose sole topic of conversation was her children, and, very occasionally, the other members of her family. Tom had apparently had to insist on Marianne coming to the opening ceremony today. She cared nothing for things outside her home and hated to leave her children, though her two maids were more than capable of looking after them.

When they reached the end of High Street, the crowds were too thick for the carriage to continue. William tumbled out of it impatiently without waiting for Robert, the coachman, to open the door. At nearly thirteen he was shooting up rapidly and he reminded Annie very much of how Mark had looked at the same age.

The lad resembled his half-brother Jim greatly, Frederick thought, watching him, but he did not tell Annie that. As he had not told her about Lizzie, though he was still not sure that Tom was right about keeping that a secret. He grinned. Lizzie and young Jim were well matched, and after a stormy first year had settled down together as if they were indeed the aunt and nephew they pretended to be. May and Jim got on less well, but May hadn't been very well lately and had had no energy for pursuing quarrels, while Jim knew when he was well off and did nothing to upset Lizzie, well, nothing beyond a few boyish pranks, and as Frederick had told her last time he visited, you had to expect such things from a lively young lad.

William was jigging up and down next to the carriage, casting anxious glances towards the station. 'Come on, Mother! We don't want to be late.'

'We're not likely to be late.' But Annie let her son take her arm and tug her along to the square, while Frederick gave his arm to Jane, who was looking her best that day in a fur-trimmed pelisse of fine navy merino over a navy skirt with a braided hem nearly as full as Annie's.

Crowds had already gathered around the station, and the Prince of Wales was doing a roaring trade in refreshments, with the gentler folk sitting at their ease in the big back room used now for concerts and musical evenings and the common folk standing crammed around the public bar or sitting out in the beer garden at the side, for all the coldness of the day. Though Tom had had the wit to provide braziers full of burning coals for them to sit around, and hot chestnuts were roasting on these at a penny a dozen.

In fact, all Tom's street sellers were out in force that day, with offerings of hot potatoes, pies, lemonade, rice water, tea, coffee and platters of pastries and sticky buns. He never missed an opportunity to earn a bit extra.

Whether they were going on the first train journey or not, the population of Bilsden had seized the opportunity to enjoy themselves. The shops that could profit from the celebrations were open and all the others were closed. The mills were closed, too, in a special whole day's holiday. The other owners had grumbled, but Frederick had insisted on that, too. He had come to see his operatives differently since he had married Annie and got to know and like her family. Or maybe it was just that he was getting soft in his old age.

'Look at them all!' Frederick murmured as they moved through good-natured crowds that opened to let them through and then closed ranks immediately afterwards so as not to lose their vantage points.

'Just look at your whole town centre,' Annie retorted, as they arrived at the station entrance. She turned round to scan the small square, now modernised and improved, her eyes filled with pride. 'Even though the trees aren't in leaf yet, the public gardens look good with the daffodils and forsythia in bloom.'

'Wait till the summer. We'll have your fountain playing there then. We're just waiting for the warmer weather to install it.'

Her eyes softened at the thought of that. Dear Frederick! He had never forgotten the suggestions she'd made all those years ago when they were chatting one day in her salon, though that had been well before they'd realised, or admitted, how they felt about one another.

'And I shall call the gardens after you. The Annie Gibson Gardens,' he murmured.

'Oh, no! Please don't. I should feel uncomfortable if you did that.'

'Nonsense. As I'm making the largest contribution to the costs, I have a right to choose the name.'

'We-ell—' she hesitated.

'Go on. What are you thinking?'

'I'd rather you called them the Lucy Gibson Memorial Gardens, if you will insist on naming them for one of the family – though I'd have thought you'd have enough things named after us with Hallam Park.'

He was surprised. 'Do you mean that? After all, the gardens were your idea.'

Annie nodded. 'Oh, yes. I don't want anything naming after me, but my mother was a wonderful woman. I'd like to think of her name being remembered. I'm sure Dad and Tom would like it, too.'

'I remember your mother slightly from when she worked in the mill. Red hair, like yours. But thin. She always looked as if she hadn't been fed properly.' But so had many people when he was a young man, and there had been bad times in the last decade as well. Life could be hard for the poor. Hard for the rich, too, when they had wives like Christine and children like Beatrice. He still could not believe how happy he was with Annie. He had never been so happy in all his life. He watched her expressive face as she spoke.

'Mum wasn't fed properly when she was a child. When her parents died, she was brought here to work in one of the other mills, not Hallam's, and she had a very hard time there.' Annie's eyes were sheened with tears. She would never forget her mother, to whom she'd been very close as a child. She only hoped she herself could develop the same closeness with Tamsin.

Frederick squeezed her hand. 'Very well then. The Lucy Gibson Memorial Gardens it shall be.'

Annie nodded and it was a moment before she could speak normally. 'And the Improvements Committee will really change the name, just on your say-so?' She still hadn't quite got used to the power Frederick could wield if he chose.

'Oh, yes.'

'You know, one day there'll be a new generation of young men running this town who won't regard you as "The Mester",' she teased, pulling herself out of her memories. 'What will you do then when people don't act on your wishes?'

'I'll be gone long before that happens.'

A pang shot through her. He had already said that his family did not make old bones. His father had only lived to be fifty-eight. Frederick had celebrated his fifty-third birthday the previous month. She had known when she married an older man that he would die before her, but not yet, she prayed suddenly. It was a price she would have to pay one day, but not for a long time yet, surely? She shivered and dismissed that distressing thought. Goodness, she was in a strange mood today.

As they walked into the new station, the brass band lately formed by Michael Bagley, who was very fond of music, began playing, making up in enthusiasm for what they lacked in skill. And from the smiling faces and tapping feet of the spectators crammed into the small square at the end of High Street, the audience was not in a mood to carp and criticise.

In the first-class waiting room of the station, some of the

other businessmen were standing around, among them Tom. Their wives were sitting on the comfortable plush-upholstered benches, chatting quietly, as Bilsden ladies always did. Frederick and Annie walked over to join the men, while Jane went over to sit with Marianne. William stayed outside with Luke and Mark, who had been waiting for him. He and Jane were to travel with the Gibsons in what was being referred to as 'Mr Hallam's party'.

Suddenly there was a stir in the crowd outside in the square and a voice yelled, 'He's coming.' John Bright had arrived in the town very late the previous evening, and had gratified Tom by staying at the Prince of Wales. Bright had declined Frederick's invitation to stay at Ridge House on account of his uncertainty about the time he would arrive. He was a well-known figure in the region, a man who had helped Richard Cobden lead the fight against the Corn Laws which might have helped farmers stay richer for many years, but which had kept the price of bread too dear for the poorer folk of the industrial towns to fill their bellies easily. Frederick had spoken to Annie of those early days, of the movement which had started in Manchester and in which he had been slightly involved.

'Did you never join anything wholeheartedly?' she had asked once.

'I was too busy when I was young winning myself a fortune and since then, I've been too busy enjoying my young wife to waste my energy on causes. There are other men to lead political movements. I'll concentrate on you and our joint children from now on.' By which he meant Tamsin and William.

'And on Bilsden. You're having a big influence here.'

'Yes. Bilsden shall be my monument. A fine healthy town for my children and grandchildren to live in. What more can a man ask?' But the warmth of his eyes spoke of his major concern, which was her. The depth of his love for her still made her wonder. But it was equalled by her love for him.

She squeezed his arm, then the chance for private conversation was lost as Frederick stepped forward to greet John Bright and Annie stepped back to join Tom and Marianne.

A voice behind them said, 'Won't you introduce me to these two beautiful ladies, Lewis?' and as they turned, Jeremy Lewis stopped in front of them, his face tight with controlled annoyance.

Annie stiffened. Jonathon Darrington was at Jeremy's side, and the way he was looking at her made her want to move away and turn her back on him. But you didn't snub a Darrington in this part of Lancashire. Not even if you were Frederick Hallam's wife.

Jeremy said curtly, 'My daughter, Marianne – Mrs Gibson now – and my friend Mrs Hallam, who used to be a Gibson. Annie, my dear, I think you know Mr Darrington by sight.'

'Yes.' Annie held her hand out, reluctant even to touch the one offered to her, and to her great embarrassment, Darrington raised it to his mouth, kissing it moistly, his lips lingering just a moment longer than was quite polite. She snatched it back and took a step away from him, hoping he would move on, but he did not. He stayed by her side, chatting, and she had to admit that he was a clever conversationalist, drawing an unwilling laugh from her several times as he told witty tales of life in London. But the tales were always at someone else's expense and the look in his eyes made her shudder inwardly.

When Frederick noticed what was happening and came across to join them, she took his arm with relief.

'Darrington.' Frederick nodded coolly.

'Ah, Hallam. I've just been chatting to your beautiful young wife.' The way he said the words, with an emphasis on the word 'young', was an insult.

Fortunately, the band blew forth its triumphant finale outside the new station just then, in tune, for once, and it was time for Frederick, with Annie still on his arm, to lead Mr Bright across the station towards the platform. The station master blew his whistle and a short distance along the line the engine that had been steaming gently began to huff and puff a little and slide forward. A barrier of ribbon closed the gateway to the platform itself, and there the dignitaries were waiting for Mr Bright to declare the Bilsden and South Pennine Railway open at last.

The smoke from the locomotive smelled both dirty and sweetly acrid, Annie thought, as rags of it blew around her face. She was not really listening to the words and would be glad when this was over. Jonathon Darrington who had followed close behind them, was proving a nuisance, glancing sideways at her and once daring to wink.

After a brief speech, in which the words 'progress' and 'good of Lancashire' figured highly, Mr Bright cut the navy and red ribbons with a pair of silver scissors and led the way to the first carriage, closely followed by the Hallams and of course, Jonathon Darrington. With some careful manoeuvring, Annie managed to sit in a window seat, with Frederick by her side and Mr Bright opposite. She breathed a sigh of relief.

There were some delays while the other passengers were settled into their places by the station staff, smart in their new navy uniforms with red piping, Annie's design, of course, then the station master again blew his whistle. It was echoed by an equally shrill and much louder whistle from the engine, then the locomotive shuddered into action and began to draw the train slowly out of the station to cheers from the onlookers and hurrahs from those riding inside it. At vantage points along the track other people were watching for the train and waved vigorously as it passed.

Annie smiled. The train was full of excited voices exclaiming as if this was something unusual. And yet most of the passengers had ridden on trains before. She hoped Laura and Jimson had found themselves comfortable seats in the open-sided third-class carriage and that they would not find it too cold. She hoped everyone was enjoying this special day. But most of all, as the journey continued, she hoped she would never have to sit in a confined space with Mr Darrington again.

The train gathered speed, and the grey, purple and dark green folds of the moors were soon replaced by cultivated fields. This time the train did not stop at any of the small new stations, but on each of them there was a man in uniform waving and inclining his head respectfully to the grandees passing through. Often his wife and children were there, too, smart in clean starched pinafores and shirts, standing a step or two behind him, waving.

Then the train moved on to a new stretch of track, which it would share with the Lancashire and Yorkshire Railway, and the outskirts of Manchester took them in a sooty grasp. Two compartments of the first-class carriages were filled with Gibsons together with Jeremy and Ellie Lewis, her brother Matt Peters and Jane Ramsby. As everyone knew one another very well, it was a lively crowd and there was much laughter.

Jane found herself next to Matt Peters, whom she knew by sight, but with whom she had never conversed before. But everyone else was talking, and the pair of them were soon deep in a discussion on the changes of the last decade, especially the railways, and the difference these had made to people's lives. It was not until they were nearly in Manchester that Jane realised she had been ignoring everyone else and faltered in the middle of a phrase.

'Is something wrong, Miss Ramsby?'

'No. Oh, no, Mr Peters.' She looked round and realised that the others were still talking just as vivaciously – the Gibsons always did when they and their friends got together – and that no one had noticed her rudeness. 'I just realised that we'd been ignoring everyone else.' She smiled as she added. 'But they don't seem to have noticed, so I shan't worry about it.'

'I've enjoyed talking to you.' Matt smiled. 'I don't get away from my work enough, I think. You've made me realise what I'm missing with your talk of books and the concerts in Manchester. My landlady has absolutely no conversation beyond whether the pork chops were tender and the iniquities of delivery boys.'

She chuckled. 'She probably has cause to grumble. When I was keeping house for my father, I too could talk at length on the vagaries of delivery boys.'

'And now you live with Mr Hallam.'

'Yes. His wife – his first wife – was my cousin – well, second cousin. He's been very good to me since my father died.'

'He's been good to me, too. He took me as an ignorant lad from Salem Street and taught me how to run a mill. He's a good master.'

'I believe,' she remarked, greatly daring, 'that he's very satisfied with you, too.'

'Good. I like to think I'm paying him back.' Matt leaned his head back against the brightly patterned plush of the seat, studying her covertly as they talked. Surely she had not been so attractive before? He remembered her as plain, pale and frumpily dressed. What had happened to her? With his usual acute observation he catalogued the fact that her hair was different, her clothes were not only stylish but extremely flattering and that she looked happier. More of Annie's magic? Annie seemed to have a gift for bringing out the best in people. Except him. Annie had brought out the worst in him.

He pushed the memories which rose at that thought firmly to the back of his mind. He had vowed not to dwell on his own foolishness again, vowed too, to find himself a wife, to stop dreaming of Annie. He needed to find himself a woman of sense, and one with useful connections. Money of her own, too, if that were possible, but it wasn't always. Especially for a man who had waited too long to settle himself in life. By now there were only widows or unattractive spinsters left – unless you wanted a very young wife, and somehow he didn't. His eyes lingered on Jane's hair, burnished chestnut, and on her face, vivacious and happy. Why had he not noticed her before?

Jane felt a sense of disappointment when they began to draw up at the station in Manchester. She was sorry the journey had ended. Not that she'd noticed much about the scenery. But she'd enjoyed chatting to Mr Peters and she had enjoyed, too, the admiration in his eyes. It was wonderful not to feel the necessity to keep quiet and withdraw into the background, wonderful just to be alive lately.

'From now on,' Frederick said jubilantly to Annie as the train came to a halt, 'several trains a day will be making the journey, and at very reasonable prices for the second- and third-class passengers.'

Darrington frowned. 'I think we're mad to allow the common folk too much freedom. We should price the trains above what they can afford. The lower classes are becoming downright impudent to their betters lately.'

Bright's expression was thunderous, but he did not take up the cudgels for the common folk he loved because Frederick had already primed him as to Darrington's unimportance in the scheme of things.

'It's the end of an era,' said Frederick, grinning across at the sulky younger man. 'You'll have to expect some changes, Darrington.'

'What do you mean, sir?'

'I mean that the common folk will not only be getting out into the world more and more from now on, they'll also stop being so willing to take orders and acting like obedient cattle. That's quite inevitable.'

'Oh, come now, Hallam, you're not suggesting the poorer classes can think for themselves, are you?' Jonathon Darrington haw-hawed vigorously at the mere thought.

Annie waited until he had realised that no one else was joining in and the laughter had trailed to a halt, then she said quietly, 'I'm from those poorer classes, Mr Darrington, and I can assure you that I'm very capable of thinking for myself, and always have been.'

'Oh, come now!' he protested. 'You can't be.'

'I was born,' she said, loudly and clearly, 'in Salem Street. In the Rows. And I'm glad the world is changing so that people like me can make something of themselves.'

'Hear, hear!' said Mr Bright. 'Well said, my dear!'

But if Annie had hoped by this to quench Darrington's admiration for her, she was to be disappointed. Her spirited defence of the poorer classes had only made the admiration deepen in his eyes.

'I think you've made a conquest there, my dear,' Frederick whispered in her ear as they got out to stretch their legs and visit the waiting rooms before getting back into the train for the ride back and the civic luncheon.

'I hope not.' But she knew Frederick was right. She shuddered at the mere thought of being alone with Jonathon Darrington, but although she made sure she did not allow him to sit next to her, Mr Bright had left them in Manchester and her unwanted admirer was now sitting opposite her by the window, staring not at the scenery but quite openly at her.

During the journey she kept her eyes away from the figure lounging opposite and answered his sallies curtly. For a time she feigned tiredness and shut her eyes. But she couldn't stop the thoughts that were ricocheting round her skull. How she hated arrogant young men who thought they only had to crook a finger for women to fall into their arms. And how dared he speak like that about the people of the Rows? Frederick never did so, and he knew his operatives far better than Darrington knew the workers on his estate.

'I'm glad I married you,' she said sleepily that night as she got into bed, 'and not a puffed-up toad like Darrington.'

'What brought that on, my love?'

But she was nearly asleep and her answer was an indistinguishable murmur, so he just snuggled down beside her, smiling slightly. He knew what had brought that on, but he would keep Darrington away from her, Darrington and all other evils.

21

Mid-March 1851

The next morning Annie stretched and yawned, then opened her eyes to find Frederick lying staring at her.

'You're beautiful when you're asleep.' He reached out to gather her into his arms.

She put her hands against his chest, stared back at him and took a deep breath. She had decided yesterday that it was more than time to tackle Frederick about having another child, really tackle him this time, make it plain how very much she wanted to have his son.

'We need to talk about something, Frederick, love. Let's ring for a tea tray and then stay here and talk for a while.'

His smile faded, but he reached out for the bell pull and when Peggy poked her head in the door a moment later, he ordered, 'Make up the fire and fetch us a tea tray, will you, please?'

Peggy nodded and went over to the fire. 'It's freezing cold outside,' she volunteered. 'Looks like snow, Mr Jervis says, and he's usually right.'

'I hope not.' Annie knew that a word here and there would keep Peggy chatting and postpone the confrontation with Frederick. 'What does Cook say?' Cook also considered herself a good weather prophet.

'Mrs Lumbley agrees with Mr Jervis. Her feet's playin' up something shocking this morning.' Peggy sat back on her heels to study the fire. 'There! It was still alight at the back. It'll soon be burning up nicely.'

When the maid had left to fetch a tea tray, Frederick said nothing, just lay back, arms behind his head, contemplating the ceiling. Annie had that look on her face, the look she got when she had decided to do something important. What on earth could it be? And why hadn't she mentioned it yesterday if it was so important?

The tea tray was with them in less than five minutes. Annie dismissed Peggy and poured the cups herself.

Frederick slid to a sitting position, accepted his cup, took a sip and set it down on the bedside table. 'You might as well say it now, whatever it is. You've been fussing and fidgeting ever since you woke up. What do we need to talk about?'

Annie took a deep breath. 'Having another child.'

He made a grunt of irritation in his throat. 'We've already talked about it, and the answer's no.'

'Frederick, I want – no, I *need* another child.'

'Well, I don't. You have William and Tamsin. I have four children living. We neither of us need another child.'

'I do need one.'

He turned towards her, anger rising in him. 'We've discussed this several times now. I will not put your life at risk again.'

'I've asked Jeremy, and he said if we were careful, the risk would not be great.'

'There's always a risk.' He laid his hand on hers. 'Annie, I couldn't bear it if anything happened to you.'

She had a new argument to face him with. 'Frederick, you keep saying that your family don't live to make old bones, and yet you expect me to cope perfectly well if something happens to you. I pray nothing happens to you, but – but in case it does – I want another child.'

He gave a snort that was not quite amusement. 'This is a new tack. But it won't convince me, love. My mind is made up.'

'There are two of us with needs here,' she said, trying to keep calm. 'And there's Tamsin as well. I don't want another child of mine to grow up an only child, like William did, without brothers and sisters to play with, without brothers and sisters to rely on as they grow older. You were an only child yourself, so you can't understand what it's like, but Tom and I have been really close since we grew up, and I want my own children to know that same closeness.'

'And after this child, you'll want another one, I suppose, with different arguments to persuade me.' He realised his voice was getting louder and tried to speak quietly. 'Annie, I am not going to put your life at risk again. You don't bear children easily. How can you even think of having another?'

Annie's anger rose to meet his. 'I can think of having another child because I love the two I have now.'

'Well, my answer is still no.'

His tone was so implacable, his anger so apparent that her temper took over. 'You're being unfair now. Dictating to me again.'

'It takes two to make a child. Who's dictating to whom?'

She flung off the covers and stormed over to the window, ignoring the chill that radiated from the panes. '*You* are trying to dictate to me again. I suppose you'd really prefer a meek little wife like your daughter Mildred.'

He threw back his head and laughed, not nice laughter. 'The last thing you are, Annie, is a meek little wife. You couldn't even pretend to be meek.' When she did not turn round, he too got out of bed, but for once he did not attempt to go over and try to bridge the gap between them. 'You got your own way about the drapery, but you're not getting your own way about this.' They had had this conversation several times already. He had tried in every way he could to convince her that he did not intend to have any more children. If they had to quarrel seriously for her to be convinced, so be it. Better a quarrel than losing her.

Over breakfast they were scrupulously polite to one another, so polite that William and Jane exchanged amazed glances. No teasing. No smiles. And an atmosphere in the breakfast room as icy as the weather outside.

Later that day, Annie threw a warm cloak round her shoulders and went for a stroll in the garden. She did not wish to go into town in case she encountered Jonathon Darrington. In fact, she did not wish to do anything but convince Frederick to let her have another child. She walked right past Nat Jervis without even seeing him, which made him stare at her in astonishment. What had got into the missus? Usually she had a friendly word for everyone. Usually she would stop to chat. Now she was pacing up and down along the gravel path that ran round the small lake like a caged animal.

When the post office lad came puffing along the drive, full of importance, he hesitated at the sight of Mrs Hallam then stopped next to her and cleared his throat. 'Shall I give it you, Mrs Hallam, or shall I take it to th'house?'

Annie stared at him blankly for a moment, then shook her head like someone waking from a dream. 'Pardon?'

The lad proffered an envelope. 'This came for Mester Hallam. He's not at t'mill, nor is Mester Peters, an' they're not at Dawton's, either, so postmaster said I were to bring it up to th'house.' When she continued to stare at him, he waved the envelope again. 'It's a telegram, missus. Urgent. Shall I take it to th'house?'

'Give it to me.' Annie stared at it. Telegrams were so rare that she had never even held one before. Folk said telegrams brought nothing but bad news.

The boy nodded and set off down the drive again, whistling tunelessly under his breath, enjoying his time away from the postmaster's stern eye. He wouldn't hurry back down the hill, though he daren't be away for too long, because Mr Burgin would be suspicious if he were too late back. But the snow was still holding off, and it'd be pleasant to stroll down the hill.

Annie stood staring at the envelope in her hand. Who was sending telegrams to Frederick? It said *URGENT* on the front. Should she open it or should she let it wait for Frederick's return? But she had no idea when he would be returning. She went back to pacing up and down beside the sullen waters of the small lake, the telegram forgotten in her hand. How could she persuade him to let her have another child? She had never thought that having another baby would matter so much to her, but somehow it did, somehow it was obscuring all her other activities. It was as if something inside her was driving her to have the child.

Half-an-hour later Mrs Jarred came out of the house, a shawl thrown around her shoulders. The servants had been peeping out of the windows for a while now, wondering what had upset the mistress. As Annie stayed outside, seeming oblivious to the cold, Laura and Mrs Jarred conferred and decided that the housekeeper should go out and see if anything were wrong. 'Excuse me, Mrs Hallam, but is there anything wrong?'

Annie blinked at her. 'What? Oh.' She shrugged. 'Nothing that you can help me with.'

'It's getting very cold. Nat Jervis says we shall have snow before the morning.'

'Yes, so Peggy told me.'

'Wouldn't you like to come inside and have a nice cup of tea? And would you like me to take that telegram for you?'

Annie realised that she was still holding the crumpled envelope and that she was frozen through. 'No, I'll give this to my husband. I hadn't realised how long I'd been outside.' She turned towards the house, shivering. What had got into her today? She would get nowhere by catching her death of cold.

As they were about to enter the house, the carriage swung into the drive and drew up beside them. Frederick got out, nodded to Annie and waited for her to go inside before him.

They've quarrelled, Mrs Jarred thought, watching them carefully. Heavens, what can have happened? They hardly ever quarrel, those two, not like him and his first wife. 'Shall I bring tea to the library, sir?' she asked as Frederick shut the front door behind him with a thump.

'Not for me,' he said curtly. He stared at Annie who stared right back at him.

'Not for me, either,' she said, just as curtly. If he thought this coldness would wear her down, he could think again. Something crackled in her hand and she looked down. 'Oh. I nearly forgot.' She thrust the envelope at him. 'This arrived for you.'

He nodded and put it in his pocket. 'Thank you. Excuse me, but I have some things to attend to.'

Annie stared at his retreating back. Never had Frederick treated her like this. For a moment, her resolution faltered, then she thought about Tamsin and set her lips into a firm line. She would not give in. Tamsin wasn't going to grow up a selfish and spoiled only child. And her argument this morning had not been just empty words. If anything happened to Frederick, she didn't want to be left with only one child and a business to keep her company. She had watched her father at family gatherings, surrounded by his children, beaming at them, utterly happy in their company. She had seen how the children comforted him when Emily died. Now that she had found herself a husband whom she could love, she wanted them to build a family together as well. A proper family. That meant at least one more baby. That was *not* unreasonable!

By the time Frederick came upstairs to change for dinner, Annie had decided that nothing was to be gained by being as cold as him. She greeted him as if they had not quarrelled and after a moment's surprise, he followed suit. When he was ready, they sat in the big armchairs in front of the fire, a habit of theirs when they were waiting for the dinner gong to sound. It was the time of day when they usually exchanged news, a time they both treasured in a house full of people.

'Did you go out today?' he asked.

He was speaking rather too politely, but at least he was speaking to her. 'No. I was a bit tired. I went for a walk round the garden instead. That's why the post boy gave me the telegram.' She waited for him to explain the telegram, but he did not. 'Er – it wasn't bad news, I hope?'

He was staring into the fire, thoughtful, distant. 'What? Oh, just a business matter. I shall have to go into Manchester early tomorrow.' He attempted to smile normally, but clearly his thoughts were still miles away. 'Thank goodness for the branch line. That makes things so much easier. I'd better tell Jimson to pack my bag while we're having dinner, just in case I have to stay overnight.'

She opened her mouth to protest that there would be no need to stay overnight in Manchester, not now they had their railway, with a last train at ten o'clock, but he stood up and went into his dressing room before she could speak.

Bosom swelling with anger, she rose and went down to the drawing room without him. He was hiding something from her. Her mind flashed back to the few times he had gone away overnight since their marriage. She had thought – once or twice it had seemed as if she could smell cheap perfume on him when he returned. Indeed, she had taxed him with it once, and he had just laughed and said something about sitting in a railway compartment with a woman who favoured cheap perfume. She had accepted his explanation and forgotten about it, but suddenly it came back to her. She remembered, too, that those were the times when he had also packed a case and said he might have to stay overnight.

No, what was she thinking of? Tom had gone with him on several occasions. Her own brother wouldn't encourage her husband to be unfaithful to her, and Tom would most definitely not be unfaithful to Marianne. His love for his wife bordered on obsession. She was not sure that she'd ever like anyone to be so devoted to her. It would be too – a word she had heard used as a child popped into her mind – too smothersome. She dismissed the telegram and Frederick's trip resolutely from her mind. She was letting her anger fuel her imagination. She *knew* Frederick wouldn't be unfaithful to her.

As she turned, a thought slipped into her mind and would not be gainsaid. He had been unfaithful to Christine. Many times. Everyone in Bilsden knew that. She pressed her hands to her cheeks. No! She must stop these foolish imaginings.

Dinner passed slowly, with everyone being very polite and careful. When Annie and Frederick went upstairs, he claimed to be exhausted and indeed, fell asleep almost as soon as he lay down. She lay awake for a lot longer, but eventually she tossed herself into an uneasy sleep.

In the morning, Frederick was dressed before she awoke, and was about to leave when she came to the door of his dressing room. 'Were you leaving without even waking me?' she demanded angrily. 'Without even saying goodbye!'

He came over to hug her. He smelled of tea and jam and the cologne he always used. 'You looked tired, love.' He put his arms round her and she leaned into the circle of his embrace. His voice was soft in her ears. 'Let's not quarrel.'

She nestled against him for a moment. 'I hate quarrelling.'

He set his hands on her shoulders and held her at arm's length. 'So do I. But I shan't change my mind, Annie. I can't bear to risk your life.'

She flung his hands off and stormed back into the bedroom, expecting him to follow. When she heard the click of his dressing-room door, tears filled her eyes. He had left – in the middle of a quarrel. What was happening to them?

An hour later, she came up from breakfast and wandered into his dressing room. 'Oh, Frederick,' she murmured, tears in her eyes. 'It's tearing me apart to be at odds with you.' She had grown to rely on him more than she had ever expected to do, grown to need his arms around her, his face smiling at her across the table, his voice murmuring in her ear at night as they snuggled together in the great bed. He was not only her husband, he was her friend, her very best friend.

Something poking out from underneath the tallboy caught her eye and she bent to pick it up. It was the telegram. She stared at it for a moment, then put it down unread and walked out of the dressing room. But a moment later, she swung round on her heels and walked back in, picked up the telegram from the top of the tallboy and took it into the bedroom. She stood by the window to read it, her hands shaking slightly.

Please come urgently. Bad trouble. Need your help, love.

L.

That was not a business telegram; that was a personal plea for help. And who was this stranger who called Frederick 'love'? Furious, Annie screwed the piece of paper up and hurled it into the fire, but it caught the side and fell into the hearth. She stared down at it, then bent to pick it up again, smoothing it out and studying it carefully. It had come from Blackpool. Who did Frederick know in Blackpool? It *must* be a woman. A man wouldn't send a telegram like that. And if it were a woman – if it were – that would explain the cheap perfume, the business trips when no business was conducted. And Tom – Tom had condoned it. How could he? How could they both betray her like this?

She began pacing the room. Well, they were not going to get away with it, either of them. She would confront Frederick and then afterwards she would confront Tom, too. Tears sparkled in her eyes, but she was too angry to let them fall. She blinked them away and stopped abruptly as an idea struck her. 'That's it! That's what I'll do!'

She ran down the stairs, passing William.

'Mother, have you—'

She didn't even see him. She flung the door of the library open and went inside. The Bradshaw guide was lying there on the desk, open at the page she needed. Frederick hadn't even bothered to close it. Did he have such scorn for her? Did he no longer care whether she knew about his – her mind faltered even as she thought the word 'mistress', then she took a deep breath and bent her head to study the page. What she saw had her searching for the new pamphlet with the timetable for the Bilsden and South Pennine Railway. Where was it? They had had several copies.

'Mother, can I just—'

'Not now, William. Can't you see that I'm busy?'

'Is something wrong? Can I help?'

'Have you seen the Bilsden railway timetable?'

He nodded. 'There's a copy in the breakfast parlour. I think Father was looking at it while he was having his breakfast. Is something wrong?'

She paused for a moment. She did not want William to

know, didn't want anyone to suspect that she and Frederick were – that they had quarrelled. 'Well, there is a small problem. Frederick – er – forgot some business papers. I thought – if there were another train – that I might take them to him. I feel like an outing. I've been a bit fed up lately.'

William's voice was sulky. 'He doesn't usually forget things.' He obviously didn't quite believe this explanation.

Her voice came out more sharply than she had intended. She had not the *time* to stand here talking to him. 'Well, this time he has forgotten them. So if you need something, go and ask Jane.' She pushed past him and went into the breakfast parlour, snatching up the folded railway guide and spreading it out to scan it carefully. 'I might just,' she said to herself, glancing at the clock on the mantelpiece, 'yes, I might just manage it.'

She ran back upstairs and set the bell pealing. By the time Laura arrived, Annie was searching for a warmer gown to wear. 'Pack me an overnight bag and send down a message that I want the carriage at the door in ten minutes' time.'

Only when the train pulled out of Bilsden station did her heart stop racing and the thoughts start crowding into her mind again. 'Oh, Frederick,' she murmured, then realised that the old lady opposite was staring at her. 'I'm sorry. I was just thinking aloud. It's Miss Finch, isn't it? How are you today?'

All the way into Manchester, she managed to maintain a conversation, though she could not have said afterwards what she talked about. As soon as the train drew to a halt, she seized her bag and fumbled with the door. A porter opened it and she grabbed his arm. 'The train to Blackpool. Has it gone yet?'

'No. But it's due out in three minutes.'

'Show me where to go. I have to catch that train. *Run!*'

She had forgotten her travelling companion who gaped after her as she forgot her dignity and raced down the platform behind the porter.

The journey to Blackpool seemed to take a very long time. As Annie's anger cooled, she began to worry. Would she be able to find Frederick? Who was this 'L' who was so important that Frederick had dropped everything at her summons?

When the train pulled into the station at Blackpool, with none of the queuing down the line to get into the station that folk had to put up with on summer trains when hundreds of holidaymakers flocked to the town, Annie sat there for a moment. Suddenly she was afraid of what she might find, afraid of Frederick's anger at the way she had pursued him. Then, as a porter opened the door of her compartment and stood waiting for her, she straightened her shoulders and got out. She could not bear to have this suspicion lying between them.

'Can you find me a cab?'

'Yes, madam.' He was as good as his word. 'Not like in the summer,' he said cheerfully. 'You couldn't get a cab for love or money in the summer. You'd have to queue up and wait for one then, you would. Or walk. Lads bring pushcarts to the station then and folk walk to their lodgings.'

Annie nodded numbly, slipped him a tip and gave the cab driver the address on the telegram.

The cab stopped outside a terrace of houses. Large houses, these, of three storeys, not at all like the small houses in the Rows. Annie sat there for a moment staring out at them, fear making her limbs refuse to move. What would she find? What would she do if Frederick was with another woman? What would he do when he saw her?

The cab driver opened the door. 'Are you all right, madam? You look a bit pale.'

'What? Oh. Yes. Yes, I'm fine.'

He gestured. 'We're here.'

'Yes. Would you wait for me, please? I'll be happy to pay double fare if you do, whatever happens, but I might just need a ride back to the station.'

'You'll have to be quick to catch the last train to Manchester.'

'I thought there was a train at six o'clock.'

'Not in winter, madam. There's not a lot of calls for evening trains to Manchester in the winter. Very quiet, it is, at this time of year.' He saw that she was not really taking in what he was saying and added, 'But I'll be happy to wait for you.' He didn't offer to get her luggage down and she didn't ask for it, which relieved his mind. Folk who wanted to cheat you didn't leave expensive leather bags behind.

Annie crossed the pavement to Number Seven with her heart thudding. She didn't even notice the snow that had started falling, but stopped at the door, reluctant to take the final step, then muttered, 'Coward!' and thumped the knocker hard several times. When a boy with a face like a poor copy of William's opened it, she gasped and took a step backwards.

'Who is it, Jim?' yelled a woman's voice.

The lad looked at Annie enquiringly, but she could not have framed a sensible question to save her life. 'It's a lady,' he yelled back.

'Go and see who it is, will you, Mr H?' the woman's voice yelled again.

Footsteps walked towards the door, the boy took a step backwards and jerked his head towards Annie as if in answer to a question.

Frederick came into view and then stopped. 'Annie!' He scowled. 'What the hell are you doing here?'

Everything seemed to stand still for a moment as the two

of them stared at one another, then a voice yelled, 'Somebody close that bloody door! You're letting all the warm air out.'

'Shall I come in or not?' she asked, her knees feeling distinctly wobbly now.

'Yes, of course.' He glanced beyond her. 'Shall I pay the cab for you?'

She could only nod. The boy was still staring at her and she tried to pull herself together. She was about to ask him who he was when Frederick returned. He tried to put his arms round her, but she drew back.

A wry smile touched his face. 'Come and meet my hostess.'

She stiffened. 'No, thank you.'

His smile faded. 'You think she's my mistress,' he said slowly, his voice bitter. 'Can't you trust me even a little, Annie?'

'I did. I ignored the cheap perfume, the sudden trips with no explanations. Then I found this telegram.' She thrust a trembling hand through the slit in her skirt to fumble for it in the detachable travelling pocket. Reticules had been easier to deal with, especially when your hand would not stop trembling. At last she found it and thrust it at him.

His face had a cynical expression, as if he had judged her and found her wanting. How dared he judge her? He took the telegram from her, glanced at it, then screwed it up, throwing it on to the floor with a sudden access of violence. 'I really do think,' he said, his voice harsh, 'that you'd better come and meet "L" yourself.' Without waiting for an answer he took her arm and dragged her along the hallway.

The boy just stood and watched them. It seemed to make everything even more nightmarish to have a face so like William's watching her humiliation.

Frederick thrust her into a room halfway along the narrow corridor that led backwards from the entrance. 'Here she is! "L" herself.'

Annie's face was as white as the sheets on the bed that dominated the room, though no whiter than the cheeks of the woman who lay there, so still, so thin that she seemed at first glance to be dead. The woman sitting beside the bed looked up, her eyes filled with tears, then she bounced to her feet and rushed across to fling her arms around Annie. She started sobbing noisily, her words incoherent.

Annie patted her heaving shoulders. 'Shh, Lizzie. Shh.'

Frederick stood by the door, watching them, his face expressionless.

He was furious beneath that calm expression, Annie knew. And she deserved his anger. She should have trusted him. She should have known that Frederick would not be unfaithful to her. But she could not tell him that just now. For the moment she could only pat her sister's shoulders, murmur soothing words and then let Lizzie take her into the front room, leaving Frederick to keep watch over May, and the boy to go and get them a drink of nice hot tea.

'May's dying,' Lizzie said baldly, mopping her eyes yet again. 'She got a bit better when we first come t'live here, but then she got worse again. This time she'll not recover. The doctor said – to expect the worst.'

Annie kept hold of Lizzie's hand. 'I'm so sorry.'

Lizzie stared at her. 'I love May,' she said. 'I never wanted a man, never. Just May. We only done that sort of thing to earn a living. I reckon she'd have died even sooner if we'd stayed in that damned mill. The fluff allus made her choke.' She gave a snort of scornful laughter. 'That's when she started, you see. With chest trouble. When she was working at Hallam's. That's why we sodded off to Manchester. An' now Mr H is the one as is helping us. Seems only fair, doesn't it? But it's too late now. Too late for May.' Her face crumpled into more tears. 'An' I don't know what I'll do without her.'

Annie could only stay there and be with her sister. After

a while, the lad brought them a tea tray, roughly set, but the tea was hot and sweet and as comforting as anything could be just then.

'Who is he?' Annie asked. 'He looks . . .' she hesitated.

'He looks like your William,' Lizzie finished for her. 'An' so he should. He's William's half-brother. Fred Coxton's lad.'

Annie gasped in shock. 'Fred's not – he's not here?'

Lizzie patted her hand. 'No, love. Fred's dead. He died two year since. Mr H and Tom brought the lad to us afterwards an' asked us to look after him, pretend he was my nephew. They were the ones who'd bought us this house, so we reckoned it were only fair. He was a young devil at first, Jim was, but we all settled down together in the end. He's like a son to me now. If it wasn't for him, I'd kill myself when May goes.'

'Don't talk like that.'

Lizzie just shrugged, her face bleak.

When they'd finished the tea, they went back into the next room.

Frederick stood up from beside the bed. 'No change.'

Even as he spoke, the woman on the bed turned her head and began to gasp for air. Lizzie pushed past them to fling herself on the floor next to the bed. 'I'm here, May, love. Just lie still and let yourself get better.'

The white eyelids flickered open and after a moment May managed to focus on Lizzie's face. She smiled. 'Not this time – love.' After a struggle, she managed to add, 'Look after her, Mr H.'

Frederick stepped forward. 'I'll look after her, I promise you, May.'

There was a long pause, broken only by May's struggles for breath. 'It's been good – Lizzie, love. I'll – wait for you,' she gave a faint smile, 'wherever I – land up.' Then she closed her eyes again.

A few minutes later, she simply stopped breathing.

Lizzie wailed and threw herself across the bed, and it was the boy watching from the door who pushed past Frederick and Annie and took Lizzie into his arms. 'Come on, Auntie,' he coaxed. 'Leave us to look after her now. You've not slept for two days. Come on. You can't do nothing more here.'

As he led her out of the room, Frederick turned to Annie. 'Satisfied?'

She nodded, tears filling her own eyes, for May, for Lizzie and for shame at her own suspicions. 'I'm sorry.'

'I am, too. Sorry that you couldn't trust me.' He didn't come across the room to her, just bent to cover the dead woman's face. 'You'd better go up and see if you can help your sister. There's a neighbour who lays folk out. I'll go and fetch her.'

22

April 1851

March went out in rain and hail and April came roaring in with more rain and very few sunny days. The folk of Bilsden ignored the weather as much as they could, for they were used to it. It was Lancashire's rain that made the area perfect for cotton spinning and you couldn't grumble about something that gave you your daily bread, could you?

For Annie, every day had been bleak since they returned from Blackpool after May's funeral. She and Frederick were living together, but it was obvious that she had hurt him deeply by her mistrust of him. When she tried to talk about it, he changed the subject. Even in bed, he was not as loving as he had been, not as demanding. They seemed like strangers, strangers who had once known each other very well, but who had other things on their minds at the moment.

Annie fretted over this, feeling desperately guilty, but she could see no cure for their estrangement, except time. And it wasn't a real estrangement, she told herself. It wasn't. It wouldn't last. Frederick was still courteous and attentive, he chatted to her, he escorted her to dinners and he told her what was happening in the mill. But the closeness had gone. And she missed it, missed it quite desperately. Give it time, she kept telling herself. Time's always the great healer.

She tried to draw her comfort from Tamsin and from William, but William was growing up and was spending rather a lot of time with his grandfather lately and Miss Rudd didn't like Tamsin's routines to be disturbed too much.

The rest of the family were inevitably aware that something was wrong between Annie and Frederick, but they, too, could only wait and hope that things would settle down again.

'The laughter seems to have gone out of the house lately,' William said sadly to Jane one day, as they sat playing cards.

'Yes.' She did not encourage him to pursue the discussion. What good would that do? But it was, she thought, a good way to describe the atmosphere in Ridge House. In the meantime, she went frequently to take tea with her friend Mary Benworth, and on fine Sunday afternoons they would go for strolls together. One day they bumped into Matt Peters in the park and Mary did not seem at all surprised when he turned round to accompany the two ladies in their perambulations.

And when they met him again the following week, Jane felt hope begin to tingle inside her, hope for – she never let herself put that hope into words, but somehow, Matt's face was always there with her as she lay dreaming unchaste dreams in her chaste little room.

Easter arrived with the prospect of visits to churches and sermons that would be much longer than usual. On Easter Saturday, William sought out his mother, who was spending a quiet hour sketching in her studio. 'Are you busy, Mother?'

She dipped her brush into the paint and gently blocked in some foliage. As Frederick had suggested, she was painting the occasional landscape and had found in herself some small talent for it, so that her paintings now graced the walls of her family's homes and one particularly nice one of the moors hung above Frederick's desk in the library.

Helen had looked at the paintings one day and said, 'Nice. You're improving.'

Annie had just shrugged. 'My paintings are not nearly as good as yours and never will be. But I still design clothes for the salon and these landscapes give me the excuse for having a studio.'

'Ah. Clever. But then you always were clever.'

Annie, who found that she still enjoyed Helen's company, just grinned at that. 'And aren't you clever, too?'

Helen had grinned back. 'Yes. But don't tell Daniel how clever, will you? He likes to think himself master of all he surveys.'

Annie nodded.

'Mother. *Mother!* Are you busy?'

A hand tugged at Annie's sleeve and she realised that William was still waiting to speak to her. 'No, of course I'm not busy. I'm never too busy to speak to you, love.'

He hesitated, then rushed into speech. 'Mother, would you mind if I went to chapel with Grandfather tomorrow?'

'No, of course not.' Though she usually enjoyed being seen at St Mark's with her tall son beside her. 'Is there some special reason for that?'

He wriggled. 'Well, I like the services better at chapel. I feel – I feel closer to God there. I like the way ordinary people can get up and speak. And I particularly like it when Grandfather speaks. He talks such sense, and he doesn't dress his sermons up in fancy words and Latin quotations so that you can't understand what they mean.' After another pause when she didn't reply immediately, he said, 'Can I, then?'

'Yes, love.' It would make her father very happy to have William with him. And she doubted whether Frederick would mind where the lad went. In fact, Frederick wouldn't mind if neither of them went to church again.

William had not finished. 'And from now on, can I go to chapel with Grandfather every Sunday?'

'I suppose so. If you really want to.' She seemed to be losing her son fast lately, he was growing so mature and independent. Though not nearly as independent and knowing about the world's ways as his younger half-brother. Thank heavens Lizzie had Jim to keep her company.

William nodded. 'I do want to. I really do.'

The fervency of his response surprised her. 'I shall miss your company at church, though, love.'

'You could always come to chapel with us.'

'No. No, I don't think so.' As Frederick's wife, it was almost obligatory for her to attend the Established Church, and she had never had any really deep religious beliefs, so she actually felt less drawn to the chapel, where religion was a more urgent personal matter now that Saul Hinchcliffe was no longer the minister there.

On the following Tuesday, Annie decided to pay a call on Marianne, which would give her an excuse for calling in at the salon afterwards to talk to Mary. She allowed Laura to dress her in style in one of her warmer gowns, a fine merino in her favourite green. It was, she thought, as she pulled on the padded crinoline petticoat and allowed Laura to twitch the frills on her other petticoats into place, another obligation for Frederick's wife to dress fashionably at all times. No tramping over the moors in an old limp dress without layers of petticoats nowadays, no throwing a shawl around her shoulders and running outside. After a glance through the window, she decided to wear a cape-style mantle, a particularly warm garment. 'I think it's going to rain, you know, Laura.'

'It's hardly stopped raining all month. And we had that snow while you and Mr Hallam were away. But it didn't settle for long, thank goodness.' Laura stepped back. 'There. You look lovely, ma'am.'

'Thanks to your efforts.'

'And your designs, ma'am. You do design lovely things.' Laura herself was wearing a dark blue dress cut out for her by Annie, who was passing on her sewing skills to the eager maid, and who sometimes sent Laura down to work with Mary at the salon for the same reason. Laura had trimmed the dress on Annie's advice with braid in two colours, twisting the braid into a looped pattern around the hem. Some ladies would have forbidden their maids to dress so smartly; Annie positively encouraged Laura to look her best.

The carriage dropped Annie at Tom and Marianne's house. She sighed in dismay when she found that the nurse-maid, Bronwen, was in bed with a feverish cold and that Marianne was looking after her two older children herself while the baby took a nap upstairs. Marianne spoiled the twins and made little effort to control their high spirits. She said children should be happy, should be the centre of their mother's universe. For children nearly two years old, Lucy and David were very precocious, speaking clearly and expecting other adults to talk to them, as their mother always did. They were a nuisance in company, however, and Annie didn't really feel like dealing with them today.

'Goodness, I'd swear those two have grown since I last saw them!' she exclaimed, hiding her irritation.

Marianne beamed at her. 'Yes, they're a sturdy pair, aren't they? And how's little Tamsin? You should have brought her with you.'

'She's very well, but she's a bit young to take visiting. Besides, Miss Rudd's routines seem to be making her less temperamental.'

Marianne nodded, but vacantly, her attention caught by Lucy, who wanted to show her mother her doll. 'Yes, dear. She's a lovely little baby, isn't she?' Marianne had made a whole wardrobe of clothes for the doll, which was Lucy's favourite toy, and the little girl changed them regularly, mothering the soft-bodied doll with its porcelain face.

After enduring fifteen minutes of child and baby talk, Annie decided that she could decently end her visit now.

To her dismay, Marianne looked out of the window and said brightly, 'It looks as if it'll stay fine for half-an-hour or so. I'll walk with you along the street and bring the twins with me. They haven't been out for two days and fresh air is *so* important for young children, don't you think?'

Annie hoped that her expression had not betrayed her dismay at this offer of company. The twins' behaviour was even worse when they were let out of the house, and the few times she had walked along the street with them, the fresh air had been punctuated by admonitions from Marianne to take care on the step, or wave to the horsey, or come back at once, or watch out for the puddles.

It took nearly fifteen more minutes for Marianne to get the twins ready, for she had to lap them in several layers of clothing and cross long scarves over their chests to protect them from the raw April weather before she was satisfied.

Sighing, Annie took Lucy's hand as they stepped outside. As she had expected, the twins both wanted to run and play, and tried to pull away from their mother and aunt. The slow walk down from Church Road to the town centre was punctuated by cries of 'No!' and 'Keep hold of Mummy's hand!' from Marianne, who was having a great deal of trouble with David today. Annie kept a very firm hold of Lucy and when the child tried to pull away, looked at her so fiercely as she said, 'Stop it!' that Lucy stopped trying to pull away and walked along beside her aunt without any more fuss.

To add to the unpleasantness of the day, Annie saw Jonathon Darrington riding towards them along High Street on one of his larger horses. This one was a real brute, with eyes that rolled to and fro in a way which made the animal look wild and barely under control. It was taking exception to the traffic on the busy main street, and at one point it reared up as another carriage came too close for its liking.

She could see that Darrington had noticed her and her heart sank as he yanked hard on the reins and turned his horse towards them. Just before he reached them, a dray loaded with bales of raw cotton and drawn by great clopping cart horses came rumbling along the street behind them towards Darrington and his restive animal. The big black horse took one look at the towering load on the dray and began rolling its eyes, whinnying and straining to get away. The cart horses, better trained, ignored it and continued their slow progress.

Just as the big horses were passing Marianne, David pulled away from his mother's hand again and darted off the pavement on to the road, with a cry of 'Nice horsey! Horsey drink. Drinka water.' He ran past the dray towards the horse trough by the side of the road, chortling happily.

Marianne gave a shriek of dismay and ran after her son.

Annie kept tight hold of Lucy and called out, 'Be careful!' Cart horses were placid creatures, so she did not expect them to take exception to the small boy who was now trotting so close to them that he could have stretched out a hand and clasped the muddy feathers on their hocks.

But Darrington's horse chose that moment to start rearing again, and although his rider used the riding crop quite viciously on him, that only seemed to make matters worse. It was as if the black horse had suddenly gone quite mad. It reared and plunged, jerking its head from side to side and almost screaming as the crop smacked into its haunches.

Even the placid cart horses were disturbed by the flailing hooves and the shrill sounds of the other horse's distress. The steady clopping sound of their hooves faltered and they came to a halt. The driver of the dray called, 'Watch out, sir!' Other cart and carriage drivers reined to a halt as well, and every pedestrian in the vicinity stopped to stare.

The little boy paused just past the dray horses, suddenly afraid of the rearing black animal in front of him with its wild rolling eyes. As his face puckered up in terror and he started to cry, he stopped moving and just stood there on the cobbled street, wailing for his mother.

Marianne reached him just as Darrington's horse started moving forward, cutting in front of the dray horses as it did so. Without even stopping to consider the danger, she interposed her body between the frenzied horse and her son, pushing him up on to the pavement. All would have been well had she not slipped on the cobbles as she turned. With a cry of shock, she started falling and twisted desperately as she fell, trying to avoid the lashing hooves. One of them struck her on the shoulder and she was thrown backwards towards the pavement. Her cry of pain was the last sound she made. Her head cracked against the edge of the water trough with a dull thud that was to echo in Annie's nightmares for years to come.

Then all was silent.

It seemed as if everyone in the street was frozen in shock for a very long time, then two men ran out and caught the reins of Darrington's horse, heedless of their own danger. They dragged it and its horrified rider backwards away from the motionless body of the young woman. The driver of the dray, shaking visibly, slowly edged the snorting shuffling dray horses sideways away from the horse trough. He kept muttering, 'Oh, my God! Oh, my God!' in a monotone, then suddenly he leaned sideways and vomited on to the road.

Annie retained enough control of herself to grab David's hand and drag him away from his mother. She tried to turn both children away, not wanting them to see their mother. There seemed to be so much blood on the white face of the body crumpled by the stone horse trough. And Marianne hadn't moved since she hit her head.

'I'll take the children,' said a voice behind Annie.

Without even turning Annie thrust Lucy and David, both screaming in panic now, towards the speaker and then went forward and fell to her knees beside Marianne, calling over her shoulder, 'Someone send for Dr Lewis.'

But it was too late. She knew it even as she spoke. She had seen death all too often to mistake it now. Marianne was lying with her neck at an unnatural angle and her eyes, her beautiful blue eyes, were staring sightlessly up at the grey grey sky.

Across the other side of the street, the black horse was still whinnying and jerking about, but the two men had him firmly in hand. Jonathon Darrington had hardly moved. He was sitting on the horse's back like a man who cannot believe, will not believe what he sees.

A howl of anguish from the direction of the Prince of Wales brought Annie out of her daze. Footsteps pounded along the street and Tom, alerted by a passer-by to the accident, ran towards them, followed by Seth Holden. Tom threw himself down on his wife's body, with a cry so heartbroken that no one who heard it ever forgot the sound. He called her name, he chafed her hands, he begged her to speak to him. When Annie tugged at his arm, he pushed her away so roughly that she almost fell and then he turned back to his wife, calling her name again and again.

Daniel Connor, who had been standing outside one of the shops, came forward and tried to pull Tom away from the body as Dr Lewis rushed up. It took all Seth Holden's strength to help Daniel hold back the distraught husband as Jeremy Lewis bent over the daughter he had idolised since she was a small child. He did not even need to touch her. Like Annie, he could see that it was too late to do anything.

A hand tugged at Annie's arm. 'I'll take the children home with me,' said Helen. 'Eva Bagley and I will look after them. I'll keep them as long as you need me to.'

Annie pulled herself together and bent to hug her niece and then her nephew. 'Go with Auntie Helen now.'

'Want my mummy!' David sobbed.

'Mummy's – hurt herself,' said Annie, then she gave the two children a little push. 'Go with Auntie Helen,' she repeated. She watched Helen and Eva coax the wailing children along the street, then she took a deep breath and turned back to Tom who was like a man insane, fighting the two men who were holding him back from his wife's body.

Jeremy closed Marianne's staring eyes and stood up. Annie would have sworn that he aged ten years in that moment. 'There's nothing we can do.' His voice was raw with pain as he raised it to add, 'Will someone help me to carry her home?'

By this time other folk had gathered round, and as they were hesitating, a man stepped forward. 'I'll help thee, Doctor.'

Widow Clegg pushed through the crowd to offer her shawl. 'Tha'll want to cover her face, sithee, Doctor.'

'Thank you.' Jeremy took the shawl, but hesitated to use it, for it seemed so hard to think that Marianne would never see the sun shining again, or feel the wind and rain on her face. To cover her up was to admit that she was dead, to admit it publicly, to close her out of this world.

With a sympathetic click of her tongue, the Widow took the shawl back and laid it gently across Marianne's face, hiding the bloody temple, hiding too the bright hair stained rusty by mud and blood.

Jeremy picked up his daughter, cradling her head against him as the stranger picked up her feet. People fell back to let them pass. On the other side of the road, Jonathon

Darrington suddenly dragged the horse's head from the men holding him and galloped hell for leather out of the town, leaving people muttering behind him.

Tom had stopped fighting the two men who were holding him and now he allowed them to lead him along the street after his wife. He was stumbling like a blind man and tears were rolling unheeded down his face. Annie bent down to pick up Marianne's hat. Impossible to leave it lying in the muddy street like that. She was unaware that tears were streaming down her face, unaware that her fine gown was stained and muddy, or that people were falling back to let her pass as she stumbled along at the tail of the sad little procession.

People moved aside, then came back together to discuss the horrifying events that had so abruptly widowed one of the town's leading businessmen and had left three small children motherless.

'It's a shame,' they told one another again and again, 'a crying shame.' 'Who does he think he is?' 'Something should be done about that chap and his damned horses.' But no one knew quite what to do, especially not with a Darrington.

At the house, they found that someone had run ahead to warn the two maids of what had happened. Megan was standing in the doorway, sobbing loudly. When she saw her mistress's still body, she gave a long moan, then shrank back to allow the two men inside.

The Widow followed the doctor inside, knowing that he would want her, and only her, to lay out his daughter. 'Fetch me some hot water,' she whispered to Megan, giving her a quick shake, 'and pull yourself together, girl. You'll be needed. Do your crying tonight. In bed. They need you now.' She held on to the maid's arm until she was sure that the girl had herself under control.

Megan gulped and nodded. Like most people from the Rows she was quite familiar with sudden death, but her mistress, her glowing happy young mistress, was the last person she would have expected to see brought home like that. 'What happened?' she whispered back.

'Accident. Horse went mad. Young Darrington's horse,' the Widow said. 'Your mistress saved her little lad's life, but lost her own.'

'Oh.'

At the front door, Tom threw off the two arms holding him and like a sleepwalker followed his wife's body up the stairs.

'He'll take it badly,' the Widow prophesied. She gave Megan a last and gentler shake for emphasis. 'Think on, lass. You'll be sorely needed here.' Then she turned towards the stairs.

Megan nodded and whispered, 'I'll not let him down.' She gulped and added, 'Or her.'

Annie followed the Widow upstairs, all her concern for Tom. She hesitated in the doorway of the bedroom. Jeremy was smoothing Marianne's hair from her face.

Tom shoved him out of the way and fell on the floor beside the bed. 'She can't be dead,' he said hoarsely. 'She can't! She can't!'

Jeremy's voice was shaking as he answered, one arm round his son-in-law's shoulder. 'She is dead. You must face that Tom, lad. There's nothing, absolutely nothing, that anyone could have done for her.'

'*No! No! No!*' Tom's cry of agony echoed down the stairwell.

In the small hallway, Seth and Daniel stared at one another. 'Best stay for a while,' said Seth gruffly. 'The doctor may need some help with him.'

Daniel nodded.

Upstairs, Jeremy had put his own grief aside to try to help the distraught husband. Later he would think of it, later come to terms with it. As best anyone could. 'She died instantly, Tom. She could have felt no pain.'

'*No!* She's unconscious. She's *not* dead. She's not!' Tom stretched out one hand to caress Marianne's cheek. 'We'll look after you, love. I promised I'd look after you and I will.' He turned to clutch at Jeremy Lewis. 'Get your stethoscope out. Listen to her heart. It's still beating. It is! I can feel it.'

From the doorway Annie watched sorrowfully, her helplessness intensifying the pain. She knew better than anyone how deep Tom's love for his wife had been, but she could not think of a single word of comfort to offer him. Sobs racked her and she muffled them behind her hand. Tears continued to pour down her cheeks, but she didn't even notice them. She just waited. There. In case he needed her.

'*What are you standing there for?*' Tom demanded, turning to shake his father-in-law's arm. '*Do something! She's your daughter. Do something for her!*' His voice broke and he pressed himself across his wife's body, calling her name over and over.

Jeremy turned to Annie. 'Go and fetch help, please. He's beyond himself. I'll need to get some laudanum into him so that we can . . .' his voice broke for a moment, then he managed to continue, 'so that we can tend her body.'

Annie stumbled down the stairs to find the two men still waiting in the hallway. It didn't occur to her that one of them was Daniel Connor. They were both large men and she saw them only as help for her brother, so that the doctor could put him out of this dreadful pain that was racking him. 'Dr Lewis needs help with Tom.'

The sound of hoarse weeping rang down the stairs as Seth and Daniel walked up them.

'Nay, it's a bad business,' Seth muttered.

Daniel said nothing. He had seen deaths, and violent deaths, too, on the railway diggings, but this – a young mother and wife cut down so suddenly, so brutally – this one had affected him more than any other death. And yet, for all his innate selfishness, it hadn't even occurred to him to leave, to get away from this house of pain, and it didn't occur to him now to refuse Dr Lewis's call for help.

With Seth and the doctor's assistance, Daniel dragged a struggling Tom away from his wife's body and into the twins' bedroom. There, he helped hold Tom down while Dr Lewis forced some laudanum down his throat, then they waited for it to take effect. The waiting seemed interminable, for the man on the bed wept and moaned and fought against them, against the drug, against a world which had robbed him of the woman whom he really had loved more than life itself.

While Dr Lewis was dealing with Tom, the Widow dealt with Marianne's body. She stood for a moment staring down and said, 'Eh, poor lass. Poor lass.' Then she began to take the soiled clothing off and wash the body with tender care. Annie helped her, weeping silently as she did so, but wanting to do this last service for her sister-in-law.

When that task was over the Widow stood up and stretched. 'What shall she wear, dost think, Annie love?' Older people had their shrouds prepared in advance, but the young gave no thought to death.

'I – don't know.'

Together the two women inspected the wardrobe. At the back they found Marianne's wedding gown, carefully wrapped in a linen sheet.

'This?' Annie asked. She had made it herself and it was a beautiful garment.

The Widow considered. 'What will thy Tom want?'

'This.'

Just as they were finishing, the door opened and Jeremy came back in. He paused by the bed to look down at Marianne. 'Thank you, Mrs Clegg. I knew I could rely on you. And you, Annie.'

The three of them stared at the pale dead face then Jeremy cleared his throat. 'Would you – leave me alone with her for a while?'

Annie nodded.

'And if Ellie comes, tell her I'll come downstairs in my own time.' For this would be his last chance to be alone with his girl.

Downstairs, the two maids were waiting. Bronwen was cuddling little Richard, who had just woken from a nap. He seemed bewildered and fretful, as if he sensed that something was wrong.

Megan stepped forward. 'Is there anything I can do, madam? Is someone looking after the twins? Do they need fetching?'

'They're with Mrs Connor and Mrs Bagley. Leave them there for a while.' Annie stood for a moment, considering. 'I think the best thing I can do is to go and tell my family. Your place is here. Your master's sleeping. Dr Lewis had to give him something. And now Dr Lewis,' her voice faltered for a moment, 'wants to be alone with his daughter. If Mrs Lewis comes round, ask her to wait for her husband downstairs, will you? And – and tell her that I'll be at my father's.'

As she opened the front door, she found Frederick standing there with his hand raised to knock. She stepped back into the hallway and allowed him to gather her in his arms for a moment, but she didn't want to lean on him or on anyone. She wanted to do something, anything, to help Tom. And that meant telling the family.

'I'm all right, love,' she said, pushing him away, not knowing how ravaged her tear-stained face looked.

'Are you sure? Let me take you home. You'll want to lie down—'

'No. I have to tell the rest of the family.'

'I'll do that for you.'

'Thank you, Frederick, but I think that's my job.' She drew herself upright. 'But you can come with me – if you want?' Her eyes looked at him uncertainly, as if wondering whether the invisible barriers were still raised between them.

'Of course I want to come with you.'

His arm was as warm round her shoulders as the light in his eyes. He did still love her.

She clasped his hand in hers. 'I'm glad.' They didn't speak again until they got to the yard.

23

Late April 1851

When the carriage stopped at the junk yard, Frederick helped Annie down without waiting for the coachman. The two of them hurried inside, where they found John and his two sons sorting through a load of junk. Tom rarely bothered about the day-to-day business of the yard now, leaving more and more of it to John.

'Eh, love! How nice to . . .' John's voice trailed away. 'Summat's wrong. Tell us, love. Tell us straight out.' He braced his shoulders, as if waiting for a blow.

'It's Marianne—'

'Not Kathy?' He let his breath out in an involuntary whoosh of relief.

She understood his fear that he would lose yet another wife or child, so she hugged him close and said in a dry sad voice. 'No. It's not your wife or your children this time, Dad. It's Marianne.'

'Our Marianne? Is she hurt, then?'

Mark and Luke were standing opposite, with the same expression on their faces as their father had. It scarred you, Annie thought, as she searched desperately for a way to soften the news. Living in the Rows, losing your loved ones, it scarred you for ever.

Frederick's arm was around her shoulders again. She looked up at him gratefully then looked back at her father and said gently, 'Marianne's dead.'

By this time, Mark and Luke were standing close to John,

as if to support their father by their closeness. Bewildered, John kept shaking his head. 'Nay, I can scarce take it in. Scarce credit it.' There was silence for a moment, then he added, 'Eh, "man's days are but grass. As a flower of the field, so he flourisheth, and so he dies, too." I've seen it time and oft, but I never thought to see that dear dear lass perish so young.' He paused to knuckle away a tear and added, 'How did it happen, Annie, love?'

Again, Frederick's arm gave her strength, but she told how it had happened herself, her voice tight and thin with the effort of controlling it.

Afterwards, they left John with the task of telling Kathy, who would, he was sure, want to care for Marianne's children until Tom could sort things out.

'We'll see to the yard,' said Mark gruffly. 'You get off home, Dad. Stay there with Kathy. She might need you.'

Beside him, Luke nodded, but the expression on his face was so strange and determined, that if she had not felt quite so sad and weary, Annie would have asked him what was wrong. But she did feel weary, her limbs leaden, her thoughts a blur of horror and death. This time, when Frederick insisted on driving her home, she acquiesced, leaning against him as the carriage horses made their way slowly up the hill.

And then it was all to face again, as Jane looked out of the window to see who was calling, saw Frederick helping a tear-stained Annie from the carriage and came running out to see what was wrong.

'I'll go and fetch William home from school,' Jane said. 'He needs to be told gently, and not by another lad gloating at the horror of it.'

'I should do that,' said Annie.

'You've done your share.' Frederick nodded to Jane. 'The carriage is waiting. Thank you, Jane, love.' Then he drew Annie into the house. There, as reaction set in and she started shaking, he swept her into his arms and carried her up to the bedroom.

The next day, Tom woke up to the horror of realising what had happened. One groan escaped him, then he clamped his mouth shut and threw his arm across his eyes. Obscene that the sun should shine today, with Marianne— He closed his mind to all thought for a moment and lay there, concentrating on self-control, grateful that no one was there to see his struggle. It was, perhaps, the hardest thing he had ever done in his life, mastering the grief that had hollowed him out, left him like an empty husk.

Jeremy, who had stayed the night, sleeping downstairs on the sofa fully dressed in case Tom needed him, came out of the parlour when he heard someone moving about upstairs. But it was a dry-eyed young man, with a face set in stony lines, who emerged from the spare bedroom.

Tom did not notice the figure below him, but went into the room where Marianne was lying among flowers and candles, beautiful in her wedding gown, all traces of the accident gone, hidden under a careful drape of golden hair.

This time Tom did not fall down and weep. He simply stood there, looking. He stood there for so long, that Jeremy, who had come quietly up the stairs, kept glancing sideways at him.

'Have any arrangements been made for the funeral?' Tom asked at last.

'We ordered the best Purnhams can provide. I – didn't choose a casket. I thought you might want to . . .'

Tom nodded.

'And about mourning. Ellie went to order it for you. The tailor will have a suit ready for you to try on by now.'

Tom gave a croak of laughter. 'What difference will that

make?' He fell silent again, then shrugged. 'I suppose it's the thing to do. What about the children?'

'They're with Kathy now. Helen Connor took the twins home after the accident—'

'And Daniel Connor helped hold me down,' jeered Tom. 'That's a turnabout for the books, isn't it? That fellow helping us Gibsons?'

He turned on his heel and walked heavily down the stairs, making Megan jump in shock as he appeared in the kitchen doorway. 'I need some breakfast, Megan. Quickly. It doesn't matter what.'

Jeremy followed him into a dining room from which all trace of Marianne had been banished by a weeping Megan.

'Where's her embroidery?' demanded Tom.

'Megan put it away,' Jeremy said. 'We thought—'

'Then tell her to get it out again.'

'But—'

'Never mind. I'll tell her.' Tom sat down at the table, drumming his fingers impatiently. Jeremy sat down opposite him, as worried about this rigid self-control as he had been about the wild grief of the previous day.

When Megan set a plate in front of her master, he nodded his thanks, then said, 'Put her embroidery back. Put all her things back. Her books, her music. Everything.' He started eating mechanically, not seeming to notice what was on his plate.

Megan looked sideways at Dr Lewis, and when he nodded, she left the room and did as her master had ordered.

When Tom had finished, he stood up. 'I'll go and fetch the children back.'

'Kathy's happy to—'

'They're my children, this is their home and they're staying here with me.' He walked out of the room before Jeremy could say anything else. By the time Jeremy got to the door,

Tom was vanishing into the distance, hatless and coatless, although the sunshine had not had time to warm things up and everyone else was still muffled in their winter things.

Face thoughtful, Jeremy went to have a quiet word with Megan. He shivered as he left the house, glad to be going home to the comfort of Ellie's warm embrace.

But when little Catherine ran to greet him, it was all he could do not to flinch away, and as soon as he could, he told Hetty to take her up to the nursery. Just so had Marianne looked when she was three years old. For a moment, he cursed Annabelle, that she had left him with a living legacy to exacerbate his grief for his own daughter.

The funeral was the most magnificent affair that Bilsden had ever seen. Plumes, mourning attendants, trailing black everywhere. And at the centre of it, Tom, with a face devoid of expression, even when he spoke to his children. He mostly ignored the people who tried to talk to him, to offer their condolences, but he held the twins' hands so firmly that they could only trot along beside him after the service and stand next to the yawning grave.

'What's in the box?' asked David. 'Daddy, what's in the box?'

'Your mother.'

'No! She's not! She's not!' David began to sob and when Tom shook him roughly, the lad screamed, which set Lucy off weeping, too. Both twins were to have nightmares about that big box being covered with soil for years to come.

Only when John came to put an arm around Tom's shoulders did he let go of the children's hands and allow Kathy to lead them away. And even then, there was no moisture in his eyes, only a dreadful blind sort of look that nearly broke John's heart. He understood how Tom was feeling, oh, yes, he understood better than anyone. Just so had he felt when he lost his first wife. And there was no comfort that anyone could offer. No comfort save the Lord. But Tom did not even attend church and John knew better than to try to bring him to salvation while the first pangs of grief were still searing him.

After the funeral, Kathy again offered to have the three motherless children, but Tom refused. 'They have a home.'

'But—'

He simply walked out of the room. It was, he had found, as good a strategy as any to deal with unwanted sympathy.

That night he called Megan in. 'I'm going out. Keep an eye on the children.'

Something about the resolution on his face made her ask, 'Where are you going, sir?'

'To beat the Honourable Jonathon Darrington senseless.'

Then he was gone before she could even exclaim in shock.

She told Bronwen to mind the children, threw a shawl around her shoulders and started running up the hill. Surely Annie or Mr Hallam would be able to talk some sense into her master. And Mr Hallam had a carriage, so he could catch up with Tom.

Just as dinner was ending at Ridge House, a subdued meal with everyone rather silent and even William lacking in appetite, there was a banging on the front door, such a loud banging that Frederick stood up and ran to see who it was himself, pushing Winnie out of the way.

Megan nearly fell through the door, gasping for breath. 'He's gone – gone to kill him – you've got to stop him.' She clutched at Frederick. 'Stop him!' she repeated. 'You've got to stop him.'

'Calm down!' he ordered, holding her at arm's length. 'Catch your breath, girl, then tell me quietly what's wrong.'

Annie was standing beside him by this time.

Megan looked at them both, sucked in air and said, 'It's Mr Gibson. He's gone to kill Mr Darrington.'

Frederick and Annie stared at one another. 'I'd feel the same,' he said. 'But we have to stop him.'

'I'm coming with you,' she declared.

He just nodded. 'Winnie, go and tell Robert to get the carriage out as quickly as he can.'

Within ten minutes he and Annie were rattling along the road that led to the edge of the moors where the Hall stood in solitary splendour. It was only a mile or so along the road, but it was a different world entirely from Bilsden, a world that guarded its borders most fiercely. Not a yard of Darrington land had ever been sold to the townsfolk, hungry as they were for space to live and build their businesses. The Darrington estate had the same boundaries as it had had a hundred years previously. Even the servants at the Hall considered themselves different to other folk, a cut above those who toiled in the smoky valley below.

Sibbson the gatekeeper rushed out and stood there uncertainly as the carriage came to a noisy halt, its lamps sending small pools of light into the darkness of a cloudy night. Robert bellowed to him to open the gates, but Sibbson did not move. He felt a bit jumpy tonight. All the servants did, for they knew what had happened in the town. Bad news travels fast.

He had heard a noise earlier and come rushing out, but he had not been able to find out what had caused it. A fox probably, or one of the stable dogs. And if it was something else, well, the servants at the house could deal with it. He did not admit, even to himself, that if someone from the town wanted to come and confront the young master, maybe give him a good thumping, then Sibbson wished that person luck. The young master was popular with no one, and never had been. As for Sibbson, his orders were to keep the gates closed, to keep everyone out, and that's what he was doing.

Frederick put his head out of the window. 'It's Frederick Hallam. I need to see Mr Darrington most urgently. It's a matter of life and death.'

'But he told me not to let anyone in.' From the gatekeeper's expression, he was well aware of what had happened in the town.

Frederick lost patience. They were here to save Darrington, though he didn't deserve it. How could even he have been so insensitive as to send flowers to the funeral? For a moment at the church when one of Purnham's black-clad funeral attendants looked at the label of the newly delivered flowers and said, 'Darrington', everyone had thought that Tom was going to explode with fury, then he had moved forward, thrown the flowers to the ground, stamped on them and torn up the card that had come with them.

'If you don't open those gates,' said Annie now, surprising everyone, 'then I'll get down from the carriage myself and do it. And you won't stop me. This is an emergency. Someone is trying to – to attack Mr Darrington.'

So fierce did she sound that the gatekeeper did as he was told, then he stood in the middle of the driveway, watching the rear lamp of the carriage bob away through the darkness towards the house. 'Well, I hope whoever it is gets there first and knocks that devil senseless,' he muttered. 'It's about time someone did.' The young master's horses had already injured the stableboys and put the fear of death into any servant who happened to be around when Master Jonathon rode out.

At the Hall, Frederick and Annie found the front door open and a group of elderly servants clustered at one side of the hallway.

Frederick raced up the steps, with Annie following closely

behind, and pushed through the crowd. 'What's happened?' he demanded.

There was a hubbub of voices as everyone tried at once to tell him about the madman who had pushed his way into the house and slammed his way into the library.

In the end the butler called for silence and said in a voice which wobbled a little. 'The intruder – went into the library, sir. And he locked the door behind him.'

'How long ago? Has there been any sound from inside?'

'Only a few minutes ago, sir. And we've heard voices, but – but no sound of – of violence.' He was ashen and shaky. He was an old man, pensioned off to the Lancashire estate. Even in his heyday, he would not have known how to cope with this

'Did you not try to go in there?'

Not one of the servants would meet Frederick's eyes. He gave an exclamation of annoyance and went forward to thump on the door 'Tom! Tom, come out!'

Annie added her voice to his. 'Tom, your children need you. Don't do anything stupid.'

There was a smashing sound, then silence. Just as Frederick was about to suggest they go outside and try to get into the library through the windows, footsteps came towards them. A key turned in the lock and the door opened slowly.

Tom was standing there, wild-eyed and haggard. 'He won't fight. He just sits there and lets me thump him.' He saw Annie and took an uncertain step towards her. 'I was going to beat him senseless. But I can't – I can't beat a man who won't defend himself.' He turned round to shout in a voice filled with scorn and loathing. 'You're a coward, Darrington, for all your breeding. A bloody coward. As well as a murderer.'

Frederick pushed past him into the room. Darrington was sitting in a chair by the fire, dead drunk by the looks of him.

He turned his eyes towards the newcomer, then shut them and covered his face with one shaking hand.

Turning round, Frederick beckoned to the butler, who came forward with obvious reluctance. 'As you can see, my brother-in-law hasn't harmed Mr Darrington.'

'No, sir.' Pity, the butler thought, but his training held and he did not voice the words.

'I'll take my brother-in-law home now.' Frederick looked at Tom, who had sagged against the wall, as if he hadn't the strength left to remain upright. Annie was beside her brother, one hand on his shoulder.

'Yes, sir.' The butler hesitated, then pulled at Frederick's sleeve. 'Is it true? Did Master Jonathon really kill a young woman?'

'His horse did.'

'And – she had three small children?'

Frederick nodded, wondering where this was all leading. He wanted to take poor Tom home, but at the same time he knew it was necessary to get the servants on their side in case anything came of this invasion of private property.

'Her Ladyship will wish to know, you see, sir. She – she is already displeased with Master Jonathon. She will be most distressed.'

Frederick nodded grimly. 'Young Darrington is a scoundrel and a reprobate. He'll hear more of this. I'll make sure the magistrate deals with it.' But the magistrate was appointed by folk like the Darringtons. He would probably record a verdict of Death by Misadventure and merely reprimand Darrington for not controlling his horse.

The butler nodded. 'He's – a difficult young man, sir. Wild. Always has been.'

When the old man cleared his throat, obviously wishing to say something further, Frederick tried to contain his impatience.

'Master Jonathon – he shot the horse. When he got back.'

'Pity someone didn't shoot him, too.' Frederick patted the butler's shoulder, then went across to take his brother-in-law's arm and urge him to leave. Together he and Annie led Tom outside to the carriage.

On the way back Tom didn't say a word till he was getting out of the carriage. 'I wish that bugger had fought back.'

'You might have done something you'd regret.'

Tom's voice was too soft for someone with that wild look in his eyes. 'Oh, I'd not have regretted it, believe me.' But he hadn't been able to beat up a drunken man who just stared at him with dead eyes, stared as if he had no humanity left within him, as if he had lost his soul long ago.

The next day, the people of Bilsden heard that the Honourable Jonathon Darrington had shot himself in the head, leaving a note for his parents. From the smallest maid-servant to the social leaders of the town, everyone was in agreement that the fellow would be no loss to the district. Good riddance to such as him. But it wouldn't help those motherless children, would it?

Tom refused to discuss the matter. He was glad Darrington was dead. But it wouldn't bring Marianne back. It wouldn't fill the empty evening hours which yawned before him every day, and it wouldn't give the distressed children who sobbed themselves to sleep every night a mother again.

As the days passed, Tom grew very gaunt, though Megan assured his family that he was eating well enough.

'But he's not sleeping much,' she added, looking over her shoulder as if she half-expected him to appear and chastise her for gossiping. 'He's up until all hours of the night.'

'What does he do?' Annie asked.

'He reads the Bible. Over and over. And he reads it aloud to the children when he puts them to bed. They're getting so that they're frightened to see him pick up that big black book of an evening. Richard's too young to notice, bless him, but the twins,' she hesitated, then said in a rush, 'it's getting so that they're frightened of their own father. He reads so loudly and with such a long face that they have nightmares afterwards. Nor he won't allow them to have a nightlight. Says they're dangerous things and he's not risking losing the children as well.' She looked at Annie helplessly. 'What can I do, Mrs Hallam?'

'Nothing. There's nothing any of us can do.' Lately, Annie kept remembering her mother dying, and how the pain had not really eased till months had passed. 'Only time can heal him,' she said sadly.

As Megan told her sister that night in bed, those children would be permanently harmed by the time Tom started to recover from his wife's death.

'If he does recover,' Bronwen said. 'He's getting that strange, you have to wonder if he's not goin' mad.'

'Don't you ever say that again! Ever!'

As the weeks passed, the two young maids grew more and more worried about their master. But it was not their place to tell tales. They kept the house nice, for their dead mistress's sake, looked after the children as best they could, and obeyed Tom's instructions to the letter, leaving Marianne's clothes where they were, laying out her nightdress each evening, putting it away again each morning. Sometimes, when they went upstairs to clean, the bedroom smelled of her perfume.

'He sprays it around, you know,' Megan said darkly. 'It reminds him of her.'

Bronwen shivered.

'And,' Megan added, 'when he used up the old bottle last week, he went and bought another bottle. All the way to Manchester. An' that was all he brought back with him.'

The two sisters cuddled up in bed, glad of each other,

glad of the normality of their days, when Tom was out of the house and when they could laugh a little and play with the children. Though the twins had been hard to handle since their mother's death, crying easily and refusing to be pleased for long by anything.

'It can't last,' said Megan. 'He'll have a breakdown.'

'Or go mad,' said Bronwen. 'If he isn't mad already. Mam says we should find ourselves new places.'

'I've told you before not to say that.'

Bronwen sniffed. 'Well, even if I can't say it, I shan't stop thinking it.'

'And we're not looking for other places, neither,' declared Megan, outraged at the mere idea. 'She was the best mistress as was ever born and we owe it to her to stay.'

'That's what I told Mam. But she said we'd regret it. She said he'd kill us in our beds one night.'

'Not him. He wouldn't harm no one, Mr Tom wouldn't. But he can't go on like this for ever.' Megan stared into the darkness. 'It's been two months now. Something's got to break.'

24

Bilsden and London: July to August 1851

O ne day Frederick said abruptly at breakfast, 'This might be a good time to plan our trip to London. After all, we don't want to miss seeing the Great Exhibition, do we?'

'Hurrah!' cried William and waved his hands triumphantly in the air.

Annie stared down at the tablecloth. 'I don't think I want to go anywhere just at the moment, Frederick. I don't think I could face it after what's happened. It would seem wrong to – to enjoy ourselves.'

William's face dropped and so did Jane's, though she tried to hide it.

Frederick said firmly, 'We're going.' And when Annie shook her head and opened her mouth to refuse, he added, even more firmly, 'You need to get away for a while, love. We all need to get away. It's been unrelenting gloom lately here. First May dying, then Marianne.'

'Who's May?' demanded William.

'Never you mind, lad.'

William ignored that and stared at his mother with his brows wrinkled. 'Emily's daughter was called May. Are you talking about that May? What did she die of?'

'Consumption,' said Annie. She might have known William would put two and two together, given half a hint. Really, Frederick should have been more careful of what he said in front of that boy.

'Grandad didn't say anything about May dying.'

'Dad doesn't know, and I want your promise not to tell him.' Annie looked at her son sternly. 'It's very important that you keep quiet about it, William. He has enough to grieve him at the moment. We don't want to upset him further.'

William sighed. 'All right. I promise. But I still don't see why—'

'Just do as you're told, for once. Hmm?'

'Widow Clegg says deaths come in threes,' William spoke in a hushed, ghoulish tone. 'Mr Darrington killed himself. That makes two. And now May makes three.'

Annie's reprimand died unvoiced. It was a common saying in the Rows, and it was true that it often did seem to happen that way.

As William opened his mouth to speculate further, Jane's foot connected with his ankle and he yelped, looking aggrieved as she mouthed the words, 'Be quiet!'

'We're definitely going to London.' Frederick turned the conversation back into more cheerful topics. 'And if I have to truss you up like a fowl for market and carry you on to the train myself, you're going with us, Annie Hallam.

William cackled with laughter at that idea.

'We'll talk about this later.' Annie then ate her breakfast in silence, or rather, she fiddled with the food on her plate until the others had finished eating, then she pushed her plate aside.

Frederick surprised her by following her upstairs afterwards instead of leaving for the mill. 'I meant what I said about going to London, Annie. There's been enough doom and gloom lately to last us all a good long time. Marianne's death was a shocking tragedy, and we're all upset by it, but nothing we can do will bring her back, so it's time we got on with our own lives again. You have a son and a daughter to raise.' He took her hand and brought it up to his lips, adding softly, 'And a husband who's been too long denied the pleasures of your body.'

She smiled faintly, a real smile this time. 'Is that so?'

He pulled her to him and kissed her thoroughly. 'That's definitely so.'

That night he brought a bottle of champagne to the dinner table and went round filling the glasses.

'Are we celebrating something?' Jane asked when Annie just sat there staring at the bubbling liquid in her glass.

'We're celebrating life,' said Frederick, pouring a scant inch into a fourth glass. 'Here you are, young William, your first taste of champagne.'

William seized the glass in delight. 'I say!' He raised it to his lips, but paused as Jane nudged him.

'A toast before we drink.' Frederick waited till all eyes were upon him and then said firmly, 'Here's to London. To the Great Exhibition.'

'Are we still going?' William asked, glass suspended halfway to his mouth. 'Are we really going?'

'Yes, we are.' Frederick reached out to clink his glass against Annie's. 'To London.'

And in the face of William's blazing joy, only a trifle marred by the choking fit he fell into when he took an incautiously large gulp of champagne, in the face of Jane's obvious delight and her husband's understanding smile, Annie could do nothing but clink her glass against Frederick's and echo his words. 'To London.'

The reaction of the rest of the family to the proposed trip varied greatly. Mark was frankly envious of them and to everyone's surprise, Luke was just as envious. But he was more interested in seeing the botanical gardens at Kew, which Nat Jervis said had been open to the public for a good few years now. Nat had seen them, gone to London specially to do so, and when he was in a good mood, he would tell Luke about their wonders, describing the strange plants from all over the world, and the tender care they received at Kew.

'You'll have to go and see the gardens,' Luke said earnestly, when told of the trip. 'Mr Jervis says they're a marvel. You can't possibly go to London and not see them, Annie.'

Rebecca was more interested in the fashionable folk in London, and kept begging Annie to remember everything she saw, *absolutely everything*, and then come back and draw sketches of the latest styles for them, so that Bilsden salon could keep right up with the very latest fashions. Even Joan shyly admitted that she was curious to see the nation's capital, and would love to catch a glimpse of the Queen and her family.

But John Gibson said that London couldn't be as good as Manchester, whatever anyone said, because everyone knew that what Manchester did today, the rest of the world did tomorrow. And from that he would not be moved. Kathy listened to their plans with interest, but told John that night in bed that she'd be afraid among so many strangers and she didn't envy them the trip to London at all.

A few days later, Annie and Frederick took a stroll around the gardens, enjoying the last of the daylight. Everything was looking magnificent, with Nat Jervis's blooms making a splendid show as usual. The little lake was reflecting the red of the sunset, birds were twittering sleepily in the trees and midges were rising in clouds near the water. Under the trees they were less troublesome, so Frederick and Annie lingered there.

'I like the dusk, especially in summer,' Annie said,

breathing the balmy air and smiling around her. 'It makes everything seem so pretty. Even in Bilsden.'

'Not as pretty as some parts of London, though. I'll take you to see St Paul's and Westminster Abbey. The architecture is quite magnificent, especially when you think the Abbey was built so long ago.'

She nodded. She knew how he enjoyed studying buildings. The designs for the hospital had been changed several times already because he wanted it to look beautiful as well as serve a practical purpose. It was becoming known as Hallam's folly in the town because its start had been delayed so many times, but he had provided the money for Jeremy and his colleagues to start a temporary lying-in hospital for poor women in an old warehouse. There, they could be looked after for a few days, given a rare opportunity to rest and then, if the baby survived, sent on their way with new baby clothes. And since the more affluent folk would not use a hospital if they could possibly help it, but would arrange to be treated in their own homes, it was only Widow Clegg and Jeremy who dared to keep pushing Frederick about keeping his promise.

'I suppose—' Annie paused and looked speculatively at her husband.

'What do you suppose, Mrs Hallam?' His tone was indulgent. Since Marianne's death they had grown closer again. Nothing had been said, but both had realised how lucky they were to have each other and the warmth had crept back into their relationship, both in their everyday life and behind their bedroom doors.

She looked up at him. 'I suppose we couldn't take them all with us, Frederick?'

'Take who?' But he guessed what she was about to say and he was already smiling as she spoke the names.

'Mark, Luke, Rebecca, Joan. My father and Kathy.'

'Why not?'

She clutched his sleeve. 'Do you mean it?'

'Of course I do.' He would do anything to bring unshadowed joy back to her face, to prevent the recurrent nightmares in which she was still reliving Marianne's death. Every time she woke and wept bitterly in his arms, he seemed to love her more, to want to protect her more carefully from the harsh realities of the world. As if his Annie would allow anyone to shelter her for more than a short time from life and its vicissitudes!

His response brought back the old Annie, for she threw back her head and laughed aloud, then flung her arms round him and danced him across the grass. 'Wonderful! Wonderful! William will be thrilled to have the others there to share the sights with him.'

'And it'll allow us some time together.'

'That, too.' She gave him a teasing smile, then shook her head. 'No, it won't. We'll still have Jane, and I'm not doing anything to make her think she's in the way.'

He suppressed a sigh. 'Of course not.'

'But,' she repeated, picturing her son when he heard, 'William will undoubtedly go mad with delight when he hears that he's to have the other children with him.'

'Your son, Annie, has been mad with delight ever since we began planning our trip. If he gets any madder, I'm sending him to stay with your father till it's time for us to leave.'

She chuckled. William's enthusiasms could be very wearing at times. But not to her. She was only relieved that he seemed to have recovered his old spirits most of the time, anyway. They all had sad moments. 'Let's walk down to Dad's now and tell them about the trip.'

She seemed, Frederick thought, to have quite forgotten that Netherleigh Cottage belonged to her and she always talked about it as 'Dad's' nowadays. 'All right. But we'd better take William with us, or he'll never forgive us.'

'And Jane. We can't leave her out.'

'No. We can't leave anyone out. Not if they have the most tenuous of connections to the Gibsons.' But he said it so softly that she didn't hear him and he didn't repeat his words. He didn't want her to think he disliked the Gibsons' solidarity in the face of an often hostile world. He admired them for that, and he was gaining a great deal of pleasure from feeling himself one of them. But he admitted now, if only to himself, that he would really have preferred to take Annie to London on her own, to wine her and dine her, buy her beautiful things and show her off to his acquaintances in the City.

John just gaped at his eldest daughter when he opened the door, for she did not normally visit them in the evening. 'Nay, there's never been another accident?'

Her smile faltered for a moment, then she said, 'No, Dad, of course not!' and planted a loud kiss on his cheek. 'We've come with good news this time – at least, I hope it's good news.'

He gave her a great hug and then pumped Frederick's hand vigorously. 'Well, then, come right in, lass, and tell us your news. You too, Frederick. And is that Jane – well, this is a treat! A real treat!' He winked at William, who was hopping up and down impatiently behind Jane, and William grinned back. 'Our Mark's just about to go off to the 'Stute, but the rest of us are here, though our Lally's gone round to see her mother tonight.' John regarded even the maid as part of the family and always referred to her as 'our Lally'. He could never have treated her differently to the rest of the family.

Annie took her father's arm and walked across the hall

with him. 'Mark will have to wait a bit before he leaves, then, because our news is for him, too.'

When they were all seated in the kitchen, which was still John's favourite room, Annie looked at Frederick, to see if he wanted to make the announcement.

He waved a hand at her. 'You tell them.'

'All right.' She turned back to her family, her eyes sparkling in anticipation. 'You know we're going down to London to see the Great Exhibition.'

Everyone nodded.

'Well, we thought – we wondered if you would all like to come with us.'

There was a moment's absolute silence, then 'Nay,' said John. 'Nay, who ever thought of such a thing? It'd cost the earth.'

'My treat, that,' said Frederick 'And it'd be a pleasure to have you all with us.'

Beside his mother, William chuckled in glee at the astonished expressions on the faces of his young aunts and uncles.

It was naturally Rebecca who spoke first for the younger generation. 'Do you mean that, our Annie?' she demanded.

'Of course we do. What about it, Dad?' Annie turned to her father who was very much the head of his family. 'Don't you fancy a trip to London?'

'Eh, how can we? There's the yard to see to, and the childer, and – and—'

Mark interrupted, terrified that his father would prevent this treat. 'Well, I've been longing to go, so if you're sure, Annie, Frederick,' he turned to his brother-in-law for confirmation, and when he received it, he beamed and finished firmly, 'then we'll *find* a way to go.' He saw John still shaking his head and added, 'Dad, it's the event of our lifetimes, that exhibition is. We just *can't* miss it. I was going to ask if I could go with the lads from the 'Stute. They're all going down there next month on a special excursion. But I'd much rather go with Annie and Frederick.' The lads from the 'Stute were taking advantage of a cheap excursion. Frederick Hallam would do nothing cheaply and would probably stay in London for longer.

Kathy clutched John's arm and whispered, 'I don't think I want to go to London, love.' She didn't want to upset anyone, but even the thought of travelling to the capital city made her feel anxious, and anyway, she didn't want to go so far away from her children. Samuel John, at two, was into everything, and Benjamin was just struggling to walk. It was one thing to go to Blackpool, from which you could return quite easily in half a day, quite another to get lost in the depths of London, from which, she felt, you might never return. It was all right for clever folk like Annie to go there, but not for her.

John patted his wife's hand. 'Nor I don't really want to go neither. But them childer do.' He turned to Frederick. 'I think the young 'uns would like to go, and I'll not stop them, but me an' my Kathy are a pair of stop-at-homes.'

'I thought you'd say that,' said Annie, knowing he'd be uncomfortable among the crowds of London. A quiet man, her father, whose world centred on his home and those he loved. 'But you'll let us take these four rascals with us?'

Four faces turned expectantly to John.

'Aye. If you can stand them.'

When Annie nodded, Rebecca got up and did a wild dance round the kitchen, partnered by William. She then dragged Luke to his feet and William dragged Joan. Mark, more conscious of his dignity at seventeen, did not join them until they all four converged on him and dragged him, laughing and protesting, to his feet.

'It's what they need,' John said to Frederick under the cover of the general noise and excitement 'It's what you all need. It's been a bad month or two.'

'Don't you two need a change as well?' Frederick asked.

John looked at him as if struck by the idea. 'Aye. Why not? But not in London. I think me and my lass will take the two little lads to Blackpool when you all get back from London. If you'll have the other four to stay with you while we're away.' He grinned, comfortable enough now with his son-in-law to tease him, 'That is, if you've got room for them all in that tiny little house of yours up the hill.'

Frederick nodded, hiding his anxiety under the urbane smiling mask he used when conducting business. If John went to Blackpool . . . if he saw Lizzie . . . if he found out she'd been living there and had not got in touch with her family, he'd be so hurt.

'What did Dad say that upset you?' Annie demanded when they were getting ready for bed that night. 'I saw your face change suddenly, then you started smiling, the smile you use to hide behind.' The smile she hated to see on his face.

'He said he didn't fancy London, but that he and Kathy might take a trip to Blackpool after we get back.'

She stared at him in horror. 'What? Oh, no! What if he bumps into Lizzie like Jeremy and Ellie did.'

'Exactly.'

'That settles it. Lizzie will just have to come over to see him.'

'And Jim? How are you going to explain him? If your father knows she's in Blackpool, he'll expect to go and stay with her. She does run a lodging house, after all.'

Annie was silent for a moment or two, then, as he was turning the bedside lamp off, she said thoughtfully, 'Maybe we could tell the family that Jim's a sort of second cousin of William's, that Lizzie knew I'd be upset to see him, because of the relationship with Fred Coxton, so she stayed away from us. Dad might just believe that.'

'And won't you be upset to see the boy regularly? Because that's what'll happen if Lizzie starts visiting your father again.'

'I'm more likely to be upset by Lizzie. She can be sharp and spiteful, our Lizzie can, if something upsets her. May's death won't have changed that.'

'She wasn't sharp last time we saw her. She looked lost after the funeral.'

Annie shrugged. Lizzie would recover from that. Lizzie always did. 'It was a good thing she had Jim. He was lovely with her after May died. I think he really considers her to be an aunt now. And since Marianne – well, I've come to think that we all have to take the best from life as we go. Because we never know what'll happen tomorrow.' She sniffed away a tear and gave him a watery smile. 'There I go, crying again.'

He pulled her into his arms. 'The memory of that day will fade, Annie, I promise you. And if you're talking of taking the best from life, well, as far as I'm concerned, you *are* the best, my love.'

The next day was Sunday, and after chapel, Rebecca and Joan made their way up the hill to their sister's. As they had hoped, she was alone in her studio, where she often spent an hour or two on Sunday afternoons, while Frederick sat in the library plotting his next business moves or even dozing in his armchair after the midday meal. He was slowing down a little bit lately, he admitted to himself, lacking the abundant energy he had had right into his middle years, unable to rouse much enthusiasm, even about making money. Dawton's would probably be his last big business venture. But he hoped he had hidden all that from Annie.

'Now, you let me do the talking,' Rebecca whispered unnecessarily as the girls were shown up to Annie's studio.

Joan smiled to herself. Rebecca always did do most of the talking, but Joan didn't mind that. It was more interesting to listen to others and she knew she'd never be a pushy person like her sister. She resembled her dad, and that suited her fine.

In Netherleigh Cottage they all had to observe the Lord's Day, or their dad would give them what for, so it was a relief to get out of the house, as far as Rebecca was concerned. She was as little affected by religion as her elder sister and got bored sometimes on Sundays.

'Our Annie,' she said, once they were settled and waiting for a tea tray, 'what are me and Joan going to do about clothes?'

Annie looked at her in puzzlement.

'For London.' Rebecca looked scornfully down at her dress, a blue and white print which was getting a little tight around the chest now and short, too, though it had been let down once and an extra flounce added to the hem. 'This is my summer best.' She didn't have to explain what she meant. It was a child's dress and Rebecca had suddenly developed into a curvaceous young woman.

'Hmm.' Annie realised that she should have thought of this herself and felt guilty. Since Marianne's death, she had not been as lively as usual. Frederick was right. They did all need a change. 'Turn round.' She studied her sister. 'Goodness, I hadn't realised how much you'd grown since Christmas.' She stood next to Rebecca and said, 'Why, you're as tall as I am now!'

Rebecca nodded. 'An' I'm still growing. My mam was

quite tall, Dad says, an' he thinks me an' Joanie might both take after her in that. His side of the family isn't tall – well, look at you an' Tom.' She stopped short, realising this might not sound very flattering.

Annie nodded agreement. Even Joan, at eleven, was nearly as tall as she was. 'What about you, Joan?'

'I'm all right. I got all new clothes this year because I'd grown so much. Me an' Rebecca made them.' And she didn't care about clothes as much as Rebecca did anyway. What she liked best was helping Kathy with her little half-brothers and cooking. She supposed that when she left school she'd go into the salon, like Rebecca, but she wasn't really interested in fashion. If she could find something else to do, she would.

'This is the best I've got.' Rebecca was still looking down at her dress. 'The others are worse.' She hesitated. 'Will I have time to make some more clothes before we leave? You haven't said when exactly we're going.'

'You won't have time to make more than one dress. Frederick wants to go next week. Perhaps Mary can get someone to—'

'We've got a lot of orders at the salon. They're all flat-out busy.' Tears filled Rebecca's eyes. 'I can't go like this! Dad said clothes don't matter, but they do matter to me! I'm not going to London in dresses that are too small and make me look like a little girl who's got too fat.'

Joan stepped forward to put her arm round Rebecca. 'We won't care what you look like, Becky, love.'

'Well, I shall. Especially in London.'

Annie stood up. 'Hmm. I might have a solution. Come with me, you two.' She led the way to her bedroom and set the bell pealing for her maid. 'Laura, Rebecca needs some clothes for London. Just look how she's grown! What have I got that might be suitable?'

Rebecca's face lit up. 'Oh, Annie!' Her voice was hushed and reverent. Their Annie had the loveliest clothes in town.

The two girls returned to Netherleigh Cottage in the carriage, together with four of Annie's simpler dresses, several padded petticoats, two mantles and two straw bonnets. The girls would be hard pressed to alter them all before they left, but Rebecca hadn't wanted any of Alice's sewing women to do it for her. 'I'm a better sewer than they are,' she insisted, and Annie had to agree with her.

As the carriage turned into Moor Close, Rebecca said to Joanie, her face fierce with determination, 'I'll get these dresses finished if I have to stay up all night. See if I don't!'

'Well, I'll help you, love. And I'll stay up all night with you.' But fortunately, that wasn't necessary.

The train trip to London was enlivened by the enthusiasm of the five young people whose excitement at their first long journey was infectious. Frederick had taken two compartments for the family, and Jimson and Laura were down the train in the second-class compartments.

William had somehow acquired a catalogue for the exhibition, dog-eared, but full of information which he insisted on imparting to all and sundry, whether they were interested or not.

'Do you know, the full title of the exhibition is The Great Exhibition of the Industry of All Nations?' he announced, as the train left Bilsden station. And from then onwards he referred to the exhibition by its full title until Mark declared that if he said those words one more time, he, Mark, would personally make William eat the catalogue.

William opened his mouth to protest at the injustice of this, caught Mark's eye and desisted, turning instead to the astounding statistics he had garnered. 'The building covers nineteen acres, you know, and it has eight miles – *eight miles* – of table space for the exhibits.'

'Yes, so you told us,' snapped Rebecca, who never bore fools gladly. 'Several times!'

'But just think of it!'

'I have. An' I don't want to think of it any more, thank you very much.'

Frederick hastily converted a snort of laughter into a cough.

William subsided, but continued to flick through the catalogue. 'I'm not bothered about machinery,' he said a bit later. 'Who wants to go all the way to London to see rotten old cotton spinning machines when we can go into Father's mill and see them any day.'

'When did *you* last go into the mill, then?' Rebecca demanded.

'Well—'

'Have you ever been inside the mill?' she pursued.

'Well, no, but I could, if I wanted to. Couldn't I, Father?'

'Hah!' She folded her arms and looked at him scornfully.

William was not subdued for long. 'There's a model of Liverpool on show, too, did you know that? With houses and streets and everything.'

'Yes,' said Mark. 'You've told us about it at least twenty times. Just shut up for a while, will you, our William? The rest of us want to look at the scenery.'

Even William was silent when they arrived at the hotel, a small family hotel in a back street of the West End, but an establishment of great luxury, with a very superior range of servants who rendered Luke dumb with fear from the moment he first had his luggage taken from him. He was petrified of doing something to incur their scorn, he could not have said why. Always a quiet person, he hardly said a word while they were in the hotel, keeping close to Mark as he had done when he was a boy. And Mark, as usual, kept an eye on him, and winked from time to time to cheer him up.

Rebecca was thrilled about the bedroom she was sharing with Joan. William was sharing with Mark and Luke, who would, Annie hoped, keep him in order and prevent him from waking everyone too early.

The next day was a Thursday, so it would be a shilling entrance day, and Frederick wondered if they should wait until the Friday to attend, at half-a-crown entrance, or even the Saturday, when there would be a better class of people there, since they would have to pay the huge sum of five shillings each for the privilege of seeing the exhibition.

Annie just chuckled. 'The children and I grew up in Salem Street, Frederick. We're not going to be offended if we have to mix with ordinary people. Stop trying to put me on a pedestal, love. I wouldn't be comfortable up there.'

He smiled back. 'I'm not fool enough to believe that it'd be dangerous to let the lower classes in, like that silly Madame de Lieven, but I do wonder if the air won't be sweeter and the atmosphere calmer on a day when entrance is more expensive.'

'I wouldn't dare tell William he has to wait a whole day to see the exhibition. If I know him, he'll be up before it's light tomorrow, he's so eager to go. We'll have to do something to tire him out.'

'Has he always been so – enthusiastic?' Frederick asked as William's voice echoed quite clearly along the corridor from the boys' room.

'Always.'

The next day they took a couple of cabs out to Hyde

Park, and Frederick made sure Jimson and Laura had
enough money to enjoy themselves at the exhibition.
Once there, Frederick handed out half a guinea to each
of the young folk, set Mark in charge and turned them
loose upon the Crystal Palace and its wonders, with injunc-
tions not to get into trouble, to look after the girls and to
meet at the Refreshment Courts at a quarter to twelve for
a meal.

Then Frederick offered an arm each to Annie and Jane,
and the adults set off to make their own, more leisurely, tour
of the exhibits. Naturally, Frederick wanted to go and inspect
the cotton spinning machinery first, but he did not linger
long by the power looms. He had always kept up with new
ways of producing and weaving yarn and there was nothing
to see that was any surprise to him, though he thought the
displays had been well set up, and that the young women
in their long pinafores were doing a grand job of it at the
doubling machines, in spite of the distractions of the crowd
around them. 'Good little workers, they are, those two,' he
approved.

Then they set out along the nearest aisle, walking
randomly and pausing whenever something caught their
attention. Twice they met the young folk and each time they
could hear William's excited voice long before they came
into sight.

'It's all very overwhelming,' Annie said after an hour of
walking round. 'There are so many things to see.' She winced
as they passed an upholstery display whose fabrics and
overstuffed furniture were set out against a garish background of no less than three different designs of wallpaper,
which might accord with the upholstered pieces placed
before each, but which clashed horribly when seen as a
whole. But she lingered near the display of French silks, her
eyes and fingers those of a connoisseur and her voice soft

with admiration. 'I've never seen silks as good as the French produce.'

'What, better than those our worthy English artisans produce?' Frederick teased.

'Yes, especially in the design – or lack of it. Just look at that length of aqua silk! Did you ever see anything as lovely? You don't need fussy prints when you have a colour and sheen like that. Just the hint of pattern in the weave is enough.'

'It's gorgeous!' sighed Jane. But she cast an approving glance down at her own cotton and silk print gown as she spoke. She had never, she thought, felt so smart or enjoyed life so much. If only Matt could see her now, parading about London like a lady of leisure.

Matt Peters was intruding more and more into her dreams, even though Mary Benworth had warned her that he had never been serious about another woman in all the years since he broke his engagement to Annie. Jane knew that Annie had no interest in Matt any more, for she was too besotted with Frederick, so Jane was cherishing some hope that Matt's attentions might mean something this time. Otherwise why would he bother to meet her and Mary so often on their Sunday walks? It couldn't just be coincidence. It was almost as if he knew where they would be on fine days.

Even Judith Hallam had commented on Jane's appearance the last time she and James had visited Ridge House. Judith had commented to Jane on several other things, too. She was not at all happy about the lavish way the servants were treated or the casual manners of those living in Ridge House. But Jane, who was enjoying her new freedom, decided that Judith had rather rigid ideas of 'the correct way to comport oneself' as she phrased it, and the sort of example one should set for 'the lower orders'. Jane preferred to model herself on Annie, who seemed to her to live life to the full, what with her home, her family and her businesses.

The folk they passed at the exhibition came from all over England by their accents, but the crowd was marked by its good humour and its willingness to live and let live. The worst the people seemed to be doing was littering the ground with the paper wrappings from their sandwiches, which many were munching as they walked round. However fast attendants swept the debris up, more seemed to appear within minutes.

'See,' Annie said challengingly to Frederick, as they walked down the central aisle making their way towards the fountain made entirely of crystal, 'you couldn't get a better-behaved crowd than this. We were right not to wait.'

'You're correct, as usual, my love. Ah! Look!' He propelled her and Jane rapidly across the aisle to take possession of a seat upholstered in red plush which had just been vacated, so that they could all rest their aching feet.

Towards noon, the three of them made their way to the Refreshment Courts.

'I think I'll use the ladies' waiting room first,' Annie declared. 'It'll be a penny well spent. Coming, Jane?'

When the two ladies came out, they were nodding their heads in approval.

'Very clean,' said Jane. 'I only wish we had a public waiting room in Bilsden. Ladies can use the salon, but ordinary women have nowhere to go.'

'Why shouldn't we build something?' Annie challenged Frederick. 'If you charged people for using a waiting room like the ones here, you could probably cover your costs.'

'Why not, indeed?' Frederick asked lazily. 'Nothing but the best for Bilsden. I'll arrange it when we get back. Now, where are those children?'

'Don't call Mark a child or you'll mortally offend him,' Annie warned. 'And Rebecca's a young woman now.'

'They seem like children to me, but I take your point. I don't see any reason to wait for the *young people*, so what would you ladies like to eat?'

'I'm more interested in a cup of tea,' Annie decided. 'But perhaps,' she studied the displays of food, also with approval, 'yes, perhaps a nice roast beef sandwich and a macaroon. I must say, they're doing things very nicely here, don't you think, Jane?'

Before they had finished eating, the five young people joined them, with William loudly proclaiming himself nearly dead of starvation. 'We found some waiting rooms over there,' he waved a hand to the right, 'where they only charge a halfpenny. We're being careful of what we spend, so that the money will last all day.'

And that must be Mark's idea, thought Annie, for you're never careful with your money, William Ashworth. Your spending money is inevitably spent before noon on a Saturday.

'In that case,' Frederick stood up, 'I'd better treat you young folk to some food, hadn't I? A cup of tea and a cake should be enough, don't you think?'

William's face fell so visibly that Annie and Jane chuckled, which alerted him to the fact that his stepfather was teasing him again. It had taken him a while to get used to Frederick's teasing, but now he entered into the spirit of things. 'Only if you want me to faint from hunger.' He clapped one hand to his chest and pretended to stagger.

'Very well, come and choose anything you want.'

'Anything?' William's eyes gleamed and he bounced along beside Frederick to help choose the food. He came back beaming and carrying a tray absolutely loaded with goodies.

The beverages with which they finished the meal were a

wonder to John Gibson's second brood. No alcohol was served at the exhibition, but you could buy Schweppes's lemonade, poured from its bottle before your very eyes, and fizzing madly in the glass, tickling your nose if you got too close, or else their ginger beer, far fizzier than any of the home-made brews that Kathy produced for special occasions. And all of these wonderful beverages were available in bottles, just like that, for instant use.

'Wonderful!' sighed William, eyeing his empty glass regretfully.

'Another?' Frederick prompted.

William eyed his mother sideways.

But they were on holiday, and she wanted them to enjoy every second. 'Why not buy them an ice-cream as well? In fact, let's all have ice-creams.'

This novelty was equally well received by the young Gibsons.

'Why did Dad say ice-cream hurt your teeth?' wondered Joan. 'It's lovely.'

'Because he's lost a few of his teeth, of course,' said Rebecca. 'It gets in the holes. Honestly, don't you know anything?' She saw that Joan looked hurt even at this mild criticism and felt guilty. Joanie was such a softie. 'I'm only teasing,' she whispered, and gave her little sister a quick hug, which made Joan smile again and address herself to the rest of the delightful strawberry ice-cream with enthusiasm.

That evening everyone was exhausted, but as all of them were eager to sample more delights the following day, there were no complaints when Annie suggested an early night.

The week flew past, for it included a trip to London Zoo, where the smell made Annie and Jane wrinkle their noses in disgust, and the dirty paths made Rebecca hold up her elegant skirts carefully. But William and Luke were utterly fascinated by the animals, and even Mark forgot his dignity at the sight of a huge elephant being fed what seemed like mountains of food.

Another day Frederick took the boys to Kew Gardens, fulfilling Luke's main ambition for the trip. It was more interesting than he had expected, though William stated several times that it was a bit slow and that he had much preferred the zoo. They lost Luke for a while, finding him at last deep in conversation with one of the gardeners about the best way of heating a glasshouse.

William would have made some loud disparaging remark, but Frederick grabbed him by the shoulder. 'Don't spoil it for him.'

William sighed, but kept quiet. 'All right.' He grinned up at Frederick. 'But haven't *you* had enough of plants?'

'In confidence, yes. But we won't tell Luke that.'

Annie and Jane took the girls round the shops that day, buying lengths of material and lace and ribbon with wild abandon, till Rebecca was in a seventh heaven of delight.

When they decided on a last visit to the Great Exhibition before returning home, Jane volunteered to spend another day at the shops with Rebecca, while Joan for once opted to stay with the boys, and Luke, greatly daring, sought permission to spend the day at Kew on his own.

'Can you find your way there and back?' Frederick asked.

'Yes, sir.'

'Then I don't see why not.'

'You'll be careful, Luke,' Annie could not help saying.

'Yes, Annie.' He nodded solemnly to emphasise his words.

'Never thought old Luke would go off on his own in London,' said William when he, Mark and Joan were wandering round the delights of the exhibition again.

'Luke will do anything when it's for his precious plants,' said Mark. 'He's surprised me a few times now.' Then he fell quiet as they stopped to study for a second time the amazing sportsman's knife containing eighty blades and attachments.

'It'd be better without all that fancy engraving,' said William.

'I think it's pretty,' volunteered Joan wanting to please.

'Pretty!' he scoffed. 'Pretty! Trust a girl to say something like that. You don't buy a knife because it's pretty.'

'Trust a boy to spend hours staring at one silly old knife,' she retorted. 'And that one's far too big to put in your pocket. I think it's daft.'

But apart from a few such exchanges, the three of them enjoyed themselves hugely.

'Well, was it worth coming to London?' Frederick asked Annie on the last night as they were getting ready for bed.

'Enormously,' said Annie. 'And it's been wonderful to see the young folk's pleasure.'

'Hmm. I just wish William would abate his pleasure a little. He's exhausted me.' As they got into bed, he said thoughtfully, 'Have you thought of sending him away to school for a year or two?'

'Sending him away! No. Why should I?'

'Because if you don't, he'll be neither fish nor fowl, neither a gentleman nor a working chap. You'll have to start thinking what you're going to do with him.'

She shrugged as she fastened the buttons on the front of her nightdress. 'I'd assumed he'd go into the family business with Tom, eventually, like the other boys have. At least until he's learned how to run a business of his own.'

'We could do a lot better for him than that, don't you think?'

'What's wrong with him going into our business? Or even yours, come to that?'

'Nothing. But the new breed of businessmen I meet in Manchester has a fair sprinkling of what you might call "gentlemen". And they're better educated than they used to be.' He pulled her into his arms. 'Think about it, my love. It isn't only the nobility who go to university nowadays. And in the meantime,' he breathed into her ear, 'think about us.' He had been longing to get her to himself all day.

25

September 1851 to January 1852

Before John and Kathy took their holiday in Blackpool, Annie and Frederick broke the news to them that Lizzie was now living there.

John's face showed a mixture of emotions. 'Well, I'm glad to hear that she's all right, but why hasn't she come home to see us?' He saw Annie hesitate and added, 'Her and May are all right, aren't they?'

'I'm afraid May died earlier in the year. Lizzie was very upset.'

Kathy gave a little murmur of distress and clutched John's arm.

He stood for a moment, shaking his head, coming to terms with the idea in his own quiet way. 'Nay, then!' he said at last. 'A young lass like that! Another young lass dead. My Em'ly's girl. What did she die of?'

'Consumption.'

'Why didn't they tell us she were ill? We could have helped out, looked after them both.'

'You know Lizzie. She always did like to be independent.'

'But she must have got in touch with *you*, love, else how do you know? Why didn't *you* tell me there was trouble?' He was very hurt by being excluded, Annie could see.

'She didn't get in touch with us, Dad. Jeremy Lewis and Ellie bumped into her and May when they went to Blackpool. Tom and Frederick went over to find her afterwards. They didn't tell even me about it. Lizzie didn't want me to know. So I didn't find out either till recently.'

'Eh, them poor lasses, facin' all that on their own!' John clutched Kathy's hand gratefully, patting it without realising what he was doing, a sure sign that he was upset.

Frederick intervened. 'Lizzie and May were down on their luck at the time and too proud to ask for help. And later – well, I asked them to look after Jim Coxton for us—'

'Coxton?'

Frederick was annoyed with himself for letting this information slip so carelessly. 'Yes. Tom and I found out that this lad, who's a sort of cousin of William's, was destitute.'

'But he's a Coxton!' John found it hard to forgive a relative of someone who had hurt his Annie so badly.

'Well, Fred Coxton's dead now, thank goodness, so he can't trouble us, but we couldn't leave the lad to fend for himself. You see, he's younger than William, but he looks very like William.'

'Oh. I see. No, I don't suppose I'd like to see him sent to the workhouse, either, then, not if he looks like our William. Yes, that were very kind of you,' John nodded his head several times.

'Lizzie and May grew fond of Jim – but they thought Annie wouldn't want to know about him, that she'd be upset about him living with them, so we kept it a secret.'

John could see that. 'It's a cruel hard world.' His favourite expression when someone was in trouble. 'But you have to look after someone as is related to you by blood, even if he's a Coxton. If you can't rely on your own folk, who can you rely on?'

Trust Frederick to smooth things over so well, Annie thought. He's good at managing people. A wry smile tugged at the corners of her mouth. But he doesn't always get his own way. She'd already started feeling a little queasy in the mornings, thanks to their trip to London. She hadn't said anything to Frederick, but he'd soon guess. And there was nothing he could do about it now. For all his precautions, nature had triumphed. She only hoped that this baby would be the son she longed for.

John and Kathy gradually stopped exclaiming at the news and agreed with Frederick that although they would be happy to stay with Lizzie when they went to Blackpool, it would be only right to pay her for their room, since that was how she earned her living.

'She'll be missing our May badly,' said John. 'The two of them were thick as thieves, right from the time they were little lasses. They allus did get on well.'

Too well, thought Frederick, and could not help hoping that Lizzie would not find another woman to love. He doubted John even knew of such predilections and was certain that it would upset him greatly to find out what Lizzie was like. As for himself, well, Frederick prided himself on being broad-minded, and he didn't see that such rela-tionships between women could do any harm.

'But should we go away from Bilsden just now?' wondered John. 'Our Tom's been acting that strange since he lost Marianne. I don't rightly like to leave him here alone. There's no telling what he'll do.'

They all agreed that Tom's grief was lasting too long, but Annie assured her father that she would keep an eye on her brother, so in the end he was persuaded to go. She was glad about that. He would give his lifeblood to help someone in need, especially someone in the family, but he wasn't getting any younger. He'd been looking drawn and older since Marianne's death. A change would do him nothing but good.

On the following Saturday, Annie brought the carriage to take John, Kathy and their luggage to the station, it having been decided that the two little boys would be better staying in Bilsden this time. She listened patiently to Kathy repeating her list of instructions about Samuel John and Benjamin, who were now residing in the nurseries at Ridge House, to Tamsin's great delight. Lally, who considered a stay there an excitement in itself, was in charge of the two little boys and even Kathy had to admit that Lally was a very capable young woman.

After she had waved goodbye, on an impulse Annie called in at Church Road.

To her surprise, Tom was at home, even though it was a working day. He was sitting alone in the parlour with the curtains half-drawn.

'I'm not disturbing you?' she asked, for he looked so sad, and had not bothered to come over and hug her.

He just shrugged.

She sat down. 'How are you keeping, love?'

'Well enough.'

'And the children?' she persevered.

'They're well, too. Bronwen looks after them all right. Not like a mother would, but all right.'

'You'll have to love them a lot, now, to make up for Marianne and . . .'

He interrupted, his voice harsh. 'There's no need to tell me what to do with my own children! And there's nothing *anyone* can do to make up for Marianne. Nothing!'

'I didn't mean—' She broke off awkwardly.

He didn't seem to have heard, for he continued, still in that hard voice that sounded so unlike him, 'I'll see that they don't forget their mother. And I'll see that they're raised properly, too. There's no need for anyone to worry about that. But what I won't put up with is my family interfering.' He raised his head to stare at her. 'Any of my family.'

Not only was the visit not a success, but in the end, Tom said he had to see a fellow and showed Annie out of the house.

'As if I had been a stranger,' she reported to Frederick that night, with tears in her eyes. 'And Tom looks dreadful. Absolutely haggard, and – and as if he's never going to smile again.'

The next morning Annie suddenly jumped out of bed and rushed across to vomit in the washbowl in her dressing room. Oh dear! she thought as she rinsed her mouth. No hiding it now.

Frederick went over to stand by the window. 'Did you do this on purpose?' he demanded when she had finished and was making her way shakily back to bed. He came to stand beside it, glaring down at her. 'Did you?'

'Of course I didn't!'

'Then how the hell did you manage to get pregnant with all the care I was taking?'

He was coldly furious, and that tone of voice had made grown men quail before now, but Annie felt too ill to bother about that, so she shrugged. 'It just happened. In London, I think. And what do you suppose I could have done? Cast a spell over you or something?'

His anger was subsiding a little now, to be replaced by a cold trickle of fear as he studied her white face.

'It's just one of those things, love,' she said softly, stretching her hand towards him.

He made no effort to take it.

'But I'm not going to pretend I'm anything but glad about it. Jeremy says there's no absolute way to be certain you don't get pregnant, except for abstaining.' She grinned at him, her spirit unquenchable, for all the pallor in her cheeks. 'And you don't exactly abstain, my love.'

He just turned and walked out of the room, and when she heard the front door slam, she got up and went to look out of the window. She could see him striding across the garden, hatless and coatless. 'Oh, Frederick,' she murmured. 'Couldn't you say you were glad?'

He returned an hour later, to find her still in bed, with an empty tea cup beside her. He knew he was being rather stiff with her, but he couldn't help it. 'I'm sorry about slamming out of the house like that, Annie. I shouldn't have got angry with you. I was just – shocked.' Worried, too. Worried sick that something might happen to her. Ironic that, for a man like him. 'How are you feeling now?'

She smiled lazily. 'A little queasy in the mornings, as usual, but so far, I'm much better than last time.'

'We must have Jeremy come to check how you're going every week.'

She bit off an exclamation that this wasn't necessary. Perhaps it was necessary, for Frederick's peace of mind, at least.

John and Kathy came back from Blackpool a week later, looking much better than when they had left Bilsden. The weather had been good to them, and Lizzie had been most welcoming. As usual, John had got on well with the lad – he got on well with most lads – and he was talking about a visit from Jim and Lizzie at Christmas.

That was when he found out that Tom was not planning to celebrate Christmas with the family that year. 'You can leave me out of your plans, Dad. I shan't be in the mood for parties.'

'Then we'll have the three children over to spend the day with our lot,' John said, trying to be helpful.

'No, you *won't* have my children. *I'll* have my children.

And we'll spend our Christmas remembering Marianne, not forgetting her.' When his son got that expression on his face, John knew better than to argue with him. Maybe, he thought, Tom would have changed his mind before Christmas.

Over the next two months, things went from bad to worse. Tom was working gruelling long hours at the yard and hotel, as if trying to exhaust himself. Anyone who suggested that he was doing too much had their head snapped off. Frederick, Annie, Jeremy, John all suffered his anger when they attempted to reason with him. Seth Holden had learned to leave him alone, except to discuss business, but he confided in Frederick one day that he, too, was worried about Tom.

'He can't go on like this, or he'll collapse,' Jeremy said to Annie, on one of his visits. 'We all miss Marianne.' There was a quiver in his voice as he said her name and he had to pause a minute before continuing. 'I think I'll never stop missing her. But life has to go on. I've tried and tried to make Tom see that.'

'He seems determined to ignore us all. He won't even let the children go over to visit Dad. And you know how much they used to love that.'

'The three of them are looking peaky and unhappy as well. Ellie went and insisted on taking them out for a walk the other week, and Tom got so angry at Megan for letting her do it that he threatened to dismiss her if she let them go out to play again.'

'Dismiss Megan! Marianne would turn in her grave. And besides, how would he manage without her and her sister? Those girls are worth their weight in gold.'

'I wouldn't put anything past him at the moment. He's not himself. Grief takes people in many ways. There are some who never recover from a loss. But I don't think

Marianne would want that for Tom. I'm sure she wouldn't. And she'd be so unhappy to see the children.'

Jeremy sighed and Annie's heart went out to him. He, too, was looking tired and unhappy. But at least he had Ellie. And Catherine, and little Arthur. Though Ellie said he seemed to be avoiding Catherine lately. 'She's too like Marianne was at that age. The resemblance is astonishing, considering.'

Christmas came and went, with Jane once again in charge at Ridge House and Annie taking things easy. The festivities were very subdued, for everyone was missing Marianne who had always adored Christmas and been at the centre of every loving plot and plan. But Lizzie came over from Blackpool for a few days, with Jim, and that helped take John's mind off absent faces, at least.

Lizzie seemed to have changed, Annie thought. She was still sharp, but she was quieter. She dressed now in plain dark garments, which she said gave the customers confidence in her respectability. 'Besides,' her smile was wry, 'the fancy clothes I used to wear wouldn't be much good with the gales we get. You should have seen the sea crashing on the shore last week. Like mountains, the waves were. May would have loved watching them. She loved the sea, May did.'

That was the only time Lizzie referred to her previous life in Annie's hearing. The rest of the time she was very quiet, though she ate well, produced a bottle of port for after the meal and gave all the adults a small gift, with a big basket of bonbons and nuts for the little children.

Somehow, Annie wasn't worried about her own health during this pregnancy. She was far more worried about Tom. They all were. The rest of the family were fine, but

Tom was turning into a cold harsh man who drove a hard bargain and who never ever smiled.

'It can't go on,' Annie said in the new year. 'It just can't go on.'

'Are you worrying about Tom again?' Frederick demanded.

She nodded. 'William called to see the children today. You know how he loves little children. And Megan wouldn't let him in. She said she had orders not to let anyone in while Tom was away, not even the family. William was so upset.'

'And that upset you.' He sat in his armchair opposite her, thinking, then came to a decision to try something that had been hovering at the back of his mind for a while. It might not do any good, but the situation was getting worse, not better, so it was worth a try. But first he had to prepare Annie. 'Look – there's something else I've been involved in that I haven't told you about, love.'

'Oh? Not another woman whom you've been helping?' She trusted him enough now to tease him about that.

'Well, yes, it is another woman, actually.' But his smile said what her heart had already told her. That she was the only focus of his affections and that this other woman, whoever she was, was no threat to their marriage.

'Who is it this time?'

'Rosie.'

There was a pause, then she frowned. 'Tom's Rosie?'

'Yes.'

Annie came across to sit on his knee. 'Tell me about it, then. Confess all.'

'It was Rosie who found William and sent him back you know, the day of Beatrice's wedding. She was still working at the Shepherd's Rest then.'

'You never said. I'd have gone to thank her if I'd known.'

'You were in no state to thank anyone. And besides, there

was another problem.' He hated telling this to a Gibson. They were so clannish about anyone who was related to them. There was no saying what they'd try to do about it. 'Rosie had a child by Tom. Just before Marianne did.'

'*What!* Do you mean he'd been unfaithful to Marianne? Our Tom!'

'It only happened the once. I gather that it was after he got angry about your father having another child. Just before John got married.'

She stared into the fire, frowning, 'Boy or girl?'

'Boy.'

'And Tom never acknowledged the child?' She didn't like the thought of that. Children needed families.

'Tom paid Rosie, but the child was the spitting image of Samuel John. There was bound to be trouble once he started getting out and about. So I helped Rosie to leave Bilsden with the child.'

Annie would not have been human if she had not felt a little jealous. 'Huh! I hadn't thought of Rosie as a scheming type, but I'm sure if you helped her, she's done well out of this.'

'She isn't a scheming type. She loves Tom dearly. More than he deserves. And I think she might understand him, now, better than we can – understand his grief and how to help him, perhaps. Nobody else has been able to do anything.'

She stiffened against him. 'You're still seeing Rosie, then?'

'Only occasionally, when she passes through Manchester.'

'Oh.'

He chuckled in her ear. 'Now, Annie. You know I'm not the unfaithful type – I wouldn't dare stray with your temper, love.'

She was still rigid in his arms. 'Then why do you keep seeing her?'

'She likes me to come and hear her progress. No, ssh, let me finish my tale. You remember she had a lovely voice?'

'I remember she used to sing down at the Shepherd's Rest. I didn't ever go there to hear her, though. It wasn't a very respectable place in those days.'

'Well, I thought her voice was quite outstanding. When she needed help, she asked me to pay for some more singing lessons. But I thought she needed more than that. We've gone on to elocution lessons as well, not to mention improving her reading and writing, and we've added a few airs and graces to give her a bit of style. And her teachers are very impressed with her progress. You wouldn't even recognise her. She's very ladylike nowadays.'

She was fiddling with a button on his shirt, not meeting his eyes. 'Why was it you who helped her? It's Tom who should be looking after her. She and the boy are his responsibility.'

'She didn't want Tom to know where she was once she left. But he is putting money into the bank for little Albert.'

'Well, and so he should. That's the least he should do. Anyway, why are you telling me about this now, Frederick?'

'Because Rosie's coming to Manchester to do a concert or two, and because I think she might be the one to pull him out of his grief. When I wrote to her about Tom, she said we couldn't let this carry on. She wants to come back, see Tom, talk to him. I said I'd ask you what you thought.'

'Do you really think she can do anything?'

'I don't know. But we've all failed, haven't we, so I think we should let her try.'

'Yes. I'd try anything to help him.'

'I'll tell Seth, then. He'll find her a room without Tom knowing. That hotel of theirs is so busy, Tom will never know as long as she keeps inside her room.'

There was a moment's silence, then, 'I love you, Frederick

Hallam.' Annie reached up one hand to stroke the side of his face, then laid her head on his chest. 'How soon can Rosie come? I'd invite the devil himself to Bilsden if it would help our Tom.'

The lady who stepped out of the late evening train from Manchester three days later was dressed all in black with a thick veil over her face and a black-edged handkerchief in her hand. She was obviously in mourning. One of the porters hastened to help her and carried her one holdall across to the Prince of Wales.

There Seth was waiting for her in the side alley. If the porter thought there was anything strange about that, he was not going to say, not with a nice shiny half-crown piece nestling warmly in the palm of his hand and Seth's 'Shh! Not a word to anyone!' still echoing in his ears. Before he had reached the station again, the porter turned round for a last quick glance at the mystery lady, but the two figures had vanished.

Upstairs, Seth let Rosie into one of the large front bedrooms, hesitated a moment, then gave her a cracking hug. 'Eh, you look so grand I hardly dare touch you, love!' he said, holding her at arm's length. 'Fine as a lady.'

'I *am* a lady now.' Her voice was as different as her appearance, low and well-modulated, though she spoke slowly, still needing to take care of how she formed the words. Then the old Rosie surfaced and she gave a gurgle of laughter. 'Well, as near a lady as makes no difference for a singer.'

He went across to light the spirit lamp under the kettle on the wheeled refreshment trolly that had a side leaf to convert it into a table. 'Still enjoy a cup of tea?'

'Of course I do! And I'm starving hungry. I've just given a concert.' She made her accent overly genteel and minced the words through her mouth. 'To a select group of ladies and gentlemen. By invitation only.'

'Oh, aye?'

'Aye.' Now it was his accent she was mimicking. 'But I can't eat before I sing, and I only just had time to catch the train afterwards, so I'm dying of hunger.'

He whipped off the cloth to reveal a plate of dainty sandwiches and another of small cakes. 'Then happen these'll do some good.'

She grabbed the whole plate of sandwiches, ignoring the small plate beside it, and went to sit near the fire, munching happily. When her hunger was a little appeased, she raised her skirts to toast her chilled feet and ate the rest of the sandwiches more slowly while Seth fussed over the kettle and teapot. 'It's a raw night outside. Will you join me in a cup, Seth? I need to talk to you.'

He nodded. He knew why she was there.

When the plate was empty, Rosie put it back on the trolley, held her cup out for more tea and sank back into the chair opposite Seth. 'So. Tell me about Tom.'

An hour later, the boy who'd been watching Tom's house in Church Road came racing down the hill to the back door of the hotel and asked for Seth. A porter, who knew what to expect, went up and tapped on Rosie's door to summon his employer.

'He's come home from the yard,' the boy gasped, still winded. 'He arrived a minute ago. An' there's a light in the front room.'

Seth nodded and tossed him sixpence. 'Get yourself summat to eat in the kitchen afore you leave. But mind – not a word to anyone about this, or it's the last time you run an errand for me.' He then went back upstairs to tell Rosie it was time and found her already dressed, veil over her face.

In silence, he escorted her down the back stairs and along to Church Road. 'That's the house.'

She eyed it. 'Bigger than Throstle Lane. He's doing well for himself.'

'Want me to wait?'

'No. I doubt I'll come to much harm in Bilsden and I don't know how long I'll be.'

'Good luck, then.'

Rosie waited till Seth was out of sight, then tapped on Tom's front door. When no one came to answer it, she thumped the knocker loudly. No passer-by was going to recognise her on a dirty night like this. Anyone with any sense in their head was indoors, avoiding the storm that had been threatening all day and which was now sending gusts of freezing air down her neck and flurries of raindrops to dampen her full black skirts.

It seemed a long time before the door opened. Tom stood there, blinking at the dark figure, an expression of annoyance on his face. Taking him by surprise, Rosie pushed her way into the hall and stood there, her eyes devouring him. She had dreamed of him so often. But this man looked years older than her Tom, and sad, so sad that tears came into her own eyes in sympathy.

'Who the hell are you?' he demanded, reaching out to grab her arm.

She let him hold one arm while with the other she unwound the fine woollen scarf she had bound round her hair and over the lower half of her face. When she had finished, she stood looking at him. 'Hello, Tom.'

Tom's hand dropped from her arm and he took an involuntary step backwards in shock. He said nothing, just stood there staring at her as if she had risen from the dead to haunt him.

She shivered. 'Isn't there somewhere warmer we can go

to talk, Tom, love? And why don't you shut that front door?
It's blowing a gale outside.'

Footsteps ran along the landing and a woman's voice
shouted down, 'Is that you at the door, Mr Gibson?'

'Yes.'

'Is something wrong?'

'No. Go back and see to the children, Bronwen.' He
moved across to slam the front door shut, then lowered his
voice to a murmur. 'I thought I told you to stay away from
Bilsden.'

'Aye.' She was too upset to consider her words or the
accent in which she spoke them. 'And I did stay away. Till
now.' She took a step towards him. 'We can't talk here in
the open hallway, Tom.' She glanced upstairs, as if to inti-
mate that they might be overheard.

He snarled something incomprehensible, hesitated, then
flung open a door. 'Come in here, then. But only for a
minute.'

Inside the parlour, she stared round in open curiosity,
taking in the signs of a woman's occupation, the half-finished
embroidery, the lacy shawl thrown across the back of the
sofa. It looked as if his wife had just stepped out for a
moment. Oh, Tom, Tom, she mourned. How you must be
hurting to hold on to things like this!

'Well?' He had remained near the door, and his expression was thunderous. 'What do you want, damn you?'

She walked slowly across to the fire, holding her hands
out to its warmth. She had always hated the cold and even
the short walk from the Prince of Wales had chilled her.

'Answer me, Rosie!' His voice was as sharp as the crack
of a whip.

It didn't sound like Tom's voice at all, she thought. She
turned to face him. 'Come over here, Tom Gibson, and sit
yourself down. This'll take more than a minute. An' I'm not

going anywhere till I've spoken to you. If you try to put me outside, I'll scream and shout all the way, then I'll hammer on the door till your neighbours come to see what's wrong.'

He moved across, grabbed her shoulder and dragged her to her feet. 'Rosie, I'm not going to—'

She moved closer to him. 'Oh, my lovely boy!'

He tried to jerk away – sympathy was the last thing he wanted, from her or from anyone – but she wound her arms round his neck and pulled him down so swiftly that he fell on to the sofa with her. And suddenly, he was gulping and saying in a thickened voice. 'Just leave me, Rosie. Please! I can't—' His voice cracked and a sob escaped him.

'Nay, Tom, love,' her voice was soft, her body warm against him. 'I haven't come to stir up trouble, but to help you.'

'No one can help me.' But he was still lying there. And her body was as warm and soft beneath him as it had always been. The temptation to lay his head down upon the softness of her breast and give in to the anguish that filled him was great – too great, far too great. The grief had wracked him, torn at him, day and night. It had denied him real sleep for what seemed like a black eternity. It had turned the world into a miserable prison that closed him in, shutting him away from his golden girl. And now – now he had no more reserves to draw upon.

Without realising how it had happened, he was weeping, with great tearing wrenching sobs that shook his whole body. And she was holding him like a mother would. His head was upon her breast, her hand was gentling the back of his head. The words she murmured were lost in the harsh noises he was making, but the sound of her voice was a comfort, as was the warmth of her body, as was the release of his pent-up agony and grief.

Megan tiptoed down the stairs, stopped in the hallway, heard the sound of Tom's weeping and whispered, 'Thank God! Oh, thank God!' Then she crept back upstairs to indulge in a few tears herself. 'He'll be better now,' she cried, her head against her sister's thin chest. 'Oh, he'll be better now, Bronwen, love. We'll all be better.'

It was a long time before Tom's sobs began to die down. Rosie still held him, but she had stopped murmuring endearments now. He would not want endearments from her, though she still loved him with all her heart, loved him just as much as his wife ever had.

When he pulled away and tried to sit up, she let him go, saying softly, 'You haven't wept, have you? Not since she died. Not properly.'

'I wept that first day, but no, not since.' He fisted the tears away, then fumbled for his handkerchief, avoiding her eyes as he did so.

Rosie nodded. 'I knew it. That's why I came. You needed to let it out, my lad. You needed someone to hold you. It's lonely when you lose the one you love. Very lonely.'

He stared at her. You couldn't mistake her meaning. 'Did you love me so much, then?' It seemed impossible. She had always been a fun person, full of laughter, taking nothing seriously. How could she have hurt for him? But something in her eyes spoke of sadness, and understanding of his feelings now.

'Aye. I loved you, Tom Gibson. I still do. But it wasn't to be.'

'I'm sorry.'

'No need to apologise. I could see how you felt about Marianne. I'm glad you had some time together. You should be glad, too, Tom. And you've got the children, her children. Children are a great comfort.'

It was another double-edged offering. 'How's Albert?'

'Bertie's well. He's a tough little devil, and cheeky like his dad. He never ails.'

Tom stood up, feeling shaky and weak, and made his way across to the sideboard. 'Would you like a drink?'

'Aye. Why not?'

'Port or brandy? That's all I can offer you.'

'Port, then.' But she only sipped at the glass to keep him company. And when he refilled his own glass, she said nothing.

'You've got to pull yourself out of it now, Tom lad,' she said suddenly. 'For the children's sake.'

He sighed and contemplated the amber fluid that half filled the tumbler. 'It's hard. I – don't want to go on – not alone.' How often had he considered ending it? How often denied himself that release for the sake of the children?

He sat there for so long that she wondered if he was falling asleep, then he looked up at her. 'Stay with me, Rosie. I can't seem to manage on my own. I'll marry you, if you like.'

Another pause, then he pleaded, 'We used to be good friends. Surely that would be enough?'

She shook her head and downed half the glass to hide her tears, choking as it went down the wrong way. He patted her back, then retreated to stand leaning on the mantelpiece, staring down at her.

When she could speak again, she did the hardest thing she had ever done in her life, even harder than leaving Bilsden had been. She said, 'No, Tom, love. I couldn't stay here with you. It wouldn't be enough. Not for me. You see, I love you like you loved Marianne.'

He was looking at her like a dog that someone had kicked for no reason, a dog that had been loved and cherished before and now didn't understand what was happening to it. 'I need you.'

She shook her head. 'You need someone, anyone. You don't need me. Nor you won't want me in a month or two, when you've recovered.'

'Rosie—'

'Besides,' she said, as brightly as she could manage, 'I've got my career to think of.'

'Career?' He took another gulp of the brandy. 'What career? Serving behind a bar?'

She punched the arm that was nearest to her, and punched it hard enough to make him yelp. 'That wasn't a nice thing to say, Tom Gibson. In fact, that was bloody unkind!'

Shame filled him, reddened his flushed face still further. 'I'm sorry, Rosie. I didn't mean to – I— Look, tell me about your career. What have you been doing with yourself since you left?' Anything to keep her here with him a little longer. He got up and filled the glass with an unsteady hand.

'I've been learning to sing.' She changed her voice, slowed down her speech and said, 'I've been taking lessons – singing, elocution, even spelling. And in the past year, I've started accepting singing engagements. Small concerts, private parties, that sort of thing. I'm getting quite well known. Don't tell me you haven't heard of Rosa Lidoni?'

He gaped, then blew out his cheeks in a puff of surprise. 'As it happens, I have. Jeremy Lewis was going to take Ellie to one of your concerts, when – when Marianne—'

'Say it, Tom. You need to say it, to face up to it – "when Marianne was killed".'

He rocked on his feet, gulped more brandy, then repeated the words suddenly, 'When Marianne was killed. When that stupid cowardly bastard let his horse trample her down. And now she's dead, and he's dead, but I'm left behind and I have to carry on somehow—' He realised that he was shouting and stopped abruptly. 'Hell, what am I saying?'

'You're talking like a human being, Tom.' She got to her feet and picked up the embroidery frame. Before he could stop her, she had thrown it on the fire and barred his way to the hearth. 'It's unhealthy to live in the past. Let her go, Tom.' She saw that the wooden frame had caught light and swooped round Tom to catch up the shawl and throw that on the fire, too. 'Let her go!' she repeated. 'Let your Marianne lie in peace.'

A smell of scorching wool filled the room. 'Oh, hell!' she said and reached for the poker to scrape the half-burnt shawl off the fire. 'What a stink!'

And that made him laugh, rusty scraping sounds, but laughter nonetheless.

After a minute Rosie joined in. 'I always was impulsive. You'll not get the stink out of this room for days. I'm sorry, love.'

He shook his head, swaying where he stood, with exhaustion as much as with the effects of the brandy. 'No. It needed doing. Def'nitely needed doing.' He nodded owlishly. 'Let her lie in peace. I like that Peace.' He began to sag at the knees and Rosie was just in time to prevent him stumbling into the fire. 'Got to sleep,' he confided, leaning heavily on her. 'Sleep.'

She pulled him down on to the floor, cradling him in her arms again. Soon he was snoring. She lay there, not moving until the fire had almost died down, then she slipped out of his arms and laid him gently down on the rug. She brushed the springy hair back from his forehead and planted a kiss there. 'Oh, Tom! I still miss you, my lad. But I couldn't take her place.' Then, as she was putting more coal on the fire, an idea took hold of her and had her scrabbling in the drawers for something to write with.

Finding nothing, she opened the door and crept down the hallway.

In the kitchen she found Megan, head on her arms, sleeping deeply, and shook her awake.

'I need a pencil and paper,' Rosie announced. 'To write a note to Tom.'

'Is he – all right?'

'He will be, now.' Rosie sighed and sank on to one of the hard wooden chairs. 'Bugger me, I'm wore out.' She liked the girl's face, so she added a short explanation. 'He cried it out of him. He'll start healing now. I knew Tom when we were both young. I knew what he needed.'

'I'm that glad,' said Megan simply. 'And will you be staying?'

'No, not me. He needs to get on with his life, learn to live without her, and I've got things to do, too.' She sat there staring into space, then roused herself. 'Now, where's that bloody pencil?'

It was late next morning when Tom awoke. His head was thumping and he was stiff from lying on the floor, but someone had been in. Someone had made up the fire, put the fireguard around it and laid a blanket over him. Groaning, he got to his feet. 'Rosie?' But the room was empty.

He ran out into the corridor. Upstairs he could hear Bronwen and the children. In the kitchen he could hear Megan humming to herself and clattering pots and pans. He went along the passage to the kitchen, standing in the doorway. 'Has she gone?'

Megan nodded. 'Yes, sir. But she left you a note.' She pointed to the mantelpiece.

Tom picked it up, but didn't open it. 'I'm hungry,' he said in amazement. 'Ravenous.' He couldn't remember the last time he had been this hungry.

Megan beamed at him. 'I'll get you some breakfast then. Do you want to wash first?'

He shook his head. 'No. I'll wash afterwards. A big pot of tea and a plate of ham and eggs, if you please, Megan. With plenty of bread and butter.'

'Yes, sir.'

At the door he paused. 'And – thank you, Megan.'

'What for, sir?'

'For putting up with me these last few months. I think I must have been half mad.' He was gone before she could answer, but he left her smiling.

The note was typical of Rosie.

Tom, love,

You snore. Did you know that? You must be getting old.

Have to go back to London now. Come and listen to me sing sometime – but not till you're feeling better. Mr Hallam will know where I am. He's helped me a lot. Bring him and your sister with you when you come.

Your friend, always

Rosie

The words were correctly spelled, the handwriting was an elegant copperplate. He could imagine her grinning as she wrote the note.

He raised his head and sniffed the air. That frying ham smelled delicious! 'I'll not forget you, Marianne, love,' he said softly, folding the note up and putting it carefully in his pocket. 'But Rosie was right. Life goes on.' After a moment he added, 'And I won't forget her, either.'

Suddenly he was filled with a million ideas. First, the children. He must go up and give them each a big hug. Then he'd take them for a walk to visit their Auntie Annie. He'd tell Annie what had happened, but no one else.

And afterwards, he'd borrow Annie's carriage to bring

the children back. He might even stop in at his dad's on the way. It was Sunday, after all. They'd all be there round at Netherleigh Cottage, the family. His family.

Tom stretched till his muscles cracked. He felt a part of the family again, and he wanted his children – Marianne's children – to feel part of it, too. They were Gibsons, after all.

EPILOGUE

May 1852

Like Tamsin, Annie's child was born in May, just before her own birthday. It was the easiest of all her births, and of course, it was a son.

'Now, will you be satisfied, woman?' Frederick teased when Widow Clegg had tidied everything up and Annie was sitting up in bed drinking a cup of tea.

'Yes. Quite satisfied,' she said smugly. 'I have no desire ever to get pregnant again.' For though she had not been as bad as with Tamsin, she had still been quite sickly.

'Thank heaven for that!'

Three weeks later the Gibsons turned out en masse for the christening. Lizzie and Jim came from Blackpool, the first time they had taken part in a public gathering of the clan. Lizzie was clad in the black she always wore nowadays, Jim was smart in new clothes and rather nervous among all these grand folk.

John and Kathy were surrounded by 'the Gibson Brood' as the family laughingly referred to them nowadays. Mark and Luke looked fully grown, and very conscious of their new suits. William trailed close behind them as usual, looking untidy for all Jane's fussing over his appearance, and yet beaming at the world, as was his wont. His mother said sometimes that he was more of a Gibson than a Hallam, and sighed as she admitted that.

Rebecca, just on the verge of womanhood, was wearing

a dress that she had designed and made herself, and was wielding an elegant parasol with rather too many flourishes. Joan was keeping close to her elder sister, nervous as always in company. Already strands of her fine unmanageable hair were drifting down over her face, escaping from under her bonnet.

Little Samuel John, three now, toddled along holding his mother's hand, and John Gibson had two-year-old Benjamin very firmly by the hand, for his youngest was already adept at slipping away and finding dirt and mischief.

Tom had brought along his two older children, leaving Richard at home in Bronwen's care. At one, Richard was far too young to participate and his lung power still astounded his father. Tom did not intend to risk any loud noises marring the ceremony. He held the twins' hands and smiled down at them from time to time. As they walked along the path from the lych gate into the church, his eyes strayed for a moment towards the far corner of the graveyard, but they did not linger there. He would never stop grieving for his lovely girl, but Marianne's children needed him, and they needed as normal a life as he could provide. As his own father said, life had to go on.

At the front of the church, Annie stood proudly as her son was christened Edgar Thomas and chuckled as he roared in fury at the coldness of the water on his brow. Frederick had wanted to use Thomas as a first name, but with her brother Tom and her daughter Tamsin, she felt that they had enough Ts in the family. Edgar. It had a fine ring to it. She was sure he would do great things with his life.

Across the church she caught sight of her brother and sent him a special smile. He was quieter than he used to be, Tom was, but he had pulled himself together, the children were leading a normal life now and his businesses were thriving again. Then she looked at her husband whose happiness had not faltered all day.

'Aren't you glad we had him?' she whispered.

'I'm happiest of all that you're well recovered,' he murmured. 'Did I ever tell you that I love you, Annie Hallam?'

She smiled. 'Once or twice. I love you, too, Frederick Hallam.' Then she turned her attention back to Edgar, heir to the Hallam fortune, last of her children.

CONTACT ANNA

Anna is always delighted to hear from readers and can be contacted via the internet.

Anna has her own web page, with details of her books, some behind-the-scenes information that is available nowhere else and the first chapters of her books to try out, as well as a picture gallery. You can also buy some of her ebooks from the 'shop' on the web page. Go to:
www.annajacobs.com

Anna can be contacted by email at
anna@annajacobs.com

You can also find Anna on Facebook at
www.facebook.com/AnnaJacobsBooks

If you'd like to receive an email newsletter about Anna and her books every month or two, you are cordially invited to join her announcements list. Just email her and ask to be added to the list, or follow the link from her web page.

Beautiful new editions of the Gibson family saga now available